He deals in the weird.

And gets to the bottom of the bizarre.

Lost Connections
The Place That Never Existed
A Cold Retreat
Beneath The Whispers
…Just South of Heaven
Noah's Lament
Mr Watcher
The Revenge of Lisa Lipstick
Mystery Island

Hudson Bell Series:
A Lifetime Ago
Come Back Home

Tall Trees Series:
Little Miss Evil

The Crazy Season

?

Question Mark Press

Jim Ody

All rights reserved. No part of this publication may be reproduced, distributed or transmitted in any form or by any means, without prior written permission.

This first edition published in 2021 by Question Mark Press

Copyright © 2021 by Jim Ody

?
Question Mark Press

This is a work of fiction. Names, characters, places, and incidents are a product of the author's imagination. Locales and public names are sometimes used for atmospheric purposes. Any resemblance to actual people, living or dead, or to businesses, companies, events, institutions, or locales is completely coincidental.

The Crazy Season Jim Ody. – 1st edition

ISBN: 9798738300233

Cover design by: Emmy Ellis @ Studioenp
Promo by: Donna's Interviews, Reviews and Giveaways
Blog Tours by: Zooloo's Book Tours

This is for anyone who's ever asked a question…

Prologue – One Year Ago

The child was bucking uncontrollably on the front lawn. Grass stains and mud patches were of no concern to her. She growled deeply, out of character. A low, feral and very unchildlike sound forced its way out. Her arms and legs flapped around like they were no longer controlled by the body or mind. Those still close enough could see her eyes roll back into her head, her eyelids flicker and dribble ran down her chin.

This was not a typical Sunday afternoon in this normally quiet slice of suburbia. The looky-loos were forming at a safe distance. Curtains twitched from the curious.

The world was changing, and this was just another example of how it had spiralled out of control.

The child's mother stood helpless; screaming nonsensically, and waving her hands without purpose like a musical conductor without knowledge of the song being played. Her actions not too dissimilar to her daughter's. Neither appeared to be in control. Both seemed possessed by different demons.

A couple of bystanders were frozen in fear, and a teen was excitedly filming on his phone. All were shocked, but still mildly entertained. The video would probably go viral in hours. Social media would send it to the far corners of the globe. He'd make money from this unfortunate event.

"No!" The mother shouted in a sudden rage. "Fucking leave us alone!" She was finally able to form the words she now spat in contempt at an evil entity buried within her own daughter.

A neighbour, a robust woman with a concerned face, and large welcoming arms, slowly and carefully walked up to her to show her support. At first the mother shrugged off the initial contact, instead going down, slightly crouched like a sprinter ready to spring forward towards her child.

The child abruptly stopped writhing and sat up. Her face was a picture of utter hatred for all of those around her. She surveyed the scene as if unaware of the spectacle she'd become. This child, normally so sweet and innocent, had grown-ups unconsciously stepping back in fear. Everything was suddenly very real.

When the girl finally spoke, the voice was nothing like that of a child. "You will all die at the hands of Satan, my saviour!" Her outstretched arm pointed a finger of guilt around to everybody. There was the sound of gasps and a mass intake of breath from all around.

The Crazy Season

The sneaky passers-by, now also remained stuck to the spot, rigid with a sideshow fascination. Another woman was sobbing. Perhaps it was for the mother and child, or maybe she was fearful for her own life. Other mothers gathered their children in closer to them, and some retraced their steps backwards, not wanting to be part of any fallout.

It was then that the police car pulled up, followed by an ambulance. The vehicles appeared alien in a respectable street with manicured lawns and perfectly trimmed hedges.

Somebody muttered that perhaps they needed a priest instead.

"Mrs Parker," the police officer called, dashing over to the mother. She was still crouched down. Her neighbour had been rubbing her back, and this began to be more vigorously. Either through her own worry, or trying to massage out any hidden demons in her, too. The female police officer was trying to disperse the crowds, or at least get them to stand back. Then two medics were on the child and doing all they could to stabilise her. The girl still writhed as though intoxicated and hurled obscenities at one of the medics as she tried to check her over. The other medic, a younger man who looked a little out of his depth, acutely aware that possession was not something covered in his training. He suddenly wondered whether he'd chosen the correct vocation.

Above them all high in the sky, birds circled as if they, too, wanted to watch the bizarre scene play out. Perhaps they thought death was near. A cold wind rushed through, its bite reminding them that man ultimately lacked control.

Jim Ody

"Mrs Parker?" the officer repeated. Her head snapped up to him from where she was sitting on the grass. She was angry and not a bit pleased to see him.

"What!" she screamed. "Unless you're a priest, you can't help her!"

The officer was used to this hostility. Verbal abuse was as familiar as his local football team losing. Calmly he spoke to her. "Eloise Parker, I am arresting you on suspicion of child abuse. You do not have to say anything…" continuing with the caution he reached down and snapped the handcuffs on her wrists.

All of the while Eloise shook her head in disbelief and repeated, "No. No. No. You've got it all wrong!"

Further up the road, a large and expensive Bentley Continental slowed to a stop. Its black paint and dark reinforced glass windows gave no clue to who was inside nor did it suggest a reason for their interest here. But ten seconds was all the occupant needed to be satisfied with what he saw. Or rather who he saw. The single man with his hands in his pockets and his head down was now walking away.

Amongst the circus of a crowd forming and now flashes of cameras, walked the man with determination written on his face. He was leaving the scene now his story had concluded. His name was Joel Baxter, and he'd just solved the case of the possessed daughter.

But instead of brimming with elation, he sighed. Craving infamy had created the scene before him. Such a sad situation.

A few weeks earlier the story had hit the news desk at the paper where he worked. Joel had been

The Crazy Season

assigned to. It was the sort of oddball story he loved to get his teeth into. The general public had watched too many reality television shows and now assumed it was their God-given right to have their fifteen minutes of fame. Except fifteen minutes was no longer an acceptable amount of time. Greed grew as the years passed. As fame became more attainable, people hungered for ways to extend their moments in the limelight.

Households stuck with terrestrial channels where single shows still commanded audiences of ten to fifteen million viewers were a thing of the past. Now, spread out thinly over dozens of satellite and streaming channels – not to mention the whole of the internet, you could be in a popular series and still not be recognised out shopping. It was no longer good enough.

The attention-seekers were now becoming more creative. They were doing shocking things to be thrust into a photo and a few columns of a gossip page. Fame gave way to infamy, proving that people just wanted recognition for being alive.

And nothing proved this more than Eloise and Trinity Parker, a mother and daughter from Thornhill in Wiltshire. It was quite simple. Trinity would be the possessed daughter showing signs of being taken over by a demonic entity, and Eloise would be the poor mother at her wits end. Soon, Eloise would be showered with sympathy and lucrative media requests.

It started out as harmless attention seeking. Wasn't that always the case? Thirteen-year-old Trinity drew graphic pictures in her lessons: animals and people dismembered but in an artistic and detailed way. And once in a while, appeared to have a seizure whilst speaking in a deep demonic voice.

Then the family cat was found ripped apart.

The pictures suddenly came to life. People began to notice, no longer putting her drawing down as a teenage phase, and unhealthy obsession with darker things.

Then scratches appeared on Trinity's body. Deep, claw-like scratches, some of which needed stitches.

Joel spoke to Trinity's friends. Most of them were shocked and scared at what was happening and no longer went to the Parker's house. They truly thought their friend had made a pact with the devil.

All except one. Claire Ball.

At first the ginger-haired girl just seemed nervous. That was completely expected from a girl whose best-friend was being possessed by the devil. But Joel saw something else. It was fear, but it seemed directed not at her friend, but at Eloise, her friend's mother.

"It's a game," she said one day. She was outside of her house with a book in her hand. A supernatural romance. She was sitting cross-legged and holding the book in both hands. She couldn't wait to get back to it again.

"A game?"

"A hoax. Mrs Parker is making her do it." The words toppled out, the way they often did from a teenage girl's mouth. Each word tumbled out onto the rest without understanding the impact of what they meant as a whole. To her it was just an annoying game. A reason for her friend to be kept away.

The Crazy Season

Joel felt the rush inside of him. He was the one who would blow this thing open. "Really? You know that?"

The girl nodded. Her complexion now flushed with anxiety. She now understood Joel's response meant her words were important. That worried her a lot.

"Trinny, enjoyed it…" she trailed off, releasing the book from her right hand as she picked up the takeaway cup with a straw poking out and took a sip of her milkshake. "Until she didn't, you know?"

Joel didn't. Kids spoke to adults like the adults knew everything. They assumed when you got to a certain age all of life's secrets would be told to you.

"What d'you mean?" Joel said, seeking clarification without admitting he didn't know what she meant.

"Until her mum began to cut her."

"The cuts that needed stitches?" The girl nodded. This was huge. Joel was torn between the excitement of the story, and the horror of a mother hurting her only child. No mother should ever do that.

From there the story and case broke open. Until the scene that played out before everyone. The mother and child refused to break out of character. The crowd was confused by the drama. The huge dedication of the main players.

Hours later, the heavy emotional burden of what they'd played out was too much. The questions and accusations underpinned by various witnesses who stepped from the shadows and revealed the truth to be exactly what Joel had first uncovered. The terrible horror was nothing but a great big hoax.

Jim Ody

For the next few weeks, Joel Baxter was an accidental hero. The storyteller now became part of the story. His usual low profile now impossible to maintain. Especially when months later he received a prestigious award for investigative journalism. The irony was, winning the award made him feel like a fraud, undeserving of the attention. Nevertheless, his family was proud of him.

"Congratulations, once again!" his wife Cherry said, patting him on the knee, as he drove.

"Thank you," he said again, but he was a little embarrassed by the attention. He was only doing his job. Uncovering the truth.

The story had done incredibly well for him. He'd received a large payment for it, a retaining bonus, and the night before he'd also won another journalism award. But now he needed a break. He craved the family time he'd missed whilst neck-deep in the case. He knew if he wasn't careful, he'd miss his daughter growing up. Engulfed by work, he'd look up to find his wife had left him and his daughter was married with her own kids. It sounded daft, but he'd been warned by others about it.

Joel and his family were looking to get away to the coast for a week. It was where her family lived. One day, they'd agreed, they'd move there.

His wife yawned beside him, and his young daughter Robyn was already asleep in the backseat.

This was what life was all about. He'd made enough money for them to be comfortable, but more importantly, he had a wife and child whom he adored. This was everything he'd wanted for the future back when he was a trainee hack, handed

The Crazy Season

scandalous tales of titillation, and told that sales by far out-weighed the editor's desire for the truth. Even then, Joel knew that these experienced men were wrong. You could only deceive readers for so long. At best they were publishing mildly entertaining fiction disguised as reality.

And now he'd expose more lies, and it felt like slowly he was cleansing the world. He didn't consider that for every case solved twice as many probably were just beginning.

It was now late in the day, but being a Friday, the roads were still full of commuters or city folk looking to get away to the coast.

Cherry had been busy at work, and wanted to tie up some loose ends before rushing off. It was now well into the evening. Joel's mind was beginning to wander, he'd a lot of offers for stories, and some of them were quite exciting. He was going to use the time to go over them all. Cherry was happy to act as a sounding board, which he welcomed as each story consumed him, and would become like a new member of the family before it was written.

Life had so many possibilities. Until everything changed.

Time slowed down.

The lights swerved and cut in front of them. Joel realised all too late that the lorry was about to hit them head on. So sure was he of his fate that his hands left the wheel and covered his face. And Cherry screamed.

The sound was loud and industrial. Although Joel would never remember it, he would be squeezed into his seat as glass, and car debris lethally shot past him.

Jim Ody

Moments later, the black saloon was unrecognisable. Finally resting on its roof, it was squashed, and concertinaed out of shape. Nobody would believe three people were still inside.

The night was lit up with flashing emergency vehicles. The bodies were cut out and flown to various departments of the local hospital. The conditions of the bodies were all very different.

The driver of the lorry had fallen asleep. Not completely, but enough to swerve into the oncoming traffic. He was Polish, and was entering his thirtieth hour awake. His gruelling schedule was the catalyst to the accident.

It was two days before Joel woke up in hospital. A stern-faced doctor frowned at him in concern. When he smiled, he did so out of procedure, not out of happiness. He had a number of emergencies that night, and time was ticking on all of them. He wasn't there for pleasantries.

"Joel? Can you hear me?" he said in a slightly accented voice.

Everything to Joel was still in a dream-like state. The Indian doctor looked frustrated, and kept glancing at his watch.

"W-where are they?" Joel managed. "My family?"

The doctor glanced over at the nurse. He was looking to pass the buck to someone else. He was more technical. Compassion was somebody else's job.

A friendly-faced nurse took a step closer, and said warmly, "All in good time. Let's focus on you, yeah?"

But eventually he learnt the truth.

His wife was in a coma. She was stable but showed no signs of coming back yet. He felt hollow. But that wasn't the worst of it.

Robyn had died on impact, her chest crushed by his car seat.

That night, from the highest heights, he'd gone from standing on the top of the world, to crashing down to the bottom. He actually began to struggle with his breathing. Later, he was told it was shock. That was the mother of all understatements.

What good was money and success without a family to share it with?

From that day forward, everything in his life changed.

Jim Ody

Chapter 1 – Joel

Present Day - One year later

Today was the anniversary of the accident. The crash. The darkest day of Joel Baxter's life.

Since then, he'd looked at the world through a darkened lens. For the past year any sort of happiness had been hard to come by. He was stuck between his life being on hold, or him wishing away the sands of time. A living purgatory was no life to lead and each day was similar to the day before, a subtle slide up a gauge of melancholy. A survivor's guilt; and a longing for the past. A year was a long time. It was a very lonely time. Quiet nights where sleep could never find him, and when it did, he relived those hours in fitful dreams.

Sadness was more than an emotion. It was like a missing organ. A deep hole that, despite what people said, didn't reduce inside. It felt cancerous. Slowly eating away at his will to live.

The Crazy Season

One day, he'd relent and give in to the darkness that surrounded him. He'd finally take his own life. The only thing that kept him going was his wife, hooked up in a sterile room and kept alive by technology.

The air was cold at six am. Not altogether unpleasant, just fresh to his face when he took a walk outside to clear his head. He'd been up all night. It hardly seemed possible, but the anniversary made things even worse. He was now struggling even more to remember what it had been like to be a family. His mind was vicious in the way it blanked out details. So mean and vindictive. The more he tried to recall details, the less his brain returned, instead only showing outlines and blurs of out-of-focus memories.

There was no one else around in the churchyard. It was still early. Too early really. Death didn't play by any rules, so why should he?

He looked at the gravestone that held the memories of his only child. It seemed too little and insignificant to hold such a precious thing below. He'd been forced to make choices without his wife. The whole concept felt awkward, strange and just plain wrong. He assumed each choice would be frowned upon like he couldn't be trusted. He didn't want to make that decision without her. In fact, he didn't want to ever make decisions about his dead daughter, with or without her.

He hated to think of his wife laid there, her mind unaware that her flesh and blood had been snatched away. It would be one of the first questions she'd ask. He'd have to tell her, and he hated the burden it bestowed upon him, but there was no way he could make someone else do it.

He spoke words of comfort to Robyn, even though he never once considered she could hear him. How could she? Only the small remains were below. She was gone. He was under no doubt that this was for him rather than her. He needed to be here. He wanted to be here.

Then he looked next to her at the space that sat waiting, the spot he'd bought for his wife. A vicar had talked him into it. Perhaps that was a negative way of putting it. They'd held discussions about preparing for the worst. After six months of no change, the vicar had suggested buying the plot. Beginning the road to acceptance. The logic was obvious, but the pain in his heart rejected it at every juncture.

Father Duggan was a vicar who looked more like a former rock star than a man of the cloth. He had a look that suggested he'd lived his life long before accepting God. What Joel liked about him was he never said phrases like *it was God's will*, *He has a bigger plan for her*, or *Everything happens for a reason*. These were not answers but excuses. Clichés for stickers not comfort. What he did offer was a father figure when Joel's was not around. Joel was brought up in care having been abandoned by his mother at birth.

His life was all about searching for answers.

The first single tear dripped from his chin. He was used to this now. A year on and it never got any easier.

The Crazy Season

His life had changed. He'd bought a new house. He was unable to live in a box of memories anymore. Maybe that was selfish of him? He didn't know. What he did know was the guilt had begun to eat him up. The stories he'd been mulling over had been written by other journalists. He'd become a titbit of gossip, a sad tale spoken in hushed voices by friends; or embellished and twisted with gruesome details by rivals. *He had it all,* they'd say. *Lost it, just like that.* Said as if he was careless and to blame. Spoken in slurred voices between a last pint and a round of shots.

His wife Cherry was still alive. If you could call it that. For twelve months she'd been hooked up to a machine that breathed for her, and ultimately kept her alive. Slowly her body had become unrecognisable. Without life to keep us alive, a person morphs into the equipment that now has become part of them. She was a living doll played with daily by hospital staff and talked to by himself. On good days he cherished the time he spent with her, on the bad days he sat and just wept, dwelling on everything he'd lost.

He moved closer to the hospital where she now lived. They were estranged without either of them wanting to be.

He'd bought a converted lighthouse that had a cottage next door. He lived in the cottage that came with it. Or maybe the lighthouse came with the cottage. He didn't know. He'd been too preoccupied with his dying wife to find out. That seemed a little more important. He didn't think the lighthouse had ever been built as one, but as somebody's folly.

Jim Ody

From his office high up in the top of the lighthouse, he could look out at three-hundred-and-sixty degrees of either sea and countryside, and feel like nothing could ever creep up on him again. It was silly, he knew. A small part of him had regressed into a paranoid teen.

He'd grown to a stage of acceptance now. He pushed aside the bread-and-butter stories and delved into a folder of potential investigations. He needed escapism. He craved adventure. He knew that sounded incredibly self-centred, but the weight of his body had been on the pause button of life. How much longer would it remain that way? He had to have hope; he had to find a reason to live.

With hands knitted together over his head, he sighed and looked out over the choppy waters. White caps topped the angry grey waters.

Many years ago, he'd been a lonely child living with foster parents - many foster parents - and constantly dreaming of a life of adventures. In all honesty, whilst it had been short lived, the years with Cherry and Robyn had been an unbelievable dream. He was grateful for them but also felt cheated and short-changed. He wasn't particularly religious, but more often than not he found himself praying to nobody in particular, wishing his wife would wake up. Maybe that was hypercritical, or perhaps he was just desperate.

If you believe, you achieve. It was a throwaway motivational comment, once spray-painted on the changing room walls of his school. He'd dismissed it back then, associating it with sports, and that was not something he entertained. Pushing your body to

The Crazy Season

overheat, your heart to overwork, and your lungs to wheeze in panic seemed detrimental to his health. He'd told his PE teacher that very thing and received three laps of the athletics track and fifty press ups by way of a response. He threw up whilst the teacher still lectured him. He kept quiet from then on.

What Joel lacked physically, he more than made up for mentally. His brain was constantly active, always asking why?

At school his friendship circle was made up of the dropouts. Not the ones that never made it to class, but the ones who half-heartedly turned up and listened to music, or drew amazing pictures instead. They were the free-thinkers. The creators. Artists and musicians. They lacked motivation but not ideas. And with them, they brought forth the darkness of the world to share with him. They had conspiracy theories aplenty; serial killer facts; ghost stories; Bigfoot sightings and a host of local legend claims and instances, etc. He was mesmerised by it all. Within this huge sage world were small pockets of the strange and unexplained. These were the places he wanted to go. Like the quest to find his real parents, he was always searching for answers.

Each and every story completely fascinated Joel.

At Bristol University, he studied journalism until eventually he married the two together.

His first job was at a magazine that specialized in sensational stories. It was easy work. Joel would follow up a lead and embellish the story a little to make it sound even more remarkable. His boss, Louis, an overweight and under-worked slimeball, successfully made money by printing lies that people couldn't disprove. The popularity of the magazine was helped by the flash of teenage skin he showcased in the centre pages remarkably under the guise of fashion. Nobody looking at the women in their underwear were in the market for what they were wearing, and he knew it. Apart from in February when a number of lucky ladies received exactly what they always wanted in the shape of peek-a-boo bras and crotchless knickers.

The day Joel told his boss he was leaving, Louis just shrugged, careful not to spill out the contents of his burger, and didn't even look up from his laptop as he stated, "You think I can't replace you this afternoon?" Joel had no idea, but wasn't in the mood to debate the point. Instead, he cleared his desk and left. Six months later the magazine folded, but Joel had landed himself a number of freelance roles, specifically now on websites. That was the future. He dealt in facts and details with not a matching bra and panty set in sight.

After his award and the exposure it gained him, he began to be inundated with stories where people assumed him to be like *The X-Files*, or rather The Hoax Files, which had been pitched to him by a local Podcast hoping to get him to sign up. The idea was intriguing, but you had to sift through a bunch of social sewage before a jewel could be found.

Through it all, as he trudged through the masses of wannabes, he found it. The one case he could really get his teeth into.

The Crazy Season, a curse that saw a number of teenage suicides over a forty-year period. It had happened every twenty years.

The Crazy Season

And now it was starting again.

Chapter 2 – 40 Years ago

1981 - The first season

Eddie took a last drag of his cigarette and flicked it out into a rockpool. He blew the last of the smoke up above him and turned his back as it dispersed into the atmosphere.

Dennis (or Denny as he was more commonly known) was still smoking his, tapping it every once in a while even when there was no ash to fall off. Micky was sitting on a rock looking out to sea, and Libby -sweet Libby - was stood, her cardigan wrapped around her as the coolness of the cave was apparent in contrast to the sun outside.

"Maybe I should get going?" she said, glancing at her small gold wristwatch. She was nervous. She was just a geek, and here she was with these older boys. She couldn't believe her luck .

The Crazy Season

"Come on, let's take a look in the cave," Denny said, grabbing her hand. She glanced up at Eddie but went anyway.

He was the reason she was there, not Denny. She went anyway.

"It's a nice day, Micky," Eddie said, but it wasn't what he meant and Micky knew it. "Why don't you stay here on lookout, yeah?"

Micky shrugged. He hated being lookout all the time, but Eddie called the shots. His dad virtually owned the town so he had a golden ticket, and with that he did exactly what he wanted. Even if that meant taking a fisherman's daughter into a cave with his mate.

Libby lived down by the docks. Her father was a fisherman who spent most of the time out on boats, mending his nets and lobster boxes, or selling his wares. It was long hard hours. He'd lost a couple of men recently. Not through death, but because they'd been talked away from the uncertainty of the fishing industry and into construction. The rich gated community called Beach View was being expanded. Eddie's dad owned the complex, and Micky's father was a major investor. There was a silent tension between Libby's father and the boys she'd befriended. He couldn't help but clench his jaw at the two boys who came from such wealth. He worked his fingers until they bled for the same money the boys threw around the Black Rock bar on the weekend. It didn't seem fair.

The gated community was a statement. It was a status of wealth, but the fact it was situated nearby but designed to keep the poor out said everything.

Jim Ody

They had gone down to the cove, the one that was attached to the gated community. A beach once free to use by the town had now been sold off.

Libby thought she was going with Eddie, but when he'd turned up his two friends were in tow. She was disappointed, but at least she still got to see the cove. Living in the town with the working-class locals, she had to be invited there.

The back of the cave was dark. Libby was nervous but stood still.

"Look at it," Denny said. "It goes on for ages!"

She looked over and saw Eddie walking over.

"You look cold," he said, and nodded to Denny. Denny walked away into the dark.

She shrugged, not wanting to appear weak to him. "A little," she said with a flash of a smile.

He placed his hands on her shoulders, and she melted into him suddenly warming up.

And then they were kissing!

She couldn't believe it. The soft warm kisses felt wonderful. She felt giddy.

Then stiffened as she felt his hand on her breast. It was under her cardigan but over her dress. She felt weird, like it was all a bit overwhelming. She wanted to stop and take a deep breath and reassess the situation.

She tried to pull away, but he clamped to her stronger. His other hand was now on her leg and finding its way up her thigh.

"Hold on," she gasped, pulling away.

"What's wrong? Relax," he said and smothered her lips with kisses again.

The Crazy Season

She wasn't enjoying it any longer. She was panicking.

"Shoo!" a voice shouted from behind where Micky was, and a dog appeared from nowhere.

"Hey!" a voice of an elderly gentleman called. "Leave her!"

"Get lost, old man!" Eddie shouted. "You shouldn't even be here!"

The guy walked over. "I was walking here long before your father stole the place."

Eddie didn't like to be interrupted. "Fuck off!" He shouted, his chest all puffed out.

"Look at you," the man said with distaste. "My son is in the Falklands, and what is your family doing? Stealing land that isn't theirs."

"Sounds the same as your son then!" Eddie laughed.

"Why you!" he swung his stick, but Micky pushed the man from behind. Denny remained rooted to the spot, but Eddie had no remorse as he kicked the man as hard as he could.

"You're trespassing!" he shouted at him.

Libby took the opportunity to break free and ran out of the cave as fast as she could, leaving the boys behind.

Minutes later they came out of the cave and walked away, leaving a man unconscious and an obedient dog sitting loyally by his side.

Eventually, the dog ran off for help. A canine unable to speak could do nothing but bark. He was taken to Bill's house where Bill could not be located.

As darkness fell, the tide lapped around the man. He became conscious but his path from the cave was cut off. Weakly, he tried to walk around the rocks, but eventually he fell and was submerged by the sea.

The old man drowned alone.

The next day, news of old Bill Hedges' dead body whipped its way around the small town. Local tragedy has a habit of that. Telephones rang from house to house with the news.

Eddie had tried to contact Libby again. He stood in his hallway with the red Trimphone in his hand and listened to the ringing of Libby's house phone in the receiver.

He had to speak to her. They had to get their story straight should anyone ask questions.

If only he could iron things out. If they all remained silent then everything would be alright.

Eddie had to go and see her. That was the only thing he could do. He jumped into his car and drove from Beach View the mile to her house.

He parked his car in the next street, smoothed his hair back and walked the few hundred yards around the corner and towards her house.

She opened it up before he got a few feet away.

"What do you want?" she said with anger. She blamed him. Of course, she blamed him.

"Can we talk?" He tried the charm that worked so well before.

"I've nothing to say to you… I can't take this." No longer meek, she was now gutsy and worked up.

"You haven't told anyone, have you?"

She looked disappointed he'd even asked the question. "Of course not." The venomous words spat. Her cute face had now turned ugly with lines of emotion, and she was flushed. "I'm not eating, and I couldn't sleep at all last night." She stared at him. He was lost for words. He wanted to throw his arms around her and hold her tightly. He wanted this to all be a misunderstanding. A cruel joke they could laugh about later. He wanted to look into her eyes and finally kiss her lips again. He wanted more.

"It's nothing," he tried. "It will blow over."

She was shaking her head in disbelief. She leant in and hissed. "Someone has died! We were there. How can you say it's nothing?"

He was getting pissed off now. "He was trespassing! If he hadn't been there, then nothing would've happened!"

"We caused it! I shouldn't have been there!"

Eddie had heard enough. "Just keep your mouth shut or else!" he made his point known with a finger pointed accusingly at her.

"Don't threaten me," she said, but she was shaken by it.

"I can do what the hell I want," he said. "My family own this town."

She went to respond, but he had already stormed off. *Typical spoilt rich kid*, she thought, but inside her stomach was in knots.

Eddie didn't head back to his car but walked down the street to the end and turned right. He was all pent-up and needed to relieve his stress.

The house was at the end of the street. It had flower baskets outside that sprayed a brightness to the rest of the drab street. It appeared to be the only house that made an effort.

He knocked on the door.

"Hey Eddie!" she said, looking excited to see him.

Jim Ody

"Hey," he replied and pushed past her into the house.

"This is a nice surprise," she said. She was his girlfriend, but they'd only been together a few months. She got that he wanted to take things slowly, that's why he only popped around every once in a while or they met down by the beach. She didn't mind, he was like a rock star. Her friends would be so jealous!

He took her by the hand and led her up the stairs to her bedroom. She liked it when he took control.

They began to kiss, but she quickly pulled away.

"Eddie, there's something I have to tell you," she said. She knew this could make or break them.

"What?" he said, clearly frustrated.

"I'm pregnant."

"You're what?!"

"We're going to have a baby." Her eyes were wide, and she waited for him to hug her and tell her how great the news was.

"You stupid bitch!" he shouted and pushed her backwards. He turned and almost ran out of the house.

No, no, no! He thought to himself. *This is not happening!* He was twenty-one, and she was eighteen, but there was no way he was going to father a child with a woman from around here. What would his parents say?

The next morning, the town woke up to more tragic news. Libby couldn't cope with the thought of being responsible for the death of someone, even if it was indirectly. She went down to the cove to pray. Some people think she got caught by the change of tide, and cut off from the safety of the rocks. Others questioned her involvement with the death of Bill Hedges and thought she committed suicide. Whatever her reasons for being there, her drowned body washed up on the rocks.

Micky spent a day frantically hounding Eddie, like a desperate wreck. Eddie quickly had enough and after an altercation, punched him hard in the face. It was too much for Micky, who emptied the family medicine cabinet of pills, and no longer grasping reality swallowed them all at once. The lethal concoction sent him into a fit at first before slowly shutting down his organs. He died alone with tears streaming down his cheeks.

That same day, after more threats and upon hearing the news about Libby, Denny jumped from a bridge onto the road. The fall broke his neck before the traffic could finish him off.

Three suicides and a murder.

That wasn't the last time the town would be struck by such bad luck.

Jim Ody

Chapter 3 - Joel

The Ilfracombe Neurological Hospital stood as a lonely building on the edge of the cliffs. A forbidding structure at the best of times, but now with angry clouds overhead and a backdrop of rolling waves, it looked more unwelcoming than usual.

The crash had been only half an hour away, and this was where Cherry's family lived. It made sense for her to be there, so Joel had made the decision to permanently make the move from Wiltshire to Devon.

Joel parked his car in the same spot he'd done for almost every visit previously to the hospital. He considered changing it, perhaps that might change his luck, but the nature of his job led him to be sceptical of such invisible powers. Even though he'd slipped into the familiar routine that did just that.

He'd been fascinated by stories that swept across the globe of many phenomena. As he grew older, he

The Crazy Season

still kept that child-like hope of wanting to believe. Most of it was to shake up the mundanity of life; whilst he also wanted confirmation the world wasn't built on lies and elaborate hoaxes. He was a dreamer and a scientist, mutated from complete opposites to an open-minded wonderer using logic to gain answers.

But after the accident, he'd lost any faith he'd ever had in God. Regular churchgoers would happily state their case for religion, but he wasn't looking for blame, nor was he looking for something to believe in. He was looking for his wife, and only then would he be able to move on. His whole life Joel was looking for something, and all the while it continued to be just out of his reach. Whatever *it* may be.

Clutching some flowers, he walked through the huge doors and into the familiar building. Squeaky clean floors audibly disliked his rubber-soled footwear, and the clean overpowering smell gave him a numb feeling inside. He jogged up the stairs and onto the floor he now considered to be his second home.

"Good evening, Joel!" said the smiling face of Jules, a black nurse who seemed to be there almost every time he arrived. Patients were lucky to have someone like her. She was an enthusiastic bundle of joy and went out of her way to be friendly with everyone she came into contact with.

"Hi Jules," he said. The staff had now become family. "How did your daughter's test go?" She'd had an important chemistry test the day before, and it was the first time Joel had seen worry on the woman's face.

Jules grinned, and motioned like she was throwing a ball into a basket. "Slam-dunked it!"

Joel nodded. "That's great news. I told you she would!"

"You did, Joel. That you did!" she glanced at the bouquet he was holding, and changed the subject. "Those are beautiful."

Joel acknowledged the words, held up the flowers, but he struggled to smile. "It hardly seems like something to celebrate, but a year… I dunno. I felt like I wanted to do something."

"Well, they are gorgeous. She'll love them! I'll get a vase in a bit."

"Thank you." That killed the conversation. The porter Josh nodded to him without any smile. He was a tall guy in his twenties with a strange potbelly, and a blown-out tattoo on his forearm. Joel thought he'd make a good undertaker.

He continued on to the room. *Her* room. Cherry's room. He almost felt like he should be paying rent. He felt guilty for taking up the room for so long, and instantly told himself off. She was just as important as anyone. The whole floor was filled with rooms like this although she was the longest resident.

Every time he saw his wife it took his breath away. The shrunken mound laid there motionless. She was attached to machines like she was the main computer powering them. That was something he liked to say to his mate, Kip. It gave her the importance that she deserved.

It was hard. He felt so much love, but there was a mix of pity there too. He hated that. *She'd* hate that. She was not one to join the pity-parade, instead subscribing to a pragmatic view of life that focused on what you could control and not dwelling on what you couldn't.

"Hey, Beautiful," he said walking over and placing a kiss on her cheek. It had taken him a few days to speak to her without crying. A part of him wished he'd still react that way. He hated to think he was getting used to her being like this, but of course he was. How could he not?

"I brought these for you. I know you love them." He placed them on the side, the softness of the petals touched his skin in contrast with the hard-crackle of the plastic holding them.

"Silly, I know," he added, and drank her in. The strong woman who was dying in front of him. The previously active person now needed to be manually moved and worked on to keep her joints and limbs supple and as mobile as possible. But there was only so much that could be expected here. Her muscle tone had softened.

He pulled out his phone and pressed the play button the same way he did on every visit. The same song.

He gulped in anticipation.

Sophie B Hawkins – 'As I Lay Me Down'

He sat down and held his wife's bony hand as the lyrics to the slow song glided over them both. An invisible bond weaving its way around them. It transported him to another time. The memories of listening to it together on their first few dates. An explosion of anxiety and excitement. Then a wash of sunlight raining down on her as she swayed in a summer dress, and he could do nothing more than

Jim Ody

look at her in awe. The top half hugged her curves, whilst below the waist danced freely with her movements. He could never believe she'd wanted him as much as he'd wanted her. But that was fine. It didn't matter. The fact she allowed him to stick around was enough, to share kisses, and intimate moments where their naked skin was pressed together, and they lost themselves in a world where only they existed. Memories flashed around him as he closed his eyes for a while: open windows with curtains flowing from an evening breeze and candles projected juddering shadows like dark fairies in the background. All the while, Sophie sang to them and only them. That's how it felt then, and that's how it felt to him now.

Then years later, at their wedding reception, this was the song that became their first dance. Cherry couldn't stop smiling at him as they swayed together, paying no mind to the many eyes upon them. They suddenly felt like the only couple left on earth. He remembered the feeling of his hands gliding over the rough and smooth of her dress, where lace sat perfectly on silk. And that was them as a couple, coming together like it was meant to be. Him the rough and her the smooth. A perfect compliment.

The track finished. He almost played it again, never growing tired of it even now. Joel gulped down the lump in his throat. Some days the tears just flowed out, and other days he just felt it in his throat and in his heart. The hole in his chest felt like it was getting bigger.

He thought back to the cases he'd looked into. The times he'd left his family to sneak around essentially being a tell-tale. Such wasted time. But you couldn't turn back time. Not even Cher could, and she'd still continued forward for thirty-plus more years. Sometimes memories and nostalgia ended up taking you to the top of a helter-skelter and that would only go one way.

He knew his wife had been proud of his work. She'd said as much on many an occasion. She also knew he struggled with being labelled as a hack, or worse still a form of paparazzi. Joel stayed away from confrontation, but abuse was often flung at him when the guilty were being led away in police custody. Desperate words trying to save face. But to Joel, what set apart what he did, and what the bottom-feeders did was all about motivation. Money wasn't it for him, nor was seeing his name in large fancy fonts. Joel was energised by a few simple things; he wanted justice and hated what was essentially con-artists desperate for notoriety by nefarious means. He also had a love of the truth, specifically when it came to legends, curses and the unexplained. The actual writing and reporting was secondary - a side line in fact - more for documenting his findings than for titillation.

"Hi Joel," a voice said from behind him. He turned and saw Carol. She walked in with her usual consolation smile. A familiarity to their friendship that had started the day he first stepped into the room and had blossomed into something that was special - and completely platonic.

"Hi Carol." She was around fifty, older than him and married. She often made time to sit down, using her breaks to do so. He enjoyed her company and the way she knew all about his situation. She said what needed to be said, made sure he ate properly, and gave him that jolt to get on with his life as best he could.

"You're such a loving husband." She grabbed another chair and sat down. "I know I've said it before, but I've seen other men in your position. They struggle with it. The visits become less and less frequent until it was just anniversaries, and finally Christmas."

Joel slowly shook his head. "That's so sad. How could you forget about them? Leave them here on their own? I mean, they don't choose to be here, do they?" He felt angry. He couldn't miss a single day himself, let alone a week, or a number of months.

Carol was very diplomatic. "Some people cannot cope. Some people have to stay away to live their lives."

"Some people are arseholes, excuse my language."

Her smile was understanding. "I've heard worse."

He reached over to his wife and smoothed her hair. "If I didn't come by… she'd know. Not to mention the guilt I'd feel…and…I'd miss coming here."

Carol nodded. "Like I say, Joel. You're a caring husband. Not everyone is that fortunate to be like you."

Joel stood up and looked out of the window. The view was from high on the cliffs, and the end of the carpark gave way to a steep drop towards the ocean. A fence had been erected when, over the last few years, a handful of people had thrown themselves over the edge onto the rocks below. They all had their reasons, but for Joel, he looked past the edge of Suicide Point - as it had been renamed - and off into the distance where further along the coast a lighthouse stood.

His lighthouse.

Some nights, he would sit up there looking out towards the hospital and imagine Cherry awake and looking back through the window at him. He'd look at his phone hoping that a nurse would ring to tell him his wife was conscious and asking for him.

The phone call never came.

"Sometimes looking out at that fence makes me know how lucky I am," he sighed. "Lost souls compelled to end their lives right there. So sad."

Joel didn't see the tears in Carol's eyes as she replied, "I know." She'd wiped away the tears before he looked back to her.

"You've both got a beautiful story," Carol said. "The ending is perhaps unknown, but the beginning was truly remarkable." She had a way of speaking that was soft and comforting. "You bought a house that looks towards your wife's hospital window. You visit her every single day. You even volunteer here twice a week so you can still be nearby. You…"

Joel held up his hand. "I'm no saint, Carol. It's nothing. It's what people do when they're in love."

Carol just stared back at him, accepting the words and not wanting to disagree.

"Not everyone."

Joel walked back over to his chair, grabbed his wife's hand and sat down once again. Not for the first time, he wanted her fingers to move just slightly.

Jim Ody

The feel of even the weakest of grips would be enough. He wanted to rub out the picture of machines and see her without them too.

Carol changed the subject. "How is your writing going? Any stories worth chasing?"

Joel shrugged. Everything in life seemed so pointless. The stories he once considered to be full of excitement and intrigue, were now nothing but cries for help or shameless attempts at fame. It just all seemed so sad. Behind every story was another one, often derived from loneliness and a feeling of insignificance.

"I have one about an alien abduction," he started, devoid of enthusiasm. He was so used to these leftfield subjects that they slipped out like banal normality.

"Oh my. How exciting," she began but saw his lack of interest. "You don't believe them?"

Joel glanced over. "That ET was coming to take him on a play-date each time?"

Carol looked pensive from how he'd become negative and sceptical of everything, and everyone. "What if it's true?" Her words were said in a subtle wonder, rather than a question aimed at him.

"D'you think it's true?"

"It doesn't matter what I think. I'm far from the expert that you are."

Joel bit his lip and remained indifferent. He turned to his wife, and simply said, "If I could prove it's true, then it would be a huge story…"

"Is that what holds you back? The worry of fame rather than chasing a dead end?"

The Crazy Season

Joel thought about it. She had a valid point. Maybe that was it. Maybe he wasn't worried about it being a hoax but was more worried about it being true. The tables would be turned, and he would be questioned, and thought of as a hoaxer the same way as those he chased himself.

And then there was the small voice he had in his head. The one with an American accent, he couldn't explain where it came from, but it posed the question, *What if it is true? And you could prove it?*

He thought of Jack Nicholson's famous line about not being able to handle the truth, and that was never a more apt phrase for this.

"You might be right. I'd never considered that before."

"Then so what? Write it under a pseudonym. Break the story, but maintain anonymity."

His gaze was drawn to the flashing lights of the monitor his wife was hooked up to whilst he thought about that. "I like it. I knew I liked you popping in each day."

Carol smiled, checked her watch, and stood up. "Break over. I must get back to it."

He nodded, the two of them comfortable enough to drift in and out of each other's lives without guilt. He'd see her tomorrow. And the day after that.

He looked over to Cherry and wondered whether he would continue this until his own last living day. That single thought scared him. Not because of dying first, but to think of her here alone without him.

He walked out of the room and waved to the nurses sat trying to make light of working in a department filled with such sadness.

Jim Ody

"See you tomorrow!" they called.

On his way out he saw the old man lost in his own thoughts. A scruff of white hair looked like it had been dropped from above and landed roughly in the right place.

"Evening, Ted," he said.

"'Lo Joel," the guy gruffly replied. He was a bag of bones, a man weakened to barely possess much more life. Each day he found his way to the uncomfortable chairs. All he wanted was the flash of interaction with relatives, even if they were other people's. He had none of his own. His wife had died there six months ago. He still turned up each day unable to move on. A habit he refused to break.

He was Joel in years to come.

Chapter 4 - Joel

Joel had resigned himself to having a microwave meal. He'd toyed with having something more elaborate and setting two places, but that seemed ridiculous. She was still very much alive. He had to grasp on to that hope.

Instead, he grabbed the plastic offering that looked nothing like it did on the packaging. Shrunk in size and merged together like some artist's impression of the food it was meant to be. All the colours dull and with small sporadic pools of boiling water that he'd have to be careful of.

When he was finished, he sat back and took in his unplanned bachelor life. He was suddenly accepting his life and needed to push himself forward. A general spring clean was well overdue. Cherry would've forced him to do it, and for the past year, he'd kept up the regimented routine in her honour, but now he'd become a bit slack. He was deciding

Jim Ody

what needed cleaning first when there was a knock at the door.

His friend Kip stood grinning from ear to ear as he opened the door.

"Joel, we're going out!" Kip exclaimed, and waggled a finger as Joel searched for an excuse.

"I can't," Joel began, but realised he was stuck for a plausible reason. He almost said he was about to dig out some ice-cream but stopped himself. Kip would laugh at that. Probably call him a girl.

"No such thing as can't," Kip said. "Melody is going to make a fool of herself at an open mic tonight."

Joel sighed. "And you want us to support her?"

"God no," he grinned. "Let's heckle her!"

"It's your sister."

"It's Melody! She'd see it as a challenge!"

Joel nodded, no longer looking to put up a fight. It was true. His sister didn't seem to possess fear but instead saw it as a feeling she needed to feel alive. If she could drink adrenaline then she would knock it back in shot glasses. "I'll get my jacket. Where's Rob?" Rob was Kip's boyfriend. He was a strong alpha male who was very much hiding in the back of the closet - as a policeman, he was fond of using that as the reason. He thought his friends and family would freak if they found out he was gay. Joel didn't think they would, but it was nothing to do with him.

"Work," Kip said rolling his eyes. Kip loved and hated that Rob was a policeman. It consumed his whole life. Kip played the cello and wrote a gardening column in the local paper. He was forty but with the interests of an eccentric old man. Rob, in

The Crazy Season

contrast, was thirty-five and loved excitement. Somehow, they gelled perfectly. Joel had met Kip at the paper they both worked at. Kip was the strange odd-ball guy and he fascinated Joel. Just like his sister, Kip didn't care what people thought. Life was much too short. Joel got that. He'd spent too much time himself trying to do the right thing only to have everything snatched away, so now when Kip turned up, he tended to drop everything and try to live his life. If he didn't, then he would give up, and the fence around the hospital car park would pull him towards it, only for him to be another statistic.

The open mic was at a local spit-and-sawdust pub in a village on the outskirts of Ilfracombe. There were a couple of other pubs, but they were either the small local pub frequented by those who saw it as an extension of their own homes or the chain pub that families would go to for a cheap meal out. This one was called The Fuzzy Duck. It tried to hold functions most nights giving the locals something different whilst drawing in people from neighbouring towns and villages. Locals would sneak in at night whilst moaning about it in the day. It was that sort of place.

They could hear the noise as they got out of Kip's car. The sound of an animal being slaughtered. A high-pitched wailing that made you want the act to be over with as soon as possible.

Except this wasn't a hurt or injured animal but a woman attempting the elongated high-notes of *I Will Always Love You*. She was neither Dolly Parton nor Whitney Houston and instead had driven a larger than normal crowd out for a cigarette break. It was noticeable that half of the people in the designated smoking area were not smoking, such was the racket within. They preferred the risk of passive smoking to the loss of their hearing and sanity.

"Are you sure you want to go in?" Joel asked, hanging back a touch. He noticed a couple of people laugh at that. They were the non-smokers.

"I don't want to go in for that," he agreed. "But Melody will be getting nervous, so now is the perfect time to wind her up."

Reluctantly, Joel followed. "I don't think I've ever seen Melody nervous," he commented. "Are you sure she has nerves?"

When they opened the door, the sound was even worse, and it hit them like a wall. A quick glance around saw the bar staff standing at the furthest point from the speakers, and all around were tables like a piss-up version of the *Mary Celeste*. People didn't seem to care about leaving their possessions out in the open.

The woman abusing everybody's ears was Masie Tounstan, a slight woman who wore a dress a few sizes too big for her. It hung off her like she was peeking over some curtains, or she was an advert for weight loss. She liked a sale, so it was more than likely the only size left.

As Kip and Joel headed to the bar, the hipster guy grinned through his manicured beard and shouted, "What'll it be?"

"Two ciders and some earmuffs, please."

The barman liked that. As he poured the cider, he leaned in and said, "I should probably ban her from these nights."

"It might help your business."

The Crazy Season

Finally, Masie finished and was met by a splattering of claps. The majority came from people filing back in and clapping out of happiness that it was over. It had now become quite a bottle neck.

Then from behind them came a sprightly voice, "Ahh, the two members of the Losers Club!" Melody didn't sound like she was nervous. In fact, she was brimming with confidence. She had on a long gypsy dress that showed off the array of tattoos down her arms. Her hair was deliberately scruffy to her shoulders, and a mix of a dirty bleached blonde, with some reds and greens in there too. All home dye-kits that she changed up probably as often as her underwear. She was quite tall and could look most men in the eyes. She had a ring through her nose and another through her bottom lip.

"You gonna clear the room, too?" Kip teased.

"I'd consider that a win if I did," she responded. Joel liked her devil-may-care attitude. He also liked the way she treated him. Like a regular guy. Everyone else stayed away from him like he had some invisible force field that didn't allow others close. A year on, and people were even less sure of what to say to him now than they were before. Their apologies had dried up, replaced by either banal small talk, or huge gaps of silence that felt awkward. Not Melody though. She quite happily berated him like a big brother, pointing out his failings. Even when Kip would glare at her she laughed it off.

Up next in front of the microphone was a guy standing with prompt cards. That was never a good sign. A couple of smokers already had made the decision to go back outside.

Jim Ody

He leaned too close to the microphone. There was a whoosh of breath and then a screech of feedback. He looked nervous, apologised to everyone and pulled back a touch. A few more people were deciding whether they needed another cigarette break, too.

"I'm going to read a poem," his shaky voice stated. "It's about love."

"Shit, here we go," Melody said eyerolling. "What the fuck does this loser know about love?"

Kip grabbed the drinks. "You'd think she'd be more sympathetic seeing as it will be her being booed off soon."

Joel quickly added. "I think they'd be too scared to boo her."

"Any reason why you losers are talking like I'm not here? Is it because I'm a woman?" She was great at that. Being a feminist she loved to press the social buttons.

"Yes, that's the reason," Kip said sarcastically. "You've got boobs."

"And yet I'm more man than you," she said as they found their way to a table.

The guy on stage was talking in a small voice as if it made the words more tender. His poem sounded like it was an anthology of verses stolen from Hallmark's Valentine's Day cards.

A group of women were stifling giggles. The white wine fuelled their confusion as to whether the guy was serious, or a comedian playing a character of an awkward man.

"…Like buttercups on a hillside, I just wish the love would find me. But alas, I'm alone. A single

The Crazy Season

heart that beats no more." The guy finished and dramatically looked up at the ceiling with his hands clasped together. The place was quiet. Eerily quiet. Confused faces looked at each other.

"Er, that's it," he said, and slowly there was some out-of-time clapping, that built up suddenly into regular applause.

From the side of the room, a guy with a porkpie hat came on. The compere for the night. He fancied himself as a character, assuming this to be a London hotspot, and not a rural village in the heart of Nowheresville.

"Next up we have Melody!"

"Laters!" Melody said to them as she jogged up to the stage.

"Evening all!" she started in the clichéd way someone might pretend they were a policeman from years gone by. It seemed completely off the cuff.

"I've a thought, and this is a little thought, that I thought, I'd share with you…I know, thoughtful, right?"

She'd already piqued the interest of a number of people. It wasn't so much as what she said but the way she delivered it. She was like one of those comedians who was funny not because of the quality of jokes, but just because she was odd.

"I am a baby," she began loudly, almost demanding this to be known. "I lie naked on my back, where I attract the desires of many. Greedy eyes and inexperienced fumbling fingers maraud my body as if it were their own. Everybody wants to touch me. To grab me. To feel me. But I am a baby and no one will leave me alone. Yes, I am a baby."

Jim Ody

She swings her arm accusingly around the crowds who chuckle nervously. Some men look scared.

"I am a baby! I am small, weak and naïve. You could pick me up and throw me around; or anything else you please! I cannot push you away, nor form words to tell you 'No'. We're behind closed doors in suburbia so no one else will know. I'm a baby." Again she pauses. A few people were beginning to look uncomfortable, but nobody was leaving.

"The years rush past, now I've grown bigger and I've got older. The faces and the grabbing hands have changed, but my soul can get no colder. I'm still laid naked on the bed, and strangers look at me like I'm crazy. But when they're done, they still pay me and most still call me baby. I AM a baby!" She stood nodding at the shocked faces, her face accusing them all. A dramatic ending to a slightly disturbing act.

Then she winked, and in a softer voice said, "That one was for all the romantics out there." She stepped off the stage to a sudden rapture of applause.

"You'd never think she had a perfect upbringing, would you?" Kip said as she strode over, looking pleased with herself.

"What d'ya think?" although she really couldn't care less.

Joel took a sip of his drink and said, "I think you might be a little bit unstable."

Kip nodded in agreement. "He raises a good point."

"Who the fuck wants to be stable?" She turned to the bar where a shot of rum was already waiting for her. She nodded to someone back there, downed it, and walked back to the table.

The Crazy Season

"How's your wife?" she said to Joel, which threw him.

"Just the same," he replied. He went to say more but stopped himself.

"See," she then said to both of them. "That's just fucked up. It makes what I do up there seem like nothing."

Kip placed a brotherly hand on her arm. "Careful. You can't justify your weirdness on Joel's misfortune."

Joel jumped in. "It's alright. I get what she's saying. I like the fact you say whatever the hell you want. I don't always get it, *per se*, but that's fine."

Melody chuckled. "Do me a favour, Joel. Don't ever say *per se* again, alright? It sounds so fuckin' pretentious."

"Fair enough. What about sarcastically?"

"You say it sarcastically and it sounds like pussy. Which in my opinion sounds a hell of a lot better!"

Kip looked bewildered. "You believe we have the same parents?"

Joel needed this more and more. The times he'd got home from the hospital and either sat down in front of the idiot-box to be entertained or else he'd gone to the top of the lighthouse and just gazed outside. He always ended up drowning in sad memories. That was the problem with the past. Everything that was happy now made him sad, and everything that was sad just made him feel worse. Nostalgia could be melancholy in disguise.

A girl with a guitar was now singing a song whilst strumming away. She was pretty good, and it was nice to see some actual talent.

Jim Ody

"So Joel," Melody began after they'd all been talking and throwing around shallow banter. "You like weird shit, yeah?"

"I don't know where this is going, so I'm not sure I want to answer."

"You know. The village fruit loops that have a tendency to make shit up. You look into it and call Bullshit!"

Kip jumped in, "That could be your mission statement – *Joel Baxter, finds crazy folk who make shit up and calls Bullshit!*"

Joel looked confused. "Was there a question there somewhere?"

Melody shrugged. "Not so much a question as a mystery."

"Go on."

"There are some crazy legends around these parts. You should check some of them out."

"You'd be surprised at the number of emails I get," Joel sighed. "Most of them seem set up from the start. I've got a guy I'm off to see who swears he's regularly abducted by aliens."

"Blimey," Melody said. "You ever want to just punch them in the face? You know, or roll your eyes at them and then whoosh, open hand bitch-slap them for wasting your time!"

Joel looked at her and then at Kip. "Oddly enough that has never crossed my mind."

They turned and watched a guy doing a stand-up routine. It was excruciating to watch. The jokes weren't too bad, but he kept forgetting his lines. The punchlines pushed to the side and lost within the

The Crazy Season

'ums' and 'ahs'. He had no delivery so he wasn't even Tommy Cooper.

"I wish aliens would take me," Kip said looking back at them. Then his phone went and he grinned.

"The husband," Melody grinned. "He's off on a promise now." She was right. Kip looked like a kid who was off to a toyshop to get whatever he wanted. He was up and out of his seat looking to move.

"You want a lift?" Kip said to Joel. "Rob's off his shift."

"Please," he said. "And no, I don't want to watch."

Melody almost choked on her drink. "He knows you, bro!"

"Funny."

"I'll walk. Don't worry about me," Melody added sarcastically. "Attacks on single females are on the increase, so when I'm found naked and dead in a hedgerow, don't you worry about it."

"You've been naked in a hedgerow on a few occasions, so I've heard. You want a lift, too?"

She glanced over to the bar. "Nah, I'll find my own way home."

Kip and Joel shared a look. They were sure she would. A guy there had glanced over a few times. Maybe he had a nice hedgerow she wanted to roll around in.

Back at the cottage, Joel walked into his bedroom and after stripping down to his underwear, sat there on his bed in reflection. He looked out of the gap in the curtains, the one he always left so as he could see the hospital. The view wasn't great as trees at the end of the garden dominated the foreground, but he could make out the box-shape of the building and the lights from within, and that was enough.

He glanced at the two pictures next to his bed. One was taken on their honeymoon and the other a week or so before the tragedy.

"Good night, Cherry," he said. Then turned off the bedside lamp.

Tomorrow was another day.

Chapter 5 - Timothy

He was fifteen. He hated being that age. The world had suddenly become a dark place. A number of responsibilities had appeared all around him, and he was forced down the route of adulthood whether he wanted to go or not.

When you were a kid the world was a magical place. You can daydream of the worlds created and shaped in your own mind. You felt in charge, even though you're under constant adult supervision. You played with toys and everyone was asking you what you wanted to be when you grew up, It was as if you really could be anything. Being a child was an excuse to do whatever you wanted and often with little or no consequence.

Timothy hated the hypocrisy of it all. The lies and bullshit. At fifteen you learnt these things. Probably earlier, but when you're younger you're more dismissive. It's like Christmas; you've known for many years that the jolly fat guy does not visit

Jim Ody

everyone in the world. You know he's just this made-up character and ultimately a symbol of greed, however you still bought into the spirit of Christmas. A recognised hysteria on a grand scale, and the world pretended it's not just a normal day and should be treated differently.

Thunderclouds moved above him. The breeze trying to clear them away. The sea was rough, dark and unwelcoming.

He sat out high on the cliff. The wind blew his hair out of place but he no longer cared. The heavy burden of life was all around him. The invisible power it had over him was overwhelming. The net closed in until he had no choice. He honestly believed he had no place else to go.

He pulled out his phone. He glanced one last time at his social media account of choice. The goodbye post sat there unanswered by all the so-called 'friends' he had. Only one person seemed bothered.

Sally.

She'd added the sad emoji. The bright yellow face had a downturned mouth and a single tear on the cheek. Her lone response was in capitals. A silent shout out to him. She sounded desperate and was pleading for him to call. He closed down the app and ignored the ten missed calls from her. He opened his palm and let the phone fall into the long grass. He doesn't need it any longer.

This was hardly the story of the Boy Who Cried Wolf. He'd never done this before. It wasn't a plea for help neither, and nor was is an attempt to get attention.

The Crazy Season

His family would be upset. They could do nothing. They were but sad faces pounding on the glass of the greenhouse he found himself in. The transparent box that had somehow been erected around him.

He'd wanted to be part of something so much that he eventually got burned. He ignored Sally and instead went after the woman out of his reach. He wasn't interested in anything else, so blinkered was he with everything she represented.

He went there that evening. He drank what he never should have drunk. He followed them down. He dressed up and held the knife in his hand.

A life of someone he didn't know was taken and before he knew it, he was part of it. He would have it hanging over him for the rest of his life.

Why did he not question anything he was doing before it had been too late.

And Sally… Sweet Sally had tried.

He glanced at the card he'd been sent. He knew what it meant.

It was small and official like a business card. Simple words that held so much power:

The Crazy Season

Timothy Salinger stood up. He looked back behind. Then up into the sky.

He edged closer to the sheer drop. He didn't jump. Instead, he just went limp and allowed his body to topple over the side.

Accepting his fate, he didn't make a sound. His limbs were flung out at all angles. Bones breaking with each bump against hard jagged rocks. Until he

Jim Ody

hit the small patch of sand with a deathly thud, and the water washed over his broken and lifeless body.

The card floated down behind him, at one point catching on a smaller ledge.

The curse had begun again.

Chapter 6 - Joel

Joel was up bright and early. He was off to meet the guy bothered by aliens later and wanted to get some research done beforehand.

He went into the lighthouse and walked up the huge winding staircase to the top. If nothing else it kept him fit. Some people might've thought to install a lift but he hated lifts. Out here, if something happened, it would feel like he was only creating himself a moving coffin. It could be days before somebody checked on him.

The room no longer had the huge light, and instead had a desk curved and facing out to sea, with a sofa behind that was designed to snuggly fit the walls. Then all around were a number of shelves for books. A couple were his own that he'd had published. He didn't think of himself as an author. It was just a hobby that provided him with a little extra income.

Jim Ody

He knew Cherry would love this place and he longed for her to see it. It was the sort of thing that would take her breath away, and he could imagine her sat back with a paperback in her hand and a smile of contentment playing on her lips. Only then would he fully feel like he was on top of the world.

One day, he thought. *One day*.

He opened up his laptop ready to do a quick search on Barry Childe. A guy who seemed sincere, but there was something very lonely about him. Sometimes people wanted to believe so much they overlooked logic and mostly reality.

It was then Joel saw another email. The subject line was simply.

The Crazy Season.

He was lucky it hadn't gone into his spam mail.

He clicked into it half-heartedly. The same way he did each time something appeared that at first didn't seem to be a sneaky spam email that had battled its way through the firewalls. He expected the usual dramatic claims from unhinged people. He'd begun to question whether it was even worth it anymore. Each month there seemed to be a new person pop up suggesting their life was fantastical, when of course, it was usually anything but. He'd even begun to have regulars who peppered him with new claims.

But this one was different:

Hi Mr Baxter

I hope you don't mind me contacting you. I don't know how to start so I'll just get right to it. I will more than likely be dead when you read this. There is

The Crazy Season

nothing I can do about it. It's the curse, and we've hit The Crazy Season.

There will be a lot of questions left behind. I really hope you will be able to answer them. My parents deserve that. Maybe you could even end the curse?! Haha. That last bit was a joke.

Please contact Angela at the Black Rock bar.

Tell Sally I'm sorry. There really was nothing I could do.

Thank you

Timothy

Joel sat back and read, and re-read the email a number of times. He tried to understand the language, and what the motivation was behind it.

There was an attachment. He tried to open it but nothing happened. It was confusing.

He wondered whether it was a joke. How could he not? But he also wondered what it meant.

He googled *The Crazy Season* but only came up with a reference to something buried deep within a forum he couldn't get access to.

Next, he searched for the guy's name. His email address led Joel to social media, and from there he was met by a smiling teenager. His pictures were set to private, but Joel was still able to see the ones previously chosen as profile pics. Naturally, he looked happy in each of them. He remembered a lyric to a song: *we always smile for the camera*. That was so true. A profile picture was carefully handpicked and was less about the person and more about how they wished to be perceived.

Jim Ody

Timothy Salinger lived in Black Rock, a small coastal town next up from Bude. Another quick search brought back the Black Rock bar, which appeared to be part of a large grand hotel. The place looked like it was haunted. It was large and dark with gothic architecture.

What Joel found to be slightly daunting was that there was nothing on the internet about Timothy being missing, or being found dead. The email had been sent the night before so it was highly possible that it hadn't hit the news; or that nobody had found the body yet. Or Timothy was perfectly alive and well, smirking behind his joke.

Joel read the email again. It was unusual that he received such correspondence with so few details. In fact, one that virtually told him nothing. All it mentioned was a curse, a pub, a couple of people, and that he would soon be dead. Usually, people were overflowing with details and claims that it was hard to cut through the bullshit.

Unless this was the hoax. Pretending he was dead.
All he had to do was locate Timothy.

Joel looked out over the sea. It now seemed to be fairly calm. The north shore was often quite choppy.

He looked over to the hospital. His eyes were always drawn there every time he looked up from his laptop. It was natural. His one true love was there. Maybe only in body now. He often wondered whether her spirit had left months ago, and she was frustrated that they wouldn't allow her to fully go. Her soul held back like a stubborn hand on her arm. That would be awful.

Joel's mobile rang.

The Crazy Season

It was Melody.

"Hi Melody?"

"Okay, so this is embarrassing. I need a ride. I'm at some dude's place down the coast. I can't get back."

"The guy from the bar?"

"Irrelevant. You gonna pick me up, or what?" She wasn't asking him, she was demanding to know why he wasn't going to do it.

"Yeah, I guess. Where's Kip?"

"Work. If this little mystery isn't weird enough for you then call me a taxi." Joel wanted to ask her why she hadn't thought about calling a taxi anyway.

"You're a taxi," he joked. With her it was a dangerous move.

"Hilarious."

"Okay, give me the address."

"Hurry up," she said after. "And bring a T-shirt." He didn't ask why.

Joel closed his laptop and popped next door to his house. He grabbed a T-Shirt, his keys and went out to his Jeep. He dropped the T-Shirt down on the passenger seat. It amused him how she didn't care about what people thought. She was such a free spirit.

As he hit the lane, he was already planning the rest of his day. He thought he'd go and see the alien-botherer Barry on the way back.

He blasted out Green Day as he headed out of the town and down some winding Devonshire roads. He didn't need to go far. He slowed at a cluster of houses until he saw her.

She sat with her arms over her naked chest like it was the most natural thing to be doing. She seemed to only be wearing knickers.

"You took your sweet time," she said, which was her way of thanking him. "You got the T-shirt?"

He got out and held it with an outstretched arm and turned his head away.

"You don't have to be scared of my breasts," she said.

"I'm not. I was being polite."

"I couldn't give a fuck. About three neighbours have already seen them."

Joel pointed to the house. "And your Romeo?"

"He's seen them. Touched them, too."

"That wasn't what I meant. Where's he at?"

"Work. I sorta locked myself out."

"With your phone?"

"God works in mysterious ways." Joel had so many responses but decided against them all. The thing with Melody was she lived her life to the fullest. She had fun. These little set backs were normal to her. However, why she'd think to step outside of a stranger's house without her dress on was beyond Joel. He wasn't sure he'd ever fully get her.

"So where are we heading?" she said as she got in to the Jeep.

"I'm taking you home, aren't I? You're not wearing any trousers."

"Bit early for that, Sailor!" she giggled. Joel felt himself go red. He didn't get embarrassed very easily, in fact he'd not had the opportunity in a long time.

The Crazy Season

She must've sensed he was slightly uncomfortable and quickly added. "I'm joking. Okay, swing by my house and I'll grab a shower, then I'm all yours for the day."

"I've got a meeting."

She clicked her fingers as if remembering. "Ah, the alien guy. I'm in! Your side-kick or what-not."

"Whoa, hold on…" he went to argue but really had nothing to say. He suddenly felt whatever he did say would come out wrong. Instead, his mumble came out as a whine. "I don't need a side-kick."

"I don't want to hear it," she said defiantly. "Besides, you'd be *my* side-kick." Although when Joel looked over, she was trying not to smirk.

Her house was on the side of the beach. It was more like a wooden bungalow. Things hung from everywhere, be it flowerpots, charms, or windchimes. It was like she was going for some sort of record in regard to how many things could physically be hung from the outside of a house. When the winds got up the place was a health-hazard. She was basically a hippie. In years to come he could see her becoming a hoarder. Perhaps that was something she aspired to be.

"Come on," she said beckoning him in. He'd only been inside once before, and that had been before a night out with Kip and Rob.

No sooner were they inside than she had the T-shirt off and threw it at him. She must've seen his shocked face.

"Relax, I'm not going to try anything." She had her hands either side of her knickers as she went into the bedroom.

Jim Ody

Joel sat down and tried not to look as uncomfortable as he felt. There were scarves draped over everything, large candles disfigured through usage, bright coloured abstract paintings, and books. Lots and lots of books.

Joel felt like he was kicking his heels a bit. Now he spent a lot of time on his own he'd become more of a control freak. That wasn't to say he couldn't learn to live by somebody else's rules, but at that moment he didn't need to.

Melody had already gone into the bathroom. She'd made a vague attempt at covering her body with a hand towel held against the front of her naked body. She loved to shock. Joel had to quickly looked away. It was all beginning to be an uncomfortable time. He could hear the shower going. She was whistling to a catchy pop song he was having trouble naming. Within two minutes she was back out and walking into her bedroom, the towel wrapped around her hips.

There was only so much to see in the small lounge. Melody had a lot of stuff, without having much stuff. Her laptop was the only sign of technology. She did most things on it. However, to counteract her loud and brash side, she was also a self-confessed bibliophile. Lost in a book, she was just as happy in silence, being absorbed into the world of fiction.

"Okay then!" she said walking out with purpose. She now wore a tight T-shirt with cargo shorts, woollen socks, and walking boots.

"You look like Tomb Raider," Joel mumbled as he got up.

The Crazy Season

"Ooh, you think?" she grinned, looking down at herself. "I like that." Joel decided not to comment further.

Back in the car, they were about to pull away when Joel suddenly said, "You don't have to come."

She rolled her eyes. "Why d'you always act like we're on a first date?"

Joel had no idea what she was talking about. She made him feel uncomfortable, but he couldn't decide whether it was a good thing or a bad thing.

"What d'you mean?" Joel pulled away, knowing she was going to remain exactly where she was.

"You always seem on edge. I can't decide whether you want to slap my face or are just itching to see my naked boobs!" She grinned again knowing she was doing nothing to make him feel comfortable.

"I've never wanted to slap a woman."

"Ahh, so you want to see my boobs?" Joel remained quiet. Sometimes it was the best way.

Chapter 7 - Joel

Every place across the country had its rough areas of town. It was easy to feel sorry for people and listen to endless excuses of how they'd come to be where they were in life.

As soon as Joel entered the estate, he worried about the safety of his vehicle. That might sound harsh, but Kip's boyfriend had only reinforced this. Joel's Jeep stuck out, not just because of the bright red paintwork, but because it was new and not up on bricks.

They parked up in the only space available outside a small block of flats. There was a patch of dried liquid on the ground. It might've been oil. It could also have been blood. It was a fifty/fifty.

"Of all the windows in all the flats, the aliens choose his?" Melody said as they walked towards the large building. "Tough break."

The Crazy Season

Turning to her, Joel said flatly, "You'll have to keep a lid on comments like that. We have to keep an open mind."

She held her hands up in a gesture of innocence. "Got it! I'm just saying, partner."

One side of the street was a terrace of houses, and each one appeared to have at least two cars. The opposite side of the road just in front of the flats, was a large open area of grass. At some point somebody had sold this as a beautiful green area, where communities could come together and socialise on a sunny day. The reality was that it was mostly used to play football, where the only rule was to score a goal - full body contact was not only acceptable, but encouraged. If anyone dared to dive and roll around on the ground feigning injury, then the others would more than likely jump on top, put a foot in, or make sure the person understood what a foul really was. The other main usage of the area was for large dogs to defecate. You could be forgiven in thinking the green had a mole issue until you got closer. More than a few of them were squashed with footprints.

Joel went to press the buzzer to be let into the building but noticed the door no longer closed, let alone locked. It had dents and nicks that suggested it had been forced open so many times that nobody was willing to throw money at repairs.

Melody looked like she was itching to comment but restrained herself. She looked ready to tut for England and was ready to jump on her high horse.

Looking at the numbering, they went up a couple of flights of stairs. The damp smell was replaced by stale cigarettes and a mild whiff of urine. More

Jim Ody

worryingly, from the dark corners came the smell of decay and sex. With those two, never the twain shall meet, as they say.

Joel went to knock on the door but it whipped open before he had the chance to raise a hand.

"Barry?" Joel asked. The guy in front of him was tall and overweight. It seemed unprofessional, but Joel wondered if aliens would really take a man of his size. It would take a lot more effort. He wasn't sure the spindly green arms were up to the task.

The guy grinned, showing a row of yellowed teeth, and the smell of cooking fat was strong in the air. The smell of sex was definitely from behind them in the dark corner of the corridor rather than inside the bachelor pad. Looking at the guy they could perhaps see why.

"You're like Mulder and Scully! Come in, come in!" He looked to be in his later twenties, but with a very rounded face that wobbled when he moved and ruddy cheeks that looked like any movement was an effort.

They were shown to a sofa that had seen better days. It was coated with food. They took their chances and sat down.

Joel saw a faded *X-Files* poster in the corner of the room and then noticed a large shelf packed with Star Trek movies. Peeking out behind some magazines was a large alien plush toy. These weren't so much red flags as bright beacons shining brightly. They suggested the likelihood of Barry being abducted by aliens was on a par with him having the Queen around for the footy and telling her to stop shouting obscenities out of the windows.

The Crazy Season

"You married? Girlfriend?" Melody jumped in. Joel threw her a stare. He was the one meant to be asking the questions, not her.

"Girlfriend," he said proudly pushing out his man-boobs.

"She about?"

Barry went red, which was to say that the rest of his face became the same colour as his cheeks. "We're on a break." He looked around the room, suddenly distracted and not wanting to look them in the face. "You know how it is?"

Joel wasn't quick enough to stop Melody. "Not really. His wife's in a coma, and I don't have a girlfriend. I've been with women, but you probably don't need to know that."

Barry stopped in his tracks. His brain was trying to process everything she'd just said. His emotions conflicted.

"You…"

"Anyway," Joel said, trying to take control. "You've been visited by extra-terrestrials?"

Barry coughed to clear his throat and finally took his eyes off Melody. He sat down in a chair that looked like the upright sort that old people favour. It made a deep sound of pain as his weight dropped down. He reached beside him and pulled up a two-litre bottle of cola and proceeded to take a large swig. When he finished, he wiped his mouth with the back of his hand and snorted phlegm in the back of his throat. He tipped the bottle towards them both like it might be a polite gesture.

Jim Ody

"You want some?" he said, wiping the bottle neck with his hands. Bubble spit could be seen on the inside rolling back down.

"Not for me, Joel? You like cola?" Melody was enjoying herself.

Joel was waving it off. He'd seen more than enough wash-back of saliva to never share a bottle with anyone again. "Not for me," he managed but felt a bit queasy.

Barry remembered the question. "Yes, a couple of nights this week. A couple last, and a one or two the week before."

"Same days?" He pressed.

"I can't remember," Barry confessed a little too quickly. Inside Joel sighed. Was this what his life had amounted to? Meetings with liars in questionable areas of the town?

"You can't remember?" Melody then said in mock confusion. "You are visited by aliens who take you away and bring you back, and you can't remember what day that happens on? That happen a lot? So much so that it's no longer a thing?"

Barry looked scared. Probably with good reason. He looked at Joel for help. Joel offered none back. Instead, Joel sat forward. Mainly so less of his clothing touched the sofa. But at this point it was to help with his conversation. It was like he was taking an interest.

"How does it make you feel? Are you scared? Excited?"

Barry took another swig of cola. The saliva infused liquid sloshed back down into the bottle. "Dunno. Bit of both, I guess."

The Crazy Season

"Explain that to me?" She snapped back the answers like elastic.

Barry looked confused by this. "Eh?"

"What about it makes you excited, for example?"

"Er?"

Melody jumped in. "They penetrate your bum?"

"No!" Barry shot back. "I, er…"

"What then? Naked alien women with big boobs ravishing your body?"

"No… I, er… maybe not so excited."

Joel continued. "So, scared then? What can you remember exactly?"

Barry suddenly relaxed. It was as if he could now slip into his pre-determined story. "I go to bed as normal, and then about three am, I wake. A being is stood over me. A huge green head, with large black eyes—"

"Teeth?" Melody pressed.

That stuttered Barry. "Er, no."

"How big was its mouth?"

"Er, normal size…"

"Normal for an alien?"

Barry nodded. "Yeah, I guess so… well, humans too."

"Carry on," Joel encouraged, although he was beginning to think that Melody was pretty good at interrogation.

"The next thing I know," Barry went on, his eyes wide. "I'm floating out of the window!"

"Okay," Melody says, clapping her hands on her bare legs and standing up. "Let's see this window."

"What now?" Barry got nervous when he was interrupted.

Jim Ody

"No, a week next Tuesday! Yes, now."

"That would be useful," Joel agreed, trying to smooth things over a little.

Barry paused and looked at them both. He then nodded and beckoned them to follow.

They took a right, and went into a room that smelt like old socks. Dirty, sweaty, old socks that had been ejaculated into. Barry pointed to the window like it seemed a pointless exercise.

The room had clothes everywhere. They were screwed up, and if they were clean before then laid on the grime of unexplained bits, they were now dirty. In the corner barely covered from under a jumper was the face of a large sex doll. It's eyes and mouth wide open in surprise. Maybe she'd seen the aliens, too, and was still traumatised. Maybe this was the girlfriend who he was on a break from. It was possible even the doll had had enough.

Melody was straight over and looking at the window. She pulled up the handle and pushed it up as it opened from the bottom.

"You floated through here?" she said using the palm of her hand to show that even fully opened the gap was not much more than a foot wide. Even Barry as a child would struggle to fit through.

Barry nodded, not understanding what she was saying. "Yep."

"You feel yourself touch the sides?"

He shook his head. "Nope. Just slipped through, then up into the sky. Then everything went black."

"That happens the same way each time?" Joel asked. "You wake up to a figure or figures standing

The Crazy Season

over you, and you float out of the window, and whilst ascending into the sky you pass out?"

"Yep." Barry was grinning now proud of the story as it came out of the lips of someone else.

"And you wake up on a spaceship or back in your bed?" Melody fired at him.

Barry looked confused. Inside he was weighing up how deep the bullshit was he wanted to spin. He played it safe. "Back in bed."

"So you might not go to a spaceship?" She responds. "You might just be floating in the air like *The Snowman*?"

Joel had to hide a laugh with a false cough. Barry looked to him for help again.

"I don't know," he said.

"When do you wake up? Any idea of the time?" Joel asked when he could begin to be serious again.

Barry shook his head. "Morning, I guess."

"You guess?"

Barry shrugged. "I mean, I might wake up before that, but I'm like half asleep."

"Are you sore?" Melody asks.

"Positive."

"No, not are you sure, but are you sore? Do you think you've been touched, poked, er, violated?"

Barry is lost for words again. Whatever his answer, he knows it will mean more questions. "Um, I don't think so," he said.

"Well, I can tell you, Barry. I've been touched and poked in probably more places than you have and I've known it, that's for sure." She then looked at her phone. "Joel, we'd better get on. We have that vampire to speak to in an hour."

Jim Ody

Joel nodded to her understanding that, like him, she'd seen enough.

"Okay, Barry, well thank you for sharing this. I'm sure we'll have some following-up questions, but we must get on."

Barry nodded as if understanding Joel was in high demand.

"When do you think you'll write the story?" Barry asked. This was his big concern. "And what paper or magazine will it be in?"

Joel was already walking out and had got to the door. He turned and said, "We have a lot of stories, Barry. Editors want details and photographs, too. This might take a while to write and sell."

Barry seemed crestfallen. "Really?"

Melody gave a good impression of disappointment. "I'm afraid so, Champ."

They said their goodbyes and walked out.

"Champ?" Joel grinned, as they got down the first flight of stairs and stepped over the small ball of foil paper. "Where did that come from?"

"It seemed right," she said. "He looked sad."

Joel nodded as they got to the bottom, and to the door leading out. "What did you think though?"

Melody had to laugh at that. "It was a waste of time, is what I thought. He's a lonely nerd whose girlfriend - if there ever was one - left him. He loves sci-fi and aliens and concocts a story to get attention. He probably gets handjobs off prossies in the corner outside his flat - judging by the smell."

"You don't buy it then?"

"What handjobs?" Joel gave her a look that was one up from eye-rolling. "Do you?" She added.

"God no. Even the logistics of him floating out of the window is just ridiculous."

"This wasn't one of your better leads, I take it?"

They walked around the green rather than tip-toe through the minefield of dog faeces.

"No," he admitted. "Not by a long shot." And then he thought about the email, and for the rest of the walk wrestled with whether or not he should tell her about it.

Jim Ody

Chapter 8 - Joel

They were heading back towards town when Joel suddenly said, "Can I ask you something?"

"Oh, this sounds intriguing," Melody replied.

"Didn't you stay in Black Rock for a while?"

"Yup," she began whimsically. "I dated a guy from there once. He was a surfer. Had a great body and he just glided over the water, but Jesus, out of the water - or the bedroom - he was as dull as dishwater."

"You ever heard of a curse there?"

That got her attention. "Hmmm. I can't say yes, but I can't say no either. There is something deep in my mind that sounds familiar. When I was dating the guy, I spent most of the time inebriated, or stoned. There are a lot of things I remember that I can't say whether they actually happened or not." She looked over at him. "Why d'you ask?"

The Crazy Season

"It's a bit weird, but I was sent an email about a curse last night. A guy from Black Rock saying there was a curse. It was just really odd."

"How so? And what did he say about the curse?"

"Well, that was just it. He didn't mention anything else about it. He told me to speak to someone who owned one of the bars there, and that was that."

"Which bar?"

"The Black Rock."

"I'm not barred from that one." She looked amused. Joel couldn't always tell whether or not she was serious. Melody often got into all kinds of scrapes. She didn't like being told she couldn't do something, and when people antagonised her, just tended to fight back, not always physically but she'd happily throw things. She once broke a window with a cue ball.

"Why not meet with the guy?"

Joel realised he was tapping the steering wheel. "That is the other strange thing. He said he might not be alive when I read the email."

"Ooh, this sounds more like it. Better than old Barry and his alien fetish."

"You see the sex doll in his bedroom?" Joel said, then felt like a gossip.

"No! Damn! I miss all the good shit! Was it an expensive one, or some cheap shit?"

"How should I know?"

"You've been missing out on the bedroom antics of late…"

"Not missing it that much!"

"I had to ask."

Jim Ody

"I don't think you actually asked anything!" He was amused again, and then added, "You were good in there, you know." He focused only on the road ahead. He meant it, but suddenly it felt like he'd said too much.

"You know that's probably the first compliment you've ever given me?"

"Shut up. I've said things before."

"Like when?"

"Your dress last night. I said it looked good…" he trailed off. He suddenly realised he hadn't, it had been in his head. He now felt awkward and weird.

"I don't remember you saying that, but thanks."

Silence fell on them again. Joel had too much churning around in his head to even realise. The first was how he could tell Barry he wasn't interested in his made-up shit. And the second was to drop Melody off and hope the weirdness between them was soon forgotten.

"So, this curse-thing of yours. You wanna take a drive down there?" She suddenly came out with.

Joel thought about it. They were about an hour and a bit away. It was probably the next logical step to take.

"Yeah, that's my next plan. I'll drop you off and then head straight there. I'll try and find that woman at the bar."

"We're heading in the wrong direction," she said. "Go around this roundabout coming up."

"Don't you have anything else planned?"

"Tom Hardy's busy being gorgeous, so my day is looking pretty clear besides, this sounds exciting. A curse! Woo! And you'll need a guide."

"Okay," Joel agreed. "Although a guide is meant to know the place, and you said yourself you can't remember what was real and what wasn't." It was nice to have someone to speak to, and Melody was just a ball of hyperactive enthusiasm.

"Yeah, I can see how that can be confusing to someone like you."

"What d'you mean by that."

"Just that. Stop making things all Avril Lavigne."

"What?"

"*Complicated.* You know, like her song… of the same name?"

"I get it. You don't need to man-splain everything to me."

"I bet your wife said that to you once in a while." He said nothing. She had. He liked to explain things to her, and sometimes forgot just how clever she was, too.

He went around the roundabout as Melody suggested. She sat back in the passenger seat with a great big fat grin plastered on her face.

Another ten minutes down the road and Melody started with the questions again.

"So, this curse," she began. "There was nothing about what it was about, or where it came from?"

"It's called The Crazy Season. That's all I know."

"And you Googled it?"

"Of course."

"But nothing?"

"No. There was a reference on some forum, but I didn't have access."

"And the dark web?"

"The dark web?" Joel repeated. He was beginning to feel old and slightly out of his depth.

"Jesus, Joel! You look into all of these crazy fuckers and you don't know about the dark web?"

"I guess I don't."

"Okay, well the dark web holds all the sites that your usual search engines don't bring up. It's like your under-the-counter stuff at some adult shop. The sordid fantasies, illegal activities, and fetishes of the weirdos from the underground."

"And you know about this, how?"

"That is irrelevant at this time. Later on, we'll take a look. I bet there'll be something there."

"What if there isn't?"

"Then it doesn't exist!"

"Really?"

Melody looked over at Joel like he was some sort of fool. "Really. I thought you were an investigative reporter?"

"That's what my CV claims."

"Wow."

They sat in comfortable silence as the music on the stereo played out. It was a mixture of pop and rock songs.

"These your favourite songs?" Melody said after a while, and it was said in a non-judgemental way. Without taking his eyes off the road, Joel quietly responded with, "No, they're my wife's."

Melody nodded and appeared uncharacteristically lost for words. They rounded a bend and saw a sign that told them they had only a handful of miles to go until they reached the town of Black Rock.

It had clearly still been playing on her mind. Melody, again without sarcasm said, "I hope I have that love one day. You're so devoted."

Joel let out a breath, the mere thought of his wife had such an emotional effect on him. "People say that to me, but it just feels natural. I am so thankful for the time we've had together."

"You see her every day, don't you?" It wasn't a question so much as an acknowledgement. "At the hospital. That is so great, Joel."

He nodded. He had nothing else to say. He didn't want, and nor did he need any sympathy.

The conversation dropped, and Melody began to hum along with the next song.

'As I Lay Me Down'

"I love this song," she said, but her smile soon dropped when she saw the look on his face. The pain supressed. "What is it?"

"I play this song every day to her." He swallowed. "It was her favourite. The first dance at our wedding."

"Wow," she began. "It's a beautiful song."

The sea was on the horizon, and the thunder clouds were rolling in. It seemed apt that they were heading towards an unexpected mystery with unpredictable weather overhead.

"You know where the bar is?" Joel asked as they passed the town sign.

"Just there!" She pointed to the end of the street where a large hotel stood. It was huge and dominating, the bar only a small corner of it.

"And you've not been here?"

Jim Ody

Melody looked over at him with a strange look on her face as they pulled into the car park. "I honestly don't know. Things are a little hazy from back then!"

The car park was half full. The cars there were dark, sleek, and expensive looking.

"I don't know now," Joel said as he turned the engine off. "I wish I had more of a plan."

"What is the name of the woman?"

"Angela."

"Angela what?"

"That's it."

"Come on, let's go!" she said as she opened the door and got out. Joel found her enthusiasm infectious. He got out too.

"Don't forget your balls!" she grinned and then laughed when he was about to look back in the car again.

"Funny."

"I think so."

They walked towards the side entrance of the bar, noticing the grander hotel entrance around the side.

Well this was certainly an adventure.

Chapter 9

He stood back in the shadows. The darkness was a cloak surrounding him from the view of the outside world. He saw the Jeep turn into the car park and pull up next to the expensive vehicles of the hotel's clientele. It stood out. It was red and an odd choice.

Nobody turned up to go straight into the bar. Most who frequented it did so having checked into the hotel first.

It looked like there was going to be a heavy downpour soon, and yet the woman was wearing shorts and he was in a shirt with rolled up sleeves. He was taken back a bit when he saw them. Both were familiar to him.

One from the internet and the other in person.

He looked up the street as if expecting to see the trouble rolling into town behind them. He was sure it would soon follow. Sleepy little coastal towns could deal with tourists. Who were looking for a break in their mundane lives. They wanted to let off steam, get a bit of sun and sea. They grabbed some meals, hit the bars or bought handfuls of seaside tat - the sort that held the town together. It was quaint. The traditional residents loved it. They put on a show and did whatever they could to make a bit extra by turning their Cornish charm.

It was a little sad, he thought. The money was further up the coast at Beach View. They didn't need to pander to anyone.

These two weren't interested in the sea, the long beach, nor the hidden coves. They headed straight into The Rock, as it was known locally.

He pulled out his phone and slipped a large weathered finger over the small screen. He hit the name and held the handset, the ringing loud in his ear.

"We've got a problem." He didn't wait for a response and instead continued. "A red Jeep just pulled up in the car park of The Rock. A man and woman have gone in."

"It's okay," the voice on the other end said. The tone level and without fear. "I've been expecting them."

"You have?"

"Of course," there was a chuckle at the end of the line. "Some people are so predictable."

"Oh, but if they see me…"

"So what? You live there. Go and get yourself a drink and relax."

He clicked off the phone and looked around again. Everything else he considered to be normal. Locals mingled with tourists. Cars were either cheap rust-

The Crazy Season

buckets owned by locals or packed up with kids and luggage.

He crossed the road and went into the bar as if he was a regular. He smiled at the guy behind the bar who nodded back.

"What can I get you?" The lad said. He was tall and skinny. He wore a black shirt like the others and had his hair pulled back into a small and high ponytail. The sides were shaved, and he had a rose tattooed on his hand. When he was that age, you'd never have got a job here looking like that. Times change.

"A bitter," he said in response and pointed to the one he wanted. They remained in character, neither one slipping their mask so others knew otherwise. They knew each other. They knew each other well.

He spotted the couple at the other end of the bar with their drinks. This was going to be interesting.

Jim Ody

The Crazy Season

Chapter 10 - Joel

The woman behind the bar was short. She could see over the bar, but only just. She had on big round glasses and wore a beaming smile. Her hair was curly and cut just above the shoulder.

"Hello there," she said, welcoming them. "What can I get for you?"

Joel ordered a cider and Melody was quick to request the same. Joel was trying to find an opening to ask about the woman when Melody jumped in.

"I don't suppose Angela is around, is she?"

The woman stopped for a second, her smile faltered at the mention of her name. "Not today. Who's asking?"

Melody laughed it off like it was a silly thing. "Oh, just a friend. Is she back in tomorrow?"

The woman placed the first pint down, and nodded slowly. "She'll be around," was all she said. Somehow the mention of the woman's name had sucked away some of the woman's cheeriness.

The Crazy Season

Although she looked almost the same, her eyes told a different story. She was now strictly business.

Joel paid, and they took their drinks towards a small round table sat in an alcove.

"This is going to be one of those hard ones," Joel said, taking a satisfying sip of his drink. "You like haystacks?"

"I've rolled around in a few," she said. Joel dropped the subject.

Melody had already gulped a couple of mouthfuls down when she replied, "Nah. We've just got to dig deeper. You see the way her demeanour changed at the mention of the name? There's something to that."

"Maybe." Joel sat back and looked around. He caught the woman speaking to her colleague, a tall skinny lad in his late teens. It could've been about anything until the barman quickly glanced over looking concerned.

The room was full of well-dressed people. They all had smiles on their faces, possibly genuine, some probably well-manufactured over the years, but each one very different. He'd been told it was all in the eyes. He didn't know whether or not it was true. He had more of a tendency to work on facts. Lies whipped through town like the breeze, but it was mostly the truth that stuck around.

There was one guy sitting on his own. He looked slightly out of place as he wore a large woollen overcoat, a black woollen hat, and his face was covered with a slight beard. The facial hair looked less cultivated for fashion, and either left to grow through laziness or deliberate to hide behind. The one thing it did do was make his eyes look like they were staring.

"Can I ask you something," Melody said, and again she sounded serious. He was so used to her joking around or verbally sparring with anyone she came into contact with, so when she showed a quiet and softer side, it almost unnerved him.

"Of course."

"I know it must've been awful what you went though. *Still going through*. How do you do it?"

Joel turned the pint glass around with one hand. The golden liquid inside now half gone.

"How don't I? is more the point. If I gave up… then what? Cherry could come out of the coma any day. If I'm not ready for her, then I'm not the husband she married. I'm not a man."

"You think she will come out of it?" She had deliberately not used the word coma. They both knew it.

"I don't know," he admitted. "I'm told the longer she remains as she is, the less likely it is she'll ever come out. But… I've had people contact me saying she is listening to me and she'll come back to me when she's good and ready."

"What, psychics?"

"I don't know who or what they are. New Age hippies, psychics, believers, crazies… it probably doesn't matter. Whatever they say won't make me change what I do."

"You're a good person, Joel." She looked sad but he didn't know why.

"Thanks," he said, and they both took a sip of their drinks as the words floated around them.

The Crazy Season

Then Melody grinned. "I can start taking the piss again now. I just wanted to get that caring and feelings-stuff of my chest first."

"Good to know. I thought you were going soft on me for a second. You're the muscle in this duo."

"You better believe it, Buster!"

"You know about this place. What's it like?"

Melody cocked her head to one side. It was a strange response, but one Joel noticed her do when she wasn't sure of the answer.

"It's a quiet town. What can I say? There's the beautiful beach and some hideaway coves. Mostly it's built around tourism. The fishermen moved on a while ago to the towns with quays. There are still a few streets of the older generation who struggle to make ends meet. Then there's B&Bs, and a sprinkling of the usual creative and spiritual folk drawn to the coast. The waves have increased over the years which has drawn in surfers, and then there's the wealth."

"The wealth?"

"Beach View. Essentially, it's a gated community, although the gates remain open. It's about fifty years old. Streets of large houses bought up by successful people in the 70s and 80s. They have access to their own cove, and of course there's the usual: golf course and country club."

"You ever been there?"

She winked. "Of course I have. I'm all about the upper-class, don't you know!"

"Of course," he took a last mouthful of his pint.

"It's exactly what you'd expect. It's posh and fancy. I was only there 'cause my surfer guy's family lived there." She bothered her glass with her hand, and seemed to leave the pub. "I spent more time there than anywhere else."

"Really."

"Like I say, it's where his family lived."

"And how long were you coming here?"

She laughed. "Nice way of putting it!" Joel hadn't realised. She continued. "We were together longer than six months but less than a year."

"Serious then?"

"It was a break from the norm, and shit, you know what? It was nice being treated as a lady."

"Did his family like you?" Joel wasn't sure why he'd asked the question and quickly added. "Sorry, don't answer that. It's none of my business. And it sounded worse than I'd intended."

She waved it away. "Don't be stupid. We're friends. We have no secrets. No, I got the impression my tattoos, piercings, and different coloured hair didn't go down well with the older generation."

"Which I'm sure bothered you greatly."

"Oh, terribly," she grinned with sarcasm.

He looked up and saw the guy was glancing over again.

"Don't look, but there's a guy that keeps staring over here," Joel said in a whisper, whilst pretending he wasn't doing exactly that.

"Is he cute?"

"God knows."

"Kip would know."

"Kip would be over there and talking to him by now. Anyway, he just stands out. I can't put my finger on it."

The Crazy Season

Melody got up. "I'm just off to powder my nose." Sometimes she was as subtle as a shotgun.

It was the age of technology, so the instant he was on his own Joel was grabbing his phone. He held it up and scrolled through some emails. He then switched the camera on and took a picture of the guy. Sometimes you just never knew when it might come in handy. Like if they found his dead body, they might look through the photos on his phone...

Then he sat back and took the place in. *What is happening around here?* He wondered, but always kept in mind that the answer might be a simple one: nothing.

Joel had come to understand that people were now bombarded with entertainment. Everywhere they looked was a temptation to show a world more exciting than their own. As consumers, we lapped it all up. We turn down the lights and scare ourselves with horror movies. We laugh at slapstick as if it's real and never question how the acts within the movie are actually making the characters feel. We are drawn in to mystery, twists and turns we struggle to work out ourselves, and yet when the credits roll and we switch off whatever media we've been absorbed in, we wonder what it would be like to be part of a life that was anything other than our own. It was sad. Perhaps fiction had a lot to answer to. A considerable rise in dissatisfaction and depression. And suicides.

Joel didn't want to admit it, but he'd experienced a pang for change. He was left in limbo. He was chasing the truth amongst stories spun by those who just wanted more excitement in their lives. Some of them weren't even aware they were doing it. He was contacted by a guy who said his house was haunted. From the outside it was a mundane slice of suburbia, but the guy heard noises in the night. He was awoken by whispers in his ears as he slept. Downstairs the kitchen was ransacked. This went on periodically once a week for a few months until Joel set up a camera. He found the guy was doing it all in his sleep. There was nothing sinister going on at all. No evil forces at work. The guy was to blame and he didn't even know it. Life could be that strange.

Melody came back to the table and sat down.

"I don't recognise him," she said quickly.

"I took a picture."

"Mr detective." She looked impressed. "Shall we make a move?" She seemed suddenly in a hurry.

Joel nodded and picked up his empty glass. The guy did his best to pretend like he wasn't interested, but he clearly was.

Even the bar staff were watching them as they placed their glasses on the bar and left. It was strange as the bar didn't come across as that sort of place. Was there really something going on? Did everyone know?

"Shall we take a drive to the gated community?" Joel asked. "See what's going on?"

"Yes," Melody said. "And I'll tell you all about my visit to the Ladies'."

"No offence, but I think I can guess what went on."

"I bet you can't."

Chapter 11 - Sally

She'd sent him ten text messages and received nothing in return. She was beyond worried now. She'd noticed a huge change in Timothy recently. He was never the loud and confident type, but of late he'd sunken into something likened to depression. He was a teenager they were meant to be depressed.

And it was all because of that girl. April Montague. Her birthday wasn't even in April. How stupid was that?

Sally wasn't jealous. Okay, maybe she was a little, but that wasn't the point. She hated the way the boys were transfixed by this girl. This young woman had some sort of hold on them.

April was gorgeous but in that manufactured way. She looked like an airbrushed interpretation of perfection. Everything about her was smooth and perfectly contrasted. Sally often wondered what she'd look like if she'd allow herself to be natural.

Jim Ody

Sally didn't get it. She was sure April had a lot of natural beauty, and yet she dyed her hair, wore make up that covered her natural glow, spray tan, false eyelashes, drawn on eyebrows and manicured nails that she tapped constantly. And the men dribbled at her sight and tripped over their tongues. It was pathetic. And if she was honest, it didn't seem fair. April was tall and slender, not skinny but she had a body she'd love. Even her lack of boobs didn't seem to be an issue. She thought boys were shallow when it came to them, but she was disappointed to realise that didn't matter.

Sally sighed. *I'm jealous, aren't I?* Sally looked at herself in the mirror. Her hair had a wave she could do nothing about. She was skinny, but failed to dazzle. Maybe she should show off her small boobs like April, but instantly she knew she never would. She didn't like the shape of hers. Not that that was the reason. Why should she want to be overtly sexual? Then she glanced at the smiling face of Timothy. She accepted that might be a reason.

That was the real issue she had with April was she'd stolen Timothy. Her Tim. The guy she'd grown up with since they were kids. He was a shy and sweet guy, but apparently stupid when it came to girls. The thing was, they'd always spent a lot of time together, and the dance was coming up. She'd hoped they'd go together. In fact, she was sure Tim was going to ask her. She'd been patient and had seen him dithering whilst verbally going round the houses. Then something happened. They were caught up in that magnetic moment where their eyes met and their heads tilted. And just before their lips touched the

The Crazy Season

door opened and Tim's sister burst in, and called Tim away to do something. When he returned the moment had gone, and she went home with only the memory of what had almost happened. But it had been enough. It was a sign of inevitability.

At least that's what she thought.

The next day he was smiling. Big, huge, giggling smiles. She felt great. He felt it, too, and this was it. This was the point they became more than friends. She was so excited. She almost kissed him there and then. Almost.

"April asked me over to hers," he said like some stupid grinning idiot. Her heart hadn't just sunk, it had plunged right through to the centre of the earth. She wasn't sure whether it was just the words he'd said, or the fact he had no idea how bad it would make her feel.

"April?"

"Yeah," he continued to grin. His voice had jumped up an octave. His narrow-mindedness was so infuriating. Bloody teenage boys!

"What for?" she snapped back, instantly regretting the tone.

He shrugged like it didn't matter. He'd go to hers to pick up her stupid dog's poo if she asked him to. "Dunno."

"You dunno? I didn't know you were even friends."

"Well, I guess we are." He must've finally realised he was being a dick as he made excuses and disappeared.

She looked out of her window at him. The way she'd done so many times. Watching him and wondering when they would finally quit playing around at being just friends. But now, he'd started jogging. She saw him doing press ups, too. He wanted to look good for April. He had high hopes for their meeting. This was worse. Not only was she still deep in the friendzone, but she'd now been relegated below *little miss thing*.

And that was only the start of things going downhill.

He went to her house all full of excitement and expectation.

But part of him never came back.

"How did it go?" she's asked him the next day. She wanted him to say he'd realised she wasn't for him. She wanted him to throw his arms around her and kiss her slow and deep. She wanted apologies that she wouldn't listen to as she'd be too caught up in the feel of his hand in hers. His breath on her cheek. That look of love in his eyes. The soft touch of his lips.

But none of that happened.

"I don't want to talk about it," was all he said, quickening the pace as they walked to the bus stop.

"Why?" she'd asked barely able to keep up with him.

For a split second she thought he was going to cave and tell her. At the bus stop he'd turned and his eyes looked at hers, from one to the other. He was wrestling with the details. But then the school bus turned up early.

So many scenarios had played out in her head. Everything from him trying to kiss April and being rejected, to the two of them sleeping together. She

The Crazy Season

wanted to be there for him, whatever had happened. They were best friends.

But she never found out.

She'd knocked on his door. His mum was always a picture of smiles when she saw her. She thought that secretly Timothy's mum wanted the two of them to get together too.

"Sally! Hello! How are you doing, love?"

"I'm fine, thank you. Is Timothy around?"

She paused for a second, and Sally wondered whether his mother might cover for him, but then she saw a twitch of worry.

"He's not. In fact, I thought he might be over yours."

They both shared a quiet smile. A knowing look between women. Did she think he'd stayed over?

"No, I've not seen him since yesterday."

"Oh," she said. Sally wondered whether she knew about April. Was that where he was? Had he stayed over with her?

Were they a couple now?

"I'm sure he'll be home soon…" but the words held no conviction, and they both had questions forming inside their confused minds.

"Okay. Thank you." Sally politely said her good byes and headed back across the road to her house.

She'd spent an hour trawling through social media.

The day had dragged.

And then later on she'd seen his post. His goodbye post. It was vague, but she was left in no doubt what it meant. She became frantic. She cycled around the small town but couldn't find him. She couldn't eat. And that night she cried herself to sleep.

Her mind went back to that night. The night of the party when she'd watched them all go into the house. That was when everything changed for them all.

That house.

Chapter 12 - Joel

They were in the car when Melody began to tell the story of the incident in the ladies', whilst also trying to direct Joel to the gated community.

"I'm sat there, taking care of nature. My knickers around my ankles, when I hear a voice in the cubicle next to me. 'Hello?' The voice calls out…"

"I'd ignore it," Joel said. "Nothing good can come of it."

"That's because you're an uncaring man. I, on the other hand, am not."

"Sorry. Continue."

"So I respond 'Hi'. And they respond with, 'That guy you're with is Joel Baxter, right?'"

"Shut up!" Joel said, rolling his eyes. "Don't bullshit me!"

"I'm not!" Melody insisted.

"You're having a pee, and a woman asks about me?"

Jim Ody

"Aright, Mr Ego, cool your jets!"

"Cool, my what?"

"Never mind. Anyway, for some reason she's heard of you. But she then goes on to say her friend had talked about you, and now he's missing. Any guesses on his name?"

"Lord Lucan?"

"Don't be a dick. No, Timothy."

"Really?"

"Yep. She slipped me a bit of paper under the partition and asked to meet us later."

"D'you get her name?"

"Left."

"Her name was left?"

"No, turn left at the roundabout."

"Oh, right."

"No, left." She grinned. "Her name was Sally."

"*The* Sally?"

"How many girl's called Sally's do we know in Black Rock?" Joel took the left and soon there were signs for Beach View.

"You probably know a whole army of them."

"What the Sally army?" Joel groaned at the joke in reference to the abbreviation of the Salvation Army.

"So why didn't Sally talk more there?" Joel asked as they pulled in through the gates. There was a guy sat in a small building who noted down their registration number but made no attempt to stop them. Joel thought that was slightly lazy, not what he'd want if he was to fall into a fortune and move to a place like this.

"She didn't want to be seen talking to me."

The Crazy Season

To the left side there was a huge playing field, and fenced off was a play park. To the right there was a sports hall.

"They have their own sport centre?"

Melody pulled a face. "I think you mean the Sports Complex. A Sports Centre is a council owned place in need of refurbishment, with skips out the back where teenage girls get fingered."

"O-kay. My mistake." He'd slowed down whilst taking it all in and realised he'd be looking more and more like an outsider if he wasn't careful.

The houses began on both sides. They were large box-shaped structures with elegant windows and a smaller building attached to the side. They had pillars and wrap around drives. Landscaped gardens, with trees and flowers.

"Wow! This is pretty spectacular," Joel said, they turned towards the sea and to the large building that dominated the area. The Country Club House.

"Behind there is a winding path down to the private beach cove," Melody said.

"And you managed to be here without being kicked out?"

She shrugged. "I mean, I probably ruffled a few feathers."

"You don't say?"

"I just did." They shared a look, and then both grinned.

Joel pulled into the car park. There were a handful of other vehicles, and not one of them was more than a year old. Most were huge and expensive vehicles that cost the same as Melody's Beach House.

Jim Ody

"Lifestyles of the rich and famous. So what does this all mean?"

Melody looked out of the window, for a second she seemed lost in thought. "Money makes people do strange things."

"But for the case. *If it is a case.* We have a missing teenager who thinks he's part of a curse and a girl accosting you in the loo."

"Then the mysterious Angela, not to mention both the bar staff and the scruffy guy."

"I dunno," Joel said. "Are we just trying to find something that isn't here?"

"I don't know, Joel. I honestly don't know…" then she suddenly shifted in her seat. "But I think we should make a move. The guy looking over from the front of the Club House there? His name is Edward Montague. He essentially owns this place. I think word about us has already made it here."

"Wow," Joel said and turned the car around as they made their retreat.

The guy in the small building let them know he was watching them as they drove by. He wasn't exactly doing a De Niro and pointing to his eyes and then to them, but he might as well have been.

"That was weird," Joel said. They turned back towards the town once more.

"Take a left down the bottom, it will take you to a small cove. Sally is going to meet us there a bit later."

They parked up and then got something to eat at a small takeaway hut. Then with Cornish pasties in hand, they walked over to some picnic tables to eat.

The Crazy Season

A guy in a yellow tabard was stopping people and trying to get them to sign up for some monthly donation. He was young and almost dancing up to people. Joel wondered whether it worked. His question was answered as a couple were all smiles as the guy jumped into his patter.

"We should stay here," Melody said. "Until we get a handle on things."

Joel knew she was right. It made sense.

"We should… but I can't." He looked away from her and out to sea. He went to say something else but couldn't.

"Your wife," Melody said for him.

"Yes." He knew in the grand scheme of things one night wouldn't make a difference, but then again when he thought about it maybe it would. Maybe she'd know? And what if something happened and he missed the opportunity to see her.

"I'm sorry," Melody said through mouthfuls of her food. Steam rose into the air. "I know when I hit a nerve as you go really quiet. More quiet than usual."

"Don't be," he replied. "It's one of the things I like about you. You don't care before you speak. You say what's on your mind." He looked to her, and smiled warmly. "Don't change that."

"What else? You said one thing. That suggests there are more than just that, yeah?"

Joel was amused by her. She got it. She could switch from tender to joking instantly and almost without thought.

"Ah, well that's for you to find out, I guess."

Jim Ody

She nodded and seemed to like that, but then said, "You did get that wrong though."

"Eh?"

"You said I'd don't care before I speak. That's not right. I do know what I'm saying, I choose to say it because it needs to be said."

Through chewing his food, he acknowledged that. She was right. She thought well on her feet.

They'd finished their food, and fended off gulls as best they could, when a small figure approached. She was pale with straight black hair. She looked younger than fifteen.

"Sally?" Melody asked.

The girl nodded. "Hello."

"You look better than a voice through the toilet wall," Melody chuckled. Had the girl been older, then no doubt the comment would've been a lot cruder.

"He's still missing," Sally said, without responding to Melody's comment.

"Hi Sally," Joel said. "I'm…"

"Joel. Yes, I know."

"Timothy?" Joel pressed.

She nodded, her face a picture of sadness. She was skinny. All straight lines devoid of curves. There was a prettiness to her face but her thin lips were lost. She looked so sad. She also looked like she'd fallen to earth directly out of Tim Burton's imagination. No doubt Johnny Depp would be around some place.

"What's all this about a curse," Joel said as Sally sat down at the table.

"I don't know," she began dismissively. "You grow up around here and you hear stories about it.

The Crazy Season

But you assume it's just a tale passed down by parents."

"So what is it?" Melody pushed impatiently.

"The Crazy Season. When troubled teens commit suicide."

Joel and Melody snuck a glance to each other although both only had faces that suggested this could be serious.

"You think Timothy committed suicide?" Joel asked carefully.

"Why?" Melody added.

Sally was fidgeting with her fingers. They were long and skinny but with sharp black nails. Joel thought they looked like the fingers of a young witch.

"It's everything that we were warned about. He went chasing after that siren. She was never interested in him, but he had stupid puppy dog eyes for her…" she stopped. When she looked up tears rolled down her cheeks, spilling from her eyes. Her black make-up was good though. No smudging whatsoever.

Melody reached out and touched her hands. "Who is she? And how does she fit in with Timothy's disappearance?"

Sally pulled one hand away to wipe her tears, but happily kept the other under Melody's hand. The two hands such a contrast. One pale and skinny, and the other covered with tattoos.

"It last happened twenty years ago," Sally said, looking up at the sky. "A party that got out of control, they said. Three teens from that party all committed suicide within days of attending. Then twenty years before that another few teens committed suicide all within a few days of each other. If you keep searching, you'll find it continues throughout history."

"You heard of this?" Melody asked Joel.

He shook his head. "I know I look into some strange stories, but despite popular belief I don't know every legend, curse, or bizarre story." He looked over at Sally. "I'm sorry, I don't mean to make this sound trivial." He paused, and his hand shot up to his head as he rubbed hard. It was his thinking pose.

"Have there been any suicides recently?"

That was when Sally looked at them both and gently nodded.

"Stevie. Stephen Molby."

"And you knew him?"

She nodded. "He was in our class. Not really a friend, but I knew him. I know everything is built on rumours and whispers but I think she was involved too."

"And by she you mean…?"

"April. She's one of those gorgeous girls that all the boys go ga-ga over. She's got like thousands of Instagram followers…" Sally sighed, then took a deep breath to compose herself. "Look, I'm not just being jealous here. It just seems important."

"What's her surname?"

Melody cut in. "Montague."

Sally looked shocked. "How'd you know?"

"I was dating her cousin for a spell."

"What, Colson?" Sally was wide-eyed. "Really?"

Melody nodded, and winked at Joel. "He's quite a looker."

The Crazy Season

Sally was clearly in agreement. "He's hot… for an older guy. So, did you live around here?" She now flipped from answering questions, to asking them herself. She'd also visibly come alive. Maybe she saw a glimmer of hope that an alternative person could be with a pretty-rich-guy.

"I rented a room for a while, then sort of stayed with Colson until it got too much."

"Wow! You were like dating? A couple?"

"You don't have to sound so surprised. I have hidden talents, honey. Yeah, I guess. I don't think we ever put a label to it."

Joel coughed. "Anyway, back to this…erm, so Timothy, you have no idea where he is?"

"No. After his last post, he seemed in a bad place. He's not answered any of my messages, nor was he at his house." She paused, and seemed to be wrestling with more details in her head, like whether or not she should continue.

"Anything you have," Melody said. "could be of great importance. Even if you don't think it is."

"I know…" She gulped. She still wasn't sure. Then she said. "There was a meeting. Some sort of club or such like. I think it was something to do with that."

"What meeting?" Joel asked. There was a difference between a party and a meeting. For a start he'd never thrown up or touched a boob in a meeting before.

"I don't know. I just know that April and Stevie were involved."

"No others?"

"There were others, I'm just not sure who."

Jim Ody

"Can you find out?"

"I can try, but…"

"But, what?"

"People don't talk to me." With the words she physically went into herself. She pulled up her leg and hugged her knee.

Joel was thoughtful, thinking about all of the details and trying to process them. "Why are you so worried about being seen talking to us?"

"There are eyes and ears everywhere. I'm worried. Timothy was really worried. Stevie was acting weird before he… did what he did."

"I just think…" her mobile began to ring. She looked at it, then looked all around. "I have to go." She suddenly jogged away.

"Jesus," Joel said. "Who was that."

"All I saw was Jordan."

"What the hell have we got ourselves into here?" Joel said.

"I thought this was your thing."

"So did I. Now, I'm not so sure!"

Chapter 13 - Sally

She was scared. No, scrap that, she was petrified. How did she manage to get so involved in all of this? But of course, she knew. Timothy.

"Where are you?" Jordan had asked, which had made her stutter. He knew she was lying. He knew everything about her. He knew everything about them all.

"I'm at the beach," she said. It was the truth, but of course the beach ran the length of the town.

"You need to go home now," he said. There was authority in his voice.

"Why? What is it?" The words formed and came out of her mouth but she knew. Deep down inside she was already aware of the news. It didn't make it any better.

"I'm on my way," she said grabbing her bike. She put the phone away and pedalled as hard as she could up the hill and towards her home.

Jim Ody

As she got nearer to her home, she saw the police car across the road. She stopped pedalling and glided towards her house. Her eyes remained fixed on the neighbours' place.

Timothy's house.

"No," she said quietly, and then repeated the words over and over again, getting louder and louder until she was shouting. Then the familiar arms of her mother scooped her up and maternally pulled her into her.

"Come inside, Sal. Come on," her mother said, trying to be as soothing as possible.

She felt herself moving but her legs were mechanical. Then her brother was by her side and helping her, too. All around her voices echoed, and the world began to spin. The helping hands got her to the safety of the sofa.

"Sal. They found him. Timothy. I'm sorry but he's dead."

"No! How can…? But, I…?" There were so many sentences vying to get out of her mouth. Her mind was creating them quicker than her mouth could release them. The bottle neck of words in her throat caused it to constrict.

"They think he jumped off the cliff," her mum said quietly not going into the details of which cliff. "It's so, so sad," she added. Her mother had a pained look on her face like she was full of questions, but it was more than that. She was full of worry that it could be her. She was now crying, too. Sally hated to see her mum cry. Despite their differences, she still loved her.

The Crazy Season

Sally fell to the side and buried her head into the comfort of the cushions. She didn't want to be there right now. She didn't want to face the truth of it. She wanted to stand and point accusingly at the adults and ask how they could not see there was something wrong with the town. Evil money was making decisions that should never happen.

Her dad was busying himself in the kitchen, ignoring everything and just pleased to have her there.

"Hey, Sals! Why don't we get ice-cream?" he said but instantly he knew she was hardly even listening. Ice-cream wouldn't bring Timothy back.

"No!" she spat, although the word was lost in the soft furnishings. She wasn't a child. This wasn't her falling off her bike or being picked last for the netball team. This was her best friend being found dead. The guy she wanted to date so badly it hurt. He was the measuring stick of all other boys to her. And now he was gone.

Forever gone.

Slowly, she sat up. She was sobbing. She got to her feet and left to find the comfort of her bedroom.

"Sal?" her father shouted after her, and then she heard her pragmatic mother say, "Leave her."

She run up the stairs and along the landing to her bedroom. She burst through the door and jumped onto her bed and cried into her pillow.

She let it all out in floods of tears. It was so heartbreaking, but even worse for his parents.

She knew then she had to do everything she could to find out what had happened.

Joel and Melody were her only hope.

Jim Ody

> Something wasn't right in Black Rock.
> And she knew just where to look.

Chapter 14 - Joel

For the first ten minutes they drove in silence. Ke$ha was singing some catchy tune followed by a song by Tori Amos. It was an eclectic mix.

"I assume your cases aren't normally like this?" Melody said as they hit the main road.

"What, more questions than answers?" She nodded. "No, more like the one this morning. A wild accusation or story, and then I can piece it together from there."

"I think we look at it first from the curse point of view. There must be some sort of pattern, right?"

Joel had wondered that, too, but people often fed a curse. They heard a story then changed the future to match it. Sometimes they didn't even know they were doing it. He'd come across that before. The mind was such a powerful thing, and there were cases where people had been unconsciously controlled by their own minds to do completely irrational things. Deep down they were children at Christmas wanting to believe in make-believe.

"Yeah. Curses are not my favourite things to look into. There are too many variables and not an easy way to dismiss them. Some things can simply be coincidences. There isn't always evil at work."

"Enough to cause someone to kill themselves?"

"Sure. The power of suggestion is a fascinating thing. It's essentially how cults work."

"What's your gut feeling here?"

"It's too early. At the moment there's a lot of teen angst. The usual complications of jealousy, and possibly the hardships of being a teenager trying to find yourself in the world. It's like anything though, it's not what we can see, but what we find when we begin to peel back the layers. What about you? You were part of this community for a short period. D'you know this April?"

"Not really. She was only young then. You could tell she had a spell on some of the boys even back then, but she would've been about twelve or thirteen. At fifteen and sixteen she knew exactly what she was doing… or maybe not. Maybe Sally is jealous that her boyfriend is off chasing some pretty little thing and she feels left out. Poor Sally looked like she needed sunlight and a good meal."

The Stones were on the stereo and giving sympathy for the devil as the familiar roads of the A39 and A361 guided them back home.

"You not raising hell tonight?" Joel said as he pulled up outside her house.

The Crazy Season

"Not tonight…" she got out, but before she closed the door, she leant back in. "You don't want to come in?"

Joel wasn't sure whether it was a loaded question, but he was already shaking his head. "Nah, I'm off to the hospital. I've a lot to discuss with Cherry."

Her smile was small and accepting as she nodded a response.

"Thanks for coming with me today," he said. "You want to help me get to the bottom of this?"

Her smile grew, he figured she thought he was dumping her.

"We're a team, aren't we? We need a title…" then he could see she'd thought of something. He thought it was a name, but instead she said, "Oh, I'm going to send you a link to the dark web."

"Oh, how nice!" She found that funny. Before turning away, he said, "I'll pick you up tomorrow?"

"You better, or I'm going to hunt you down!" He raised a hand to her as he turned around and drove off. He was at the end of the road before he realised how much he was smiling. Despite all of the questions and the mystery of it all, he'd enjoyed himself. It felt like he'd finally found a purpose for life again.

He pulled into the hospital car park, and straight into his space. He got out of the Jeep and walked into his second home.

He had a spring in his step as he jogged up the stairs. He pushed open the doors to the corridor that held the strong and familiar clinical smell.

There was the usual hustle and bustle at the nurses' station. Gemma was stood waving a folder around which may or may not have been part of the story she was telling. Behind them was a picture of them all taken for some celebration he never thought to ask about. Jules was sat down with a mug in her hand and almost spilling the contents as she laughed. She turned and spotted him.

"Hello, Joel!" she said. "You look different?"

"I do?" he said.

Gemma was nodding in agreement. "You look a little more upbeat. It suits you."

"Thank you," he replied, a little embarrassed. "How is she?" It was the question he always asked. One day he hoped they'd throw their arms around him and proclaim that she was awake.

"She's good, Joe. She'll be pleased to see you."

He raised a hand that could've meant anything from thanks to good bye and walked into the room.

"Hey, beautiful," he said walking towards her. He bent and placed a lingering kiss on her cheek, then sat back and sunk into the chair.

He put his mobile on the side and set Sophie B Hawkins off singing, transporting him back to a magical time. Nostalgia hugged him tightly, and despite his day, nothing could replace this feeling. He wished he could bottle it to keep for eternity. He also wondered the price he'd pay to have a VR headset that would immerse him into that world, and if he did, would he ever come back?

There were so many things that made him sad. The tubes that were a permanent feature of her face. Her lips never free for him to kiss as they provided life for her. Her body wired up. He longed to hold her tightly, but more so for her to hold him back. To

The Crazy Season

feel the tickle of her breath on his neck. To hear her call his name. These were such simple things he'd taken for granted for far too long. *But didn't we all?* he thought.

You don't know what you've got until it's gone.

He reached out and took her slim hand in his. He remembered the first time they'd held hands. They walked side by side, and one hand brushed another. And then he touched hers, and she slipped her hand into his. He remembered holding her so tightly and having to remember to loosen his grip as they walked along the river bank. That was a lifetime ago. He choked up. He felt love and loss all at once.

The song finished and he placed his phone back into his pocket. There was nothing more important than sitting with his wife.

"We've had a busy day," he began. He chuckled ever so slightly. "We met a guy who has been abducted by aliens. We didn't believe him." He paused and faltered. "I went with Melody. You know, Kip's sister. She had nothing else to do. It was nice to speak with someone else." He then looked at her. "We talked about you," he added feeling guilty. It was all tearing him apart.

"Knock, knock?" he turned around and saw Carol. "Can I come in?"

"Of course you can," he said, and realised that spending the day with Melody wasn't so different from seeing Carol every time he came to the hospital. "You're always welcome here."

She walked in and pulled up a chair. "Everything alright?" she asked.

Joel nodded. He always did that whether or not he was okay. She knew it, and he knew it. They both knew he'd eventually tell her the truth.

"I was just telling Cherry about my day. I spent it with Melody as we looked at a couple of cases. But I…" he struggled to turn his worries into words.

"But what, Joel?"

"It feels wrong that I spent the day with another woman."

Carol reached out and patted his hand. It was a maternal act. One that was meant to reassure him.

"Was it a date?" She asked gently.

Joel looked shocked. His eyes darting first to Cherry and then back to her. "God no!" he said.

"So why are you beating yourself up about it?"

Joel ran his hand through his hair. "But, I… it was a good day."

"Did you want something to happen?" Carol pushed, and then added. "It doesn't matter."

Joel shook his head quickly. "No, it's nothing like that. I've not had a female friend, outside of Cherry, who I've enjoyed the company of so much."

"Really?" she said with a sly grin.

"Oh, apart from you, obviously!"

"Haha! I'm joking. Look, Joel, don't fret over what others think. I can tell you now that Cherry appreciates you coming here every day. She'd want you to be happy. Not moping around."

He glanced over at his wife. He knew she was right. His wife wasn't the jealous type, she was pragmatic and to the point. Some of the many things he loved about her.

The Crazy Season

"What happened today then?" Carol asked with interest. It was what he liked about her. She worried about him and was genuinely interested in his life.

"We saw the alien-botherer."

"You see ET, too? You think he's lying?"

Joel shrugged, but inside he was screaming yes. "He says he floats out of a window that when fully opened he could not fit through. He loves sci-fi… I don't know. It felt like it was more a fantasy for him than a memory. He just seemed lonely."

Carol nodded her head. "Maybe that's your answer."

"What? I tell him he's a liar?"

Carol laughed at that. It was one of the first times he'd heard her properly laugh out loud. "No, silly! Maybe he just wants a friend. He doesn't want to be mocked; he wants to share that fantasy with someone."

"Ah, okay. That does make more sense."

"What else did you do? With Melody."

"We took a drive to Black Rock. The next case is more complex. It's basically more questions than answers… I don't know. Teenage suicides."

She looked sad. It was a horrible subject.

"You'll get to the bottom of it. You don't rush things and you don't leave stones unturned. That's the way to find answers."

"I don't want *an* answer, I want the *correct* answer." Joel regretted how he'd said it, even if it was *true*.

"Exactly."

"How is your husband?" Joel asked.

"Not so good, if I'm honest." Her usual sunny-disposition was absent. "He gets so lonely now he's not working."

"And you're here working long hours."

She smiled. "I cannot leave this place, Joel. Look around at all the people who have no one." She looked over at Cherry. Joel couldn't argue with that. "It's more than a job, it's my home."

"You do such a great and important job," Joel said, although it was something he said often to her over the past twelve months. "You deserve to be paid so much more."

"You're too kind, but money isn't always the answer."

"You need me to check in on him?"

"No, no. He'll be fine. But thank you." She looked down at her watch. "Right, I had better get on." She got up and was gone, just like that.

Joel sat and talked through the mystery of Black Rock with Cherry. He wished she'd answer, even to tell him to shut up.

Chapter 15 - Stevie

Before the party

When he got the note, he instantly questioned it. Why wouldn't he? It was a technological age where everything was electronic or digital. The last time he'd had a note passed to him it had been from Jilly, the small girl with a shock of curly brown hair and dimples. She had asked to meet him at the park. They had been thirteen. He'd gone, but after ten minutes of it feeling awkward and weird, he broke the news that he wasn't after a girlfriend. It wasn't strictly true, as he was desperate for one, just not her. It wasn't that she was ugly or anything, but she just seemed like a little sister. She'd grabbed his hand, and he felt nothing and pulled away before their history made a second paragraph.

But he was no longer thirteen, and this was not about little Jilly. This was Becky inviting him to a party.

He'd looked at the note, and then looked around the room of his science class fully expecting a group of girls to be pointing at him, ready to tease and ridicule. Instead, he saw Becky and April sat together smiling. They pointed to the note, and then gave him the thumbs up. He took that to be a question in regards to him attending the party. He put his thumb up and was surprised to see they looked relieved and actually happy. He wondered whether it was his dad's aftershave he'd stolen a spray of that morning. He was going to wear it again if that was the case. Girls were all about smells and stuff, weren't they?

He sort of knew them both. Becky and April. He'd been to comprehensive school with Becky. And everyone knew April. They came as a pair. That in itself spurred many a late-night fantasy.

His mind was playing out all of the things that might go on at a party - specifically with April. He'd heard rumours. She'd kissed a lot of boys. Some of which had cars and loud mouths. He'd heard them speak about what she'd done and he wanted a part of it!

Later, when school was over, Becky called out to him. At first he thought he'd misheard her, but she called again.

"Stevie?"

He turned and saw her walking over to him. She had blonde hair that had begun to go more mousey brown of late.

"Hey, Becky."

The Crazy Season

"I'm excited that you're going to the party," she said. She would be even more attractive if she wasn't constantly in the shadow of April. It was a shame. He wondered how she felt about it. He tried to stop dribbling.

"You are?" he said, annoyed that his voice had come out higher than he'd expected it to. He wondered if they'd sneak in alcohol and play spin the bottle or some such game. He didn't care if it was fate that placed his tongue in her mouth. Or April's.

"Yeah. There aren't many people who've been invited. It's exclusive... and secret!" she placed her fingers to her lips.

"Really?"

"Oh, very much so. What goes on there, must stay there... if you know what I mean?"

Stevie's mind was conjuring up all kinds of things. The sort of things a teenage boy dreams of. *Would this be when he lost his virginity?* He wondered.

He struggled to respond to Becky and instead nodded and grinned like the village idiot.

Once again, Becky placed a finger to her lips, winked, and then wiggled her fingers as a goodbye, as she turned and disappeared.

He was left smiling to himself.

His friend Timothy walked up. His head was down, but he looked up and nodded to him.

"What you grinning at?" he said. "You just farted?"

That only made Stevie laugh even more. "Hah. Nah, mate." He was desperate to tell his mate, except Timmy would never get it.

Jim Ody

"Your shadow is coming," Stevie said instead.

Timothy turned and saw Sally. "Don't be mean. She's alright."

"I'm not," Stevie said. "Just saying." The truth was he was a little jealous that his mate had her following him around. She clearly wanted to be his girlfriend, but his mate was too much of a dipshit to realise. He seemed to think he was going to get the attention of one of the older girls. Or April.

Sally lived over the road from him, too. She was basically gagging for it. She wasn't that bad looking either she just seemed so... I wasn't sure. So *fragile,* he thought.

"You free at the weekend?" Timmy asked him.

"I dunno," Stevie said. His mind was on the party. The one he couldn't tell Timmy about.

The problem with secrets is that they dig deep inside you. They fester and grow. For Stevie, he was focused on the party, and it made him even more secretive. He couldn't tell anyone, and because it was suddenly all that he could think about, he withdrew. He made excuses and slunk off into the shadows.

On Friday night, he ignored the call from Timothy. He was going to the party and didn't have the time nor energy to spin a further web of lies.

"I'm off to see Timothy!" he called to his mum as he ran down the stairs. The lie slipped easily out of his mouth.

"Okay," she called back without looking at him.

He was nervous. Really nervous. He'd even stolen a condom from his brother's wallet.

He left early. He was going to take his bike, but leaving it propped up outside would look stupid and lame. It was one up from being dropped off by your mum.

His phone buzzed, and he stopped to pull out his phone and look at the message.

Hey Stevie! I can't wait to see you. Change of plans…

He read on. The address wasn't just down the road in Beach View but a bit further away. He didn't like the way it made him feel, but he thought about Becky. He thought even more about April. He had to stop acting like such a pussy.

He turned round and walked off in the opposite direction. His heart still beat hard in his chest. It was a mixture of fear and excitement. The wandering into the unknown.

This was what he'd been dreaming of. He'd squirted a double dose of his dad's aftershave this time and even had a go at shaving. He looked no different, but when he ran his fingers over his top lip he was sure he could feel the tiny needles of stubble.

This was the night he finally became a man.

Jim Ody

Chapter 16 – Joel

Joel had grabbed himself some chicken out of the fridge and diced it. He tossed it around in the wok and had added chopped vegetables before finally adding a sauce.

A year ago, he'd stopped eating. With his wife and child snatched away from him, he refused to accept the feeling of hunger. Instead, he'd eat a piece of bread and an apple. Within a month or so he'd lost a stone in weight.

Following on, the tables turned and he grabbed fast food and takeaways, suddenly indulging in comfort food. Homesick, the weight soon returned.

But over the past six months, he'd regained a hold of his life again. He'd been forced into cooking. He found quite quickly that being on his own, he found it quite therapeutic to cook for himself. He tried different things. He discovered new recipes and soon was able to change and adapt them to his own tastes.

The Crazy Season

He couldn't wait to show Cherry exactly what he could cook. He longed for her to sit down and talk to him as he would chop, stir, and mix various things, before pulling it all together. It was another thing that kept him going.

He sat down to eat his food in the small but cosy lounge. He wasn't one to blow his own trumpet but the stir fry was delicious. As usual he'd done twice as much. Each recipe he learnt for two so when Cherry returned he would be a whizz at it. Until that day, he'd box up the remainder and reheat it the next day.

He watched the fate of the world through biased eyes on a chosen news channel. You could be forgiven for thinking it was all doom and gloom outside the window. Nobody seemed to want to spread news of happiness, in fact the way we feel better about ourselves appears to be by hearing of thers'misfortunes.

He took his bowl out to the kitchen, and then made his way outside and slowly up the stairs to the top of the lighthouse.

He clicked on his table lamp. It was a full-size skull with a bulb coming out of the top, a treat he'd bought himself when he saw it on eBay. He then opened up his laptop. True to her word, Melody had sent him a link. He hovered over it not wanting to fully commit. It was stupid, he'd looked up weird and crazy things before, so why he should now be scared to click was beyond him.

He picked up his phone and rang her.

"Oh, you missing me already?" she said, surprisingly upbeat. "Hold on," she said.

Jim Ody

"Eh?"

"I was doing naked yoga. I was balancing on my head." It was a picture he found hard to get out of his mind. He stuttered slightly as he said, "I got your email. The one with the link."

"I only sent you the one."

"Yeah, that's the one I'm on about."

There was the sound of a muffled giggle. "You're funny. You can just reply thanks, or some such meaningless response. You didn't have to ring me."

"No, it wasn't that," he said. Why did she always have to make even the simplest of conversations hard. "It's okay to just click, right?"

"Seriously?" she was definitely amused. "You confronted a woman whose child was possessed. Didn't you once go to a haunted house? Even today you've met a guy claiming to have been abducted by aliens, and then driven to a cursed seaside town, and yet you are too scared to click on an email link?"

Joel huffed. "I mean, it sounds bad when you put it like that."

"You left your balls in the car again? You want me to come over and find them?"

"I think I can locate my own balls."

"Shame. You want me to click your button?"

"Uh... no. Thank you." There was silence; they were each waiting for the other to speak. As usual, Melody was too scared of the silence and had to fill it. "Just press the link. I'll stay on the phone just in case something comes out of your laptop to kill you."

"I'm not *that* worried."

"So why'd you call me then? You wanna know what I'm wearing? Zip. Nada. Nothing."

The Crazy Season

"No, it's…"

"A small lacy bra," she said breathlessly. "My nipples are poking…"

"I've clicked it. You can stop now."

"What a big brave boy you are. You gonna be alright now?"

"Thanks."

"Good, in this position I've realised I need to shave the old nether regions…"

"Night, Melody." He put his mobile down on the desk and hovered over the search bar before biting the bullet and typing in: The Crazy Season.

The page filled with results.

"Wow," he said out loud. He wasn't sure quite what he was expecting, but this was now a lot of stuff to go through.

The first thing that jumped out at him was the name Timothy Salinger. The boy's body had washed up on the shore less than a mile from where they had sat. He jumped off the cliff and, judging by the reports, had hit the rocks long before the waves got him.

Another suicide.

He slowly navigated his way onto forums, quickly making accounts and using the same generic avatar. He lurked in the background reading through the conversations. Some were harsh. It was easy to be rude when hiding behind a laptop away from the world.

The little prick deserved it, someone called CursedChild666 said.

Harsh, bra, was the response from BRockFamous.

Jim Ody

He knew what he was getting into,
CursedChild666 went on.

Joel looked down the forum. CursedChild666 spoke a lot but there were a lot of inconsistences and speculation in what he was saying. He sounded like someone with few facts but a huge imagination. BRockFamous, on the other hand, said less but appeared to know more. There was the feeling he was holding back a little. It seemed to Joel that he also lived there but was careful to say what he knew was second-hand. That could be true, or he might know more and was getting off on that fact.

Joel continued. Slowly he was drawn into the black hole that pulled him in deep and kept him there. He hit another forum but there was only one conversation. Again, it was one person who seemed to enjoy knowing more than the rest.

He took some screenshots, copied the web addresses, and hovered over the send button on his email. He thought about the implication of sending links to the dark web. He almost rang Melody again but thought about how she'd take the piss, especially when he went over what he was asking – *can I send an email with a link in it?* She'd berate him with some response designed at attacking his masculinity.

He threw caution to the wind and pressed send.

He picked up his phone and sent his IT guy a text. He was deliberately not calling him. The guy had no social skills. His name was Gareth, and he looked and acted like a serial killer. Minus the killing part. That he knew of. He rarely smiled. It was as if the muscles in his face didn't work properly or they were too much effort to flex.

The Crazy Season

Within minutes he got a response.

"No. Watching GoT. Try Jez." It was frustrating. Joel had asked him to do a simple thing and he couldn't be bothered as he was watching *Game of Thrones*. He didn't really know Jez. But he'd heard rumours.

He bit the bullet and rang the number that Gareth had passed on.

A loud and enthusiastic voice rang out. "Yo! Pedro's Pizza Parlour. How can I help?" Joel paused, slightly confused until he heard a woman's voice in the background saying, "Hurry up, Jez, or I'll have to finish myself off again!"

"Jez?" Joel asked.

"It is I! Who is this?"

"Hi, my name's Joel Baxter. I'm a friend of Gareth's. He sent me to you as he was... never mind. Can you help me find out the identity of someone via their online name?"

"Oh... Spook?" Jez said.

"Eh?"

"Dr Spook? Isn't that what people call you?" Then there was some fumbling. "I've put you on speaker phone." Joel was about to answer but was distracted by some heavy breathing in the background.

"Sorry, are you in the middle of something?" Joel said.

"Yes!" a voice in the background said loudly. At first it sounded like anger, but then she repeated. "Yes! Yes! Ugh! Ahh!" There was also the sound of bedsprings squeaking.

Jez however, in a normal upbeat tone simply said, "It's okay. I'm multi-tasking."

"Uh-huh. Okay. So, can you help?" The woman sounded like she might need medical attention now. Joel wasn't sure whether she was religious but she'd now said the words God, Jesus, and Almighty, a few times now.

"Yes, of course. Have you got my email address?"

"No, I haven't."

"Okay, let me text it to you."

Then suddenly the female voice said through quick breaths, "You stop now, Jez and I will punch you in the face. Hard! Oh, Jesus! Very, uh, hard!"

"When you're done will be fine," Joel quickly added, feeling embarrassed for the second time that day.

"Right you are," Jez said, sounding as if he was grinning from ear to ear. "D'you think you could hang up though, as I have my hands full at the moment."

Joel hung up just as the female let out an almighty scream. He sat and looked at his phone, unsure exactly what had just gone on. He felt like he needed to shower, though.

Chapter 17 – Ethan

Ethan finished his shift at the Black Rock bar, stuffed the tips into his wallet, and walked out into the cool night air. He was taking each day as it came. He really had no idea what the future held for him.

He glanced around at the huge car park. It was half full. These would be owned by hotel guests. More rich people flashing their cash.

He felt eyes on him.

It was strange as he'd done this shift hundreds of times and never felt like this. This sudden state of paranoia was new.

There had been some patrons that day who had put him on edge. The ones he didn't recognise who asked one too many questions. If people would shut up then everything would remain covered. The secrets hidden. He could then continue with his life.

Part of him wanted to get out of this town. To run away to a big city and make loads of money. It was a

Jim Ody

popular dream around these parts. A fantasy shared by most. And that was the problem.

The thought of something new felt exciting. It was easy to get caught on that hook and reeled in. Before you knew it, you were going in a direction you weren't comfortable with, and there was no way of unhooking yourself.

That's exactly what had happened to him. To the others, too.

It was all about the party. A false rumour that whipped around the shadows and drew people in. He drank up the lies with youthful expectation. He asked no questions. The worst part being how much of it was his fault. The keeping quiet and not warning them was as bad as doing it.

The town was small. He'd dated a handful of girls, and this promised more for him.

Hook, line and sinker. He fell for it.

He sometimes worried that when he was older he'd never be satisfied with just one woman and would become a womaniser crippled by infidelity.

Now, of late, he worried whether he would ever make it to the age he worried about. He knew too much.

But he trusted him. Maybe it was a blind faith, but when you're a teenager you need to find a hero, and he certainly fit the bill.

He walked over to his car looking all around as he went. When he sat in the driver's seat, he looked over his shoulder. Not that he was expecting to see anyone, but he just wanted to be sure.

The Crazy Season

He started the car and pulled out of the car park, and turned onto the road that would take him up and out to his family home just outside of Beach View.

He couldn't help it, the whole while he looked in his mirror expecting to be followed. He eyed pedestrians suspiciously and looked at oncoming cars to see whether the drivers were looking back at him.

This was no way to live a life. He knew that.

And that was the point.

He parked his car and with a last look around him went into the house.

Like most teenage lads, he headed straight for the kitchen. His stomach was full of knots, but he wondered whether it was just a mixture of hunger and anxiety. He'd never felt anxious before. He was pretty good at most things, and whilst he wasn't often the best, his confidence was always high.

When he closed the fridge, he saw the note saying his dad was out. *No surprises there*, he thought.

His dad was so focused on his work that he sometimes forgot he had a son. Until he was useful to him.

He took his plate of food up to his room.

He'd closed his door and turned back towards his bed when he saw it.

A note.

Keep quiet. Speak to no one.

It was short and to the point but scared him nevertheless. He felt himself being pulled in deeper. Being implicated in this whole thing. The finale was to come. It scared the hell out of him. Not for the first time, he thought about chucking his stuff in a bag and driving out of there. He struggled with having

Jim Ody

the same beliefs and motivation, but he was now a major player whether he liked it or not.

He pulled his curtains shut and grabbed his phone.

He probably shouldn't call anyone but he was panicking.

"What are you doing!" the voice hissed back at him in an angry whisper.

"I need to see you," he said.

The words stopped them in their tracks. "We can't," they replied, even though inside it was the last thing they wanted to say.

"It's getting too much."

"Only a few more days, then it will be over."

"Do you believe that?" he said and realised why the conversation was so strange. This should be them saying these words to him.

"It's what he wants."

"It doesn't mean it's right!" He was struggling to keep his voice down, and even though he thought he was alone, he couldn't be sure. Walls have eyes and ears.

"It doesn't matter. We're too far in. People have already died for this. What we should be doing is finding Natasha and Becky."

"I know. That's what worries me."

"What if they've already gone to the police?"

"No, the police would've been here by now, wouldn't they?" There was a paused on the other end and the sound of movement. They were checking out of their window, he thought.

"Can I come over?" He felt desperate saying it. He wanted to see someone else who knew what he was going through. He hated to admit it, but he

The Crazy Season

didn't want to stay in his house on his own. Safety in numbers and all that.

"You can't," the voice replied but there was little conviction. He wanted to say more. Maybe lie a little, but he knew his intentions were purely selfish.

"Are you sure?"

"Aren't you? We need to stay apart, Ethan."

He hated being told what to do. Especially when they were right.

"Okay. Maybe I'll see you tomorrow?"

"Maybe."

He placed his phone on the side and walked to his notice board. It was full of photographs printed from his phone or from his friends' social media accounts. To look at it you'd think he was one of the happiest lads alive. He was grinning in virtually all of them. Some he was holding bottles of alcohol in. Around him were other popular men and women. Girls in bikinis or small vest tops hanging off of him. They were all tans and white teeth; highlights and manicures; despite their tender ages some had already had nose jobs and breast implants. Daddy had bought them a little more self-esteem. Ethan had slept with some of them, but kissed most of them. That was just the way it was.

It was also from a different place before he moved here. He'd gone from being popular to being unknown. He had to start again, and it just didn't seem fair.

He traced a finger over the glossy collage. This was the past. It was the happiest time of his life.

He didn't want to think that it was all gone. He wanted it again.

Jim Ody

That was the promise that had been made to him, and that was the fantasy he held on to so dearly.

He scrolled through his phone and deleted the pictures he had of some of the girls from the collage.

The pictures of them naked.

It wasn't the sort of thing you wanted discovered after you'd been found dead.

He had to get rid of everything before it either became too much for him or they decided he was no longer of use.

He wished he was young again. The way his mum would do everything for him. How easily satisfied he was.

Before he'd come here and been talked into a plan that could only be evil.

Chapter 18 – Joel

Joel had tossed and turned all night. One minute he was plumping up his pillows, and the next he was smoothing them out flat. The covers were pulled up, and then they were flung off. He couldn't get comfortable. But it wasn't his bed.

It was never about his bed.

There was so much going on inside his head that he almost got up.

The biggest issue he had was to do with the case. Or more so to do with Cherry.

Joel had decided the best way to get to the bottom of what was happening in Black Rock was to go and stay there overnight. Really commit to it. Driving back and forth was not going to work. It was all about getting the facts quickly. They were dealing with missing people, not misplaced objects.

What kept him awake was missing out on seeing Cherry that afternoon. And that then sounded selfish.

Jim Ody

He was prioritising one life over another. He felt awful for even thinking about it.

And then he would be with Melody. That seemed like a double-blow. It was almost rubbing it in her face. *I'm not coming to see you today, oh, and I'm spending the next couple of days with another attractive woman. Ok?*

He felt like the world's biggest loser. Even thinking in his head that Melody was attractive seemed like cheating. These were all emotional conundrums he'd not experienced before.

God, he missed Cherry. He wanted so badly to have her next to him when he woke up in the morning. The times he'd wake up cold to find she'd pulled the covers from him and cocooned herself. He'd have a flash of frustration before seeing how cute she looked asleep. He'd get up and get another blanket instead so as not to wake her.

The sun was cutting through the gap in the curtains when he grabbed his phone to check his emails. Jez had come through for him. He had a name. In fact, it was the same single name to all of the profiles. Martin Davidson.

He lived in Black Rock a few streets away from the Black Rock hotel. The plot thickened.

He responded back with a thanks to Jez. What was it with IT guys? The two he knew were both at the opposite ends of the social spectrum. One never smiled, and the other did nothing but smile. Maybe it was the bright lights from staring at monitors all day, or the complex algorithms and coding. Or maybe they were both a little weird.

The Crazy Season

His finger hovered over Melody's name in his phone. For a fleeting moment, he wondered whether he should just go on his own to Black Rock, but logically it made sense to go with someone else. If he was digging into a town's secrets, then people would soon find out. In his experience it didn't take long for locals to determine whether or not you were a tourist. They were happy to take your money but not so happy to tell on their neighbours. Most just wanted to be left alone and isolated from the world.

He took a deep breath and pressed her name anyway.

"Twice in twenty-four hours!" she said, sounding bright-eyed and bushy-tailed. "I was just doing my naked yoga again."

"You're trying to shock me," he said out loud. He'd meant to keep it in his head.

"Not at all. If I was trying to shock you then I'd go into the details about the body hair I removed after you called last." She sighed. "Clothes are so restricting!"

"No, it's okay. I believe you."

"What's up? I've already told you what I'm wearing, so what about you?"

"Is this how our conversations will go each time I ring you?"

"Probably. I like the squirm in your voice."

"The squirm in my voice?"

"There it is again." He could picture her smiling. He tried not to picture anything else.

"Okay. Anyway. The reason I called. Maybe we should stay over in Black Rock."

Jim Ody

"Like a dirty weekend?" When she heard the silence she quickly backtracked. "Sorry. Continuez."

"Was that French?"

"*Oui.*"

"Anyway. I'm going to go to the hospital to see Cherry this morning, then we can get going."

"You don't have to worry," she said after a beat or two. The humour had gone, and she was being serious. "I know it feels strange going away with me, but it's to help others, isn't it? She'd get that. From what you say, she's a wonderful person."

Joel was nodding, and barely managed to respond, "Yes. The best."

"Please tell me she farts though? I know she's perfect, but surely every once in a while…"

"Nobody's perfect."

"That will do. You check out the dark web?" she said quick to change the subject.

"I did. I'll tell you all about it later."

"Cool. Okay, go and see your wife, and I'll pack the condoms."

"Eh?"

"Joke."

Joel didn't realise he was smiling until he caught himself in the mirror. The fact that Melody came out with these things probably just meant she was comfortable with him. He liked that. He also liked that she didn't pussyfoot around him.

Joel sipped his coffee and ate his toast, all the while he jotted down notes on a pad and looked on his other laptop (the one he kept in his house) about Martin Davidson.

The Crazy Season

He was fifteen and, despite all of his cyber-aliases, was quite happy to let the world and his mother have access to his social media pages. Joel saw this with youngsters. They longed for validation in their lives, and whilst they knew all about covering their tracks, they often consciously left the window to their lives open for the world to see. They wanted to be known. They craved to be famous. Martin was one of these. His posts were boastful, and he spent most of the time showing off and grinning at a camera he was holding himself. That spoke volumes. The only person who wanted to shoot a picture of him was him.

Joel washed up his breakfast stuff and then threw some clothes into an overnight bag. He was about to leave the room when he looked at the wedding picture on the side. For almost a minute he stood still, transferred back to that happy day. Then with a consolation smile, he snatched it up and placed it in his bag.

Fifteen minutes later and he was pulling into his spot in the hospital car park.

It felt strange being there so early in the morning. A disruption to his routine. The cars around were not the ones he'd grown familiar with. The light from the sun was different, and when he eventually got to the familiar floor, the nurses were polite but less personable. He still knew them, as they often changed shifts. An older lady sat behind the desk today. She looked up and smiled a hello without engaging.

That was okay with Joel. He had a lot on his mind.

Jim Ody

He walked over to Cherry and smoothed her face with the back of his hand. He glanced over his beautiful wife now surrounded by pipes and wires.

He pulled out his phone and wondered whether there was any point to the sentimentality of the song he played daily.

But he played it anyway. Those four minutes and eight seconds gave him a moment of contemplation. He took in his wife in her current state and thought about a time when she was so much more.

He'd tried singing it to her once, many years ago, but he would never be confused with a singer. She appreciated the gesture, but fell into a fit of giggles that told him it was something he'd be best not to repeat.

The sun shone in through the window upon her. It felt like heaven was opening up its gates welcoming her. Energising the small light that still shone inside of her.

When the song was over, he placed the phone back into his pocket and leant over and whispered into her ear, "I want you back, Cherry. I really, really do… but if that is not possible, then please don't hang on for me." He kissed her cheek again. Each time she seemed to get colder, and he wondered whether she was getting further away from him rather than closer.

"Robyn needs you." His voice quivered as he thought about his dead daughter all alone. He wondered if there was an awful struggle going on where Cherry was stuck between life and death. Her daughter and her husband.

The Crazy Season

Joel sat back down on the chair that felt more familiar than ones he owned.

"I am going away for the next day or so," he began. It felt like a confession, and he was surprised at how emotional he felt. "There's this case," he continued, and remembered he'd already told her about it. "The boy, Timothy. He's been found. He committed suicide. Something isn't right and I need to get to the bottom of it before more people die..." he looked at her. Her eyelids twitched very slightly. It was completely normal. He'd seen her fingers move before. The feeling of elation and disappointment within a space of a few minutes was awful. Now, he just accepted it.

There were some footsteps from the doorway followed by a voice he'd come to know well.

"You're early," she said, sitting down wearily in the chair he'd decided was hers. "But you still look like you have the weight of the world on your shoulders."

"I can't make it this afternoon. I need to go back to Black Rock."

"Your case."

"Yes. I was thinking about it all night. The only way I can solve the case is by being there and following up every lead, but..."

"You wanted to still come back each day."

He nodded. "Yes. You always seem to know. How is that?"

"I'm a nurse. It's what I do. I observe and make judgements."

Joel looked at her. The kindness in her eyes. The way she came to see him each day. "You know," he said to her. "I think doctors are fantastic at what they do. They train, and learn, but nurses, the most important thing they bring cannot be taught. It's not academic, it's a natural intuition."

Carol almost blushed. "Well, you're a charmer, aren't you?"

He ignored the compliment. "You're always here, helping others. You know, I'm not sure how I would've coped had you not been here each day, too." He nodded gently to her hoping she understood how important she'd become to him. He continued. "There are suicides, and I don't know why. What is so bad that it makes somebody take their own life?"

Carol looked over almost speechless. "Everybody has a reason. Try not to judge them on that."

"I know but it's so… final?"

This time it was she who ignored him. "Joel. You need to do what is best for the greater good. If that means going away for a few days, then Cherry here would be fine with that. She'd be proud even. You are no use to anyone moping around these rooms when you could be out in that huge wide world getting to the bottom of all the oddities of life." She knew he was listening and taking it all in. She didn't even look at her watch, but stood up anyway. "Go. Bring happiness to someone else, and then come back when you've succeeded."

"What if I don't?" he questioned.

"You will," she winked. "I just know it." She walked away, but as she got to the door, she turned. "You're doing the right thing, Joel."

"Thank you." The words meant so much more than they sounded.

He turned back to Cherry. "This is it," he said flippantly. He kissed her again, and held her hand.

"I'll see you soon." The words echoed around the room as he disappeared.

Chapter 19 – Joel

She was already outside when he pulled up. Melody had a huge grin that almost wrapped around her head. She looked like a woman looking for adventure. She had a rucksack on her back and was wearing another pair of cargo shorts with a vest and a shirt over the top.

"How are you doin', Joel?" She asked as she opened up the back and chucked her small bag in.

"I'm good," Joel responded before adding, "How long you going for?"

"Clean knickers and a few girlie things. We like to rough it with you boys, but there are those essentials that we just can't do without. Feminism hasn't managed to do away with them yet."

Joel was aware he made a vague grunting sound. One of those that could be taken whichever way the listener decided. If a woman mentioned feminism in a sentence then there was a likelihood they had no interest in his opinion. He had no idea on Melody's views but had a feeling within a couple of days he would. Inside and out.

"I'm embarrassing you," she said out loud, which ironically enough only served to do just that.

"I've lived with women," he added as she got in. "Don't forget that." Instantly he regretted it as it sounded more boastful than factual.

"Before your wife?"

"Yes, I don't think Cherry would've taken too kindly to me shacking up with other women while we were married. We're not one of *those* couples."

Melody nodded then clearly remembered where he'd been that morning as she said, "And how is she?" then to soften any tension added, "Your wife, I mean, not the harem you're beating from your front door."

Joel found her to be strange, but replied with, "The same, I guess."

"Sorry, that sounded flippant."

"No, no," Joel said and puffed out his cheeks. "I have to get used to the fact she may never get any better. She may end up like that for years to come."

Melody had a way of looking out of the window when she was saying something sensitive. "How does that make you feel? Again, I don't mean it to sound like such a stupid question." She finished by looking at him.

The car had now turned onto the main road that would take them south. There were still some thunder clouds high in the sky that looked like they may be chasing them, but behind them was a gorgeous blue sky and a memory of the earlier sunshine. Maybe that was the analogy of how he felt.

Jim Ody

"I'm getting used to it," he said slightly defeated. "It doesn't get any easier, but I accepted it weeks ago. It's part of my routine, which I suppose is why I… you know…"

"Freaked out?"

That was it, he thought. *Freaked out*. "Yeah. Freaked out when I thought of breaking that cycle. We like routine, right? Or at least I do. Eating and sleeping, but also all of those little things we do, too. Any break in that can make us anxious."

"You know that most of the time when you talk to me it's like a lecturer to a pupil?"

He whipped his head around. "Do I?"

She laughed. "It's not a bad thing. You're always looking to teach me the deep workings of the mind."

"Sorry, that sounds condescending."

She was rolling her eyes. "Take the stick out ya arse. It's nice, and educational. I was merely pointing it out, not criticising you."

"I see."

She then turned to the window and mumbled. "I hope you don't do it in the bedroom."

"What?"

She then put on a voice he assumed she thought to be like his. "I'm now going to gently rub your nipples, as I believe there are sensory glands that may well bring you pleasure."

"I get the point."

She continued, clearly amused. "I see your eyes are rolling back into your head in a way that would suggest the foreplay is of a pleasurable quality."

"I don't even speak like that!"

The Crazy Season

She was on a roll now. "I observe you're nibbling your lower lip and your face has become flushed I therefore wish to whip out my hard..."

"Okay, okay. I get the point."

They both chuckled to themselves, neither wanting to show their amusement.

"I'm not sure I'd cope," Melody said after a while. At times her honesty was refreshing, and at others she could come across as being rude.

"But what would you do in my situation?"

"You know what? I don't know. I really don't know."

Creedence Clearwater Revival were now singing about a bad moon rising. Coming up to midday, it seemed completely out of place. To Joel, it would always remind him of the horror movie *American Werewolf in London,* but Cherry loved it. Her dad played it when she was young.

"Your brother sent me a text this morning," Joel said, tapping the steering wheel. "He thanked me for picking you up."

"He worries too much."

"That may be so, but it's nice to know he cares, right?"

"Yeah. It is. Although I don't know why he worries so much."

"Yesterday, I picked you up from outside a stranger's house where you were wearing a pair of knickers and a grin. I kinda get why he might worry."

"At least they were my good knickers. And don't try and tell me you didn't notice."

"I'm not even going to bite."

She seemed thoughtful for a second. "You know, despite all of my escapades, I know Kip's always there. I probably don't deserve him."

"That is the wonder of families. Blood thicker than water and all that."

"We put our parents through hell. A homosexual and a tramp, just what every parent wants."

"They're okay with Kip's sexuality though, aren't they?"

"Yeah, to start off with I think my dad struggled with it. He had these preconceived ideas of Kip bringing home girls, and it was almost like he had to reconfigure his thoughts before he fully embraced it."

"And you being a slut?"

"I said tramp, not slut!" She threw him a mock frown. "He used his denial on me. What he didn't see didn't happen!"

"It's good you have them though."

"What about your family?" she asked.

"I guess I have one somewhere," he admitted. "I was abandoned and sent into care. I went to a few foster homes. It was okay."

"You say that, but honestly, man to woman, did you have it hard?"

He shook his head. "You know what? It was fine. Each family was nice, and I was treated completely fine…"

"But?"

"I wasn't theirs. They knew I was temporary. I guess nobody got too close because they knew I'd be gone in a few years."

"That's sad," she said bothering her nail and then chewing it.

The Crazy Season

"Is that why you help people?"

"I don't know. It sounds like pop-psychology. I'd say it's more selfish than that. It's not helping people, it's exposing the truth. Searching for an answer."

"That's not selfish."

Joel looked out of his driver's window. He didn't see any of the cars on the other side of the road though. He was thinking. An upbringing of trying to fit in. Of searching for who he was.

"I just like answers. Hanging questions are the worst thing for me."

"Have you ever tried to find your parents?"

"No." The answer was short, he realised that. He'd been asked it before, and it always remained the same.

"Can I ask why?"

"What if they are bad people? What if they have done awful things? Wouldn't it be better not to know?"

"You're a walking contradiction. You hate hanging questions, and yet the biggest question of your life you are not willing to find the answer for."

"I don't have to know everything." His words slipped out.

"And yet, Joel Baxter, I think you do."

A few more miles down the road, and the music had changed pace to the political angst of Rage Against The Machine. They were both nodding their heads to the heavy beats. This was his choice and a song Cherry had tolerated in the past.

Jim Ody

"I probably should've mentioned," Melody said in the way she was prone to do, "I booked us in to a place to stay."

"Really? Where?" It had totally escaped Joel to even think about booking somewhere. In the back of his mind, he assumed there would be loads of places available. It was hardly the height of the season.

"A B&B down by the coast. I booked us in for two nights, but obviously if you need to get back tomorrow, then…" her words trailed off. Joel didn't want to think about it. To miss a whole day without seeing Cherry seemed awful. He'd have to build up to it, but in all honesty, he couldn't see it happening.

"We'll see," he replied anyway and then quickly added, "Thank you for doing that."

"You're welcome." And then she quickly changed the subject. "I can't believe Timothy is dead."

"It certainly makes the case seem all the more real now. We were working on speculation and one suicide, and now we have two. In a small town like Black Rock, that is unusual. They both went to the same school and were the same age, so there has to be a connection."

"Well, it could still be a number of things. Bullying, social media, drugs, teen love, sexuality. D'you forget what it was like to be a teenager?" She was right. It might not be anything sinister at all. It seemed the pressures of being a teen meant you were under the microscope more. The expectations of how to act and what to do seemed to be that much stronger.

The Crazy Season

"I do," he admitted. "I had a crush on a girl called Heidi. She was popular, but the quiet one of the 'In-Crowd'. A mass of dark hair and these cute dimples."

Melody chuckled when she added. "I assume there was no happy ending?"

"I think there rarely are with crushes."

"I wouldn't say that. At school, I had a crush on Peter Brown. I gave him a handjob in the bushes of the school fields. He certainly got a happy ending."

"How romantic."

"I thought so at the time. Until my friend did the same the very next day."

"Wow! Our lives growing up really couldn't have been more different, could they?"

She grinned. "What happened with Heidi?"

"Nothing much. My friend asked her out for me, and she said no. She never had a boyfriend as far as I knew, but it crushed me."

"Hold up," she threw her hands up. "You got your friend to ask her out for you? Jesus, Joel, how did you ask your wife out, by email?"

"I was short on confidence."

"But still…"

"It didn't matter anyway as a month later I was with a new family and enrolled into a new school."

They both were smiling and thinking about those school days many years ago. Joel had assumed Melody had been a wild child. He also knew she had taken a lot of crap for her brother being gay. He may not be flamboyant or camp in any way, but he had never hidden who he was. It was good to hear, but Melody had felt the need to fight anyone who dared look at him funny, and became loud and aggressive by way of a defence.

When the now familiar sign for Black Rock appeared, Melody sat up to attention and gave Joel directions to where the B&B was.

"For someone who claims to have been in a drugged out, drunken, sexual haze for the period she was here, you seem to know your way around this place."

"Strange as it may seem, it wasn't a drugged-out orgy for the whole time. Sometimes I wanted some time alone without being groped or penetrated."

"You have a unique turn of phrase," he said as they followed the road along the sea front.

"Turn here," she said. "It's this house on the left."

The word house was an understatement. It could easily have been a hotel. It was that big. There were a number of floors, and was as wide as three normal-sized houses.

"Jesus, how much is this place?"

"You're cheap."

Joel frowned at her. "It's not that," he said, getting out of the car. He offered nothing else. It was that, and they both knew it.

"Look, don't sweat it. We can sort something out later, okay." Joel wasn't quite sure what that meant, but he was fed up of second guessing everything.

"Come on. We're here to meet the owner, Miss Shannon."

"Have we slipped back into the 50s, suddenly?" Joel was amused by the quirkiness of some people. The Cornish were certainly quirkier than their neighbours in Devon or further up in Somerset.

The Crazy Season

They pushed open the double-door and entered by a reception area. This was a simple high desk with a bell on it, and behind looked to be a computer.

Melody of course bashed the bell with her palm without waiting to see if anybody was around.

A noise from down the hallway was followed by a sweet-sounding voice of an older lady. "Just coming!"

"Miss Shannon," Melody mouthed, and Joel nodded. He'd figured that out for himself.

When she appeared, she looked like an older motherly figure. She was a slight woman with a cute face, lined with age and laughter, and her grey hair was up in a bun. She had large wire-rimmed glasses that made her look elegant but with a youthful glow. It was hard to age her.

"Ah, Melody wasn't it, and this is a strapping fellow. You did say two rooms, didn't you dear? Only that's what I've booked, but I can change it?"

Melody looked at Joel.

"Two rooms," he confirmed, at which Miss Shannon glanced at Melody with a frown.

"Shame," she said and produced two keys from a box. She held them out.

"Thanks," Joel and Melody said together.

This made Miss Shannon grin and clasp her hands together. "Ah, you young ones certainly lead complicated lives!"

Joel and Melody couldn't help but look at each other. It was only a quick glance but they'd already perfected a subtle recognition.

"Well, I'll leave you to it." She clicked her heels, turned and was gone.

Jim Ody

"Wow," was all Joel had to say.

Chapter 20 – Martin

A week ago

It was a fucking joke, Martin thought as he saw his mate Stevie become all mysterious. He always turned into such a dick when it came to women. He was obsessed with April, and of course Becky. Yeah, well, join the queue. April was the school fantasy. He thought she was totally banging. Most of the boys there had thought about her at some point. Mostly, when locked in their bathrooms pretending to be checking their balls for lumps. And those with brains outside of their pants knew she'd be nothing more than a wet dream. Even Stevie - to his credit - recognised as much which was why he was now following Becky around like some soppy idiot. She was still a league too high, but she was the type that was slightly more attainable. Hope springs eternal, and in the right environment, with no one around and some flowing alcohol, anything was possible.

Stevie was hoping he was the saddo-got-lucky character in a rom-com movie, but it would inevitably be so corny that it would never make it past its initial pitch, let alone to casting.

Martin had tried to talk him out of it, to save face, but Stevie was having none of it. He was deluded by lust.

"Fam, let her go, init. She's Gucci, she ain't interested!" he said in the school hallways after Becky had gone to her class and Stevie was left stood alone, unsure what he was meant to do without her to follow.

"You're jealous," was all Stevie said.

"Nah, my G. Not at all." But Martin had to admit, it sounded a little that way. The only action he'd had was touching Brenda Bolton's boob, and that had cost him a Mars bar. She'd still been wearing her T-shirt, too. He'd heard rumours that he'd have to supply her with a tad more confectionary items for the good stuff, but he also wasn't comfortable with doing so. The whole transaction part didn't sit comfortably with him. Then, when he was grabbing and poking away, like a kid with a new toy, she'd been munching on the chocolate bar and stuffing it into her chubby face acting like he wasn't there. He didn't like it. When she'd finished and licked all the crumbs, she turned to him and said, "Unless you've got more sweets, that's your lot." Embarrassed, he got up and mumbled thanks. It had been more humiliating than exciting.

He wanted to say, "Babe, Man got mad skills but man all outta treats. Laters, yeah?" But instead he skulked off.

Rumour was, she got a lot of snacks free. Someone once gave her a tub of Quality Street. It was unclear what he got in return, but the story went that the lad in question didn't wash his hands for a whole week afterwards.

Martin wondered what Becky had promised Stevie. Whatever it was, it had made him wander around like someone from that old movie *Invasion of The Body Snatchers*. In a trance.

The thing was, he knew it would end badly.

He didn't realise just how badly.

Chapter 21 - Joel

The B&B was grand. All mahogany with dark red and cream paisley carpets. The outside didn't do the inside justice.

"Hello there!" A voice sang out. "New guests, I presume!"

Joel turned and was met by a guy with wild white hair and a cultivated moustache and beard combo like he was a mad-professor with a liking for General Custer.

"Hi," Joel said.

"Hello, sir," Melody said in a completely out of character way. Joel had noticed her ability to morph into whatever character she deemed fit for each situation.

"I'm Charles," he said, striding over. His arm already outstretched ready to shake. "I run this place with Miss Shannon."

"I see," Joel said, more as something to say.

The Crazy Season

Charles had already clasped hold of Melody as she told him her name.

"Well, that's a rather fitting name for a beautiful lady," he smiled. A twinkle of a gold tooth peeked out from his mouth. He was older than Miss Shannon but had no less energy.

"I'm hardly a lady!" she winked, which set him off into a loud and throaty guffaw.

"Wonderful! Those are the best kinds!"

Joel then took his hand and pumped it. "I'm Joel," he said.

"Joel? Joel?" he mumbled looking up to the high ceilings just in case what he was trying to remember was written on the simple but impressive chandelier.

"Joel Baxter," Joel added, if that was what he was trying to remember.

"Of course. The Mystery Man! Dr Spook, isn't it?"

"Well, I… er."

Charles grinned, which sent the twirls of his moustache up north. "I'm joking. Pay me no mind. When you get to my age, life requires gallows humour to get by! Anyway, perhaps we'll catch up at supper? I've read a lot about you!"

"Yes," Joel said, as the old man raised a hand, nodded at them both, and walked off with a spring in his step.

"O-kay," Melody said.

"If someone is found dead in the study, then we're not staying here. It already feels like an Agatha Christie novel."

Jim Ody

Melody remained tight-lipped as they took another flight of stairs. They were now on the top floor.

A coat of armour stood rigid and sinister with a large battle-axe in its hand.

"Great," Melody said nodding towards it. "Just what I need outside of my room."

"The fearless woman does have a weakness after all."

"Doughnuts, mainly. Oh, and when someone touches my…"

"I get the point." He laughed at the way she spoke so freely. He walked up to the armour and peered at it closely. "I think you've been watching too many Scooby Doo episodes! D'you know how long it takes to put one of these things on?"

"Never had a cause to think about it," she admitted. "I'll leave the analytics to you."

"Well, it's a faff. Let's just say that. It might seem to be a good way to pull a prank, but highly inefficient."

"O-kay." She sounded bored.

Joel looked down at his keys and then up at the door on the right with a matching number.

13.

"Right, well. I guess I'll see you in five minutes."

She looked at her own keys as he pointed to another door as a hint.

"Yeah," she said, glanced again at the coat of armour, and turned to wrestle with the key.

Joel turned his key and pushed against the heavy door as it swung open into an impressive room. There was a large wooden bed with more linen than seemed necessary, real or faux antique looking furniture, comprised of a desk, a wardrobe and a chest of drawers. There was an *ensuite* on the far side, and a large window that allowed the light to flood in.

Joel placed his bag on the bed and walked over to the window.

It was a sea view. Choppy waters were devoid of boats. The wind whipped up a single item of litter that looped-the-loop in the air like a cheap kite.

He took a deep breath.

What am I doing here? He thought to himself.

He felt like part of him was still an hour or so up the coast. Of course it was. Laid in a hospital bed with nothing to do but stay alive and wait for him.

Had he made the right decision?

Would she know?

Would she care?

He looked to the side where there was a small cluster of houses. He tried to focus on the case at hand. Suicide was an extremely hard thing to get to the bottom of. People were complex and at other times just plain simple. The appetite to take one's life at times appeared trivial. Most people couldn't understand it.

It's often said that everybody has the ability to take their own life. They have a rational tolerance that ensures this doesn't happen, however sometimes that scale reduces drastically when psychological distress is introduced.

That was the key.

A movement down below caught his eye. A dark figure disappeared out of view. It might've been completely innocent, but Joel had this niggling feeling that the person had been watching him.

A small rap on the door shook him from the thought.

He walked over and opened it up to see Melody grinning from ear to ear.

"Sea views and large beds. Didn't I do well!"

He nodded. "Very impressive. Are you going to suddenly produce a huge itemised bill at the end of this?"

"Now there's an idea!" She was then looking past him into the room. "Nice!"

"Yes. Not wanting to increase the size of your head any further, I will admit you appear to have done well. Did someone die in here or something?"

Melody looked suddenly shifty. "Er, come on," she said. "We've people to keep from dying and cases to solve!"

He pulled the door closed. "Really? Someone died in there?"

"It's just a rumour really."

"Tell me it didn't make the papers?"

"It didn't make the papers." Her voice went up at the end. Either it was a lie or she had turned Australian.

"It did."

"Just a small one." Joel was intrigued rather than worried. He'd uncovered enough hauntings to be sceptical for both of them.

"You ain't afraid of no ghosts!" she then sang a bad version of the Ghostbusters' song.

The Crazy Season

"Busting makes me feel good," he replied unenthusiastically and in his normal voice. They got to the bottom of the stairs.

"Here they are!" Miss Shannon declared as she walked with an armful of clean bedding. "Usually, the lure of the big beds are too much for young couples!" She gave a coy grin that had nothing but dirty thoughts behind it. "But of course, you two are not a couple, right?" Without waiting for a response, she turned and walked off chuckling to herself.

"I'm not sure she's all there," Melody said as Joel looked puzzled. "Gin or pills, is my guess."

The fresh air hit them, as did a light drizzle.

"Where to, boss?" she said, putting on a flimsy, almost transparent raincoat.

"Let's go and visit Martin, shall we?"

She nodded then stopped. "Hold on. Do you mean at his house?"

"No, on the moon! Yes, at his house. The place he lives."

Melody raised her eyebrows. "O-kay, I see how we are playing this. Sarcasm, is it? Well, Inspector Morse, what do you think will happen when we turn up at this lad's house?"

Joel knew he looked as confused as he was. "I dunno. He talks to us?"

"Jesus," she shook her head. "You got much experience with teenagers? I'll tell you what will happen! Either the parents will answer the door, ask us who we are, and then tell us royally to piss off, or Martin will answer the door, deny who he is, or tell us royally to piss off!"

"You think?"

Jim Ody

"Well, more like," she cleared her throat and got herself into character. "I know nuffin', innit fam? You's might be bangin' an all peng, but ahh swear down, bruv. It ain't even like that! Manz bait cause beef, innit? Nah, get out ta endz!" She ended by flipping her wrist and clicking her finger.

Joel just stared at her, his mouth hung wide. "What the hell was that."

"Youth-speak."

"Are you able to translate that for those of us who remember three channels, and the loud screeching sound of the internet!"

"I'm told he speaks like that. I said, 'I don't know anything about that, madam. You might be highly attractive and good-looking, but honestly, I think you are tricking me into some trouble. Please leave the area.' Okay?"

"When I was a kid, we thought we were fooling adults by saying fan-dabby-dozy!"

Melody laughed out loud at that. "Things have moved on since the rib-tickling anarchic antics of The Krankies, Joel."

"So it would seem. I've forgotten how this all started again?"

"Do you want me to get you a pen and a paper? Shit, the old couple from the B&B have more get up and go than you, and they've lived through two world wars!"

Joel frowned. "I'm not sure that's true, is it?"

"That's not the point. Okay, dummies guide to teenagers. Ring him and get him to meet us somewhere."

The Crazy Season

Joel understood that. He wished she'd made that point clearer to begin with and not put on that very strange pantomime whilst they were standing in the rain.

He pulled out his mobile and quickly found the details from the strange guy, Jez. He'd not thought to put the lad's telephone number into his phone.

He then pressed the call button and wondered whether he should try using some slang.

"I didn't see nothing," the voice said with panic.

"Hello?" Joel countered back.

"Oh, uh, yeah? Who this?"

"Is that Martin?" There was a pause. Martin was thinking things over.

"Who this?" he repeated.

"My name's Joel, and I'm trying to get to the bottom of things in Black Rock."

"I...er, I don't know..."

Joel cut in. "We know. Meet us somewhere. Anywhere you want." Again, there was silence at the other end. Joel glanced at Melody who was motioning her hand in a circle, presumably as encouragement for him to continue.

"Martin? We can help you."

"Okay," he said. "I'll DM, innit."

"Thank you." Martin cut the call, and Joel was trying to work out what DM meant. In his day it was Danger Mouse. He assumed that to no longer be the case. He soon worked out it would be a text message.

Melody looked relieved. "I'm not sure whether I was more worried about him not meeting us or you trying out some street slang."

"I thought about it."

Jim Ody

"I know. That's what worried me."

They took a walk over the road to a storm wall that had the beach behind it. They needed to give Martin a few minutes to think things over.

There was then a sudden movement, and Joel turned to see the guy from the day before dancing over and wearing a different tabard. This one was yellow and was about water shortage in Africa.

"Hello to you, beautiful people. What a lovely couple!" He began. "Are you having a good day?"

Joel hated this sort of talk with a passion. Small talk that people used only as a bridge towards their more pressing question, or rather the task in hand of signing up new donors.

"I was at the hospital this morning to see my wife who's in a coma. She's still alive so I think we can confirm it's a good day."

The smile fell from the guy's face. "Oh," he said, his mind now quickly calculating his sales patter to save his commission. "You'll understand then about helping others, right?"

Melody was unusually quiet. Joel got the feeling she enjoyed it when he was the one being slightly outspoken.

"And who is it I'm helping exactly? You were all about the elderly yesterday, I believe, right?"

The guy gulped. He realised he was going to have work for his percentage today. "I help a number of charities," he conceded. "I like to reach out to a number of people and make them aware of as many causes as possible. You'd be surprised at how many fortunate people don't feel the need to spare just a small amount of change each month in order to help

The Crazy Season

others…" he paused but it felt like for dramatic effect. Joel thought the guy might actually try and cry on the spot. "I think you'll agree these are good causes, right?"

Joel glanced at Melody, and then replied, "A question that's very hard to respond to in a negative fashion. Good training. I suspect you'll now say that many people have been giving generously, which is a last ditch attempt to free me of some cash by means of guilt. A sign up you'll hope I forget about so I continue to pay until the day I die."

"If you can't afford it…"

Joel turned to Melody and cocked a thumb back as he said, "You believe this guy? He now tries another line in a passive-aggressive manner. A direct dig at the fact he knows I can afford the amount he's trying to fleece me for, but this time he is directing his sales pitch at my alpha-male side. He thinks I'll not want to be shown up in front of you so I will sign up, and not for the minimum amount but more in puffed-chest pissing contest win that secretly he doesn't mind losing."

The guy grabbed his clipboard, "You'll sign up then?"

"No. I won't."

Melody was opening up her hands in a suggestion that said she was no longer interested in the conversation. She was gazing off into the distance at the people coming out of shops with their smiling children and flimsy bags of tat.

Then Joel felt his phone buzz. It was Martin.

Jim Ody

"I have to take this!" he said to the guy, who now looked relieved and was shuffling off with a lot less style than he'd had when he danced over to them.

Melody was laughing, properly grinning and almost bent over.

"What was that all about?" she said when she'd caught herself before an asthma attack.

"When I came into money last year, all I had was people trying to take it from me. It was the most popular time of my life. I hated it. I was in a dark place, and all I had was people pushing more guilt on me!"

"Chill out, Scooby-Doo. Joel, the guy was just trying to earn some cash. He only gets paid when people sign up, and then half of them pull out after a few days meaning he loses that commission."

"But he was here yesterday touting another charity that was the biggest cause in the world, and tomorrow it will be something else."

Melody held up her hands again. "Look, I'm not saying it's the best job in the world, and personally the morals are a little sketchy, but he's a salesman creating cash for charities. Yes, they lose a bit in commission. No, he probably knows nothing more about the charities than what was in the leaflet on the back of his clipboard. But so what?"

"I dunno. I just didn't trust him."

She laughed again at that. "What is Martin saying?"

Chapter 22 - Natasha

A week before

Natasha looked longingly out of her window as she saw April walk by. She was all dressed up and looked amazing. Like that didn't come easy for her! Natasha wasn't sure she'd seen her ever look bad. Even in joggers and a T-shirt she looked great. Her unbrushed hair looked deliberately tousled. Some people were just so lucky.

She looked back at her bedroom door. It was halfway open. Her dad made her keep it that way so he could slip in and out to make sure she was doing her homework. Even when she had nothing due, he was on to her to go over what she'd learnt. He meant well. He just wanted her to succeed.

It was a Thursday night. She knew there were parties going on. Well, not so much parties as such, but gatherings of her peers. They got together at the

Jim Ody

park, or down by the beach. She was left cold on the outside.

"Tash, why don't you come?" Becky had said to her once. Nobody ever called her that. It felt nice. Sort of friendly.

She'd paused, wanting so badly to nod her head and say she'd be there. Instead, she pictured her father sneering at her and raising a hand ready to slap her. He didn't want her going out when there was revision to be done. Of course, he didn't want her going out at all.

Natasha got up and strained to still see the perfect figure of April sashaying down the road. She was gorgeous. Then, as she went out of sight, Natasha sat back down at her desk and looked carefully at the work in front of her. She read and reread the lines of philosophers on the screen. It was a subject close to her father's heart and one he pushed her to study further.

She'd enjoyed it earlier in the year. The lucid thoughts on perception had made her question the motivations of others. The complete being of mankind and everything that surrounds it. But for the most part it was confusing and conflicting theology. The views of men dead a long time ago. And with their revelations had the world become a better place? Natasha didn't think so. She now questioned her life. Her childhood was slipping through her fingertips. She'd never get it back. Someday, she'd be sitting, staring out the window and wondering where her life had gone. Her husband out, and a couple of kids demanding her attention. She thought she'd be on antidepressants like her mum. It seemed to be a topic of conversations held regularly by her mum and her friends; which pills worked the best.

Her gaze wandered from the textbook and then past her laptop out into the street again.

She thought about the curves of April. The way she made the boys fall at her feet and do whatever she wanted. She wanted that. That power.

Or perhaps she was also part of the crowd in awe.

She'd never had a boyfriend. The boys at her school just didn't attract her. She wondered if she'd change when she went to university.

Although the thought of April made her feel different. She didn't just want to be friends with her like the other girls did. The ones who followed her around agreeing with everything she said. It wasn't like that. She didn't want to be part of the group.

She wanted to be with her alone.

She wanted to kiss her; and that was what really scared her. She figured it was a stupid crush. Nothing more.

"Natasha!" a voice boomed from behind her. "There is nothing outside of the text!" He was quoting Jacques Derrida, the deconstruction theorist.

She turned and in a small voice from memory replied, "Imagination decides everything." A quote of her own playfully volleyed back to him. Blaise Pascal, a probability theorist.

Her father smiled at that but added his own Blaise Pascal quote in return: "Imagination leads us astray." He seemed pleased with himself as he pointed to her and then down at both the laptop and the open text book.

"I *am* working," she whined.

Jim Ody

"When you're my age you'll be thankful of the hard work you put into your study. You reap what you sow!"

She was very close to asking him which philosopher said that, but proverbs were often dismissed by him. If there was no definitive person attributed to a quote then he held little to no value to it. Instead, she nodded and sadly said, "I know."

He sighed and walked over. "Natasha," he said, trying to come across now as caring. "I know some of your friends go out. You're young. You have your whole life ahead of you." He went to smooth her hair, but his hand remained outstretched and empty. An action he'd decided against. Instead, a sympathetic smile appeared. He nodded as if an unspoken understanding had passed between them and left her to it.

She watched him go, unsure of the relationship they had anymore. She'd grown up, and he'd not wanted to accept that. It was expected. Daddy's little girls would always remain just that.

She looked at the large text book filled with other people's ideologies, and then at the laptop screen, and decided right there and then she would look to take control of her life.

She wanted more from it. She wanted excitement.
She wanted April Montague.

The next day her actions changed everything in her life.

She stood outside class looking at April. She was trying to be subtle about it, but she knew she was staring nevertheless.

The Crazy Season

"Hey Tash. We had a great night last night..." Becky stood there letting the words hang as she saw where Natasha's eyes had been. "She was asking about you."

Natasha tried to contain her excitement. "Who?" Her mouth was wide, her cheeks flushed.

Becky nodded over to where April stood. The centre of attention, surrounded by both males and females. Everyone wanted a slice of her but for varying reasons. "April, who else?"

"Wow! I mean, oh."

"You free tonight?" Becky said almost expectantly. Like, why wouldn't she be free on a Friday night?

Natasha thought about her dad. The look of disappointment on his face if she went out. She wished she knew someone she could say she was going to study with. There would be the slimmest of chances.

"You wanna say you're coming over to mine?" Becky asked, almost reading her mind.

"Uh, um... *could I?*"

She shrugged like it was no biggy. It probably wasn't, her parents practically lived down the country club. April's parents owned it. So who cared?

And just like that she was invited. It was a party. Small and exclusive. Natasha couldn't believe it.

"Who else is going?" she asked before Becky slipped back into the crowds.

"You'll see," was all she said. "Only a select few," she mouthed back.

Jim Ody

The rest of the day dragged. She daydreamed more than she'd ever done before. She was anxious but excited.

She wanted to tell someone. She almost spoke to her friend Sally, but Sally was too caught up in Timothy, who in turn was also following April around. The last thing Sally wanted to hear was another friend was obsessed with April.

Chapter 23 – Joel

Joel looked to Melody and said, "You know where Dead Man's Cove is?"

The look on her face suggested that not only did she know of the place, but it held a number of memories for her. She nodded. "Yep, this way."

They followed the beach as they walked a trail that took them up and down a coastal path.

"I still don't get why he wouldn't just speak to us at his house," Joel muttered.

"We've been through this. The fact he's taken us out of the town says a lot, too."

Joel had to agree. It wasn't lost on him that not only was the town now left behind them, but this was the opposite side to the gated community.

"Did you like it here?" Joel asked when silence found a home between them.

Melody seemed to think this through, perhaps going over the thoughts in her head before deciding on how to respond.

Jim Ody

"You know how you felt about your wife when you were first together?" He did. Of course he did. A scent or song could transport him back there. The feelings alive and real. "It's intoxicating - in a good way, but the strength of feelings blurs the surroundings and dulls your opinion."

"Blinded by love."

"I don't know whether it was love." She turned to him. "And I'm not just saying that because we're no longer together. I was blinded by this overwhelming attraction to something new and exciting. Eventually it evaporated and disappeared. To me, that shows it wasn't love."

"But you must've had an opinion about this place despite your infatuation."

She half-chuckled to herself. "Infatuation. Makes me seem like some wet-knickered schoolgirl. I don't know what you'd call it… And Black Rock?" She stopped, and they both looked back at the town. "I got the feeling it lost its identity, you know?"

"New money."

"Exactly. This was a fishing village. It grew to be a fishing town, and then the money appeared. The docks were developed into a marina. The gated community and the country club then overshadowed everything this town had built."

Joel had heard this story in many coastal towns across the South West. Farming and fishing were not the thriving industries they were generations ago. The rich retired early and moved to the coast, bringing with them a lavish lifestyle that attracted others. Like a cancer of commerce, it ate into the

The Crazy Season

town killing off the history and principles the town was built on.

They had a little climb now. The coastline went from being almost ground level near their B&B, to undulating cliffs and back down again.

More benches appeared when they climbed up another hill, suggesting a place to rest and look over the sea. Then it dipped, and some steps took them down to the small beach. Large rocks sat amongst the fine sand. Small pools filled with sea life and seaweed were below.

Joel glanced at his watch. "It's midday, and we're still no further forward."

"Let's see how this goes with Martin before you get all Mr Sulky-Pants."

Joel tried not to smile at her, and did his best to suppress the grin, but she was a lot of fun.

"Thanks for coming," he said. "It is nice to have a partner."

"I've nothing better to do." She tried to sound dismissive. "My red light doesn't go on until after dark."

He ignored the last comment. "No, you and your brother have been brilliant. You both treat me normally. I get it. Others find it awkward, but…"

"Kip thinks you're great. He's in awe of the work you do. He gets treated differently just because he's gay, so he knows what it's like."

Joel could understand that. People weren't great at communication. The ones that liked to talk often talked about themselves, and the ones who listened didn't want to burden others with their problems. Then you had the ones who didn't realise they were

Jim Ody

being selfish. They stayed away as they assumed it would bring pain to speak to others, when in fact all they were doing was saving themselves. Too scared to interact and understand what the other was going through.

"Here we go," Melody said as they both saw the lone hooded figure walking in a strange speed walk style and periodically glancing over his shoulder.

"He couldn't look any more suspicious if he was dressed as a chicken and holding up a sign saying 'nothing to see here'."

"Youths, eh?"

"Dusty Utes."

"Eh?"

"Forget it."

The lad glanced behind himself again, before he came within talking distance. He had a black hoodie with a logo that might've been a band or a brand. Joel wasn't sure. He was medium height with skinny dark jeans and bright white trainers on his feet. His eyes looked shifty, and his skin was pale and pockmarked from acne.

"Martin?" Joel said, although there really could be no doubt.

"Yeah, big man," The lad said by way of salutation. His voice deeper than they were both expecting, and his voice was street, and nothing like the local accent.

"You wanted to get out of the town before speaking to us?" Joel began. "Why's that?"

"Peeps everywhere, init?" he said hovering awkwardly and shifting his weight from one foot to the other. Joel wondered whether this talk was

The Crazy Season

roadman. The urban slang derived from the streets incorporating a mash up of cultural styles most commonly associated with London. He might need Melody to translate.

"Be straight with us, Martin. What's going down?"

Melody coughed slightly. Joel realised it was a TV phrase, and not something spoken in the English West Country.

"Eh?"

"What's happening around here. I've seen your posts on the web. You either know something or you're bullshitting. Judging by this sponsored walk you've got us doing here, my guess is there's some truth to what you're saying."

"I dunno, Bruv. I'm no squealer, ya hear me?" He glanced over his shoulder again.

"We're not the police, and we're not part of…" he waved his hand struggling to put a name to something he knew nothing about. "…whatever it is that has you jumpy. Tell us about the curse, okay? The fact that you've agreed to meet us tells me you want to help."

"It's a curse, init. Makes people kill themselves." He ran his finger over his own throat dramatically.

Melody jumped in. "What, anyone?"

He shrugged, but Joel felt it wasn't out of not knowing, but rather a reluctance to speak.

"I dunno. I heard there's like some party. Shit went down. It's that, ya get me?"

"What sort of party?"

Jim Ody

"Man's not party to that intel. Secret an' shit. Selected peeps from ma endz. They targeted or some shit."

Joel was processing the words. There must be a link. "Is this gang-related? Drugs?"

Martin held up his hands and looked almost hurt. "It ain't like that, bro. We ain't into nuffin' like that, ya get me?"

"And Timothy, how did you know him? Classmate?"

"Yeah. I knew him. He's cool. Was alright, init. He went to the party, though."

"What about Stevie?"

"Yeah, him and Timothy were tight. Man…" He genuinely looked hurt by it.

"Who else went to the party? D'you know?"

Martin paused, but definitely looked like he was full of information. "I heard some names, init. I dunno whether it's right, an' that but…"

"Okay. It's a good start."

"Timothy, ovs…"

"Ovs?" Joel wasn't sure what he meant.

Melody leaned over to him. "It means obviously."

Joel looked at her frowning. "What, a silent B now is it?"

Melody grinned then looked at Martin apologetically.

"This guy for real? You's like some geriatric, Fam." Martin laughed.

Melody cut in. "He's lived a sheltered life."

Martin grinned again, and seemed a little more at ease. "Is it." Joel wondered what sort of a response

The Crazy Season

that was. It was a question, even if the words suggested so, but said like an answer.

"You were saying... the party?" Joel said trying to push the conversation on.

"Yeah, yeah, right. April and her like BFF Becky... erm, I heard Natasha, but man, she like a nun, or summit, dun leave her endz and that..."

"Okay, so April is April Montague, right?" He nodded.

"What's the full names of the others?"

"Becky Longton, Natasha Barr and some other geezer, Ethan Fuck-knows."

"Fuck-knows, interesting family name."

"Pog bants," Martin said, shaking his head.

"All classmates? Friends? Enemies?"

"I mean, Stevie, Timothy and I were alright. Though they woz like proper sneaky last week. Everyone knows April and Becky, they're like the popular girls. Natasha is sort of a nerd. I mean, she's fit an' that, but..."

"She doesn't go out to parties."

"Yeah."

"And Ethan Fuck-knows?"

"I dunno, he turned up here last year, init. He sort of keeps to himself. Thinks he's this big man. Came from Bristol so he's a city boy." For the first time, Martin's accent dropped, and when he said Bristol he pronounced it Brissle the way the locals there would.

"You're not from here are you?"

He smiled at that. "Nah, city, init. 'rents moved here a cup'la years back."

"Which city? Bristol?"

Jim Ody

"Yeah, Fam. I din't clap eyes on that Ethan geezer, though."

Melody then jumped in. "You said you were friends with Stevie and Timothy. How much did they tell you about the party?"

Martin pulled a face. "Nuthin'. I mean, it ain't like that. We don't have to tell each other everything, init? Like I say, they woz acting proper shifty beforehand. Both thought they woz gonna score, I reckons. Ya get me?" He looked up quickly with the head movement that was opposite to a nod.

"You said you heard these names, and considering none of them confirmed it, you do appear quite confident they all were at this party. Where were you getting the information from?"

"Nah, nah, nah. I ain't no snitch, yeah? It don't matter."

"But a reliable source?"

"Yeah. Gucci."

"What do you think went on at this party? Any ideas?"

Martin's whole demeanour changed. Any cockiness slipped away and a scared child was left trying to put on a brave face.

"I wanted to go so bad… yeah? I dunno."

"So you knew about it beforehand?" Joel jumped in.

"I knew something was happening. Look, I can't explain it but I'm good at picking up whispers, an' that. I get a sense of something. I notice the way people act. Like I say Stevie was suddenly clammin' up. He was following Becky around like a real saddo.

I told him that, too. I said, 'You look like a proper dickhead, Bruv!'"

"And how did he take it?"

"Said I was jealous. Shit like that."

"And were you?" Joel pushed.

The look on Martin's face said it all. There was a flash when it looked like he might lie, but his shoulders noticeably dropped when he conceded. "Sure, I guess. Becky's fit. She's not April, but April isn't gonna be lookin' at us. We know that. With Becky there's always a chance. Stevie saw that, and…" his words dropped off as he was scanning the cliffs. He was still worried about being spotted talking to them.

Melody then said with a calming voice, "Go on, Martin. What was it you were going to say?"

Martin turned back to them. "I saw them talking. Becky and Stevie. Those two never spoke. I couldn't hear what they were saying, but she was leaning in and he was grinning. There was something similar with Natasha. She didn't hang around with Becky and April, but suddenly I noticed them smile at each other. Becky would say 'hi'. Plus, I think Natasha has a crush on April. I've seen her staring at her… you know, in like some stalker way. What was that movie, blood? Single White Female? Yeah."

Melody was careful how she worded her next question. "Was she into girls? Natasha, I mean?"

Martin made a face that said he had no idea. "Who knows," he eventually said. "She kept to herself. Like I say, she sat at the front in class. She kept out of trouble, and she never went out. No one knew much about her."

"She's still alive, Martin," Joel said. "You talk about her in the past tense."

"I've not seen her for a while." He looked cross that he was being accused of something.

Joel looked at Melody. "When was the last time you saw her?"

The side of Martin's mouth turned down and he slowly shook his head. "A few days, I guess."

"And Stevie and Timothy?"

"I saw Stevie day before he died. Timothy? A few days ago."

"The others?"

"I saw April today, and Becky a couple of days ago."

"And…" Joel looked at Melody for help.

"Ethan," she said.

Martin nodded. "He's working at the Rock."

"The bar?"

"Yeah."

"He doesn't go to school. He's older than us."

"So how do you know him?"

Martin was supressing a grin. "April."

"They're together?"

"April's not like that. I don't think they hooked up. She's… I dunno. She's a fantasy, ya get me?"

"I'm beginning to."

"And Timothy? What can you tell me about him?"

"Man, that was tough. Good kid, he hung around with a girl called Sally. I thought they were like a thing, but I dunno. I guess he got pulled in by April, too. You know, I see it, yeah? She's not interested in us," he was repeating himself but they let him continue. "All these people were infatuated by her.

The Crazy Season

She's like some, I dunno what you call it, from a horror movie." He clicked his fingers.

"A siren?"

"Yeah, yeah, Fam. That's it. Like she put a spell on them. Look, it's some crazy shit but, you ask me bro, it's like she got a group of people under her spell, took them off some place and it fucked them up."

"You think that's possible?" Joel had to ask the question. Partly it could be true. Add alcohol and drugs and you may have the pieces of the jigsaw. Although the motivation was questionable.

"I dunno. Sounds like summit from the Horror Channel, or what's that old guy called? The writer? King?"

"Stephen King?"

"Yeah. Sounds like him without no spooky clown!" he laughed at his own joke.

"Okay, Martin," Joel began. "What do you think is going on? You think this talk of suicides all come back to a party attended by kids infatuated with April?"

"I guess that's it."

"So no curse then on this town?"

Martin looked uneasy. "Them kids in the millennium all topped themselves. I heard it happened in the 80s too."

"Coincidence?" Joel tried. Life could be full of coincidences that people read too much into. This goes back to people wanting excitement and adventure in their lives. What-ifs? And other such wild theories.

"Suicides? All together? I dunno." He glanced too quickly at his watch, to take in the time. He was getting worried.

"Okay. Thanks for meeting us, Martin. Can we speak to you again if we have any follow up questions?"

Martin looked like he wanted to shake his head and run off, but stalled for too long and instead mumbled, "Sure." He nodded.

"Man's be true, so Bro, you missed someone."

Joel looked perplexed and looked at Melody for help. "Eh?"

"Who are we missing?" she asked.

"Mr Townsend, init. Teach be all over them. Summit not right. Pulled them into detention and shit. You need to be checkin' him, ya feel me?"

"Okay. Will do."

"Alright." He turned and walked off, again like a power-walker desperate for the toilet.

"What d'you think?" Joel looked at Melody, not wanting to show his cards first.

"What about his accent?" she grinned. "It's put on."

"I got that. It slipped once in a while. He sounded like Ali G." Melody grinned at that.

"April Montague seems to be in the centre of this. The daughter of the most influential and powerful man around here. I agree she is the one who attracted the partygoers."

"The Honeytrap," Joel mumbled, looking out to where Martin was now a long way away from them.

Melody snorted, which made Joel whip his head around to her. "What?"

The Crazy Season

"Honeytrap? Where did you get that from? Some Raymond Chandler novel?"

Joel wasn't sure. "It's a thing, isn't it?"

"From about 1950! But yes, I guess she was." Her giggles died down.

He dismissed her mocking. "The question is, who threw the party and where was it held? If it was April, then what was her motivation?"

"She liked being adored?"

Joel thought that, too, but it didn't seem strong enough. "Maybe, but it doesn't feel like she was the one in charge."

"Then who? Ethan?"

Joel raised his eyebrows. "Interesting. An interested party looking to kill off the competition. Although, as Martin would have it, Ethan appeared to be the only one to have got anywhere with her."

"Seems drastic though."

"You're the one who said about teenagers. *'Little things to us are huge things to them.'* Maybe we need to speak to Sally again and see whether she knew who was the dominant person with April and Ethan."

"How about we go and visit Ethan?"

"Let's do that. Fancy a drink?"

"Sure. We need to get a bit more information on the teacher too."

"Yes, the mysterious Mr Townsend."

Chapter 24 – Stevie

The day after the party

He'd fallen straight to sleep with exhaustion. His body stank of sweat and fear. It had eaten into his clothes and hung in the air like bad thoughts. After the initial deep sleep, his slumber soon became fitful. He was only slightly conscious of wriggling like a dying fish on dry land. The events of the evening before playing heavy on his mind. His dreams twisted the horror of it all into different scenarios. Each one worse than before. His mind was in a war to suppress them. It was a war it lost.

At one point, he awoke with a start. It was a little after three. He wasn't covered in sweat like in the movies, but his heart felt like it was going to explode through his chest. Like that old guy in the movie where the alien suddenly freed itself from inside of him.

The Crazy Season

Images flashed through his mind. Cloaks, masks, darkness, naked flesh, and blood. So much blood.

Everything had spiralled out of control, and he didn't know why. At times he felt like he'd been under a spell. Or a curse.

He tried to go back to sleep. He turned from side to side but his once soft mattress now felt like gravel beneath him. His pillow a tool to suffocate. It no longer brought him comfort but instead worry that it might wrap itself around his face.

He'd gone to the party with hope. He'd been so excited. A sense of adventure beckoning. Late on, he'd found it and a whole lot more. He'd slowly gone deeper and deeper until there was no return.

He remembered flashing lights in a darkened room. He had been kissing someone. He'd touched a boob. He'd danced and drank and at some point passed out.

He had awoken in the early hours, shirtless. He watched April pulling on a T-shirt having been topless. They all looked confused, slightly embarrassed and unsure of what had gone on.

Could he have stopped? Refused to be a part of it? Turned and walked away? These questions seemed so obvious now. *Why? Why? Why?*

It hit him hard. It wasn't whether he would be able to distance himself from what had happened. He'd seen enough crime programmes to know he was in trouble. *Deep* trouble. It would only be a matter of time before he was sitting in a small room with the question *why?* being shouted at him by the police. He'd cowardly reply with *No comment*. Not because he wanted to, but because his legal advisor would say so. Everyone would hate him.

He'd got up at lunchtime and was unable to face his parents. He went for a walk but stayed away from the beach. He didn't want to speak to Timothy, even though part of him did. He wanted to forget about it.

He felt sick. Permanently sick. They'd killed someone. It was as simple as that and there was no getting away from that fact.

Eventually he came in telling his parents he'd been with Timothy. He went to his room and sat in his wardrobe sobbing. He felt like a little kid again.

Eventually he fell asleep and the night embraced him.

His life was basically over. No one would believe his side of the story.

He got up before anyone else was awake in his house. He couldn't face them. Whether the guilt of the smiles or the pain of their disappointment. It was too much.

Grabbing his rucksack, he got onto his bike and pedalled away from his house. He didn't know where he was going, or indeed whether he'd ever come back. The world around him was a blur, devoid of detail and suddenly inconsequential. He felt alone. So very alone.

The cold air was fresh against his cheeks. The neighbourhood was still asleep. All around him the world seemed to know. The day was different. His whole perspective on life had changed. He didn't have a plan. His mind blank of his actions. He just wanted to get away from it all.

The Crazy Season

At fifteen, running away from your troubles seemed to be the only option. Well, one of the options.

The town was now behind him. He left the road and cut through a path that glistened with morning dew.

He got off his bike, placed it carefully against the railings, and walked to the bridge over the main road. He watched the traffic below. Despite the early hour, commuters were already hitting the roads to get to places they needed to be. He wanted to walk down and hitchhike. Get into one of the cars and go wherever the driver was going. Get swallowed up into the depths of a city. He could blend in and pretend the town of Black Rock never existed. Or, he'd stow away in the back of a lorry. Head off around Europe. Warm beaches and sun-kissed skin. He allowed a small smile. He realised he'd probably never leave the country ever again.

He didn't have much in his life he'd miss. His parents were too distracted with their own lives. He was only ever a burden to them anyway. His dad had said as much. *A useless teen who'd amount to nothing*, those were his actual words. Anything he did have was overshadowed by the guilt from *that* night.

He spoke in a whisper about what had happened. His voice barely audible. His confession stolen by the wind. Out loud made it final. Awful. Shocking.

An idea came from nowhere. He rummaged through his bag and pulled out a piece of paper and a pencil. He had to write it down. He needed to see it in his own amateur scroll. Scratchy words of truth. If

Jim Ody

nothing else he could hand it over instead of having to actually speak it out loud. He knew he'd be in tears if he was made to do so. A snivelling sad little boy.

He sat cross-legged on the cool stone surface of the overpass. Each word formed in shaky handwriting. He wanted to add a picture. Something to liven it up, but it felt wrong and inappropriate. A selfish act to make him feel better. Like tickling the corpse of the person you've just shot. Or stabbed.

Once he started, his pencil moved with speed. Words formed quicker from the pencil than those that were in his mind. His writing changed slightly as the pencil became blunt. He shifted it around in order to use another edge of the lead. The contrast between previous and new now obvious.

When he finished, he held it up. That was it. His confession. Everything about what he'd done and why he'd done it. At least, that's how he'd remembered it. The vague bits he'd tried to fill in with detail he didn't even know was true. It just felt right. Or was that bit a dream? His confused mind not sure what was real or not.

But somehow, without knowing it, his grip had loosened. A gust of wind snatched it from his hands and it danced over the side of the safety rail. It came to rest precariously. Now the gentle breeze teased it a little, threatening to send it floating below.

He gasped and in panic rushed over. The shoulder-high cage was made with small wire squares. His fingers were unable to grab it. A strong breeze almost lifted it again.

He had to get it. It couldn't be found.

The Crazy Season

Another day and another stupid act. It was becoming a habit.

He looked all around. No one. Just a desolate country landscape. The bridge wasn't a main walkway. Later joggers and dog-walkers would come by. Now, it was only him and his thoughts.

He did the unthinkable. He slowly climbed over the edge. Then holding on with one arm, he bent down slowly and just managed to grab the tip of the paper between his thumb and forefinger. Then he clamped it.

Relieved, he pulled it into him.

And that's when he lost his footing. And fell.

The world was suddenly light around him. The air rushing past. Time slowed down.

His body smashed to the ground. His back felt the ground first, followed by the back of his head. White pain flashed through him. Then the huge and heavy wheels of a lorry squashed the life out of him. Cars screeched and smashed to miss the bloody mess now graffitied all over the asphalt. Whatever was left of Stevie was now in many mangled pieces that nobody would ever be able to put back together again.

The note fluttered and got caught in the tarpaulin covering the back of a lorry heading towards Plymouth docks.

Days later and the note, now wet and smudged, was in another country, swept up and thrown into a skip.

Forever forgotten.

Chapter 25 – Joel

Joel held the door of the Black Rock Bar open for Melody. As usual, she walked confidently in front of him. He admired the way she was able to go anywhere and look like she fitted in.

Joel scanned the bar and saw Ethan standing at the far end replacing an empty rum bottle. The tall lad clocked them and there was something that could pass for recognition flash in his eyes. He quickly looked away, but it had been there.

The same woman was also serving, but thankfully she was caught up with another order. Her back was turned as she dropped slices of lemon into a handful of tall glasses.

"What can I get you," Ethan asked, a professional smile fixed on his face. His eyes were unable to pretend. He knew before they spoke.

"You got a break coming up, Ethan?" Joel asked. The smile dropped suddenly.

"Who are you?" Ethan said, leaning over and lowering his voice.

"We know all about the party. Last Friday night."

"I don't know what you're talking about." Ethan busied himself with cleaning glasses that already shone. A clichéd response.

Melody placed her hands on the bar to show she meant business. "Ethan? Come on. We know. The families need to know."

He flashed a glance over to his colleague who was still busy with her order - she was now adding lemonade to the glasses. He was weighing up his options. It didn't take long. He knew he had only the one.

"Five minutes out the back. But only if you don't stay."

Joel nodded, looked at Melody, and without further words they left.

"What do you think," Melody said as they got outside.

"There is something different about him. Aside from him being older."

"Like he might be behind this?" They continued to walk around to the back of the huge building.

"I don't know about that, but the others we've spoken to looked scared. I'm not sure I saw fear, but he was definitely worried about who was watching."

"Small towns have many more eyes."

Joel shook his head and grinned to himself. "You read that on a fortune cookie?"

A crow swooped down and landed on the post of a garden fence. It seemed to be watching them and only added to what Melody had said.

Jim Ody

They heard movement from behind them, and Ethan stood there looking shifty.

"I haven't got long," he warned. He now had a hoodie on and was quick to pull out a cigarette.

"Noted," Joel said. "So, what do you know about these suicides?"

He shrugged as he bent over the lighter, the cigarette balanced expertly between his lips. The flame gave way to a thick plume of smoke before he started puffing, and he eventually took what appeared to be a long and satisfying drag.

"Okay," Joel nodded. "Let's put this another way. We know you know about them. We know you know April, Becky, Timothy, Stevie and Natasha. We also know you all attended a secret party. Of the six of you, two are dead and two are missing, one is keeping a low profile, and the other, which is you, is getting on with their life. Care to fill in the blanks for us?"

"Who are you?" he said defiantly. It was the same question he'd said inside, except it wasn't said like it was a question, but as a statement to confirm what he already knew. The hand with the cigarette balanced between his fingers scratched his eyebrow. "You're not the police."

"We know something went down. Two kids are dead, maybe more. What happened at the party?"

"It was nothing to do with me," he began. "Look, I was there because of April. I wasn't expecting the others to turn up. It was a complete surprise to me."

"Where was the party? Was it a party?" Melody then cut in.

The Crazy Season

Ethan looked at her. There was a twinkle in his eyes. He liked what he saw. A small part of his defences melted away. "It's a secret place. It's hard to explain... No, I mean, I dunno if it was a party..." he looked off towards where the crow was still sitting. It cawed, and almost appeared to look over. Further down the fence another couple appeared. It was almost a sinister symbol. A murder of crows.

"What *is* a party?" Ethan muttered. "How would you define one?" He was suddenly cocky.

"Music, alcohol, and a gathering of people. Sometimes laughing and joking, and usually some fun," Melody said straight-faced and remained that way even when she added, "A good one has some nakedness. It's not a good party if I don't end up flashing my tits at some point."

Ethan looked at her, his draw dropping open slightly. Like Joel, it appeared he'd not met many women quite like Melody.

"I mean," Ethan tried to compose himself. "We had some drinks. I remember music coming through some speakers, I dunno, rock and rap from what I can remember. We laughed and joked. I mean, I was there to see April, but once they were drinking, the others seemed okay." The sides of his mouth twitched with the memory.

"Go on."

Ethan took another drag. This one long. So long, in fact, that when he spoke smoke expelled from his mouth and nose for most of the sentence. "It all suddenly went weird. I don't know. My memory is not so great from that point."

Jim Ody

"Okay," Joel surmised. "There is a large missing piece here, Ethan. You go from drinking, laughing, and listening to music, to suicides, disappearances, and shifty behaviour. I've been to some parties in my time, but not one of them that's ended up like that."

Ethan was still puffing away, the only true sign that the conversation was making him uncomfortable and nervous.

"All of you have acted differently," Melody said softly. "We are trying to establish why." She then made a show of puffing out her cheeks and raising her voice slightly. "I've gotta say, Ethan, you seem to be taking it better than the others, so I've got to ask myself, is he good at hiding his feelings? Or is he the reason why the others are acting, or have acted, the way they have?"

Ethan was already waving the stub of the cigarette at her. "Nah, ain't nothing like that."

Joel said. "April is an attractive girl. She want to try something new that involved others? Get them drunk? That sort of thing?"

Melody continued. "Things got out of hand. Some were into it, others panicked? We see it all the time in our line of work." Joel was impressed by the way she lied. Her line of work was either painting alone and naked, or standing up in a pub shouting out poetic statements at people.

"D'you know where the missing girls are?"

Ethan was looking at them. His eyes going back and forth. His lips parting ready to speak.

"Ethan!" a voice called from behind him. "Break's over!"

He snapped out of it. The short woman looked at him with real anger. Joel wasn't sure how much she'd heard.

"I've gotta go," he said and flicked away the butt of the cigarette.

As he turned, Joel asked. "Who's Angela?"

Ethan turned and narrowed his eyes. "She's the devil." And then he was gone.

"What the fuck?" Melody said.

"I couldn't have put it better myself."

Chapter 26

He spied them again. They were up to no good. Despite the discovery of Timothy's body, the waters around Black Rock remained fairly calm and still. The police were happy to put it down to unrequited love, a teenager so overwhelmed with rejection that he threw himself off the cliff in despair.

They didn't even connect it to the unfortunate suicide of Stevie. Why should they? They were friends, but nothing further linked them.

But somehow these two strangers had got involved. They were poking around in the shadows and swirling up the waters. No good could ever come from that.

A town needed its secrets.

Things went on in a town that locals accepted and understood. They could take care of it themselves.

The Crazy Season

He'd seen them on the beach speaking to Martin. That in itself was interesting. They'd not just met up in town but had deliberately gone far out to share whispers. The boy had disappeared as quickly as he'd appeared. He was a fucking joke. A caricature parading as some multi-cultural gangster, when he was a mixed up white kid in a fucking Cornish town.

He now watched them talking to Ethan. A guy who did his best to look normal and innocent. An outsider trying to fit in.

He watched them now. The two co-conspirators planning and watching, grabbing the pieces and trying fit the puzzle together.

They'd never get it. He was sure of that.

And if they did? He smiled to himself and let the thought spin around his head some more.

Disposing of the bodies of outsiders was easier. Erasing them from the earth was not hard when you knew all the dark deserted places of the area. The sort of places nobody ever went to.

He rubbed his rough hands on his beard and smiled again to himself.

If he had to get his hands dirty, then he would.

Jim Ody

The Crazy Season

Chapter 27 – Becky

Before the party

She loved her life. It sounded stupid for a fifteen-year-old to say but that was it. Like, the total truth.

School was a breeze. Well, she wasn't the brightest, but she was far from dumb. She cruised by hitting the minimum grade requirements to keep the teachers off her back and giving her enough time to enjoy her life. Her socialising. Her popularity on Instagram and Tik-Tok was rising. It made her feel like, validated.

Everybody wanted to be her friend. She knew a lot of the time it was because of April - she wasn't stupid - but that was fine. It didn't matter. She found it funny. That might be odd to say, but April was not easy to get close to. What was it her father joked? She was aloof. Walked around with her head in the

The Crazy Season

air and pushed her little tits out. So people spoke to her instead.

Boys would cuddle up to her and she'd let them. Why not? She loved the attention. Who wouldn't?

Becky had grown up always being on the chubby side. She couldn't help it. Her mother had one of those gastric bands fitted and had gone off a number of times to get the excess fat sucked out of her. Her father was a large bear of a man. Her genes, therefore, were always against her. As were her cravings for sweet things. But she worked out, so whilst she might be considered too big to be a model, she was shapely. It meant she had a large butt and big thighs, not to mention boobs that had a mind of their own. Her waist - though never considered small - gave the impression of being much smaller than it was. So whilst April was tall and athletic looking, Becky was shorter but full of curves.

Life was what you made it. It was funny how much boys would do for you if they thought they'd get to fondle your breasts or even more... The thing was, she felt empowered. She was in control. She attracted the nervous ones and as such was the dominant one.

There was something about the look in the eyes of the hungry male. The sweet talk and the gifts. The handjobs and fumbled touches of inexperienced hands. But she was only fifteen, so there were limits to what she'd do.

April was different. She looked so much older that schoolboys were of no interest to her. She wanted older men. She felt she deserved them.

Jim Ody

"You want to know what it's like to be with a real man," she'd whispered in her ear.

"Of course," Becky had replied. She was nervous but excited at the thought.

"I can set it up for you," she almost purred as they drank her mum's Prosecco.

Nervously, Becky had considered it. "I guess," she'd said.

"Don't be scared." Her voice was soothing as she smoothed away Becky's long brown hair from her face. "I'll be there, too."

"You will?"

April nodded. "He wants us both together. That's okay, isn't it?"

Becky wasn't sure what that meant. She could guess, and that was fine. To do that with her best friend there instantly put her at ease. "What? Like you watching."

"Is that okay?" April actually sounded slightly worried. Becky wasn't used to it. It was almost a vulnerable side that was rarely seen by anyone.

Becky nodded. "Of course. I'd love you to be there."

"It will be fun." April didn't realise that Becky needed no convincing.

They'd drunk some more. April talked about what it was like to be with a man in great detail. The difference now was it wasn't boastful. It was said like something special shared between friends.

It was after another glass that April spoke about the party. A gathering of a few of them.

"How many people will be there?" Becky asked. She was trying to gauge the size of the party.

The Crazy Season

"Just something small. But different people. Like a secret party."

Becky was intrigued. She looked up and held April's gaze. "Secret?"

April was biting her lip. "Sounds good, right?" She reached over and placed her well-manicured hand on Becky's thigh. Becky didn't want to admit she liked the feeling of it there. She assumed it was just a crush. April had something about her. It was almost a star-quality. Becky had no doubt she would one day be famous. It was highly unlikely she'd hang around Black Rock any longer than she needed to.

The thought of a secret party seemed exciting.

"Whereabouts is it going to be held?" Becky asked.

When April told her, it seemed the perfect location. There was no doubt Becky was going to let her hair down and open herself up to things she'd never done before.

What she didn't realise was the things she'd end up being involved in would change her life forever.

If only she'd known.

If only.

Jim Ody

Chapter 28 – Melody

She felt guilty that she was enjoying herself. Her life had become slightly mundane. She'd isolated herself from others, her decadent ways had distanced her peers from her. She'd had a lot of good times. Some of it was lone adventure, and others were just senseless fun. Her mind tattooed with memories that for the most part she didn't regret.

She felt sorry for Joel. He was only part of the man he once was. That sounded bad and not something she'd ever say out loud to him, but it was the truth.

He used to be this action hero. A guy who went into all kinds of situations without care, and came out of it unscathed grasping the truth by its hair.

The car accident had hit him hard. Really hard. She got it. He was still mourning his daughter, and each day he mourned a wife who wasn't dead yet. She wondered whether it wouldn't do him good for

The Crazy Season

his wife to finally leave this world. Only then would Joel have the chance to slowly return to the man he once was. Now, he was a little lost. A man in need of guidance.

Kip had spoken to her the night before. "Look after him," he'd said. "He needs a friend, not a lover."

At first, she'd been shocked by his words. But deep down, did she really want to scratch her nails down his naked back?

"Just help him get back on his feet," Kip had continued. "He trusts you."

So here she was. Her nose deep into someone else's business and completely intrigued by the whole story.

They were walking away from The Black Rock Bar when Joel grabbed his phone.

"You know who we need to speak to now?" Joel said.

"April."

"Correct. She is one of the most important missing pieces in all of this."

"You want me to ring her?" Melody asked. April liked the company of men, but that didn't necessarily mean she trusted them. She understood the young a lot better than Joel did. She also knew her from way back when.

"You think that would work better?" Joel said.

"I dunno. Until we try, we'll never know."

They crossed the road towards the beach, but instead of walking onto it, they sat down on a bench both with their phones at the ready.

"Here you go," Joel said. "Her mobile number is on her social media. That speaks volumes. Risky, but typical for someone craving attention."

"It won't be her only mobile. Trust me!"

"Really? I'm not sure I'll ever understand teenagers nowadays. I didn't have a phone until I was in my twenties, now kids have a handful of them."

Melody added the number to her phone and then pressed the button to call her.

It rang a few times before a confidant voice responded.

"Hello?"

"Hi, is that April?"

"Who is this?" the voice still remained confident but also slightly defiant.

"It's Melody."

There was a pause, then she said, "Oh my God! I can't believe it's you!"

"It's been a while. I'm looking into the disappearance of a couple of people. I wondered if I could ask you some questions."

Just as quickly her tone changed. "I don't have anything to say." Her voice still remained strong. For a fifteen-year-old she was far from rattled.

"You can tell me. You were at a party with them both, as well as the two lads who committed suicide."

"Other people were there, too. Ask them." Her voice was suddenly small.

"We have. You seem to be an important piece of the puzzle."

The Crazy Season

"You're not the police," she said matter-of-factly. "No offence. I'm underage so I'm afraid I can't answer your questions without an adult present."

"Come on," Melody replied. "It's me you're talking to. You're not under arrest. The other people we've spoken to were very nervous. All of them mentioned you." It wasn't quite the truth, but April had no way of knowing that. "The question we have to ask ourselves is why?"

"What? Ethan, you mean?"

"Ethan wasn't the only one. We've spoken to others."

For the first time, something else crept into her voice. It might've been doubt. It might've been guilt. "Who else have you spoken to?"

"You tell us. We know who was there. We know who is dead and who is missing."

"It wasn't my fault," she said suddenly, a switch in her stance. It was a childish response. She was sounding younger by the minute.

"What wasn't," Melody replied carefully.

"What happened... I didn't know."

"What didn't you know?"

Melody heard April breathing. She wondered which way she'd go. Confession or lies. The crossroads for the accused.

Another pause, followed by sobs. They might've been crocodile tears, or April might have been genuinely upset. In person you could often get a pretty good read of people, but on the end of the telephone with almost a stranger it could be anything.

"It wasn't supposed to be like that," she said, sniffing back her regrets. "It was meant to be a fun night."

"Go on."

"It all started when… shit," she suddenly said, a panic now prevalent in her voice. "I gotta go."

"Wait…" Melody said, but April had already gone.

"Well?" Joel asked impatiently.

Melody tapped the mobile on her thigh. "She's definitely the key. She knows a lot more than she's letting on. She was about to say more but suddenly had to go."

"You think she was going to say more? Or did she get spooked?"

Melody shrugged. It was a good point. "Hard to say. She had started sobbing, but that might've been a good act."

Melody picked up her phone again and tapped out a quick message to April.

Can we meet? Your choice of place. Thanx.

"I've asked to meet her. We need to get a read on what she knows." Melody looked around at the people walking about and minding their own business. Did any of them know what was going on here?

Melody added, "You know what? Everyone else seems scared. Like really scared. I didn't get that feeling from April. She was worried about someone, and I don't think she's the instigator, but she's on a different level to the others."

"The others have already painted her as this untouchable goddess. Maybe she thought that would be enough?"

"True."

Joel got up. "Come on. Let's head back to the B&B and get some research done. I think we need to look into the old cases, too. I just have a feeling that there must be some connection somewhere along the line. Even if it's just being used for inspiration."

"You could be on to something there."

"But first I need something to eat. And a coffee!"

"Now we're talking."

The two of them walked slowly along the beachfront. To onlookers they appeared to be a couple in love, chatting and close enough to be holding hands. But they had a case that was building up quite a momentum. One with still more questions than answers.

One person stood watching them and spoke into a mobile phone.

"They're walking away now." The words slowly delivered to a person on the other side of town. "I'll follow."

The sleepy beach town, once a fishing village and now sparkling with new money, looked like an innocent escape for city folk from surrounding counties. But dig a little deeper and what bound the money together was lies. Deep, dark and dirty lies.

Chapter 29 - April

Before the party

Her heart was beating fast. Really fast. And she was nervous, but excited. This was a new and special feeling. It's what she should be feeling. It's what she deserved.

Her mum had spoken at great length about her teenage years. She'd confided to her the liaisons she'd had before April's father.

"April, you have to live your life," she'd said. At the time, April wasn't sure whether this was advice from mother to daughter, or a justification on her tainted past. "Don't limit yourself to just one man. You'll never have a comparison if you fall for the first man you meet."

April liked the chats she had with her mum. Her father was often out at the club or playing golf with his buddies. His life had slowed down in recent years, and the balance of work and play flipped over.

The Crazy Season

That was to be expected. Her father basically owned the town. He was the mayor without the official title, or indeed duties.

Even at fifteen, April and her mum would sit in nothing but bathrobes at the country club spa, drinking Prosecco, and giggling about boys. Her mum, Evelyn, or Evie as she was known, fancied herself as April's BFF. It kept her young. The skills of a plastic surgeon could do only so much. In fact, often the remit of her surgeon Raul wasn't to make her look young again, but just to make her look appealing. Too many of her friends had skin so tight it shone, permanently raised eyebrows, and lips twice the size than needed. They became caricatures of a privileged middle-aged woman. Not that Evie considered herself middle-aged, of course.

"You look tired," her mum would often say. "You're the one who should be keeping the boys awake at night, not the other way around!"

Her family was the blueprint she wanted for herself, and why not? She'd grown up with nice things, so it was only natural she'd expect to continue to have these things as an adult.

"You're a beautiful woman," her mum would also say. "Use what you've got to get what you want. You think your father would've looked twice at me if I was ugly and let myself go?" When April was a tween, she'd thought this to be a harsh ideology, but come thirteen and fourteen she saw how boys looked at her. The looks were different from before. They noticed her. Really noticed her.

At fifteen men noticed her too.

Jim Ody

Now here she was. Taking a big step into unknown waters. The waves appeared gentle, but the water was deeper than she'd ever known before. Who knew what lay beneath the surface?

Her parents were out. Their family seemed to have extended into the lives of everyone at Beach View. She was familiar with them all. Huge smiles and little hand waves greeted her from each person she met.

Mostly, she thought they were nice friendly people. They adored her father, and she by proxy. A few flashed false smiles. It was an act of expectation that went against their true feelings. No doubt behind closed doors they spoke freely hating that they were down the social pecking order, but unable to do anything about it. Felicity O'Brien was one of them. She always asked after her mother like she wanted so badly to hear of some unfortunate news. She was a grade A bitch.

April sneaked out. Her profile in high society meant she couldn't just wander around unnoticed. Roving eyes would follow her every move. Whispers and tales sweeping back to her parents before she even finished her journey.

She took an Uber into the town centre, making sure it dropped her in a busy place. From there she got into a car, and silently they drove back out of town and towards an isolated house.

"You look very nice," he said to her. His confidence excited her. He wasn't a pathetic boy from school following her around and trying to hide his hard-on. This was a man. He seemed to like her but in the same instance could make her feel like one wrong move and she'd be history. She didn't want

The Crazy Season

that. She wasn't stupid enough to think this would be something, but whatever it was she wanted to experience it fully.

"I love your house," she said. She instantly regretted it as he ignored it. It was probably a line he expected. What she needed to do was something unexpected.

The house was large and new. It was close to the cliff that looked out over the sea. She could see the gated community only half a mile away. She liked that. A man on his own. Next to the house was the strange structure of a tin mine's wheel house. Its ruins a reminder of another of the industries that was prominent fifty years ago but was now lost to a world that's moved on.

He didn't wait for her. He walked to the house and opened it up.

She followed, not used to being led. She was nervous. Incredibly nervous. She wasn't expecting that.

He walked up the large staircase. She followed, her eyes wandering around at everything, trying to take it all in.

He walked into a room. He turned towards her and smiled. That very thing calmed her.

"Welcome," he said with open arms. There was a huge bed with black iron posts and a brilliant white backdrop behind.

"Wow!" she said, taking in a large window that showed the sea.

He looked her up and down and said, "Okay, why don't you take off your clothes."

Jim Ody

At first, she thought he was joking. She smoothed her hands against her hips. It was a nervous trait she'd picked up from her mum.

"What's the matter? Don't you want to?" He didn't seem cross. In fact the tone almost came across as apologetic like he might've misread the signals.

"Oh, no. That's not it," she said trying to regain her composure. She thought about what her mum had said about new experiences.

"Then what? You're a beautiful woman. Of course, you don't need me to tell you that. Show me your full beauty."

She gulped and tried to pretend she'd not just done that. Carefully, she removed her T-shirt and slipped out of her trousers. He sat down on a chair and hungrily watched her.

For the first time in a long time she felt self-conscious. Really self-conscious. She hated that her boobs were small, a padded bra doing its best to double up anything that was hidden beneath. She'd hate to see any disappointment on his face.

"Bravo," he said calmly as she stood there in just her underwear. "This calls for a drink!"

"Why?" she asked. It all seemed strange. Nothing like she'd imagined.

"Beauty must be celebrated!"

He stood, and she bent to retrieve her clothes.

"No, no," he grinned. "I'll take those. Relax."

He disappeared from the room and she was left stood there trying to understand what was going on. She wondered if it was a game. A way to show domination.

The Crazy Season

When he returned, he was bare chested. He held a bottle in one hand and two glasses in the other. He poured her a glass and handed it to her.

She took it in a slightly shaky hand, unable to take her eyes off his chest. He wasn't exactly toned, but with some hair sporadically placed, he looked so much more manly than the boys she'd seen before. Either scrawny, or else flabby.

"How is it?" he asked as she drank more.

"Nice," she replied, although it felt strong. She'd not eaten since lunch, and it was already going straight to her head.

"Why don't you remove the rest," he said nodding to the small amount of material she was still wearing.

Her head felt fuzzy. She was excited and suddenly drunk. Clumsily, she unclipped her bra and then slid down her knickers.

She lay down on the bed. The sound of a camera clicking was the last thing she heard as everything went black.

And that was that. Caught in the web and forever tainted with her decision to be there that day.

Jim Ody

Chapter 30 – Joel

The coffee shop was a long, narrow, independent shop. It had everything the chain coffee shops had but with individuality and a little more soul. The décor was a mix of clean white walls and old items that were once an important part of the town's history. It looked like some TV show had just left having given it a huge costly makeover.

Coffee shops were the new pubs. Bright and welcoming, and turning over customers more quickly and efficiently.

"Hey!" The guy said as soon as they walked in. There were a handful of other people sat around, and a woman busy walking back and forth with trays of dirty mugs and plates.

"Hi," Joel said as they walked up.

The guy was about medium height, he was thick-set and had tattoos down his arms. He wore a T-shirt with the name of the coffee shop on it, and smiled constantly.

The Crazy Season

"What can I get you?" His voice wasn't local.

"Let me see," Joel said, scanning the immense menu. He remembered a time when the decision would be between white or black coffee. The world had now experimented themselves into a realm of complexity when it came to hot beverages. Even milk had over half a dozen variants.

Melody didn't wait for Joel, and so said, "Whilst he's deciding, I'll have a cappuccino."

The guy nodded and got to work, "No rush, mate."

Joel was stuck. Not that he didn't know what the things were. He wasn't that stuck in the past. Before the accident, he'd gone to the chain shops a few times with Cherry and Robyn. Since then, when he went out he had a purpose. Specific things he needed and so bought them and went home. Now, standing in front of the board it all came flooding back, just how long it had been since he'd stood like this staring at fancy drinks and wondering what he desired.

The last time he was holding Robyn's hand with the other on the back of his wife. Now, he stood with a woman he'd known only since the tragedy and a hole in his heart that would never mend.

"You okay?" Melody said, noticing Joel had gone quiet.

He nodded. "Yeah. It's been a while since I came to a nice place like this." He looked at the guy who took in the compliment. "I'll have a toffee latte. There was a time when I only drank black coffee. Seems like everything has changed."

Jim Ody

"Embrace it, big guy!" Melody said as the guy placed her drink down in front of her.

"You here for the day?" the guy asked, throwing them a glance and then filling up a huge metal jug with milk.

Melody looked at Joel like for once she wanted him to speak.

"A couple of days. We're looking into the missing teenagers," he said, but the word suicide was silently there, too. Unspoken, but everyone knew it.

A plate smashed behind them. The women looked apologetic. A couple of people stopped talking and looked over.

Then everyone carried on.

For the first time the guy stopped smiling. He looked over at the woman and said, "Yeah. That's my wife, Josie. Her sister is one of them."

"Becky or Natasha?"

Josie walked up. She was a slight woman, but looked strong. She had Italian features and deep brown eyes. "Natasha…Who are you?" There was more accusation in her voice than anything else. "What do you want?"

"My name is Joel, and this is Melody. I look into strange happenings and try to get to the bottom of things. I'm here to find out what is going on, I'm not here to cause trouble or get in the way. We're just looking for the truth."

Josie went to speak, her face still hard and looking ready to argue, but the guy stepped in. "We'd love the help. The police…" he looked over at Josie, not sure how to finish it.

"They haven't got a clue," she said.

The Crazy Season

"We're not blaming them," the guy said, although the look in Josie's eye's suggested otherwise. But they just don't know.

"Do you have a contact?" Joel had the police on his list of people to speak to, but it was never easy. People might ask why they hadn't gone directly to speak to them, but the police never looked too kindly at civilians playing detective. He'd been called many things by them in the past. Of course, Dr Spook seemed to be the name that stuck. He liked to form his own opinions first, look at the details, and then approach the police. He actually held the police in high regard, so Joel always came at an investigation from a new angle. He looked at people and their motivations. Which wasn't to say the police didn't, but everything revolved around evidence, which was completely understandable. They couldn't charge someone without the evidence to satisfy the CPS, and that was often incredibly difficult.

"D'you want to pop out the back?" Josie asked.

"I'll bring your drinks through. You want anything to eat?"

Joel and Melody both ordered paninis before following Josie out of a door marked Private and into a room with a farmhouse table and a selection of cakes surrounding it.

"Are you a journalist?" Josie said as they grabbed some chairs around the table.

"Of sorts," Joel admitted. "I hate that term though, as it's always associated with hacks looking for stories at the expense of people's feelings."

The look on Josie's face suggested she agreed. "But you're different. You have morals?" It was a question, but said as a statement, perhaps with some hidden sarcasm.

"I don't write for tabloids. I have no interest in celebrities or who anyone is sleeping with. I get sent details of strange cases, often these are quite fanciful and the claims huge. What I usually find is a lonely person or persons wanting attention."

She nodded as the guy walked in with the drinks. "I'm Mike, by the way," he said and disappeared just as quickly.

She looked at him and a sad look appeared on her face. "He's great. I love him to bits. He makes such an effort to be nice to people." It sounded like there should be a lot more to her sentence, a second part left unsaid. It was also kind words that were somehow said as if they were a complaint.

"Sounds like the type of guy I need!" Melody quipped.

Josie looked from Melody to Joel and back again.

Melody got it. "No, we're not a couple. Partners."

Joel felt the need to flash his left hand. "I'm married," he said and instantly felt like a prick. Who cares? This wasn't a cheap TV show like *Jerry Springer*.

Then Josie said something strange. "He tries to understand us. Those who grew up in Black Rock, I mean. Bless him." She seemed disappointed, and her words resigned as she added, "An outsider will never know."

"What d'you mean?" Melody said.

"This place has changed so much. Farming, fishing, and tin mines have now given way to fancy

The Crazy Season

country clubs, golfing, and spa retreats. It's completely changed."

"What do the older generation think?"

Josie turned her hands over to show her palms. "What d'you think they think of it? Hard work that has left grandparents and great grandparents crippled, or worse still dead, has been pushed to the side. Glossed over with rich money. It's like that era never happened. Mike just sees the wealth that rolls in. It boosts our business here, but it erases our past."

"You tell him that?"

She shook her head. "I shouldn't even be telling you that. I'm sorry, it's an area I struggle with…" she stopped and took a deep breath. "Maybe it's nostalgia. Some whimsical fascination with the past. It's not Mike's fault, so I'm not angry with him."

Just then Mike appeared with the paninis, unaware of the conversation they'd just had.

"There you go," he slipped each plate in front of them.

"How much do I owe you?" Joel said. He hated not paying for things.

Mike waved it away. "Don't be silly. If you help us then that's all the payment I could ever want." He turned and was gone.

"You sure I can't have him?" Melody grinned, glancing to where he'd gone and then back at Josie.

That brought a smile to Josie's face. "Definitely not."

"What do you think happened to Natasha?" Joel said clearing his throat and getting straight to it.

Josie began to chew the inside of her mouth. It stretched her cheek and gave her a determined look. "I don't know."

"Her friends know anything?"

At first, Josie pulled a face. "She didn't really have any, I mean. Our parents are strict and want her to do well. They didn't want her slacking off to go to parties or hang out with her friends."

"You think she might've run off? You know, had enough of it all and disappeared?"

The way Josie shook her head it was obvious she didn't agree. "No way. She'd have told me, if nothing else."

"She tell you everything?"

"Maybe. I don't know. I guess all teens have secrets, right? There's ten years between us. I moved out long ago. I live down here in the town. They live up in the high and mighty Beach View community."

Joel was surprised. "So you used to live up there?"

"Yes. Look, the thing is my mum lived down here in a small fisherman's cottage. There were six of them in a two-bedroom house. She met my dad and suddenly there was money…"

"Money's not for everyone," Melody commented.

"She's right," Joel said.

Melody then added quickly, "Says the guy who owns his own lighthouse!"

Josie looked impressed. "Really? It's not in a gated community, is it?"

"Certainly not." Joel sometimes felt compelled to relay his own story, but this wasn't about him. He knew he had to stay on track.

The Crazy Season

"What about the others? The other missing girl and the two boys who died?"

"I don't know. She went to school with them so she knew them. I mean, she knew April. Everyone knew April. My parents love her parents. I guess she knew Becky as the two of them came in a package, but the boys? I have no idea…" she then looked deep in thought. Her mind searching for something she knew was important. "Wait… they were all involved in something. A school play. No idea what it was all about. In fact, Nat really didn't want to be involved."

"So why was she?"

"Something she was made to do. That's all she said."

"And the others were in on it too?"

"April was lead, of course. Becky was in it too. I heard that Stevie was doing the curtains, and the other lad…I don't know. Miss Simons thought she was some director extraordinaire! Seemed to think she was putting on a production for the West End."

"She live locally?"

"Yes. In fact, take a right out of here and follow the road to the end. She lives in the cottage with the huge apple tree outside."

"How was Natasha the last time you saw her?"

"She was Nat. She was focused on her work, annoyed at our parents, but generally fine. A typical teen."

"Any specific issue with your parents?"

Josie looked alarmed. "God no. Like me, she'd grown out of the high life. All she saw were the things she was missing out on…" Josie bit her lip again maybe wrestling with the next line. "You know how it is to be a teenager. You want to enjoy life. You don't want to stay in your room for hours when your friends are out meeting up and going to parties. She wanted to chase boys."

"But she didn't really have any close friends?"

"Not close. She told me she got invited out, but dad wouldn't allow it. He instilled discipline in us showing how hard work pays off, I guess. I hurt him by moving down here, so he was even more strict with Nat. Look, he only wants the best for her. For me, too."

"He like Mike?"

She glanced out the door even though she couldn't see him. "He likes his work ethic. He thinks he should expand, but Mike's not like that. He goes surfing, and reads books. These are all pointless activities to my dad. My dad's a social butterfly, surfing and reading are solo past times, not to mention not money making." She laughed to herself at that, but it was a slightly embarrassed gesture. "But he's a good man," she added quickly.

"I have no doubt," Melody said as Joel listened and drank his coffee.

Melody grabbed her cup and took a satisfying sip.

Joel took over. "Do you know much about the other kids?"

"I'd heard of them," she began, her eyes looking up as she tried to think. "Only April really, but then everyone knows April."

"Had any of them, Natasha included, ever spoken out of turn about her father, or Beach View in particular?"

"I don't think so. Like I say, I didn't really know them. There's no way April or Becky would. I don't think Nat hated it, she just didn't like the work she had to do. I'm not sure I could see her living down here!"

"You have a lovely place here," Melody said through mouthfuls of food. She waved her panini in salute. "And this is amazing!"

"Thank you."

"Have you been here long?" Joel asked.

"Only a year or so. In spring and summer the place is heaving. We have to take on more staff, and the queues go out the door. Autumn and winter are slower; we get a steady flow of regulars and day-trippers that just makes us a profit, but it's nice. We love it."

Joel liked that. The silver spoon had been replaced with one she'd handcrafted herself. It might not be as fancy, but arguably it was more satisfying.

They talked some more whilst finishing up their drinks and food, Josie told them more about Nat, and Melody spoke about her house by the beach and love of surfing and books too.

"I'm definitely keeping you away from Mike!"

When they finally left, they did so as friends. Not that they required any further motivation, but it all felt more personal.

"Let's go and see whether Spielberg is home," Joel said.

"Eh?"

"Miss Simons."

"Ah."

Jim Ody

Chapter 31 – Joel

Melody was checking her phone as they walked down the road.

"Nothing from April," she said, and began to tap away. "I'm sending her another message."

The road had long rows of terrace houses on either side. They were the two-up-two-down type built a little before WW1. Most of them now had new roofs, loft-conversions, or extensions. It was funny, nowadays fewer people lived in the houses but society demanded they be larger.

The apple tree was easily recognisable. It peeked out over the hedge that surrounded the cottage. It looked like it had been plucked out of the countryside and placed here on the edge of town.

Joel pushed open the small gate, and they followed the sandstone path up towards a bright orange front door. As he pressed the brass door bell, Joel noticed the battered Volvo parked in a strange

The Crazy Season

manner in the driveway. It was slightly at an angle. Probably an example of a haphazard person.

"Hello?" A voice boomed as the door was swung open theatrically.

"Miss Simons?" Joel asked, taking in the plump woman who was twisting the long dangling beads around her neck. She had wispy brown hair with a shock of white streaking through in places.

"Yes, I'm not interested in buying anything."

"Neither am I." Joel tried for a bit of humour. "I wondered if I could ask you some questions about some of your students?"

"You don't look like the police, and you're far too handsome to be the press." she stated tossing her head back and swinging the beads some more.

"I'm an investigative journalist. More on investigation than the journalist part. I want to solve a case rather than sell a story."

"I've already spoken to the police," she said defiantly. "I'm not sure I can offer anything further."

Melody stepped forward. She had a habit of doing that. Joel was beginning to think she had a real skill. "If I may ask a couple of things? I'm not a journalist. In fact, I'm a painter, not a dreamer. We're friends of Josie and Mike, from the coffee shop?" she turned and pointed up the road.

Miss Simons nodded. "I know them." It was unclear whether this would help or hinder things.

"We're just trying to find Natasha, and trying to find out what happened."

"I see." Miss Simons stood rigid. She made no attempt to move to the side to let them in. "Perhaps I can offer a couple of minutes. I really must get on.

Jim Ody

My schedule is extremely busy. I'm five people down now." Her words were slightly insensitive, even if factually correct.

"Please," Melody smiled warmly. "If you don't mind?"

Miss Simons huffed and reluctantly let them in. "Come, come," she said like she was speaking to a couple of students. Joel wasn't sure whether they'd get much from her, but they had to cover all bases. Sometimes answers came in the most unlikely of places. These were what could change the pace and direction of an investigation in an instant.

The cottage looked small and confining as they stepped into a dark room with stone walls and a small window. There was a huge fireplace and an attractive iron log burner underneath. Miss Simons might've been in her fifties, or she might've been in her thirties. It was hard to tell. She dressed conservatively, doing her best to keep as much of her body covered as possible. Joel wondered whether her hard exterior ever softened.

"As I told the police," she began. "Kids are kids. Outside of school they are hardly my responsibility." She slowly shook her head. The thoughts inside her were troubled. "You see," she continued, "in my day, to be part of the arts was an honour. To stand and perform in front of audiences was something only the best were able to do. It's a real skill. They were the first greats… Now? They talk nonsense into their phones and look to become famous that way. It's absurd. No thought into the message they're trying to convey, often just some nonsensical rambling. Worse still are the ones who think art is stripping down to

The Crazy Season

next to nothing and wiggling like they have some sort of skin irritation." Joel had to suppress a laugh. She was very animated about it, but he couldn't help but think she may spend a lot of time watching these videos just to get herself worked up. A professional complainant.

"You're right," Melody agreed. "I played Calpurnia in our school production of Julius Caesar. An underrated role, if you ask me. My parents were so proud."

Miss Simons' face lit up like she'd just seen her long-lost sister. "Bravo!" she clapped her hands. "Underrated indeed. I bet you were wonderful," her eyes looked Melody over. "You have a certain presence about you."

"Thank you," Melody almost blushed.

Miss Simons turned to Joel. "And you?"

That caught Joel on the hop. "Er, I was sheep-three in year 4's nativity play… I, er, was a midfielder mostly for the football team."

Miss Simons was not amused by this. "Another problem today. The theatrics appear to have snaked their way into sport instead. No longer do men see the real artistry in dominating an audience at the Theatre Royal, no, they'd much rather kick a bag of wind around a field and roll around on the grass feigning injury." Without realising it, Joel shrunk back slightly.

"So, Miss Simons. What were the roles of the five children?"

They all sat on a sofa that was more antique than comfortable. It was hard faux-velvet and had small gold tassels hanging around the seams. Similar tassels adorned plump cushions that had a shine to them making them more for show.

"April, of course, is a natural. She has charisma that will carry her further than a stage. She has a Midas touch…" there was a sudden play of a smile to the side of her lips as she thought of this child who was beginning to get a God-like state for everyone.

"Did her father donate to the school?" Joel said. It stood to reason that someone with so much money and influence would want to shape the youth of today too. The subtle act of a megalomaniac. Control the young to control the older.

"Of course. A very generous man," she agreed, the point lost on her.

"And the others?"

"Becky was a little clumsy. She tried hard, maybe a little too hard," she grinned at a memory. "She had a tendency to overact. Every move was over exaggerated and unnatural. Natasha, let me see. She didn't want to be there. She had been asked to attend by Mr Townsend. He thought it would give her more confidence. I wasn't sure myself. He seemed to think she was just a little shrew." Dramatically, Miss Simons hunched over and looked meek clasping her hands in front of her, before almost exploding out. "And needed coaxing out of herself. She was okay. Nothing special."

"And what does Mr Townsend teach?"

"History. He has a good rapport with the kids. I think he goes too far myself but…"

"How d'you mean?"

The Crazy Season

"Oh, don't mind me. I'm just being overly picky." She seemed to be a little worried with what she'd said.

"There must be something for you to say that. Please expand for us."

She looked both of them in the eyes, choosing her words carefully.

"We are there to teach. We come in, we go out, but Mr Townsend... he likes to be all buddy-buddy with them. Some of the girls had crushes on him, and I'm not so sure he didn't encourage it!"

"Did he ever step over the line?"

"Oh no, nothing like that."

"You had no suspicions at all?"

"None whatsoever. He just... he liked the attention as much as the girls did."

"Stevie?"

"He stood at the back and stared at the girls. I don't want to speak ill of the dead, but there was always something a little off with him. He wasn't interested in the production. That's why he was working the curtains. It was hardly a taxing role, although to watch him huff and puff you'd think it was!"

"And Timothy?"

"Much the same. He was interesting. He always had his little friend Sally there near him. It was sad. She looked at him the way he looked at April. Teenagers, eh? Hormones and unrequited love! Food for the dramatics, no less."

"Did they hang around together after? Those five, I mean?"

Jim Ody

"I have no idea. After rehearsals there are a lot of things to do, I have no care to be babysitter any further, nor worry about what teenagers are getting up to."

"Was there any tension between them?"

"I didn't see any. More with Sally towards them, if you ask me. She was a pretty little green-eyed monster."

Joel and Melody shared a look, before Melody said. "And what was the production?"

"Romeo and Juliet."

"Really?" The thought of forbidden love and suicide wasn't lost on either of them. Nor was the character's name. "Romeo Montague," he said.

Miss Simons grinned wide, and chuckled for the first time. "I know! How apt!"

Joel looked at Melody. "How apt indeed."

"Okay, that's about it. Thank you for your time."

They all got up. "You're welcome," Miss Simons said, happy to move them on.

They walked outside, and Miss Simons was about to close the door when in true Columbo style, Joel suddenly asked, "Oh, and another thing. Who was playing the role of Romeo?"

Miss Simons looked slightly nervous for the first time. "We couldn't get one initially. Then someone recommended a lad to come in."

"From the school?"

"No, he was a little older. His name was Ethan."

"The one who works at the Black Rock Bar?"

She nodded. "Yes, correct."

"Thank you, Miss Simons, that's been very helpful."

"Oh, and where might we find Mr Townsend, if we wanted to speak to him?"

She was ready to close the door. "He'd be over at the school now, or at his home. I understand he's got some building work going on so he's usually somewhere between the two."

"Thanks again," Joel said nodding good bye.

With a slight nod, she closed the bright orange door.

"Well, that's interesting," Melody said as they walked away.

"Yes, indeed. Shall we take a trip to the school?"

Chapter 32

He watched them walking along the road. They weren't holding hands, but they seemed very close. Friends? Lovers? He couldn't be sure.

The guy said something and she laughed. He wanted that little head shake she did when she didn't actually find it funny but was acting like it. It didn't come. She struggled to stop.

He knew that laugh. He'd enjoyed that laugh. Another man was making her do the same. It seemed so primal, but that made him mad.

He wanted to go to them, punch the guy directly in the face and ask what the hell he was doing.

The act would more than likely blow up in his face. It wasn't a clever move. He had to bide his time, set it up carefully and then he'd swoop in like the superhero she once thought he was.

They continued to talk. She was holding eye contact, and periodically touching her hair. She had eyes for him. She longed for him to whisk her off to a room and have his way with her, his large hands ripping her clothes off.

He felt his jaw clench. He suddenly didn't know what to do.

What he did understand, though, was they were going from place to place poking their nose into things that were none of their business.

He didn't like that one bit.

He especially didn't like the fact she thought he was a fool. Some local who didn't know shit. Surely that would be her downfall. He could slip under the radar and attack when everything was just right. *You'll keep*, he thought, and slipped back into the shadows.

Chapter 33 – Joel

Joel began to walk back up the road. He wasn't sure why.

"You don't know where the school is, do you?" she grinned. "It's the other way."

"Ah."

They turned in the opposite direction and headed towards the main road that sliced the town in two.

"How far is it?" Joel asked. He'd had more exercise in the past 24hrs than he'd had in the last month.

"You know when you look at a map and 'um' and 'ah' whether or not to take the car? Well, it's about that far."

"Wonderful."

Melody checked her phone again. "Ah, April," she said, as her thumb tapped and slipped over the screen.

"She'll meet us later. After we've been back to the B&B."

The Crazy Season

"Okay."

"Where we were going about an hour ago."

Joel raised his eyebrows but saw she was being sarcastic. "That's the nature of digging. One thing leads to another." He laughed to himself and commented, "I didn't know you did acting by the way?"

Melody grinned. "I didn't. It sounded good though, didn't it?"

"What? You were telling porkies?"

"Yep. I wasn't even sheep three."

"Not everyone could pull it off."

"I'll bet."

The clouds had cleared above them. The sky was hardly blue, but it no longer looked angry. There was even a warm breeze whipping around them.

"D'you think we need to speak to Sally, again?" Melody said as they walked on. "She seems to be on the periphery of all this. It might be coincidental, or it might've been deliberate."

"It's possible. She knew them all, and she had a thing for Timothy. Maybe she does know more than she's saying."

"And the big production? Is that the key?"

Joel idly scratched his cheek, then said, "Maybe, maybe not. It could be how Ethan comes into it."

"*Romeo and Juliet?* Really?"

"There is nothing normal about this case. It's not so far fetched that Ethan and April have a fling, Ethan wants more, and April doesn't."

"How do the others come into it? And how come April is one of the only ones unscathed?"

Jim Ody

"What if April was the one who wanted more and set up some elaborate web to catch Ethan?"

"That is more likely."

The road was long but the signs for the high school gave Joel hope they might reach it before sunset. Then just as he was thinking about the comfort of his Jeep, the school was finally in sight.

Joel looked at his Fitbit and tapped it a couple of times. "I'm killing the step count today!"

"That's because you spend most of the time at the top of your lighthouse staring out at the sea and dreaming of mermaids."

He chuckled at that. "You think that's the extent of my daily routine?"

"It's what I'd do," she confessed. "I'd probably paint them in watercolour. Your lighthouse would make such a great studio."

"It makes a pretty good study."

"Mermaid lookout."

"Or mermaid lookout."

The school was beginning to look tired. It had been built in the 60s and had large coloured panels between the concrete columns. It was a boxy sprawl of a building with little to no architectural flair. It was built for purpose, and arguably that purpose had now passed.

There was only a handful of cars, all spaced out in the car park like they'd had a disagreement.

A woman with a huge tight blonde perm was placing a large box into the back of her car. She stopped what she was doing when they got closer.

"Can I help?" she asked, ever the helpful one. You could always tell a teacher, Joel thought. They took control of a situation and constantly searched for answers.

"We're looking for Mr Townsend. Is he here today?"

She nodded slowly, and then looked out towards the school. "Yes, he's around somewhere."

Joel was about to thank her when she suddenly added. "Ah, there he is, behind the older gentleman."

The older gentleman had a shiny bald head and wore a mismatched suit that was probably the height of fashion fifty years ago.

"Thank you," Joel said with his best smile.

Mr Townsend was a handsome man in his forties. He was old enough to show authority but young enough to still look cool.

"I can see the attraction," Melody muttered.

"Please don't swoon. It often distracts from the investigation."

"I'll try."

"Excuse me," Joel called out. The teacher looked up at them. He looked wary, but then flashed his million-dollar smile.

"Hello. Can I help you?"

"Mr Townsend?"

"That's correct. Who wants to know?"

Melody then spoke out. "We're looking into the disappearance of a couple of your students," she said. "Can we ask you some questions?"

"Of course." Joel expected him to invite them back into the school, maybe into an office, but Mr Townsend was more than prepared to speak to them right there in the car park.

"When did you last see them?" Joel asked.

Jim Ody

Mr Townsend made a point of thinking hard. "Last Friday, I would say… in class. Or in the school grounds anyway."

"The day of the party?" Melody stated.

"Party?"

"You didn't know they all attended a party?"

Mr Townsend chuckled at that. "I'm not their father, Ms…?"

"No, of course not," Joel jumped in. "We appreciate that, but still. You must hear about parties, right? Kids struggle to maintain their composure when excited."

"We hear a lot of things, but what we hear and what actually happens are often two different things! Teenagers bullshit more than anyone. They are in constant need of affirmation from their peers. Forever hopeful for acceptance, even the loud ones - in fact, especially the loud ones! The stories I hear are tall to say the least!"

"But you heard nothing specifically about a party last Friday?"

He looked like he was giving it more thought. "I can't say as I did. The two boys were both obsessed with April… I can't tell you what happened, but fantasy and hormones can be the death of a teenager. I can tell you that!" He was making light of it, but Joel thought it was just his style.

"You don't think there was anything - I don't know - strange about it?" Melody asked.

Mr Townsend shook his head. "I've asked around, but I've heard nothing. Like I say, kids talk, even if the stories are filled with holes and pulled together

The Crazy Season

with lies. But I've heard nothing. The whole school is still in shock."

"And the two missing students?"

"I don't know… I wish I did."

"Did they hang out together?"

"I don't think so. Natasha and Becky were too different."

"How so?"

Mr Townsend puffed out his cheeks, he was picking through his answers carefully. "Natasha was a grade A student who was quiet and got her homework done, Becky, was more vivacious. She aspired to be April but held a limited number of tools… but it didn't stop her from trying. She was a B-minus student, happy to scrape by."

"Did she speak to Timothy or Stevie?"

He seemed to find the question funny. "Sure, she spoke to them. They were both little boys with big dreams. They followed her and April around like they might have a chance. You know, they weren't alone, there were other boys who did the same. Martin for one, but he'll tell you different. You can't believe a word he says."

"Really?"

"Yeah, he said he was friends with David Beckham last year. He had some photo of the two of them together. Said it was taken at his house."

"But it wasn't."

"No," he grinned. "It was a poor photo edit. I felt a little sorry for him. Kids can be cruel, and he clearly just wanted attention."

Jim Ody

Joel nodded, and wondered how much of what Martin had said could now be disregarded. "Gut feeling, where d'you think the missing girls are?"

"London probably. It wouldn't surprise me if Natasha had enough of her family and got talked into some adventure to piss off both of their parents."

"It's been days since they went missing. Don't you think they would've called?"

He held up his hands innocently. "I'm just answering your question. Honestly, I have no idea."

"Okay. Thank you for your time."

"Anytime."

They turned and began their long walk back to the B&B.

Chapter 34 – Joel

The road ahead of them was long, both physically and metaphorically.

"What do you think about his comments on Martin?" Joel said.

"He's a teenage boy, lying and exaggeration is the nature of the beast."

"True. The missing girls bother me though. There is something we're missing. I just can't quite put my finger on it."

"Yeah, I know what you mean."

They continued in silence until the end of the road. Joel was processing all the answers he'd been given by a number of people.

"I just don't get that Natasha wouldn't have spoken to her sister. It's one thing being mad at your parents - and I still think just under a week is a long

Jim Ody

time to remain mad - but her sister was devastated, wasn't she? There is no way she'd not tell her."

It was surprising to Joel how comfortable they'd become with each other. A few days ago, she'd been Kip's baby sister, someone who generally stayed out of his way, but now they'd become good friends.

Melody did have a habit of coming out with random things: "I used to walk all the time when I lived here. It kept me fit. I ate some great foods and spent a lot of time without clothes on, so it was a benefit."

"Too much information."

"You know what it's like, don't tell me you don't. I bet you jumped Cherry's bones at every opportunity when you first met."

Joel struggled not to smile. "Jumped Cherry's bones, what a phrase. Sure, bone jumping happens to be something I enjoy."

Melody went suddenly quiet. "You don't mind me bringing her up, do you?"

Joel turned to her, "Of course not. I like talking about her."

"Okay, cool."

"I'm not so keen talking about all my sexual techniques with you though."

"Why? You have pictures instead?"

They continued the light-hearted banter until the B&B was in front of them.

Joel wasn't sure why, but something drew him to look at his Jeep. There, under the wiper blades was what appeared to be a note. It was folded over a couple of times.

The Crazy Season

"What have we here?" he said reaching over and tentatively freeing it.

"An offer to scrap your car, I'd think," Melody quipped.

"I can always do with the money…" he began to joke, but as he opened up the note, he saw it was a statement. One made in cut out letters like some clichéd ransom note.

Leave it alone! Or the curse will get you too!

Joel held it open so Melody could see it, too.

"Wow! A threat that has the power to cast the curse on us!" She was trying to make light of it, but Joel could see she was a little shaken, too. She glanced all around just in case she saw someone sitting looking at a newspaper with large eye holes cut out.

There was nobody around.

"Come on," Joel said. "Let's not stand out here in the open." Even Joel felt a little uneasy. With most cases he took on there was something happening he had to get to the bottom of, but people were so wrapped up in their own story, he'd never been threatened before. When he thought back to some of them it was a little surprising.

But this was different.

This was teenage suicides and disappearances. A host of secrets and fingers being pointed in all directions.

And the curse. The huge accusation that some sort of evil spirit could float around and affect the lives of those it chose just felt like fiction. Small town minds, overactive through boredom and the mundane. They had to get to the beginning of the curse. Where did it originate?

"Here they are. The lovebirds!" The jovial voice of Miss Shannon said.

"We're not…" Joel began, but saw Miss Shannon grin mischievously.

"So you keep saying! He doth protest too much!"

"Because it's not true."

"She's winding you up," Melody said, elbowing him.

"Ah, right."

"It's a lovely day for a walk," Miss Shannon continued, ignoring her playful open line. "D'you go anywhere nice?"

Melody was quick to speak up, and when she did it was with much enthusiasm. Any sarcasm was deep and covered like the local tin mines. "Yeah, down to the beach to start with. Oh, it's so nice to blow the cobwebs away! Then we went for coffee. I'm not sure why we don't come here more often!"

"I see," Miss Shannon said. "You know this place though don't you?" her tone changed slightly.

"Sorry, I don't follow?"

"I've seen you before, have I not? Or am I mistaken?"

Joel could see that Melody was caught off guard. For a second she almost faltered. "I was around a few years ago for a while."

"Things didn't work out." The line was flat. Neither a question or a statement.

"Life rarely does."

Miss Shannon nodded and made an accepting face. "No, dear." She then uncharacteristically

The Crazy Season

winked and said, "That's why you sometimes have to grab the bull by the horns and fight for what's right."

Charles appeared through the archway of the sitting room they'd not yet ventured into.

"I can't stop and talk," he said. "Much too busy to gossip!" He slipped past and went out the door.

"The stupid old fool," Miss Shannon said. "He's not been busy since the Falklands! Anyway, I am, however, so I'll leave you to it."

Joel and Melody were left there bemused by it all and wondering whether that was a snapshot of the two of them in years to come.

Then Joel thought about Cherry, and his stomach dropped. He'd usually be thinking about seeing her about now.

"Come on," he said, and they went up to his room.

As they got up to the top, Joel was hoping that Melody would want to pop to her own room. He didn't want to admit it, but he was going to call the hospital. However, she was right behind him when he opened up the door.

"If I log on to my laptop, do you want to have a look into the suicides in 2001?"

"And what is so pressing that you are looking to run off?"

He showed her his phone, and admitted, "I'm going to give the hospital a ring… you know, just in case…"

She was already nodding. Like him, she probably knew that had there been a change then he would've been the first to know. But it was something he had to do.

He hated thinking of her being so far away.

Jim Ody

He spoke to the receptionist who put him through to the correct department. He felt himself lift as the loud friendly voice of Jules was heard on the other end.

"Hi Jules, it's Joel. Joel Baxter."

"I know who you are, you silly man!"

He laughed nervously, and once again wished he was there. "I can't make it there today… how is she? Cherry? Any changes?"

He realised he was firing questions at her.

"Joel, your Cherry is in good spirits, but there's no change," she said. "I was going to ask. Would you like me to play her your song?"

Joel was nodding into the phone. It broke his heart when other people's kindness filled his life. "Would you?"

"Of course."

"I'll be there tomorrow."

"Joel. I know you're on a case. If you have to stay away another day, Cherry will understand. I never got to speak to her, but I'll tell you this, I bet she's the proudest woman on earth to have a husband who spends so much of his life looking out for others."

"Thank you," was all he could manage.

"Alright then. We'll see you soon. Take care."

"Thank you. You, too."

Joel took a moment. He didn't think not seeing his wife would affect him so much. He went over to the window. He knew they had to get on, but to go from speaking to the hospital straight into the case seemed too hard a transition. He wanted to take a moment. Pretend that Cherry was there with him, maybe taking a shower as they dressed to go out for a meal.

The Crazy Season

He remembered back to a time in Bournemouth, when they'd done just that. He was hungry, and looking out of the window whilst she was still doing her makeup. He'd been frustrated with her but had remained calm. He was glad he had. How could he be cross with a woman who just wanted to look her best for him?

It had been the last time they'd been away together before Robyn was born.

Sporadic dark clouds were rolling in, they threatened rain, but could just as easily pass on by.

It was a good few minutes before he heard Melody speak. "Are you okay?" she asked.

He turned and nodded, although he was far from okay inside. He ignored her question, not wanting to dwell on it, and instead took a more pragmatic approach.

"Have you got anything?" He could tell she understood. It was another thing he liked about her. She got when he was feeling uncomfortable.

She was on her front, laid out on the bed with her legs curled back in the air. It was the last position he'd put himself in to go on his laptop. His neck and arms hurt just looking at her. But she did do all of that yoga.

"Bits and pieces," she said. "This is the third time. In 1981, three teenagers committed suicide. All three were friends, but they died in separate locations. It was investigated as some sort of pact, but there was no indication that was the case. No suicide notes were ever recovered, and all three seemed like promising students. Although there was a strange death at the same time of an old man. Most reports dismissed any connection but one… well, this is interesting…" She looked up at him mischievously.

"Go on."

"Not only did it try to link the cases there was a fourth person that day. Edward Montague."

The recognition was instant. "April's dad?"

"The one and only."

"Interesting."

"Jump forward to 2001, and three teenagers again commit suicide. All were friends, and all died in different locations. No notes, and from what authorities could tell, no reasons. They were average students, one minute joking around in school, the next all buried in the local cemetery."

Joel sat down on the bed and looked at the screen. "There must be a link."

Melody's fingers hovered over the keys, but instead of tapping them, she rested them on the side, turned, and stated, "But this time there's only two suicides."

"That we know of. There are two missing, so it could end up being two, three or four suicides. The time frame of twenty years feels significant, although it could be coincidental."

They looked at some pictures of the boys from 2001. No matter whether or not the lads were smiling, the pictures remained sad. To know that at some stage they took their own lives was awful.

"Hold on a minute," Joel said looking over Melody's shoulder. "Scroll back up to that photograph."

"Which one?"

"The one with all three and the people in the background."

The screen moved and then stopped at the picture he was talking about. The boys were smiling and in the park. A couple stood behind them, talking unaware a picture was being taken.

"There. Stood to the side." Joel couldn't believe it. There next to a tree and almost out of sight was a teenager scowling at the boys. He looked familiar.

They'd spoken to him earlier that day.

"Mr Townsend?"

"I think so."

Jim Ody

Chapter 35

The Previous Season – 2001

Stuart had been hiding out in the shed at the bottom of his garden. He was trying to tell himself that wasn't the case but he knew deep down it was. Sometimes you can lie to anyone, but you really can't lie to yourself.

He had his headphones on listening to Blink 182. It was almost a resurgence of happy songs again, however where the rock songs were boastful and misogynist, pop/punk was songs about losers drooling over girls too good for them.

Stuart was fifteen and sat huddled in the corner wearing his baggy jeans, a hoodie, and Vans trainers. He was definitely not okay. When he looked around, he thought the shed walls were going to come in on him.

He thought he was looking for adventure. He was a teenage boy, and that was his rite of passage.

The Crazy Season

It started with a story, the way it always does. Him and his mates were sitting in the park drinking whisky they'd hidden in opened cola cans. Richard had stolen a bottle from his dad's drink's cabinet. There were enough half empty bottles that he would never know. They'd split it between cola cans and held them proudly as they walked down the road to the park.

"You heard about the suicides?" Trev had said. He was always looking to come out with something huge. He once scratched a swastika on his forearm with the sharp point of a compass. He knew no more about the Nazis than he did about the rapper Nas, but he knew enough to know it would shock. And shock it did. Mrs Peabody, the science teacher, took one look at the bleeding symbol and sent Trev to his head of year. Stuart didn't see Trev for a week. He'd been suspended.

"What suicides?" Phil said, taking another swig. He'd already drunk enough, his eyes were no longer able to focus, and his limbs were moving in a strange slow and fluid way that he apparently couldn't control.

Trev looked at Stuart who shook his head.

"It was like 20 years ago. It was called The Killing Season.1980-something."

"What happened?" Stuart asked, stalling. He didn't want any more whisky. It was strong stuff and he was having waves of nausea.

Trev pulled a face like it was something really bad. "Man, it was awful. Three kids killed a man then committed suicide all within a few days. They were teenagers like us!"

Jim Ody

"Why?" Phil asked.

Trev shrugged. "They killed a man! Didn't you hear me, you bonehead?"

Stuart looked at him dubiously. "What man?"

"Some old guy, though that was never proven."

"So why did they kill themselves?" Stuart didn't get it.

Trev held up his hands in defence. "Don't shoot the messenger. Fucked if I know."

"They were probably druggies, or idiots."

"I don't know about that," Trev said, and leaned in closer. "Apparently they all came from rich families. The case went cold. They all knew each other but weren't all friends. No one knew what had driven them to it. Apart from the curse."

"The curse?" Stuart was interested now. "What curse?"

Phil rolled his eyes. "There's no curse. It's bullshit."

"You try telling that to their parents!" Trev said. Phil and Stuart looked at each other, but they had no response to that.

"Let's look into it then!" Phil said. For some reason even though professionals could not get to the bottom of it, Phil figured some dumbass teenagers could.

So they did.

This was years before the internet was in everyone's homes. It meant hard graft. Hanging around the town library and looking suspicious. Asking older people in a covert way, until they caught a break. Except that break only led them into the eye of the storm.

The Crazy Season

To a point where they wished they'd never pushed to uncover the truth about the curse. Meddling kids as a popular cartoon was fond of saying.

Much had happened, and now Stuart was here alone. His friends long gone. His friends were dead.

It pounded with rain outside. A complete downpour. If nothing else it stopped the world from being so silent.

Why had they poked their noses in? Why couldn't they have just left it alone?

He slipped out of the shed, the cold rain penetrating the cotton of his hoodie. He turned and was shocked to see the figure standing near his house and staring at him.

He was frozen to the spot. Rigid with fear. He began to sob. How? How? He mumbled to himself, but they were foolish words. Of course, the person knew where he lived. Stuart had been told he had no place to hide, and his home was the guaranteed place for him to be found.

With purposeful steps the figure walked towards him. Their face under the hood of a rain-mac. The darkness from the night covering them further.

Stuart suddenly found his feet. He turned to run but tripped and hit the hard ground. The concrete of the garden path abruptly stopped his fall and knocked the wind out of him. It might've been funny, had the situation not been so serious.

Stuart went to get up but was struck to the floor again. He felt his legs being grabbed as he was dragged back into the shed.

Jim Ody

Inside the shed, he went to scream. Something that felt like a pill was placed into his mouth and a glove covered his nose and mouth.

He was consumed by the strong smell of leather as he tried to get air. He swallowed. The tablet well on its way to begin its role of shutting down his organs.

Something was dropped with a clatter. Later it was discovered as a picture of his friends. Next to it, a letter of confession.

The stranger slipped out into the night. Moments later through the sound of the rain hitting the shed roof, the sound of Stuart's mum could be heard desperately calling out his name.

He tried to respond, but his limbs were too heavy to move. The world became fuzzy, and then went black. The last thought in his mind before he finally died was *why did we have to find out about The Crazy Season?*

The police couldn't understand the confession. It sounded like Stuart had talked his friends into committing suicide, too. But each boy killed himself in a different place and at a different time.

It made no sense. Nothing about the case made sense.

Despite a brief media interest, the case soon went cold. Even the parents accepted the fate of their sons as that of misadventure. Some sort of teenage naivety that went wrong.

Out loud, nobody wanted to draw comparisons to the events of twenty years previously.

At least it would never happen again.

Chapter 36 - Joel

Was the teacher really around the three boys all those years ago.

Melody looked up from the laptop. Joel was sitting on the bed with his back resting against the headboard.

"What d'you think?" she said. "Is that really him?"

"It looks like it."

"He never mentioned anything." Her voice was weak, she knew like he did that it meant nothing.

"For a start we never asked him about the curse, did we? And all this suggests is that he was at the park when they were. He doesn't even look like they were friends or anything."

"You're right," Melody agreed and toggled the page back to another story about the original season.

"It's a whole bunch of coincidences though, isn't it?" she said, reading down the page.

"Yes, and a lot open to interpretation."

Jim Ody

"A body of an old man found down on the beach, and three teenagers seen around that area all commit suicide. I'm not so sure of a curse but more of guilt. That's where it started?"

"Including the king of Beach View."

Melody tipped her head to the side, and puffed out her cheeks. "The thing with curses is that no one can ever be sure on where they began. I've had a look on the dark web. There are of course a number of theories. One suggests that the old man placed a curse on the kids, and from there all teenagers caught up in murder would be victims of the same fate."

"Sounds like standard curse fare."

"Another suggests that the cave they were in held some evil spirit, and when they went exploring, they unleashed it."

Joel shrugged at that one. "A little vague and very unbelievable."

"From there they get a bit fantastical."

"Of course they do. Lonely people without the discipline to write fiction."

Melody grinned at that. "More than likely. We have a cave troll. The dark witch of Black Rock. Sea sirens. Oh, and a number of tales of revenge. Parents having affairs, the industrial change of the town. If you can believe it, hit men making murder look like suicide…"

"Any mention of Mr Montague?"

"Only when you dig really deep. There are a couple of suggestions that his family covered it up. They paid off whoever they needed to for it to go away. One person even talked of an affair he was having…"

"But no actual motives?"

"No, it's all speculation."

Joel got up off the bed. He walked again to the window and looked out. "News was news back then. If they had no details then they didn't fill in the blanks themselves. There was slightly more integrity to journalism back then." He turned his head to see Melody looking at him dubiously. "Well, not quite as bad as today anyway!"

A lone figure walked by. They were covered from head to toe in a large fishing jacket and big boots. Then quickly, the person turned and looked at the B&B. Then stopped and stared.

However, just as quickly, they turned and walked away.

"And what about the suicides in 2001? They are even more vague."

Melody clicked a few keys, and then mumbled to herself as she read through what was written in front of her. Her finger was following the words on the screen like a child deep in concentration.

"Three friends again. The details again are pretty vague… All three died in separate places… no one really knows why."

"This is the millennium, there must've been speculation?"

Melody raised her eyebrows, and gave a small nod. "Not much. Drink and drugs are mentioned, but I think that was a default of being young. Friends and family deny both, and any medical reports must've come back clear as there's no further mention of it."

"Nothing about Devil worshipping?"

Melody chuckled. "Funny enough, no. If this was America in the 90s, then rock music would've been held accountable too!"

"And the suicide methods?"

Melody changed position. She sat up crossed legged and put the laptop on her lap. "Well this is where it gets a bit interesting. Stuart was found in his shed having taken some pills, Trevor jumped from a bridge, and Phil drowned."

Joel looked at her like she'd just given him a huge clue. "Timothy jumped off the cliff into water and Stevie jumped off a bridge…"

"What are the chances that either Becky or Natascha have overdosed somewhere?"

"Shit," Joel said, pulling out his phone. "I'll ring the police for an update on the case, you start ringing around the local hospitals just in case a body has been admitted, and they don't know who she is?"

Melody held up a hand. "But the police would've already checked that, right?"

"It doesn't hurt to be thorough."

Ten minutes later and the case had moved nowhere. Melody had spoken to the nearest three hospitals in the time it took for someone to reluctantly speak to Joel. There was no Jane Doe in any hospitals who was unaccounted for. The contact Josie had given them was treating the case as top secret, and prizing anything from him, was to Joel like trying to gain proof of Christ. To a point it was understandable, but frustrating nonetheless. Some people knew of Joel, and most people didn't. Neither appeared to be a greater advantage at getting information.

"Maybe we should just concentrate on what's happened in the past month. We really don't know if there is a connection to the past other than the rumour mill being at full steam ahead."

"Perhaps." Joel paced the room. His mind was whirling around. Inside his head was a montage of scenarios, scenes and details playing out. Each flashed with colours, and it felt, at times, like they were reaching out to connect.

Then he caught something out the corner of his eye. He turned to the window and saw her walk fast, her head whipping around to see if anyone was watching her.

Sally.

"Oh…" was all Joel said as he ran to the door. "Back in a minute," he called as Melody was left open-mouthed on the bed, not the first time she'd ever been like that.

Chapter 37 - Becky

After the party

Everything in her life now seemed irrelevant. When she looked into the mirror, she no longer recognised the girl staring back at her. She'd changed. She was damaged. There was absolutely nothing she could do to make herself feel alright.

It wasn't just the smudged make up, and the black line of depression left by tears. She looked and felt older. She'd learnt a lot the night before but was certainly not wiser. She'd not changed her clothes, instead feeling the added comfort in still remaining in them rather than stripped down to next to nothing.

There were visions she couldn't get out of her head. She thought about raiding her mother's drinks cabinet. She wanted to numb the pain. She reached into her drawer and pulled out her glasses case. She'd got contact lenses as soon as she could. The only

The Crazy Season

time she wore her glasses was when boys requested it. Some stupid fantasy they had.

She picked up an Adderall and with one swift action popped it into her mouth and dry-swallowed. She laid back on her bed and waited for it to kick in. She wasn't hopeful. Her head still hurt from whatever she'd been drinking.

She picked up her phone and looked at the messages. There was nothing new. That was odd. Often April would send her a message. A small comment on the night before. Or even a quick invite to breakfast or something the next day where they could talk about things. Relive the night before and giggle at what they'd done.

It felt like her friend was ghosting her.

She clicked onto April's name:

Hey A? You ok?

She was about to send it but then decided to delete it instead. The message seemed too flippant. After the night before it needed to be much stronger, but she had no idea what to say.

A lot of it was a blur. She remembered music and flashing lights. She remembered a dark room. She'd been kissing someone and at some point had removed her top. Then there was the deep dark feeling of sickness as she thought about the blood. A body.

How did it all come together? How had the scenes come together?

Tears had escaped before she realised it. Her throat closed up. She felt sad and emotional for herself. And then for the others. They were all bound

Jim Ody

by their actions. Old enough to go along with it, but too young to understand the repercussions.

The looks on her friends' faces would haunt her for the rest of her life. The way the room spun round. The shadows danced.

The flashes from the camera.

The pictures.

Evidence of what they'd done.

She grabbed her phone again. Her finger looking at the picture of April. She wanted to call her. Hear her voice. She needed reassurance that everything would be alright.

Her heart beat fast, but her fingers worked faster.

We need to talk.

Short and direct. She pressed send before she had a chance to think about it and delete it.

She looked accusingly at her phone. The smiling faces of herself and April no longer brought her the comfort they once had. She willed the phone to vibrate and the cute picture of her friend to fill the screen to say she was calling.

But it remained still. Just an object of much promise.

She gave it a minute. Two minutes. Five minutes. Nothing.

The walls of her room closed in on her. The air slowly sucked out. A tightness in her chest made her gasp for air. She turned into her pillow and wept. Well and truly wept. Invisible hands pressed her closely and refused to let up.

How had it all come to this? She wondered.

And then her phone vibrated. She snatched it up without thought. A single tap opened up the message.

The Crazy Season

Don't contact me again.

Her stomach dropped. Her lifeline severed.

It was at that point Becky decided she no longer had a reason to live. Her best friend hated her.

What else had she done last night?

She stopped crying. A numbness took over. Her sadness drained from her body and was absorbed into the perfect world she'd leave behind.

Nothing mattered in a world without April.

The next day she looked at the pictures on her wall for the last time. She delved into the deep dark corners of her wardrobe and found her backpack. She yanked a couple of items of thick clothing off the hangers and stuffed them into the bag. Normally she'd roll the clothes after carefully folding them, but now nothing seemed to matter.

She slipped out of the house. She didn't like goodbyes. She guessed this was it.

She walked to the outside perimeter of the community. She knew exactly where she was going.

Momentarily, she hesitated, thinking she'd forgotten something. A quick pat on her cargo trousers told her that her packet of pills was there.

Each step took her away from her life, and she wondered whether it was right to suddenly feel so serene about it.

Gulls circled above, their cry now mournful. She could hear the sea and it struck her then that she hadn't appreciated her location enough in life.

She walked almost robotically away from her house and away from the toxicity of Beach View.

She approached the building.

She slipped inside.

Jim Ody

She was alone. She was scared.

She thought of her friends and family.

The room was bright white. She pulled out a pen and pad and began to write out everything that had happened. A confession of sorts.

When she was done, she read it over. Again, and again. Tears ran down her face, and she wondered whether she was doing the right thing. *What was the right thing?* The question seemed too hard to answer anymore.

She unscrewed the cap of the bottle, and placed the pills in the shaking palm of her hand.

In her mind she counted down from ten. Each number flashed another picture of horror from that night. Regrets sat with her, each taunting and prodding with invisible fingers. They laughed and goaded her to continue.

When she got to one, she slapped her hand to her mouth and slowly swallowed each of the pills. Then, on her hands and knees, and with the empty bottle in her pocket, and the note in her hand, she slid under the large bed and out of sight.

She used the backpack as a pillow and realised just how pointless it was. Deep down this was how she was always going to play it. She would never be April, nor even Natasha for that matter. She wasn't pretty and she wasn't smart.

She was Becky, and if she was lucky, her sacrifice would take her to heaven.

If not, it might just lead the authorities to *him*.

This would tell her whether or not he really was a God.

Her thoughts became harder to grasp. Her body was heavy and her mind now thick and hard to focus. Her breathing was harder and her heart felt like it was slowing down. She felt drowsy.

Where am I? She thought, having suddenly forgotten.

Becky slipped into a dream. One she'd never awake from.

Jim Ody

Chapter 38 - Joel

There were so many stairs to run down. Joel began to try and miss a step each time but when he almost toppled over, he decided against it.

"Careful!" A voice called, but he ignored it.

Pulling the huge front door towards him, he ran out into the cool air and looked up the street.

The slight figure of Sally was now jogging in a strange fashion. By the looks of things, sport wasn't one of her strong points.

He took off after her. It wasn't one of his strong points either.

She was now a dot at the end of the road. She turned to head down some steps and out of sight.

He continued to pump his legs. Running was something that felt almost foreign to him. At one stage he'd played a lot of football, but stories had taken him away from the commitment required to be part of a team. Then middle-age had crept up behind

The Crazy Season

him and slowly drained his energy. Whilst walking up the stairs of his lighthouse each day was a great workout, you couldn't replace the fitness of running. Thrusting the air in and out of your lungs.

Joel got to the steps and looked down. The beach was down there, but he saw no one.

He wiped his brow, took a deep breath and jogged down the steps. He slowed to almost a standstill and scouted all around. There was a sprinkling of people. Dog-walkers and families mostly, but nowhere could he see a girl on her own, walking or running.

How had she disappeared?

He shook his head in disappointment and turned around.

That's when he saw her again.

She'd been hiding beneath the steps and had now double-back and was almost at the top.

"Really?" he said in frustration, and set off again. He was getting too old for this. He should've sent Melody after her.

His legs felt heavy as he finally got to the top.

She was gone.

Only a Black BMW could be seen pulling away.

He pulled out his phone to take a picture of it, but when he looked back at the photo all he saw was a black blur in the shape of a saloon that could be a BMW.

He walked back along the seafront towards the B&B. In the distance Melody jogged towards him.

"What was that all about?"

"I saw Sally," he gasped.

"And?"

Jim Ody

"She took off… She knew I was following her… I lost her, but I think she got into a car." He was now bent over with his hands on his hips.

"She was meeting someone?"

Joel was still trying to get his breath. "I think so."

"Are you going to keel over?"

He coughed once, and then again. "There's a distinct possibility."

Melody maternally patted him on the back. "She knows something. The fact she took off running suggests that."

Joel took in some big deep breaths and then stood up. "Jesus, I think I might survive."

"Sally, Sally, Sally." Melody looked back up the road as if expecting to see the girl standing there taunting them.

"She's another key. She knows a lot more than she told us."

"But?" Melody started but stopped herself. "You are piecing this together, aren't you?"

Joel turned and looked back to the beach. The one that eventually joined the area of Beach View. "The picture is beginning to come clearer now."

"You gonna tell me, or keep me in the dark?" She looked annoyed.

"I'll tell you soon enough. There are just a couple more gaps I need to fill."

They walked back to the B&B, Joel was deep in thought, and it was only when they got nearer, he thought perhaps Melody didn't like that he wasn't telling her everything.

There was still a while before they were off to meet the elusive April.

The Crazy Season

"You know who we should speak to," Joel said, turning to Melody.

"No. Who's that Sherlock?"

"Miss Shannon."

"Did I hear my name!" the voice sang out as they walked into the lobby.

"Yes, just the lady. We wondered whether we could ask you a few questions?"

She looked troubled by the request and glanced down at a small watch, as if something more pressing might be about to take up her time.

"I suppose I could spare ten minutes."

Melody suppressed a smile, but Joel was more understanding. His grandmother did the same. Well, he called her his grandmother, but she was the mother of one of the foster parents he had stayed with. She was retired and had nothing more important than a luncheon club or a hair appointment, but these were written on her calendar in capital letters and underlined twice. Both she considered to be an evil act to miss and assumed she'd never be allowed to book them again should she cancel. She missed a wedding once due to a luncheon.

"Can I get you both a tea?" she asked with a smile that was as broad as they'd seen before. If Joel didn't know better, he'd think she might be coming around to them.

"Only if it's no trouble," Joel replied.

"No trouble at all." She turned her head slightly, and suddenly shouted. "Charles! Charles?"

Charles walked in like a man in trouble. "What d'you want, woman?"

Jim Ody

Miss Shannon then smiled sweetly and said, "Be a dear and make a pot of tea, would you?"

He rolled his eyes and walked out. Joel and Melody sat down at the large mahogany dining table.

Miss Shannon looked over at Melody, "You have to use a stern voice with the menfolk once in a while, don't you?" Her turn of phrase was older than she was and Joel could see that she was in fact younger than he'd first thought.

"Very much so. Sometimes I even beat them a touch!" Melody chuckled.

Miss Shannon clasped her bony hands together and laughed. "You know a thing or two, young lady."

Joel clocked her hand and noticed for a person named Miss, she had a small gold band on her ring-finger.

"Okay then. What is it that you wish to speak to me about? Is there a problem with the rooms?"

"No, no. The rooms are lovely."

Joel had considered how to begin. Not that he thought Miss Shannon knew much, but she seemed wily, and he wondered whether she was prone to suddenly snapping shut and refusing to speak. He wanted to tread carefully.

"What do you know about the suicides around here?" he began. "There are quite a lot compared to other larger places in the county."

"Awful business," she said leaning in. "Drugs, I was told, but those kids were so sweet."

"Really?" Joel said. He'd heard nothing to back that claim up so far.

"You sound surprised, too?" she said. "Have you been to the school?"

The Crazy Season

"Yes, we spoke to a couple of the teachers. Some of the children, too. Drugs have never come up." Saying children felt weird. Of all the ones they'd spoken to, they were all closer to adulthood than anything. Transitioning.

Miss Shannon pursed her lips. It wrinkled all around her mouth like deep cracks. She then glanced at Melody, "It seems like you did a bit more than walk to the beach and grab a coffee." She looked pleased with herself to have caught them in a bending of the truth.

"We've spoken to a few people. That's why we're here," Melody confessed.

Miss Shannon nodded, looked at them both, and then said in a sad voice, "Why would any of them tell you? The teachers don't want that fact to be known, and the kids know they'll get into trouble." She took a breath, and stared off past them. "There are predators out there preying on innocents."

"What do you mean? Have you got any evidence?" Melody said but in a gentle way.

"My dear, the evidence is all around you." She spread out her arms. "Youngsters with too much money and nothing to spend it on! They all want to be stars."

There was the sound of china on china and Charles came in with a tray full of tea cups, a teapot, and milk and sugar.

"Thank you." Miss Shannon was polite and thanked to him. There was a kindness to her. Sometimes it felt a little misplaced, but she had a good heart.

"You're welcome, m'lady." He didn't wait for a response, just looked pleased with himself and disappeared.

"What about the other suicides over the years?"

Miss Shannon poured the tea into three cups, not even asking whether or not they wanted it.

"What about them?" she said, and added. "Tragic. All of them."

"Do you think they're connected in any way?"

She had carefully poured the tea, and then placed the teapot down. Everything she did or said was careful and with purpose.

"Twenty years is a long time to connect something, don't you think?"

"Perhaps," Joel agreed. "But you have to admit it's coincidental. Especially with a similar thing happening twenty years before that too? What do you know about the curse?"

When she laughed, her eyes showed a liveliness Joel hadn't seen before. If you looked at her as a whole, you'd see a mature woman, but here was a flash of youth burning brightly, and he was now convinced she was still in her fifties.

"Curses are for fairy tales and campfires. It would have to be something spiritual or supernatural to control the minds of others, don't you think?"

"Or persuasive people with hidden agendas," Melody added with a smile. Joel had come to recognise the smile as being one less of humour and more to defuse the impact of the aforementioned statement.

"Hidden agenda? Oh my, child! This is a small, poor fishing village that has grown into a tourist town attracting some wealth. None of that is a secret."

Joel frowned at her. "Would that in itself not be enough?"

"What? Do you think people here would want to remain poor and not welcome a better economy? You must understand, I'm in the hospitality business, so I can only see the benefits! In twenty years' time I won't be here. I'll be in some home left to die with others."

"No offence, Miss Shannon, but I find that hard to believe," Joel said.

The side of her mouth twitched which told him she didn't believe it herself.

Joel added milk to his tea, and a little to Melody's.

"Did you know the boys who died in 2001?" Melody asked, flashing a smile of thanks to Joel for the milk.

"Did I know them?" Miss Shannon spoke to herself. "I knew of them. They lived down in the town. It was almost the last time most of us knew one another. Even though new people come in from afar, Beach View was still integrating with us. Now not so much. They are continuing to build along there."

"I see," Joel said. It was interesting to speak to someone who had seen the changes first hand.

"Let me ask you a question," she said, a sudden cheeky look on her face.

"Okay," Joel said.

"Are you looking to solve the curse? Mr Baxter, I know my way around a computer, and there are some quite insightful stories that concern you." She reached out and patted his hand.

"I'll give it my best shot."

She then looked over to Melody and said quite wistfully, "But not so much about you on the internet? I wonder why that is?"

"I keep a low profile," she said.

"Maybe that's it," Miss Shannon said suddenly standing up, but Joel had a feeling she was far from satisfied. He thought perhaps the whole love of what she did revolved around understanding her guests. Maybe it was the injection of excitement she craved. Living other people's lives vicariously.

"Well, I thank you for coming to our aid. I really hope you find the answers you're searching for. Don't rush your tea."

Joel was already holding his cup; he looked at Melody and tried to read what was going on inside her head. Miss Shannon had decided the meeting was over and had dismissed herself.

"What's up, have I got something on my lip?" A flash of self-consciousness that caught Joel by surprise.

"No. Sorry, you caught me in a contemplative moment. Today has been a long one, filled with new people and information. Sometimes I need to let it all slowly filter into my brain."

She seemed to dismiss this, and instead admitted, "It's been fun. Dare I say I feel like I've had a little purpose."

"What's it like being back here though? This place must be filled with memories. And don't give

The Crazy Season

me any bullshit about not being able to remember. I'm beginning to read you quite well!"

"Are you now. Well, I'd better not lie then."

"Lies only hurt," he muttered and took a last swig.

She began to fiddle with the rings on her fingers. He'd not paid much attention to them before. She had rings on every finger except one. The finger a lot of people only had a ring on.

"It's a nice place. It's slow moving and chilled. I had a lot of fun here. I also had a lot of occasions to feel lonely and out of place."

"And April's family?"

"They are probably everything you think they are. They are full of smiles and wonderfully charming, but behind the mask is a lot of power."

"Enough to make school friends disappear or kill themselves?"

"I don't know. It sounds like a Netflix documentary, but I can't completely say it's not possible."

"When are we meeting April?"

"Another half hour or so."

They finished up their tea and continued getting to know each other. It was surprising how well they got on.

"Do you think you should meet April on your own?" Joel said. "You know her, right? D'you think she'll say more if I'm not there too?"

"It's possible."

"I was thinking. Maybe I'll use the time to go and speak to Sally again."

"As long as she doesn't run away from you again."

"She had a head start." Melody tried not to laugh.

Chapter 39 – Natasha

A few days ago

She sat there on the bathroom floor hugging her legs tightly and rocking back and forth. She gulped back the tears that felt like they themselves might choke her.

The bathroom was in a hotel she'd sneaked into. The Black Rock.

She knew the place and how to get in without being caught. Considering what she'd been through this had been relatively risk free.

But now she was feeling it. Incriminating pictures flashed into her mind. Flashing lights, hoods, darkened rooms, and blood. So much blood.

She'd not slept all night. She'd barely slept in days. She locked herself in the bathroom with a view to having a shower. Her mother had always said that a shower makes you feel a hundred times better. But

Jim Ody

once inside, she'd slid down the door and had remained the same way until morning.

Now she was hungry. Really hungry. She couldn't remember the last time she'd eaten.

She looked down at her hands. She panicked seeing something there that had gone long ago. She shot up and went over to the sink. She scrubbed her hands over and over. The water got hot and she could barely stand them to be under the stream any longer. She turned off the taps and rubbed her sore hands with the towel.

But when she pulled her hands away, all she could see were the crimson stains. The fresh blood was no longer there, but the residual marks remained.

She walked to the bathroom door and slowly pulled it open. Part of her expected people behind it with guns.

Or hooded people in white masks.

She walked to the window and peeked behind the curtains into the bright morning. She was high up above the ground. The sea was in the background but the picturesque view meant nothing to her.

Again, she expected a line of police cars. Men in black outfits huddled behind the cars, all eyes trained on her window. Lips moving into walkie-talkies. Sweeping hand gestures. Guns. Many guns.

Or worse. Nobody. Just the invisible cloud of the curse that floated above her and laid to rest like a blanket.

You knew where you were with armed men. But the silent assassin gave away nothing. It could be watching and waiting.

It could already be there.

She stumbled over to the bed. She was all out of tears but cried nevertheless. Broken promises that had turned into nightmares.

At some point it was all around her and taking over her body. It might've been exhaustion. Her body finally giving in to sleep.

Or it might've been the curse.

The card sat beside her on the bed, its vague words brief but weighing heavy on her mind.

The Crazy Season.

Was this the beginning of the end?

She slept through exhaustion.

She didn't hear the door open and the figure enter the room.

She woke to a cloth against her nose and mouth and bucked in her best attempt to fight back. But he was strong. Too strong.

She passed out and her body was taken from the hotel to a place away from prying eyes.

Chapter 40 - Melody

She was feeling a little uncomfortable now. She didn't want to say it to Joel, but too much had gone on. Why she thought this would be a good idea, she'd never know. But she liked Joel. He was just a nice guy. One of the good ones.

She hated lying to him. She knew she should just be honest, but sometimes honest came around and bit you on the arse.

Melody had left him going over things in his room. Now here she was outside in the open and feeling vulnerable. Not to mention bad.

It was a good idea to speak to April on her own, and she was really pleased he'd suggested it, but she was nervous, too. April knew.

April and her family were a huge part of this. She wasn't joking earlier, either. She was pretty sure the family had made people disappear before. She sure as hell didn't want to be another one.

The Crazy Season

She followed the road to the end and walked along the path that took her into the new money. It was interesting that everything from that point on seemed cleaner and more cared for. The private area boasted more money than the council-run town it pretended not to be part of.

She knew the short cuts and also, like tonight, an area that would take her away from the back of the country club. The kids had learnt this knowing their parents were often at the club, the last thing they wanted was to be caught sneaking out.

The last time she'd walked down here she had been in tears. She felt embarrassed about it now, even though it was only she that knew. She thought she was stronger than that. She'd been so guarded for so long that she'd kicked herself for falling for a man's charms. And she did. Just that. Hard and fast.

It was quite a walk. She never noticed it before.

The house was huge. Most of the houses on the estate were large, but this one you could tell was something different. It had huge pillars on a large overhanging porch. A double-garage the size of a bungalow housed cars more expensive than most people's homes.

She felt self-conscious as the door swung open and the pretty teenager stepped out and flung her arms around her.

"Melody, I've missed you," the girl said. The last time Melody had seen her they'd been the same height, and now she was taller and looked like a perfect woman. She greeted Melody like a long-lost sister, but in truth the two had only spoken a few times.

Jim Ody

"You look good, April," Melody found herself saying. The words were absorbed without return. It was of no surprise to her, and she was probably used to hearing it. Compliments were an expectation to the beautiful.

"Come in," April said, and just for a minute glanced over Melody's shoulder just to see if she was being watched.

Melody had been inside the house only a handful of times, and each time she felt out of place. The last time she'd been holding on to *his* hand. Colson. April's cousin. She felt like some movie where the girl-from the-wrong-side-of-the-tracks gets caught up with the rich guy. The awkward comedy element of when she realised just how different she was. Sitting down to eat was no longer about food enjoyment and indulgence, but a show of etiquette. The roles of the sexes were rolled back fifty years, and the lack of evolution wasn't acknowledged nor discussed about.

They skipped through the hallway, past the open entertaining room, and up the huge grand staircase. It wound around until they were facing a landing that could have had walls added to become two more rooms.

They went towards the door at the far corner, just before another staircase that more than likely went straight to heaven.

As soon as they were in April's room, April shut her door.

"I'm in trouble," she said immediately and looked panicked. This was wealth. All smiles outside, but behind closed doors worry and panic.

"Okay, slow down. What do you mean?"

The Crazy Season

For the first time ever, Melody saw tears in April's eyes. They weren't the crocodile type like an actress who could roll them down her cheek at the click of a finger. April now looked like the little girl Melody remembered. The one coming to terms with being attractive.

April pulled out her phone. The small charm dangled off it as well manicured nails slid and tapped the screen.

She held up a picture.

It was April laid completely naked on a huge white bed. The pose wasn't even artful but crude and pornographic. April was smiling in it.

"Oh, April," she said. "Who took these?"

April was already shaking her head. "I can't say. He'll kill me. He said I couldn't tell anyone."

"So how come you've got that picture."

"He sent it to me. Said if I didn't do what he said then this would be all over the internet and sent to everyone I know. He said he could get it flashed up on screens at the country club!" She began to sob. A girl who finally allowed herself to be natural.

"This isn't right," Melody said. "He cannot treat you like this. Tell me who he is and I will stop him. This sort of thing only snowballs and gets worse."

"I can't have people seeing this…"

"When was this taken?"

April was sitting down on her bed now. She'd reached over and grabbed a teddy-bear that had been well-loved. The little girl with big troubles now seemed so vulnerable.

"Just over a week ago."

Jim Ody

"Before the party." April visibly jerked at the words.

"What? What d'you know about the party?"

"We've been speaking to a number of people. My partner and I came here to help."

"Partner? What? Are you a cop, or something?" She went from sad, to defensive, to an underlying anger in a flash.

"No, we're not the police. He's looking into the curse. About your friends." Melody realised that April was completely caught up in the photograph and her own issues to not have even mentioned her missing and dead friends. It was interesting.

"The curse?"

"D'you know about it? The suicides over the past forty years?"

April was in deep thought, but her eyes dropped to her phone. Again, she was struggling to see the importance of death and disappearance on other families when she had the dark cloud of humiliation hanging over her head.

"Sure. Everyone does. Nothing much in it." She turned her phone around in her hands. The charm flipping over and over.

"And Timothy and Stevie? What do you know about their suicides?"

She was blank-faced and hard to read. "I don't know… I mean, it's sad and all, but I don't know."

"But they were at the party? The one you were at with Becky and Natasha… and Ethan."

The last name got her attention. She looked up trying to understand what Melody knew.

"Who took the photos, April? Was it Ethan?"

The Crazy Season

She was already shaking her head, She got up and walked over to a pin board filled with pictures. She unpinned one and brought it back over.

"I wish I could go back to then," she said and handed it over.

Melody looked at it. She knew which one it was. She felt sick. So many faces smiling. Everyone dressed in their best clothes, most with tall glasses of champagne in their hands. Real champagne, not sparkling wine.

"Do you miss that day?" April asked, and Melody stared at it. She was happy then. It had been a whirlwind, but she was happy. The smile was not a lie. What happened later had been.

"This doesn't matter," Melody began. "It's the past, I'm here for you. I'm here for your friends."

"Do you still love him?" April's voice was expectant. Like she needed to know that true love existed. Perhaps if Melody still loved Colson, then whoever was behind the pictures still loved her. It was a big leap, but the mind of a teenage girl isn't always so complex.

"You know what, April? Through life there are a few people you'll fall in love with. Or only a couple. But you will always have a small bit of love for them, no matter what else happens."

"Or what they've done." The words were flat. Confessional at best.

"Yes, but that doesn't mean you should forgive them. Nor does any emotional and physical past mean you should remain connected."

"But Jesus says…"

Jim Ody

Melody felt angry. "April! Come on! Don't start with Jesus on this. You and everyone else around here bring him up when the argument falls flat or the price is too high. When you stripped off for those pictures was Jesus on your mind?"

April flashed anger, but it passed, and she sat back down and buried her head in her hands. "He made me…"

"You're fifteen. You shouldn't be in these types of pictures, but I agree, you trusted him and he persuaded you to do it."

She was shaking her head. "Yes, I was scared… but I…"

"Go on, tell me."

"I liked it. I really liked the feeling of being naked in front of him."

"I can stop him, but you have to tell me who he is."

April looked up. "But that's just it. I can't."

"April, you can. Tell me and I will help you. I can stop him."

"He wouldn't like me telling you." She looked serious. "He'd kill me if he found out I'd told you."

"He won't know. I'll keep it between us." Melody placed a hand on April's shoulder.

April slowly shook her head. "He'll know."

"How can he?"

That's when an arm thrust around her and a cloth was placed over Melody's nose and mouth.

"Because he's behind you," she said, as Melody tried to kick and swing her arms.

Her airwaves became closed, her breathing quickened, and she began to feel light-headed.

The Crazy Season

And then everything turned to black.

Chapter 41 - Joel

Inside his mind everything was still a jumbled mess. For the uninitiated it would look like utter clutter. A mass of information piled on top of each other. Chaotic and unorganised. But to Joel things had been carefully placed into piles. There were a few things becoming clearer, and he had a hypothesis that he was working on.

People and their motivations are complex beasts. We cannot always understand why people do the things they do, but experience and the laws of averages can give you a good idea.

Joel had phoned Sally, and it had taken some convincing to get her to speak to him. Teenagers closed up so easily, and to them the ostrich-effect still held some weight as a viable option.

The guard at the entrance to Beach View made no effort to stop him as he slowed down and went past, but Joel knew his details had been taken down and recorded. Maybe even a phone call made.

The Crazy Season

He felt eyes staring through lace curtains. His red Jeep stood out against expensive saloons, sports cars, and Range Rovers that garnished the expansive driveways.

He looked over at the large house on the other side of the road. Timothy's house. He knew inside was a family coming to terms with their son's suicide.

Sally was out of the house before he had even stepped out of his Jeep.

"Maybe we could walk," she said urgently. Her house was clearly out of bounds.

"Okay."

At first, they did just that. Silently walking down wide pavements that ran outside houses on huge plots of land. Some had gates, trees, and hedges to properly stamp down their plot's boundaries.

Finally, Joel spoke. "We've spoken to a lot of people over the past day or so. I think there is more to what you told us."

"I told you everything I know."

"Is that right," Joel began. "If that was the case then you wouldn't have agreed to meet me again, would you?"

"You talked me into it."

"As I recall you didn't need much persuasion. In fact, it was either you knew that I knew more now, or perhaps that sick feeling in the pit of your stomach. Maybe deep down you want to tell me. You know it will make you feel better, and you know I can help."

"I don't know." She looked down at the floor, admitting nothing. She wore some expensive trainers, and at that moment they seemed to hold her gaze like they were the most beautiful things in the world. Maybe to her they were.

They came to an open space. It was a field with a play park in it. On the other side of the field was a fence that proved to be the boundary line for the gated community. Beyond that, the land opened up with only a desolate road, a house, and an abandoned tin mine. Joel wondered whether one day the house would be bought up too, as Beach View grew, hungrily eating everything in its path.

"I saw you earlier, didn't I?" Joel said, turning to her. She was so small and shapeless. Her pale skin made her look ill.

She immediately turned away. "I don't know what you're talking about."

"Well, a girl who looked very much like you was walking past our B&B this afternoon. I came out to speak to you and you took off. My question to you is why?"

Sally was thinking this through. Wrestling with whether or not to lie. He could tell she wondered how much he knew. That was the problem with lies. They had jagged edges that could cut or catch in your skin each time you came into contact with them.

"It's time to be honest. Your friends need you."

"They're not my friends." She responded with anger. "I wasn't invited to their little get together. Look at me! Sally-Strange they called me. April said I was a dyke. Timmy couldn't see past friendship…" She sat down on a bench that gave a view of the park and out to where the hill went down towards the sea.

"But you knew about the party?"

The Crazy Season

She smiled at that. "It was never a party. That's the bullshit that April wants people to think. She wants to say they were all having fun. Then after their drinks were spiked, they didn't know what was happening. She's manipulated everyone since she was born. Just because she has money! I fucking hate her! She has it all and still plays the victim!"

"Hate her enough to hurt her? To hurt her friends?" Joel was treading carefully. It wasn't the route he had thought things would go, but sometimes you had to go with the ride and hope your balance held out.

Sally stared at him. She looked frustrated and upset. "What do you think I could do? Really? I'm this small, little, insignificant bitch with no money and no friends."

"You live in the gated community."

"So fuckin' what?"

Joel glanced away as if the words were throwaway. "I'm guessing your parents have money. Friends and influence attracts those in different ways."

"We're not poor, but we're hardly the Montagues!"

Joel laughed with her on that. "My understanding is that no one is quite like them."

Sally glanced behind her. "No…" she began but her thoughts never materialised into words as they were lost in the wind.

"If you're not friends with them, then how d'you know so much about the party?"

Sally looked down at her lap. At first Joel thought she was about to cry, and then he saw she was turning around a brightly coloured friendship band around her thin wrist.

"Have you ever loved someone so much it hurts?" she said, still fussing with her band.

"I have," Joel admitted, the face of his wife came into his mind.

"Then you'll understand that you'll do anything for love, right?" The conversation was beginning to sound like lyrics to a number of power ballads he'd grown up with.

"I understand the feeling. But I also understand that there are lines that cannot be crossed, right?"

"I don't agree." She seemed adamant. "Love is all powerful. It's like God. It's everything."

"God? Do you go to church?"

"In my own way," she said. "You don't need a place of worship to worship."

"So what has this got to do with anything? If God is so important then how come the Montagues never built a church up here too?"

"The Montagues aren't religious. The queens head is the only thing they pray to. Cash is king."

The invisible lightbulb above Joel's head lit up. "The one thing in life more powerful than money is belief…" he muttered to himself.

She smiled as if happy he got it.

He looked at her. "Who is he? You know he's grooming you."

She was shaking her head and her face changed. "You don't know him! You'll see!"

"What? This isn't a game, people are dying, Sally!"

The Crazy Season

"The weak are dying, Jo-el!" she said his name in disgust.

"Timothy, your friend, is dead!"

She was still shaking her head as she got up. "He was weak... that's why he's dead. You think I didn't try to save him? You think I didn't do everything I could to make him understand? He didn't care. He was only interested in her! That slut! And that is why he had to die!" She began to back away from him like it was he who had suddenly changed.

"Whose car did you get into earlier?" Joel asked. He didn't think he'd get a response, but he needed her to know that he was piecing things together.

"Do your best, Dr Spook, it's too late." She looked him up and down and laughed. "She's gone. You're much too late!" she ran off. He let her go. What use was it to try and stop her; she wasn't going to give up the name and nor where she was going.

Who the Hell was the '*she*' that Sally was talking about?

He pulled out his phone and dialled Melody's number. It rang a handful of times before going to voicemail.

"Hey, it's me. I'm in another universe at the moment. I'll call you back if I ever return home."

He pulled the phone from his ear and pecked out a message.

Are you okay?

He sent it and then looked around. The hedges and trees that had once been planted when the development was designed were now mature. The wealth was now part of the landscape with the natural patina adding to the feeling it had always been there.

His phone vibrated.

I'm okay. With April, met up with some people I know. See you later.

He felt disappointed. And then he was cross with himself. The case was so important to him, but it wasn't her case. She'd lived here before. She'd probably not seen these people since the last time she'd been here.

As he walked back to his Jeep, he had to wonder whether April was a pawn in this. Everything still surrounded her, but like a magic-eye picture, if you stared long enough then it wasn't the mess of shapes and colours you saw, but the background creeping to the forefront and producing a sudden clear picture.

That was beginning to happen now.

He looked across the field to the tin mine. Would Beach View take that, too, one day?

The house next to it looked grand but contemporary. It had recently had work done to it, there was a large skip outside. And a car. A black saloon that looked like a BMW.

Was that why she'd walked him here?

Chapter 42 - Natasha

At first, she'd been frightened. In fact, that didn't even come close to how she felt. Petrified was closer.

It was surprising how quickly humans give up. She couldn't remember at what point she'd stopped fighting. That point when she'd conceded that she might never see daylight ever again.

She looked at the door. It was metal and locked. A single light illuminated the room in a dirty orange glow. The light wasn't always on. At night it was turned off and the whole place was thrown into darkness. It felt damp. She had only a metal-framed bed and a stale mattress that was thin enough to feel the springs underneath.

She had stared at the four walls for a few days now. She had nothing to occupy her time. Only her thoughts and the demons inside.

Jim Ody

And the literature. The well-worn pages of the large paperback were face down from where she'd last hurled it at the wall.

She'd trusted him. Sneaky messages of promise, and yet this was all it had brought her.

She didn't get it. What the fuck was the Gospel of Jordan all about! Her aunt was deeply religious and had insisted on reading chapters of the Bible to her. She'd also been forced to attend church on dozens of occasions. If she was honest, she didn't hate it. She just didn't subscribe to it either.

She had absolutely no recollection of the Gospel of Jordan, and that was the worrying thing.

The town of Black Rock had hidden this secret for years and the truth was still nobody knew. She couldn't even take solace in knowing. She had no way of telling anyone.

In one corner was a bucket. She'd never felt so humiliated than the first time she'd used it. The degradation was awful. She'd cried a lot recently. With no seat she had to hover over the top. The smell now was thick, strong and pungent. Near it, was the litter from food chucked in. Sandwich wrappers, crisp packets and plastic water bottles.

But whilst she was on the edge of giving up, there was a single glimmer of hope.

If he was still feeding her, then he wanted her alive.

With each possibility of the door being opened, her optimism grew. She had to think about how she could be ready. Her chances were less than slim. But she was a fighter. And even a slim chance increases with hope.

She glanced at the book. Or faith.

How had she not known before? How had no one else known what was going on?

She wasn't dead. But really, was she any better?

He was this within the community, embedded and trusted, and all the while he had nefarious plans.

He'd given her the opportunity to escape and she'd passed the test. A single mission. She'd taken it. Knowing he could press a single button at any moment.

And now she was here. Almost forgotten and left wondering whether she could've got away without him knowing.

If today was Friday then soon she'd know.

Everyone would know.

Chapter 43 – Joel

Having spoken to most of the people, now it was obvious that he would have to do a round-robin again.

When you have nothing, you are happy to have something. However the more people you speak to the versions of events appear slightly different.

Sometimes the best people are gossips and snitches. There was someone he needed to speak to again.

"Martin!" he said in surprise when the lad answered with, "Who dis?"

"I don't think you were completely straight with us earlier. I have a few more questions to ask."

"I dunno, Bruv," he said. He didn't sound nervous, just unsure.

"Well, the thing is I'm hearing a lot of noise, and I think you're the guy who can tell me what it is I'm hearing, right?"

"Crystal, but I don't want beef. Ya feelin' me?"

"Okay, let's cut the sweet talk. Who else was going to the party. And what do you know about the party?"

"Like I say. I hear stuff, but dun' know it kosher."

"Go on."

"Party is a bit of a stretch. I heard it was more of like a recruitment. You know? Like some initiation."

"What? A gang?" This was a new one, Joel thought.

"Not so much. It's like God an' shit?"

"Which gospel is that from?" there was silence as Martin was clearly wondering whether or not that was a question for him to answer. "Ignore me, I'm joking."

"Ah, I get ya, Fam. Good one."

"So it's religious?"

"Cult, init. Charles Manson stuff, or that G from Texas where the Feebs shot the place up." That got Joel's attention.

"Really? How so?"

"It's secret, init. They recruiting but not through posters an' that."

"Martin? Why didn't you tell us this earlier?"

It went quiet at the end of the phone. "I gotta go."

"Who is it? Who runs it?"

"He knows, Joel. He knows you're here, and he knows all about you. You think it was coincidence that you found me? And that Timothy emailed you? Read it again."

Jim Ody

"Wait!" Joel said but Martin had gone.

Joel sat there for a second. That changed everything. It wasn't a party that they'd gone to but an initiation for some religious cult. It sounded bizarre, but what if it was true?

Joel thought about Melody going off on her own to see April. He looked at her message again. He went to send her another text, but as he began to type, he stopped, shook his head and deleted it. She could certainly look after herself.

What if April was the leader? Martin said 'he' but what did he really know? Was he trying to put him off? Was Martin part of it? But a fifteen-year-old lead seemed farfetched. She had a following but her being a cult leader was ridiculous.

He started the engine, and then slowly pulled away from Sally's. He glanced one last time, and left her house behind him.

Joel drove slowly out of the gated community. The guard again watched him carefully as he slowed next to his building before departing. Joel almost waved.

It was late in the afternoon, and he was in need of something to eat. He was happy for Melody but felt a little on his own now. It was funny how quickly he'd become used to having her around.

He pulled into the only petrol station in the town. It was one of those that doubled as a convenience store. He filled up the Jeep, mostly out of habit. He always liked to have at least half a tank of diesel just in case he had to go somewhere in a hurry. It was another of his overthinking traits, but he considered it

The Crazy Season

to be good logic. Always be prepared, that's what the good Cub Scout in him knew.

When the fuel pump clicked, he returned the fuel-nozzle to the machine and closed the fuel cap. He walked into the shop and gazed at the food. There wasn't a lot on offer, but he settled on a sandwich and a pork pie. Remembering the run earlier, he momentarily thought about something healthier, but he had time. When life changes in a split second your will to sacrifice small vices becomes harder.

As he paid, he wondered whether in years gone by the shop assistant might've struck up a conversation. An observation that he wasn't local, but now the guy barely looked at him. His robotic motions moved on autopilot as if he wasn't even there. In fact, had the shop suddenly been held up at gunpoint, Joel wondered whether the guy would even bat an eyelid. Would he shrug and move to the side, and then when they'd gone, just continue on as if nothing had happened? It was a sign of the times. The difference between a minimum-pay employee and a fully-invested owner.

Back in his Jeep, Joel drove the few streets towards the B&B. He pulled in just as a guy walked out.

Joel recognised him as being the guy who had been in the Black Rock bar. He was the eyes in the shadows.

He let him walk off before getting out of the Jeep.

Instead of going into the building, Joel carefully walked after him.

With the beach on the right, the guy was following the same path Joel ran along earlier after

Jim Ody

Sally. He took a gamble hoping that the guy would be heading towards the steps at the end of the road. Joel turned to the nearest set of steps, and jogged down them.

There were people on the beach, and they may have found it strange when Joel ran as fast as he could along the beach hoping to overtake the guy. Sometimes you needed a subtle approach, and others you had to go out and grab your chance.

Joel got to the steps, and just as Sally had done, he hid underneath.

Sure enough, the guy came down the steps. There was the dull thud of shoes on metal as he descended towards the sand.

Slowly, Joel walked behind him. Then quickly he snaked one arm around his throat, and with his other arm he poked the guy in the back with his mobile, pretending it was a weapon.

"You want to tell me who you are?" Joel said in his best Action-Hero voice. He was trying to Jason Statham.

The guy struggled. He was strong, but Joel was stronger.

"Quite struggling and answer my question."

When the guy spoke, his voice didn't match his look, in fact now that Joel was closer to him than he wanted to be, the guy didn't smell as bad as he looked, either.

"What do you want?" he asked, his voice had a slightly posh edge to it.

"I want to know who you are!"

"Okay, okay," he said. "My name is Colson." But it was his next words that left Joel shellshocked.

"I'm Melody's husband."

Chapter 44 – Joel

Joel couldn't believe what the guy had said.
"Sorry? Run that past me again?" He said to this guy.
"I'm Melody's husband, Colson." Behind the scraggly beard was a face that now looked a lot younger. His eyes were a piercing blue.

Joel knew he must look confused to this man. This was a shock. Was the man lying? Or was Melody?

He realised Melody hadn't lied, she'd just omitted this information. Was she involved in this too? Again, it was coincidental that out of the blue he received the email, and it was a place that Melody hadn't just been to, but had lived and married someone there.

"...read the email again..." Joel suddenly reheard the voice of Martin before he terminated the call.

"Colson, I think you better tell me what's going on."

A couple of dog walkers were hanging around, pretending that the small area of the beach was suddenly full of wonders. They knew something was going on. Maybe they hoped to witness a fight.

"Okay," Colson said as they turned and headed for the steps. This was the second time today Joel had run down to this beach, and he was hoping it would be the last.

"Melody didn't tell me she was married. In fact, no offence, but she's never mentioned you by name until we got here."

Colson sighed. He seemed disappointed, but also resigned to the facts. "Oh," he said and stroked his beard as they walked.

"So?"

When speaking about Colson, albeit somewhat fleetingly, Joel had pictured this huge confident guy. Film-star good looks and oozing charisma. It was hard to morph the guy next to him into that. He looked like a former movie star who'd fallen on hard times, which was to say had been reckless with his life. Maybe that was part of the story.

"We had a good relationship," he began, finally opening up. "It was what they call a whirlwind. I fell hard and fast for her, mainly because she didn't give a shit, you know?"

Joel nodded. "Oh, yes. I know." He grinned as he thought of some of the things she'd done since he'd known her.

"She turned up here with these dirty dreadlocks and tattooed arms. She grabbed a surfboard and proceeded to almost drown herself for an hour. I watched her. I was grabbing some waves, and there was something about her determined way. I swam over and gave her some pointers."

"Sounds like a movie." Joel's words were a gentle observation, and if anything, slightly sad as he thought about Cherry again.

"Not really. I think she told me to go fuck myself a few times before she allowed me to speak to her."

"That does sound more like her."

"But anyway, you don't want to hear about that…" Then the air between them felt strange. Different, almost. Suddenly there was a bond, but were they enemies or allies? That was the real question.

The sun was dropping now behind the large building in front of them, and the darkness of evening had begun. Colson said. "You two dating?" It seemed like a question he'd wanted to ask for a while.

"No, nothing like that. I'm married."

"Does she know?"

"Yes, she knows." Joel stopped before his narrative on car accidents, hospitals, and comas kicked in. That only brought sympathy and a complete change in the dynamics between him and whomever he was speaking to. He didn't want that. He refused the sympathy points. He saved that card for real arseholes.

"What happened between you two?" Joel asked innocently.

"Honestly, it felt like it was everything. I mean, it was great. Electrifying in fact. We got together and we were there in front of each other all day everyday…"

"And the drink and drugs?"

"I mean, we…"

"I'm not judging you. Melody told me that. She said a lot of her time here was a blur because of it."

Colson accepted that. "Okay, yes. There was drink and drugs. This place is great, but sometimes I think it's a curse…" He looked at Joel. The word connected with them. "But sometimes you have to live young."

"And what do you know about the curse? Not the curse you're talking about, but the town's curse? Surely you've heard of that?"

"Sure. I've heard of it, and I don't believe it."

"What do you know about your cousin, April, and the teens that died?"

"It's fucking scary," he said and sounded genuinely worried. "She's my little cousin. The problem with her is she thinks she Paris Hilton or someone. Like her looks and wealth will carry her throughout life. That is what's so scary. But those guys… that was a real tragedy."

"You know what happened?"

He was shaking his head. "No, I've tried to speak to her but the thing with my family is they close up and circle around each other. If something happens, they are there to protect."

"But you're part of the family, are you not?"

"I'm the black sheep. I'm not interested in being a financial mongrel…"

Jim Ody

"Mogul," Joel corrected before realising Colson had meant it as a joke. "Ah, I get you. It was deliberate."

"You've seen some of the women from the country club no doubt. They look like this is the Beverly Hills of the South-West. My family wanted me to find a woman like that, not a hippie-chick who I'd get wasted with."

"It was family pressure that split you up?"

Colson went quiet. Joel didn't rush him. It seemed like there was a lot he wanted to say.

The B&B came into view.

"I split us up by being a dick... I cheated on her."

"Oh."

"Look, I'm not proud about it. My parents kept on about Annabelle Swanson. A very pretty and single woman at the time. Her father worked with mine. It was all about joining forces. For years, they'd talked about her. She's a nice enough woman... then Melody came along... but I felt the pressure of my family. The levels of expectations I was failing on. I know how this sounds. Whining excuses, right? Yes, you'd be right. I don't have any defence. I admit, Melody and I..." he stopped and looked out over the beach below. It was as if he hoped the words would come rolling in with the waves. Perhaps that would be less painful. As the light died, so did his argument.

"I was confused. I love Melody, but living against the grain was hard. Then one night, Melody was gone and Annabelle was there. From there it was just easier."

To his credit he looked regretful.

The Crazy Season

"I'm going to have a stab at this," Joel began. "but would I be right in saying it didn't work out between you and Annabelle?"

"How can you tell?" He seemed genuinely surprised.

"The way you talk about Annabelle and your family expectations leads me to think of her as a woman who is permanently made up with make-up. She probably considers calorie counting a hobby, and rarely swears. No offence but the way you look at the moment suggests to me you're no longer together. I'm not sure Annabelle would like your hipster-slash-hobo chic. And secondly, you're looking for your wife."

"All good points," he conceded.

"God, I have so many questions… Okay, so when were you married? How did that come about?"

Colson smiled to himself. A happy memory surfacing, no doubt.

"It seems stupid now. We went away on holiday just the two of us. Yes, we were caught up in our own little world. We'd only been together for six months. We'd fallen deeply for each other, and when we were away from this place it was amazing. Despite what everyone thinks, we both were changing. Melody was trying hard to fit in with the High Society, and I knew she felt awkward doing it. In return, she took me to seedy clubs and meditation retreats, and I was equally awkward, except when we were away, we just did what we wanted. We surfed, and sunbathed, explored, and drank. It was like an adventure romance novel."

Jim Ody

"What did your family say when you were married?"

"They weren't happy. They put up with our relationship because they knew it would crash and burn. Perhaps not as spectacularly as it did, but hey, there you go. My dad walked out mumbling something about inheritance. It was the only thing he had over me. I know, standard rich troubles, right?"

"We're all different."

"Melody picked up on the tension straightaway. I felt sorry for her. None of her family was around, and she already felt guilty that Kip didn't know, and she suddenly felt very alone. I think she always knew I'd end up trying to please my parents. Kip came and picked her up and they went back to Ilfracombe, but evidently, she missed me and came back early. Just as Annabelle was in the shower."

"Ooh!"

"Yes. What a dickhead, right? Well, that was it. She left, and like an idiot I never went after her, choosing the quieter life instead."

"And you're still married?"

He nodded. "I have divorce papers. I haven't signed them. She stopped chasing me."

"Wow. Are you looking for her in order to reconcile?"

"I don't know, if I'm honest. I've not seen her in eighteen months. I miss her. I miss how we were."

"You were in the Black Rock bar yesterday," Joel stated. They were now standing on the other side of the road to the B&B. Joel still had a lot of questions, but to invite a stranger up to his room would be weird.

The Crazy Season

"Yes, I saw you arrive."

"So who is it that April is seeing? Is it anything to do with Ethan, the barman at the Black Rock Bar?"

"Ethan?"

"You seem surprised by that."

"D'you know him? I mean, I saw you speak to him so I know you've spoken. What did he say to you?"

"Like most people around here, not a lot."

"He's some Jesus freak. He doesn't look it but he is. His mum is dead and his dad… He's the reason Ethan is the way he is. He works at the school."

"The school? What? A governor, teacher, janitor?"

"Something like that." It sounded like he knew but didn't want to say.

"I heard rumours Ethan and April were an item."

Colson chuckled at that. "Not likely."

"Why d'you say that?"

"Dig a little deeper. You'll see."

"Where should I dig?" Colson looked like he was about done with the conversation. "Where's Melody?"

"She went to see April. She hooked up with people she knew and they went for a meal. I assumed at the country club."

The look on Colson's face worried him. "What?"

"She doesn't know anyone else really. I mean she knows who people are, but I was the only person she knew apart from April, her parents, and my parents."

"Maybe it's April's friends," Joel said, but the words sounded wrong as he said them.

"Yes, that will be it." Colson's whole demeanour changed. It was like he'd just talked himself into something.

Joel took Colson's number and promised to let him know when he saw Melody. He then almost jogged into the B&B and up to his room.

He grabbed the laptop and got ready to pull it all together.

But first he had to ring Kip.

The Crazy Season

Chapter 45

Before the party

They were a sorry looking bunch. A millennial Breakfast Club of sorts. Perhaps not John Hughes' choice as characters, but all individuals nevertheless.

April was sitting at the back of the classroom giggling with Becky. They were huddled around Becky's phone. She was always connected to some social media site. The two of them often filmed themselves dancing to songs in break time, uploaded them, and by lunch were squealing at how many views and likes they'd had. The trend had now meant that anyone could gain acceptance no matter who they were or where they came from.

Stevie walked in, looked at them both, and sat down close enough to stare, but not so close that

Jim Ody

they'd tell him to move. He pulled out a pad and was doodling. He thought he was a cartoonist. In truth he had a long way to go, but desire and dedication went a long way.

Timothy was sitting a bit further down. He was also at the back, but with his headphones on. Sally was next to him trying to engage in conversation. He nodded once in a while, but found a way to throw sideways glances over to where April sat. Sally either didn't notice, or pretended not to notice. When there was silence, she was lost gazing at his eyes. The ones focused anywhere but on her.

In front was Natasha. She was hunched over an open folder and was scribbling away at her philosophy homework. She had a notion that if she could finish it there and then, she could show her dad and maybe he'd let her go out for an hour or so. Her phone buzzed; she glanced around before looking at it. She smiled when she saw who it was from and slipped it away out of sight.

Benny Choi was sitting alongside her and was humming loudly. He always had trouble staying still. The other kids teased him that he was on drugs. He was, of course, but prescribed for ADHD. It was a vicious cycle. The more they teased, the fewer tablets he took and the worse he got. Kids are cruel. Very cruel.

The teacher walked into the class with his usual friendly face and an air of authority.

"Welcome everyone to detention! So nice of you to make it here today!" He clapped his hands together and looked over them all. "What a motley crew we have today." Years ago, that might've made

The Crazy Season

a slight giggle erupt from those who knew their rock bands. The faces in front of him were not up on Mötley Crüe and more than likely had never heard any of the band's multi-platinum selling songs. At some point the genre he'd grown up on had turned into granddad rock.

"I see we have some old favourites," he looked to Benny. "Benny, nice to see you here. You looking to set a record, or something?"

Benny grinned and saluted back.

The teacher continued. "You come here many more times and I might have to change the name of the room to Benny's room!" A couple of giggles came from the back. Everyone now wore a smile.

"Stevie, I see you're here again!" Stevie stopped his drawing for a second and acknowledged the mention before returning back to it.

"April and Becky! Always a pleasure to see you two here!" Becky had placed her phone on her desk, but was still glancing at it like it might suddenly turn into gold or diamonds.

He then looked over at Natasha. "Ah, a newbie," he laughed. "You mistake this place for the library?"

She looked up from her text book. "No, I wanted to crack on with my homework." Her voice was small.

"Swot!" Becky called, but as Natasha glanced back at her, Becky winked to show she was joking.

"Interesting," he said, and turned his attention to the last two. "Ah, the lovebirds. Timothy and Sally. The Sid and Nancy of the bunch?"

Jim Ody

"Who?" Sally said grinning. She genuinely had no idea who he was talking about, but loved the reference to them being love birds.

"The Sex Pistols," Timothy said not looking at her. "Sid was in the band, and Nancy was his girlfriend."

"Cool," she said, unaware of the tragedy of it.

"Okay, well, first things first!" He said, addressing them like a stage production. "I am giving a free pass to two people because that's the type of guy I am. He looked down at a piece of paper he had fussed about with on his desk.

"Sally and… Benny! Congratulations! You are free to leave."

"Really?" Said Benny, already standing up.

"Yep! See you again!"

Sally was a little more reluctant in moving and looked at Timothy. He looked back, shrugged, and said, "I'll see you later."

"Chop-chop!" he said to her. Benny had already gone. He ran out just in case it was a joke and he was going to be called back.

Then when Sally had finally left the room, he closed the door, and looked up with Jack Nicholson eyes.

"This detention we are going to do a bit of history," he looked each one in the eyes.

"Who here has heard of The Crazy Season?"

Heads turned to each other but nobody said they had. Even Natasha closed her book to hear something new.

Chapter 46 – Joel

When Joel got into his room he flicked on the light and pulled the curtains. He sat on his bed and pulled out the food he'd bought earlier.

One minute he thought he was getting somewhere, and the next he wasn't so sure. The blurry picture kept changing. And the surprises kept coming.

He ripped open the sandwich packet and took a bite. The bacon in the BLT was cold and chewy, but he munched it down nevertheless. He pulled out his phone, slipped his finger down the contacts and pressed Kip's number.

"Hey Spooky!" Kip said in a jovial voice after not even a single ring.

"Were you waiting for my call?"

Jim Ody

"I'm psychic. Haha! Not really. I don't want you lumping me in with your weirdo clients! How's things?"

"Confusing. Since when did your sister get married?"

Whereas before Kip was quick with his response, this time he was definitely unsure of what to say. "Ah."

"Yes, ah."

Joel heard Kip breathing. He took a deep breath, as Joel looked at the wall in front of him without taking it in.

"The thing is," Kip began, his words were slow and careful. "She doesn't like to talk about it."

"I get that. I'm not prying, it's just… I would've thought it might have been worth mentioning considering the case, don't you think?"

"Joel, I get it, mate. But you know Melody. She's a closed book to things like this. People misunderstand her. She is this gregarious hippie-surf-chick who doesn't give a fuck about anyone or anything on the outside, but inside she's curled up and protecting herself. You can tell this when you listen to what she says. You'll know more about what she doesn't like rather than what she does."

"I guess…"

"Wait? Why are you ringing me and not speaking to her? Have you two had a fight?"

"No, no, nothing like that. She went off to speak to someone and she got caught up with friends."

"Friends? As far as I know, outside of Colson she had none."

"Colson said the same thing."

The Crazy Season

"You've spoken to him?" Kip sounded like he'd just suddenly taken more notice of the conversation.

"Yeah, he was looking for her."

"Joel, look... that town is something. Melody spoke about it. Why she went back there I'll never know, but she has. I didn't worry when she was with you... but now..."

"You're worrying me now."

"Just track her down. Send me your address I'm coming down there."

"What? Really? Why?"

"It's all Stepford wives and corrupt men... I just don't like it. It's probably nothing, and I'm sure she's fine, but..."

"I get it. I'll text you the address."

Joel put the phone down and pushed his laptop to the side. He took another bite of his sandwich and didn't even close down the lid of his laptop.

Had he looked he would've seen the page that had loaded whilst he was on his call to Kip.

The page that had the details of who Ethan's father was.

Joel went to his bag and rummaged in the side pocket. He pulled out a small phone. A really small phone. It wasn't fancy, no bells or whistles, but it served its purpose by being small. He slowly stuffed it down the front of his trousers and into his Jockey boxershorts. It seemed weird but he'd had to use it more than once for an emergency.

Joel quickly went down the stairs as quietly as possible. He suddenly trusted no one. It was almost like stepping into *The Twilight Zone* or *American Horror Story*.

Jim Ody

When he got to the bottom, he'd taken one step forward when he heard hushed voices. It was the loud whisper that caught his attention, the irony being had the voices been at a normal level then he wouldn't have thought anymore about it.

He walked towards the room.

"You have to tell them," Charles was saying.

"I don't see what good it would do!" Miss Shannon responded clearly irritated.

"If they can find those missing children!"

"Keep your voice down, Charles!"

He was getting angry too. "Angela! Stop being a stubborn old bird!"

Joel stepped into the room and saw the pair look as guilty as an older couple could. Charles looked relieved, but Miss Shannon seemed to lose the wind in her sails as she collapsed into one of the easy chairs.

"Who wants to tell me what's going on? Charles? *Angela?*" Was this the Angela who they'd been searching for?

Miss Shannon was shaking her head. "We don't know." Joel thought at first, she was denying it all, then she looked confused. "I just have this feeling…"

Joel looked at her, and then at the picture of Jesus on the wall. Around her neck was a small gold cross.

"Your name is Angela," Joel said the words but they came out as an audible thought.

"Angela Shannon," she confirmed. "Why would that matter?"

"The boy Timothy. He told me to come and find you at the Black Rock Bar."

The Crazy Season

Miss Shannon looked at Charles who nodded with encouragement towards her. "Tell him."

"But…"

"Come on. You can't go on protecting him if you have suspicions."

"I go to the Black Rock Bar a couple of times a week." She looked from Charles to Joel.

"Go on."

"I go to see Ethan…"

Joel was about nudge her on when Charles did it for him.

"Her grandson."

"Oh," Joel said as a piece of the puzzle slotted into place. "He's only moved back recently? Is that right?"

The feisty woman now just looked sad. She'd aged suddenly, just in the last few minutes.

"I suppose I should start at the beginning. Many years ago, I had an affair. I was young and naïve. I mean, I knew what I was doing but he had it all, and he was everything a girl could want…" she looked away from Joel and up at the picture of Christ like she was now confessing.

"I got pregnant. It was stupid, and I was too caught up in it all. I thought we'd be together…" she sighed. "A typical girl with fanciful ideas. I suppose I thought I'd live up there in Beach View… and then we had a talk. Well, he talked and I mostly just cried. My whole world collapsed when he told me to give up the child. I went full term and had a beautiful baby boy. It broke my heart when he left my arms for the last time."

"I'm sorry to hear that," Joel offered.

Jim Ody

"He grew up in a religious family. I must confess, it had been one of the requirements I'd insisted on when told new parents had been found. He came back here one summer when he was a teen and worked up at Beach View helping to expand the place. But then he was gone again. The next time he contacted me was to say I was going to be a grandmother."

"Wow, that must've been a surprise."

Her eyes had already welled up, and both let loose tears at the same time. She smiled happily at the memory. "It was!"

"Did he come and see you?"

"He did. He brought Ethan over, but then... I don't know, something happened and he split up with Ethan's mother. She took Ethan away. I guess life moved on."

"That was hard?"

Once again, she glanced from Charles to the picture of Christ. "I had my faith. I'd given him away, so every new minute I had was a bonus. Jesus brought him back."

"Who is it you're protecting? Ethan or your son?"

Miss Shannon clammed up, and looked down at her hands. She dabbed her eyes but remained tight-lipped.

"Tell him, woman!" Charles said.

"My son Jordan. He moved here from Wiltshire. He was a teacher in Religious Studies. He started as a Christian, but when he sent me emails, he began to talk about small groups and sects. I thought it unhealthy, and to be perfectly honest somewhat blasphemous. He was being drawn in by these people

The Crazy Season

who weren't accepting Jesus as their saviour, but looking to replace him with charlatans in the same guise. It was like they would roll a dice and decide someone was the new Messiah! Religion doesn't work like that!"

"Then they came here," Charles added moving things along again. Sometimes you needed a Charles around to keep the flow going.

She nodded. "Yes, he came here and began to teach at the school."

"What's his surname?"

"Townsend. Jordan Townsend." Joel nodded picturing the confidant man at the school. Tall and handsome he had the charisma to be a religious leader. Why had nobody told him that Ethan was his son?

"What does he teach? Religious Studies?" Joel asked.

"No, religion has moved on a touch here, it no longer holds the importance it once did... the congregation is but a dozen people now when fifty years ago, you'd struggle to get a seat... No, he began to teach history, and Ethan worked at the bar."

"What suspicions do you have?"

"One night he told me he was going to reignite religion around here. I was so proud to hear those words, I cried... but then he told me he had no intention of going to a church. He was going to run his own."

"His own church?"

"His own religion."

Charles once again chimed in. "A cult."

Jim Ody

Miss Shannon threw him a scolding look. "It's not a cult!"

"Has he started it?"

She sniffed slightly, and then looked up at Joel. "I don't know. All I know is those children were his students. Two are dead and two are missing."

"And Ethan is one of the ones that is still alive and accounted for."

She nodded. "He won't say anything. I've asked him. He won't lie to me so he doesn't speak at all."

"What about Melody. Did you know her before we came here?"

Again, Miss Shannon looked at Charles who nodded to her encouragingly.

"It's a small town, Mr Baxter. She was dating a member of one of the biggest families around here. Everybody knows her."

"What did people think of her?"

"From down here, everyone liked her. She was funny, a little wild, but that was okay… but in Beach View, I got the feeling they thought of her differently. She was a threat to everything they believed in."

"Like she wasn't good enough?"

"Exactly that. She didn't come with money or a blue bloodline."

Joel nodded. He wanted to hear more but he was suddenly even more worried about her safety. "Whereabouts is April's house?"

"You can't miss it. Head to the country club, and her house is the huge one right next door."

"And your son. Where does he live?" Joel said, beginning to make a move. "I assume he's not in Beach View?"

She laughed at that. "God no. He hates that place. Although considering he does hate it, it's strange he bought a house right next to it."

"He lives up there too?"

She nodded, and Charles spoke out. "The one with the abandoned tin mine."

Joel felt the panic inside him. He'd been here talking and not considered how much danger Melody was in.

"Thank you both."

Chapter 47 – Melody

Her first thought when she came round was that the room smelt damp. She thought about Miss Shannon, and was ready to tell her exactly what she thought of her room. And her head hurt. She felt like she'd been out overdoing the tequila again. The last time she'd done it, she'd woken up with a tough-looking guy asleep with his hand on her boob.

TripAdvisor will be getting a harshly worded review of this dump.

Then she opened her eyes. That hurt even more.

If this was her B&B room then the place had been shot to shit.

The walls were made from either mud or dirty concrete. She turned all around to take in the room.

There were no windows, just a door, a bucket, an unopened bottle of water, and a bed that looked like it might have come from the first world war.

The Crazy Season

She went to her pocket for her phone but of course it was gone. She sat back against the wall and realised just how stupid she'd been coming back here.

And how she should've told Joel.

Two years ago she'd come here. It was the summer of love. It may have spanned from February to October, but that year seemed to be filled with sunshine and laughter. It was everything she'd wanted, and then everything she didn't.

Colson was a good guy. For the most part. He fell in love with her. He rebelled against his family. Nothing mattered. They surfed, they partied, and they drank too much. Both of them experimented more than they probably should have.

When she thought back it was like a dream. Or some Rom-Com on Netflix. A typical tale of boy meets girl, then boy fucks up and loses girl, but where in those movies the final act would see the reconciliation of the two, for them that had never transpired. She ran and he never bothered to chase her.

Maybe this was it.

A sick twist to the genre. She didn't think so. It didn't make any sense.

That day, when she saw Annabelle coming out of the shower wrapped in nothing but a towel, her whole world fell around her. Her heart had sunk to the floor.

Annabelle was a perfect woman in Melody's eyes, and the whole time she lived in Black Rock, she'd looked to her as the blueprint of who she should be. She knew she never would, and that was fine. But this was the woman his family wanted her to be. So to see her there fulfilling the wishes of local royalty, stung. And of course, the betrayal of it all was much too much to take.

Kip had been wonderful. But then Kip always had been wonderful ever since they were kids. He'd accepted her moving to Black Rock. He'd not complained when she'd eloped with Colson to a foreign land to get a ring on her finger. And nor had he worried about getting in his car and driving an hour in the middle of the night to pick her up and bring her home. That was Kip. He joked around and called her names, but he loved her.

A few days ago, she'd received the email from Colson. It was out of the blue. She couldn't help it, she felt excited. She knew it would be stupid to get involved again, but inside those fires reignited. How could they not? It had been amazing. Only now could she admit the things that attracted her to him. It was his good looks, his body, and the fact he could buy her whatever she wanted. She'd grown up saving every penny. They weren't exactly poor, but if she wanted something, then someone had to work a lot of hours to be able to afford to buy it. Not for Colson. He could dip into a bottomless well of cash. It was exciting. But thankfully, this was the first of the attractions she grew tired of. She would only have to mention something and it was hers. It was a cliché, but it instantly devalued all objects.

Everything was wonderful through the natural honeymoon period. The relationship tag, not the official period. It was like an extended holiday romance. Living day to day with a new person. But

The Crazy Season

slowly, everything falls away until you are left with the basics. What she found was ugly.

Other people looked down on her. Jealous eyes wandered over her, judging her every move. Whispers behind hands, and giggles at jokes poked at her. It zapped away her energy. Being happy became a chore.

Colson was really the problem. She couldn't blame him. He was in the same position as her, except they assumed he'd get bored. Melody felt like she was a nasty little habit they'd turn the other cheek to until he got himself back on the straight and narrow. She could only imagine the wave of relief that moved throughout the community once he found solace between the legs of Annabelle.

Melody had run away. The poor little girl ran back to her own kind, the hippy beach hut and her gay brother.

Colson had said he was sorry. The apology written in an email was weak. He sent a text but she soon changed her phone.

She had almost forgotten about him.

Until she'd got to know Joel. She couldn't explain it. The love he had for his wife was something she thought she'd had with Colson, but she wasn't so sure. She tried to console herself into thinking that the longer Joel's wife remained in a coma, then the rosier his glasses became as her memory lifted her into a goddess-like status.

She tried to think of the last time she'd heard him say something negative about her.

She looked across the room. Where the fuck was she?

Instantly, she thought about the missing girls. Was this linked? How could it not be? And more to the point what was it somebody wanted with her?

With nothing else to do she sat there and thought about all the ways her life had led her to this point.

Everything always came back to April. Why? What was her connection other than her father - the most powerful man in Black Rock.

Her heart jumped as she heard movement from outside the door. The sound of the lock being turned.

She stood up on edge ready to deal with whatever, or whomever came through the door.

If she was going to die, then she was going to die fighting.

Chapter 48 – Joel

It was a conundrum. Walk or drive. Driving would take the road up and out of Black Rock. A large golf course split the town from the road to any of the houses in Beach View, and it was deliberate that the entrance appeared outside of the town. The benefit being he'd have his Jeep with him. The downside was by the time he got to April's house everyone inside would know he was coming. The surly gatekeeper would make sure of that.

He knew there was a shortcut by foot that followed around the side of the beach and then up through some trees towards the huge country club.

Joel was a man of strong build, but he was a little wary going there on his own. If there was one thing he'd learnt in life, it was that money ruled the world. It was enough of a motivation for normal, logical people to do stupid things. With money you could bend the rules, break the law, and more importantly, make people disappear.

Jim Ody

He'd seen it before. The case of the missing vicar. A man seen walking into a hotel and never coming out again. The security cameras had stopped working in parts of the hotel, and it had been Joel who had narrowed down the rooms that were affected by the cameras. Then by a process of elimination three rooms were swept by forensics. In room 976, the bathtub lit up when tested for blood. The occupant of the room had given a false name, but had left a perfect fingerprint. Upon arrest, Jasper Jonas 'no commented' his way through his first interview before, hours later, finally admitting to cutting up the vicar in the bathtub, and wrapping him in bin-liners before stuffing him in a couple of suitcases and wheeling them out of the hotel. He even stopped at the reception to check out with a number of people walking past the cases unaware of their grisly contents. That had been all about money.

Before leaving, Joel sent a text message to Kip telling him where he was going. He wasn't going to be some dumb scream-queen in a low-budget movie, and get himself into a bad situation.

At the beach, instead of going down onto the sand the way he'd done twice before that day, he followed the path around the side. Instantly, when he went through a gateway the place changed. The path was freshly swept of sand. On the side were large beach huts, and on the front of the beach were expensive looking loungers.

The path led around some rocks that jutted out from the hillside. Above was the golf course. When he got around it, there was a large bar on the beachside, and above it an even larger building that was clearly the Country Club.

You could follow the path directly up to the bar, and the Country Club, or you could follow the winding path with its lamps around the side and up through a corridor of trees.

He wanted to be inconspicuous, or as stealth-like as a man clearly not a local, could be.

The gradient wasn't too bad because much of the hill continued slowly afterwards. He turned to the right towards the road, and saw the large house next to the Country Club. It was prominent and told everyone the owner was a person of importance. All around there the houses were grand, but this one sprawled back into a further wing.

He walked up to the door and rang the bell. He stepped back leaving a little personal space between him and whoever answered.

There was nothing.

He stepped forward and rang the bell again. He could hear the clear ding-dong of it inside. He added a couple of raps too for good measure and again stepped back.

Nothing.

He tried one more time, but wasn't hopeful.

He glanced over towards a gap that showed him the Country Club. If Melody was meeting friends then they'd be over there, but if they weren't then he was showing his hand and making himself known.

He looked up the road. Fancy houses lined it, and the road branched off to more streets and yet more houses. Eventually it would end up at the park.

Joel pulled out his phone.

Jim Ody

"Hey, Colson! Look, I'm at April's house, but no one's home. You know where she might be?"

"Uhm…" he responded, but he seemed to be playing for time. "You're at April's house?" Joel didn't like it when people repeated things he'd said on the phone. It often meant they were retelling the call to someone else.

"Yes. Where are you?" Joel could hear something muffled.

"I'm… at the club. You know…"

"I see," Joel said. He wasn't at the club. If he was then it was the quietest club in the world.

"Yeah… I'm just having a beer and getting food. There's a match on the telly… and, yeah." He was babbling. Liars tend to speak too much.

"Okay, well you have a good evening."

"Yeah… yeah, you too, Joel."

It was a shame. Joel didn't mind Colson, but now he knew he couldn't trust him. The guy was too caught up in this place. His poisoned bloodline influenced his decisions.

Joel looked back at the house and realised even if someone was in there, they were not going to open the door anytime soon.

He made a decision. He was going to see if he could find a back entrance to the club. He wanted to go in and see if he could see April, or Colson for that matter. If he could, then he'd wander through and make himself known. He'd speak to Melody and remind her of the missing teenagers.

He walked back down the path the way he'd come, but this time, he stepped off the path and between some trees following where the side dipped

The Crazy Season

down to a loading bay. There were no windows here. There didn't need to be. The view was trees and a hidden incline to where the golf course was situated.

A lorry was there and a guy was putting a tablet device away before getting back into the cab.

Joel used the sudden deep throaty noise of the diesel engine to hide his footsteps, as he got nearer.

A guy with a comb-over was walking back inside and glancing at his watch. He was in a hurry.

Joel snuck in the open double doors. It was a stock room with a large door at the end. He watched as the guy walked through it. He looked around and was glad he was alone.

He knew this was the hard part. When the large area packed with hiding places became corridors and small rooms.

He amused himself by thinking if this was one of those country clubs with jackets, then he'd find one, slip it on and pretend he was hired help. But it wasn't like that. Everyone knew everyone else. Blending in would be impossible.

He got to the door and took a deep breath. He opened it and turned left. He could've gone either way, but logically, left took him to the largest area.

He passed a room where he heard two people talking. Their voices were muffled and the door ajar. He went by unnoticed. At the end, he went up some stairs and through a door. He was now in a main area with toilets and a staircase, then through two large doors he could see the huge expanse of a bar and restaurant. It was packed.

He took another deep breath and walked through the door. Instantly he saw a telephone at the side in its own little booth. Open sided, but a little privacy nevertheless. Nowadays it was probably hardly used.

He walked confidently up to it and grabbed the receiver. And pretended to press the buttons.

He turned and slowly scanned the area.

There were tables and booths all around. It was split between dining and socialising, at the far end was a stage. The bar was one side with doors to the kitchen next to it, and on the right was a huge wall of glass that showcased the sea.

Near the stage, tables were being arranged and covered with cloth. Something was happening.

Joel then noticed the poster on the wall:

Beach View Charity Gala: 8pm

It was tonight.

Faces flashed smiles, and everyone seemed in a buoyant mood. Maybe money does buy happiness, he thought, and for a second almost bought into it.

But there was no TV on playing the match, as Colson had suggested, and of course, neither Melody or April could be seen.

Then a slightly husky female voice spoke up.

"That thing's not worked since 2003, handsome." He turned and saw a woman in her late forties, or perhaps she was older The makeup and surgery made it he hard to guess her age.

"I'm beginning to realise that," he smiled back politely.

"You've been stood there a while for someone who seems quite clued up."

"Enjoying the view," he said, looking at her. He wanted to leave. And quickly.

The Crazy Season

"Well, you should come over to my table and enjoy it some more."

He put on his best false grin, and replied, "I might. I just need to check my car for my phone."

"Wonderful," she purred. "I'm there in the corner."

She made a show of wiggling her hips as she walked away. She was attractive by numbers, her unique attributes cut away and disposed of by a surgeon years ago.

He took one last glance around and headed out of the main doors, down the steps and back up towards April's house.

Melody wasn't there, but he had a good idea where she might be.

He walked past April's house and turned right to follow the road all the way round. Within a couple of minutes, he walked past Sally's house. Timothy's house was opposite. He wanted to go and knock on the door. Offer his condolences and assure his parents that he'd do all he could to find out what had happened. But he couldn't. He had nothing concrete. Just a bunch of hunches, a theory, and loose alibi.

But sometimes, that was all you needed.

When he got to the play park, he walked past the equipment and one of the benches towards the fence. He didn't even bother to look around. So what if he was seen? He was leaving the grounds of Beach View, albeit in an unorthodox way. He climbed over the small fence. He was surprised that they'd not built a huge wall around, but apart from the house in the distance, there was nothing but a long road that eventually fed into the main road. To build a fence

Jim Ody

would be a deliberate act of distrust to those living outside of it.

Joel shook his head in disbelief as he spied the camera up on the pole and had to wonder whether the gatekeeper was watching his every move and writing a report to his boss about him. Joel didn't care. By the time any sort of action was taken, he'd be gone. Surely, they weren't paranoid enough to send people out to get him? The gatekeeper had seen him pass a number of times and had made no attempt to stop and question him.

He stepped through the undergrowth of the thick and slightly boggy grassland. There wasn't much you could do with land like that. He stopped and took another picture of the house, making sure the tin mine could be seen in the background. He sent it to Kip, too, with a quick description of where he was.

Safety first and all that.

There was no fence when he got to the house, it just turned into a gravel drive and a beautiful house, one that wouldn't look out of place within the outstretched arms of the gated community.

There was no black saloon in the driveway, but there was a garage attached to the house.

He was about to walk up to the front door when he made a final decision on something he'd been wrestling with ever since he looked out towards the house.

It made complete sense.

He continued along a well-worn path towards the tin mine. Wouldn't that be a kicker?

From the outside it looked derelict and a forgotten ruin, but as he got closer, he could see a door had

The Crazy Season

been erected. There was a padlock but it was unlocked and the door was open.

Joel wished it was America and he had some sort of weapon. Walking into a dark place that would take him down underground seemed incredibly foolhardy. He contemplated waiting for Kip, but he could hardly stand around whistling and looking at his watch for the next hour or so.

He opened the door wide enough to get through and walked into the unknown.

The top was open to the elements, exactly how you'd expect. There was a yellow caged lift, and behind it a yellow staircase that descended into the ground. Probably hell for all Joel knew.

There was no way he was going to take the lift. For a start, he could only imagine the noise it would make. It would hardly be a sneaky entrance. And secondly, the lift wasn't there, it was already down below.

That meant potentially someone was down there.

He took the stairs. The metal seemed loud despite his careful steps. He tried to stand on the edges of the steps as this would make the least sound.

Down he went, turning around as the staircase took him deeper underground.

Only the odd orange glow of a small encased light showed him where to go.

He stopped at the first level. There was a tunnel with more lights leading down underneath.

He stepped onto the level cautiously. He still couldn't quite understand the motivation behind it all, but at that point finding Melody was his goal.

Jim Ody

The '*pfft*' sound, and the sudden sting in his back happened almost instantaneously. He reached to try and find the cause of the pain and saw a figure holding an outstretched gun.

"Who are…you?" Joel managed as his legs gave way and he collapsed on the floor.

"I'm the Messiah," the deep voice said, walking confidently towards him. Joel didn't hear the words; he was already unconscious.

Chapter 49

Before the party

Timothy stood at his locker wrestling a chemistry book into his bag. He didn't understand why they still needed books. It was the fucking millennium not the bloody olden days! They should have laptops with the text books uploaded to them, not still going back and forth to lockers that were stuffed with huge fat textbooks.

"Hey," she said, walking up to him. It was Sally.

"Hi," he replied, but she wasn't getting it. He didn't want to be horrible to her, but… he'd outgrown her. They'd been friends since forever, and it was nice, but she had these thoughts of them becoming a couple, going to prom and shit… He sighed at the thought. He wasn't against it, in fact he'd almost conceded that these were inevitabilities of his future. It wasn't so bad. But then April and Becky had invited him to the party. And that *was*

Jim Ody

exciting. From then on, he realised that was what he was missing in his life. He didn't have to settle for the strange girl-next-door when the popular girls were beginning to realise he was well on his way to becoming a man.

"You wanna come over tomorrow night and watch Netflix?" she said. "There's this great new documentary."

He looked at her, then past her at Becky who threw him a little wave.

"Sorry, I can't," he said. "I'll see you later." He walked off leaving her open-mouthed and watching him jog up to Becky. She was heartbroken. She hadn't seen that coming. The week before they'd almost kissed and now… and now what? It was like she no longer existed.

"Still on for tomorrow?" Timothy said, catching up with Becky. He was trying to play it cool, but he was still a nerd. And she was a cute girl with nice tits.

"Hey dick!" One the huge guys above him said. "You lost your way to Loserville?"

There were so many things Timothy wanted to say, but most would end up with him on the floor with either a black-eye or a broken nose. Or maybe both.

Instead, it was Becky who spoke up. "Leave him alone."

"Oooh, what? He your boyfriend now?" The guy said, nudging his mate for approval.

"Yes," Becky said, completely shocking Timothy. She turned to him, grabbed his shoulders and kissed him slowly on the lips.

The Crazy Season

To Timothy, it was the most magical thing in the world. The guy just said, "Weirdos," and grabbed his mate's arm as they turned and walked off.

Behind them, Sally stood and wondered how she would be able to pick up the pieces of her life that had just shattered all around her.

"Tomorrow should be fun," Becky grinned answering his original question. "Anyway, I've got history and you know how Mr Townsend can be!" She rolled her eyes, but they both knew that Mr Townsend wouldn't do anything. Not to them.

Timothy nodded, still lost for words, as she walked off.

"Dude, what the fuck?" Timothy turned to see Stevie.

"What?" he replied but couldn't stop grinning. He hoped everyone had seen it. He was completely high with what had happened.

"She kissed you?" Stevie didn't hold the same thrill and looked disappointed. Timothy couldn't blame him. He'd been walking around after her, too. They both knew that April was totally out of their league, but Becky... well, technically she was, too, but she was a fantasy that could be manipulated into being an outside possibility.

Stevie walked off swinging his bag which hit a couple of people talking.

"Loser!" One shouted after him, and without turning around Stevie put his hand in the air with his middle-finger up high. An American influence for all to see.

April gave Becky a knowing look as they got into class. "Good move," she said.

Jim Ody

Becky nodded. "I told you I'd get them to come, too."

"That you did. What about Nat The Rat?" she hushed her voice down a notch, but didn't really care who heard. They were careful. They were always careful.

"Check. She's up for it, too."

"Really?" April looked surprised.

"You're not the only one with skills," she made a crude gesture of oral sex, and both girls giggled.

Mr Townsend came in and clapped his hands to get their attention. Teenagers had an inability to remain quiet and grabbed whatever free seconds they had to gossip, joke around, or just generally test their vocal cords.

"Settle down, settle down!" He said, and the whole class stopped and focused on him. He was able to control them with ease, unlike Mrs Kemp, who got all flustered when the boys challenged her authority. Or even Mr Rowley who would suddenly dish out detentions like confetti, and yet they still pushed him to the limits.

"What shall we do today?" Mr Townsend said out loud looking like he was pondering this thought like a mathematical equation.

"Something easy!" Barry grinned and looked around the room for his applause.

"Really? What? Like your mum?" Mr Townsend retorted and everyone laughed.

"Funny," Barry said looking embarrassed. The way Mr Townsend got away with his comments was a true skill of his charisma. In black and white it would seem unprofessional and bordering on cause

The Crazy Season

for a formal complaint, but the class got it. They all secretly liked him. Of all the teachers, he was the crush a lot of the girls had. The boys saw this, and wanted to be like him. The banter, therefore, was seen as playful, rather than hurtful.

So perhaps that was how he could talk the students into his project. At first the girls, and with their help he could recruit the boys too.

It was just the beginning, but that was the thing with all big projects. It started with only a handful of dedicated people, and from there it spread until the new joiners had no idea of what the point of the project was. They just wanted to be part of it.

The brilliant thing about the plan, Mr Townsend thought to himself, was that it was all completely about self-destruction. The great leaders of the past were not the ones who got their hands dirty, but the ones who planted the seeds.

"Okay. Today, class, we are going to study Mr Charles Manson!"

The class looked at each other. Some wondered whether it was right that they should enjoy a lesson so much.

"Who can tell me what crimes Charles Manson committed?"

Mr Townsend stood in front of them all and looked at every single member of his class. Each in thought some with small smiles on their faces. All of them fully engaged.

This was the crime that Charles Manson was guilty of and he would be the same too.

The next evening his flock would come together, and that's when things would really change.

Chapter 50 – April

He stared at her like she was the most important person in the world. She liked that. Even her father didn't look at her in the same way. She was pretty sure she'd do anything for this man.

It was all pretty real now. But she still felt incredibly excited by it all. She was part of something. She got it. The photos had to be taken as insurance. She was here for him. She believed in him. It was all about power and less about money. Whatever he needed she would do.

They both expected Melody and Joel to show up armed with their inane questions. They had no idea what was going on. Let them ask their questions and then they would eventually go. Those poor teenagers unable to cope with their privileged lives. It made her laugh. They all moaned and complained about their parents but went running to them when they needed something.

The Crazy Season

The two of them had planned for the two inspectors to come snooping around. Joel and Melody, who thought they were Fred and Velma, or Fred and Daphne, whichever of the Mystery Inc. characters they favoured. But they had a secret weapon, and he'd always been a crucial part of the plan.

Colson. He still loved her. And Melody wasn't over him either. Easy pickings.

They couldn't believe it when she'd said she was coming on her own. All April had to do was keep her talking whilst he crept up behind her.

"Eh-up, it looks like we've got company," he said looking out of the window. The lone figure walked purposefully towards the house.

"What are you going to do?" she asked with a little twinkle in her eyes.

His grin turned evil when he looked at her. "Hmm, good question." He walked over to a large case and clicked it open. His hands hovered between the two weapons. "Kill or keep…. Kill or keep?"

He wasn't talking to April but she replied anyway. "Keep, definitely."

He shook his head. "If he was a short fat old man you wouldn't say that."

"But he's not," she replied.

"No. No, he's not." He grabbed the weapon of choice and checked the window again.

"Time to go hunting…, Sis," he said with a grin and walked off.

She watched him leave. He was a perfect specimen. A strong and charismatic man you wouldn't tell on first glance the power that he held.

But soon everyone would.

It was such a crying shame they could never be together. Everyone else it seemed would always be in his shadow. He came into her life only a couple of years ago. He meant nothing then, but soon they built up quite a bond.

And then she found out the truth.

He was her half-brother. They had different mothers but shared the same bastard father.

Chapter 51 – Sally

Before the party

He had avoided her for the rest of Thursday. Then on Friday, he was quiet as they walked to school.

"What is it about her?" she asked him directly. She was fed up with playing these games. The ones where she was the shrinking violet hanging on to his every word.

"Who?" he said but refused to look at her. She hated that. He was deliberately avoiding the question.

"Becky of course. And April."

The guilt was painted all over his face. She could see him fighting it, but it was an impossible task. You couldn't hide the truth for long.

"Nothing," he said again weakly. She was making him uncomfortable. And that was what really hurt. All those evenings they'd spent talking about random things. Relationships, their bodies and sex, but now he couldn't even look at her. "It doesn't look like nothing. You were there drooling all over them."

"Was not," he said defiantly and walked away in a huff. She'd blown it again. Or maybe it was never there.

Only a week or so ago they'd laughed all the way to school. For a moment they held hands. Their fingers brushing together and both grabbing at the same time. She felt the electricity jolt through her body. She felt something deep inside she'd not felt before. That day they sneaked smiles and their obvious intentions telepathically shared in a world only they knew. She'd mentioned the prom, and he'd spoken about it with words like *together* and *us* and *we*. She wondered what the prom held for them now? She'd daydreamed through Geography, scribbling a sacred heart design and adding their initials above and below the barbed-wire. Everything was on track. They would soon be the couple she dreamed of…

But then he changed. And it was him, not her. She was no different. She still loved him. Yes, that was right. Sally loves Timothy. She reached out and grabbed Mr Cuddlesworth, her ragtag bear. She pulled him in close and pulled up her knees before rocking slightly and crying unashamedly.

"Boys will break your heart," her mother had said in a way that suggested she had to accept it and suck it up. Except that wasn't something she was willing to do.

Why did boys always dictate what happened? At fifteen they didn't know what they wanted. They thought with their you-know-what. Sometimes a woman had to show them. That was it.

The Crazy Season

On that Friday she tried to catch his eye, but Timothy was ignoring her. At break time he was sitting on a table with Becky and April. He looked stupid, like he was trying to fit in. He'd brushed his hair differently too. Added some sort of product. On some level he figured a blob of styling wax and a spray of his dad's aftershave was the route into her knickers.

He wasn't the only one, though. The weird kid Stevie was there too and the quiet girl Natasha. All three looked like they were sitting there for a dare. They smiled awkwardly, and when they laughed it looked forced.

Something was definitely going on.

On the way home she saw Timothy and jogged up behind him.

"I'm sorry," she said backtracking on her conversation from earlier. "It's no business of mine."

He shrugged. "'salright." But he didn't look like he had forgiven her.

"Why don't we do something this weekend? Whatever you want?"

"Sure," he said but he lacked enthusiasm. She wanted to grab him by the shoulders and shake him until the spell was broken. He wanted her before, and now it was as if she didn't exist.

"So what did you say you were doing tonight?" she asked casually as they walked up their street and towards their houses.

"I didn't," he said. "See you later."

"Sure," she said but couldn't hide her disappointment.

Jim Ody

When he got to the other side of the street, he turned and called back. "I'll text you tomorrow?"

She nodded and felt a wave of relief inside. Maybe he did still like her.

After dinner, she excused herself and sat upstairs in her room peeking out the side of her curtains. She wasn't exactly spying, just taking an interest in her neighbourhood. That's what she told herself, but who was she kidding. She knew the minute she dug out the black hoody from the bottom of her wardrobe what she was going to do. If he wouldn't tell her where he was going that night, then she'd follow him.

Her heart skipped when she saw him. She wasn't sure whether it was love or disappointment. She was fifteen, she didn't always understand what her body was trying to tell her.

He was looking all around and even glanced up at her room. Luckily, she was looking out of the crack of her curtain with the lights off. She was more than happy he couldn't see her. As if to confirm this, he looked away, and with his hands in his pockets, he turned right and walked away from the Country club and the town, and out towards the park.

Sally wasn't expecting that.

Both April and Becky lived in the other direction. Where was he going?

She moved quickly out of her bedroom and ran down the stairs. It was Friday night, and her parents had already left for the club: the place they frequented more than their home.

She left the house and walked quickly up the road. A car drove past, but she was too focused to look to

The Crazy Season

see who it was. Whoever it was waved. They'd get over it.

At the top of the road, it curved around, and she could make out Timothy walking on the grass in the park. As she continued, he got to the fence, ducked through the middle gap, and began to walk across the field in the direction of the lone house.

What is he doing? She thought. She knew the house. It belonged to her teacher, Mr Townsend.

She jogged towards the small climbing frame with the slide coming down. She was too exposed there, and could be seen from all around, so she climbed up the frame with ease, and now hidden, sat down. There, she watched him as he walked.

That wasn't the only strange thing.

There was already a figure at the house walking inside. It looked like Stevie.

What were Timothy and Stevie doing going to their teacher's house on a Friday night? She thought Timothy was sneaking out on some hot date.

And then from behind her, she heard some laughing. Remaining hidden, she looked back and saw Becky, April, and Colson laughing together as they walked into the park and towards the fence.

She wanted to go, too. Sally felt left out of it. But what could she do? She couldn't just turn up, could she? She could imagine April and Becky shouting insults at her, and Timothy would shy away in the background looking mortified. She couldn't take that.

Life wasn't fair!

When she saw them enter the house, she sat back and felt like crying.

Jim Ody

She was alone again on a Friday night. Not even her family wanted to stay with her.

She jumped down and thought about getting a pop-tart and watching a movie.

She was looking behind her when she almost walked straight into someone.

Natasha.

"Sorry," Sally said. Natasha looked guilty.

"S'okay."

"Where are you off?" Sally asked but the penny had already dropped.

"Just taking a walk," she lied.

"You too? Seems like a lot of people are taking walks tonight…" Sally wasn't looking for a fight. Natasha never went out. And yet she'd still managed to be invited and worse still, had gone.

"Okay. Well, enjoy your walk." Sally didn't wait for an answer and instead walked quickly home.

When she got into her house, Sally curled up on the sofa and cried. She really did feel left out now.

If only she knew what a lucky escape she'd had.

Chapter 52 – Joel

Joel's body ached terribly. He was laid on a cold dirt floor and his first thought was he'd died. His second thought was despair as he knew he'd never see his wife again.

He managed to open his eyes, and slowly his vision returned. His head was pounding hard so he figured he must still be alive.

He tried to sit up but, that was a mistake.

Where the fuck am I? he thought.

He looked around and saw there were no windows and all he could see was a door. It was like some sort of prison.

He grabbed his crotch and was happy to feel the small hard phone still stuffed under his balls. It was an effort to get it out, and he hoped to God no one would come bursting in and accuse him of a last act of pleasuring himself before doing something drastic. Finally, his hand came out with the small phone which was now incredibly warm.

Jim Ody

If memory served him correctly he was located down some mineshaft. He thought it was about one or two floors below the surface, so even now the phone was probably useless.

But there was a single bar of reception. It might just be enough.

He hovered over the buttons unsure of his next move. He could ring the police but would they believe him? He didn't want to speak for fear of someone outside the door. He also wasn't massively keen on putting an object near his mouth that had been cuddling his balls for god-knows how long.

But he wanted to check on Melody, and he wanted to check on his wife.

Instead, he sent a text message to Kip.

Where are you? I'm being held in the tin mine at the house in the picture.

Joel looked at the phone and thought of all the times he'd received a text message and ignored it, knowing he'd look at it later. Please don't do that, Kip.

Still nothing.

He looked at the phone to make sure the text hadn't failed. As far as he could tell it had been successful.

He placed the phone in his pocket this time and walked over to the door. He placed his ear against it.

Suddenly, louder than he was expecting he heard a shout.

"Haaaaay! Let me out of here!" It was Melody. He didn't know whether to laugh or cry. He'd found her, but she'd been caught, too.

"Melody?!" he shouted back.

"Joel!"

"Yes!"

"Well, this is a fuck up, isn't it!" The emotion of the situation had him laughing, but they were still in deep shit.

And then another voice. This one small, female and unsure. "Hello?"

"Who's that?" Melody shouted.

"N-Natasha."

"Hi Natasha! How long have you been here?"

There was a pause, then sobbing. "I don't know," she said through her tears.

"It's okay," Joel said, but really it was far from that.

And then a loud and confident voice cut through the scene.

"Well, what is happening here!" His voice turning angry at the end, and the sound of him banging each door with his fist could be heard. "You are all captive. This is not a social gathering!"

Joel didn't know what to say to that. He wanted answers but he didn't want to make the guy angry.

He heard a door open but it wasn't his.

"Face the wall!" he demanded. "You move and I'll shock you!" There was the sound of scared sobbing. Natasha.

Everything went quiet. Or at least that's what it seemed when you couldn't see anything and you were stuck behind a locked door.

Then, Joel heard another door go and Melody's voice with a slight quiver of panic say, "Keep that thing away from me."

Jim Ody

"Do as I say and there'll be no need for me to shock you!"

And then a minute or so later, there was a sound outside of Joel's door and the sound of a bolt being slid across metal.

"Stand back, and face the wall!" the voice said.

Joel turned to face the wall. He heard the footsteps enter, then as he sensed him get close Joel jumped into action. He turned quickly with an outstretched arm, and threw his hardest punch with the other.

At some point, the worst pain of Joel's life erupted around his body. Blue flashes of electricity lit up the room brighter than the light bulb. He was paralysed in pain, and then everything stopped. His muscles gave away and he collapsed onto the floor. The residual pain was still humming all around him, and his muscles hurt from the way the electricity had fully tensed them.

"I did warn you," the voice said. "Men are always the worst. Trying to be macho in front of ladies!"

Joel went to speak but found he couldn't. He was trying to get his bearings again.

"Give it a few minutes and you'll be fine." The guy grabbed Joel's wrists and snapped on some handcuffs.

Joel looked up at him. It was the teacher. Jordan Townsend.

"What's this all about, teacher?" Joel managed, sitting up. "You're trying to start some cult or something, right?"

This seemed to amuse Jordan. He stood back tapping the electroshock baton on his leg. Joel wished to God it would go off.

The Crazy Season

"A cult. All of this is a cult? No, not quite. Mr Baxter... Joel. We're friends, right? You felt the electricity between us, yeah?" He grinned at that. He moved his arms around like he was taking centre stage. A megalomaniac.

"So tell me. Help me to understand."

"Hmmm. Now where do I start, I wonder?"

"The Crazy Season. Start there."

"Yeah, you're all over the weird stuff aren't you, Joel. The Crazy Season. The curse! The teen suicides! Cults!" he laughed but something was lost in his eyes. "Sex, drugs and rock'n'roll! Boom! Boom!"

"What happened in 1981?" Joel spoke the words carefully. He was still not in control of the situation.

"The summer of 1981 was when two people fell in love. Or at least that's what they thought. Angela was a beautiful woman whose family was from a long line of fishermen. She met a handsome man from a rich family..."

"Montagues," Joel said, still feeling some discomfort. Jordan looked shocked.

"Yes, how d'you know?"

"I've pieced it all together. Your father is the great Edward Montague, and your son is Ethan."

"He's not great!" Jordan spat. "He's an awful man!" Everything had suddenly changed about him. "He left my mother when she was pregnant because he didn't want to be associated with the working class. It would've been frowned upon."

"Like Colson with Melody?"

"Hardly! My mother was a respectable woman. She may have been working class but she worked extremely hard. Her," he pointed out into the general direction of where Melody might have been imprisoned. "She's a party girl. She came looking for wealth. Typical. I've come across so many like her. She wanted to bring him down to her level, and bleed him dry. No, for them, I understood it."

Joel shrugged. "Sounds a bit hypocritical, if you ask me."

"Well, I didn't!"

"Okay, continue."

"As I was saying…" and then it hit him. "I'll speak and say whatever I want to say, whenever I want to say it, alright?"

Joel nodded. It was one of the best ways to deal with men like Jordan. They wanted centre stage so you gave it to them. Eventually they would talk themselves into a confession.

"Okay. My father's friends were weak. Why they killed themselves was anybody's guess."

"I heard he threatened them, and his family - your family - covered it up."

Jordan shrugged. "I'm afraid I was still in my mother's womb then so I cannot comment on your hearsay."

"Whatever."

He continued. "I was given up for adoption. I was put into a family of Jesus-freaks who tried to force-feed religion to me. I grew up hating it all, but then I met Layla, a girl whose parents were part of this religious off-shoot. I was amazed by it. The guy in charge commanded such respect from everyone, and the whole life seemed idyllic. They had this large house with smaller houses coming off it. I guess a commune, but less hippie. Layla and I fell deeply in love. We had Ethan but somewhere along the line we changed..." he paused like he was waiting for a reaction.

"So you came back to Black Rock?"

He nodded, and then his eyes turned dark. "The first time since I was twenty."

"You mean 2001? The last Crazy Season?"

He was grinning now, enjoying the fact that he knew more than Joel. It was all about control. Feeding the facts as he went.

"They liked to send you off as a teenager into the towns. The idea was to put you off the standard way of life. If the youngsters of the commune felt like prisoners then they would rebel and leave, but if they were given the opportunity to have some time away, then they could leave... I found Ma, and she let me stay with her."

"And the three lads. What happened?"

"They were suicides."

"Twenty years after the first ones. And you had nothing to do with them?"

"They were suicides," he repeated. "But..."

"You were looking for your father, weren't you?" Joel's mind was flicking through the facts. "These kids... their parents were opposed to Beach View. You coerced them?"

"You can't pin them on me." But his face told a different story. He suddenly had a bit of swagger. He loved to hear how great he was even if he wasn't fully admitting to anything.

"Maybe not, but it's always about money, the gated community, and your father, right? What happened? Now, it's the rich kids you've targeted. So either you are looking to have your own commune with kids who are from a similar bloodline or…" The light-bulb in his head shone brightly. "Shit. What have you done? What are you planning to do?"

Jordan looked pleased. "Well, Sherlock. This is where it gets clever. You'll like this. You went into the club today," he made a tutting sound, and shook his head. "Awful. You snuck in the service entrance and planted a bomb in the basement there."

"What?"

"I know. April took some pictures of the club, specifically the service entrance and the basement, but of course the police won't know that!"

Joel didn't realise he was shaking his head. "No, that's not going to stick…"

Jordan shrugged. "The one thing you've underestimated the whole time, Jo-el, is the love of a mother for her son. She's already planted the plans of the country club and the camera with the photos in your room."

"They won't believe you," Joel's words were as weak as they sounded. He'd been caught. The net was well and truly around him.

"Oh, and the email from Timothy? The attachment you opened that had nothing there? Well, it did," he was grinning again. "It attached files to your laptop. Internet searches about bombs, history of my father, and most importantly, an email from Natasha asking you to blow the place up."

"Why would she do that? What would be her motive?"

"My father was in a sexual relationship with her. I mean, he *wasn't*, but he liked the ladies, so it's believable enough."

"When is the bomb going off?"

"When do you think? Tonight, of course. At the gala."

"Why would you want to murder your father and all of those innocent people?" Joel couldn't believe it. The more he heard, the more he considered Jordan to be either mentally unstable or a psychopath. Or both.

"They are all greedy nobodies. He clicks his fingers and they all do what he says! He's nothing without his money."

So that was it. He wanted to show he was better than his dad. All of this came down to a child being rejected by a parent.

Chapter 53 - Jordan

2001

He was a teenager having been brought up to not care about possessions. The world didn't exist outside of the church. Everything they did somehow ended up within the religious building. The harder his adoptive parents worked, the more they gave. Jordan didn't get it. What was the point?

At twenty he ran away. He found his real mother, and she gave him the money to come and stay with her. He was amazed at the B&B when he saw it. The hustle and bustle of the town and the way his mother smiled constantly. But she, too, had a picture of Jesus that was the most important picture in the house.

And then she dropped the bombshell.

The Crazy Season

She told him who his father was. Edward Montague, the most powerful man in the whole of Black Rock.

At first, he felt great about it. His dad ran the town! How cool was that?

One day he walked boldly up to the country club and demanded to see him.

"Yes?" the large man said. He was handsome in a 50s film star way. His clothes were immaculate, and he held such a powerful swagger about him.

"Sir? I wanted to speak with you about something important."

"Is it about money or girls?" The man laughed, lighting a cigar.

"Neither, really."

"Then why do I want to know? Go on, beat it! If you want a job here then get an application form from down at the bar."

"No, it's not that. It's Angela Shannon. She's my mother."

Montague shrugged, but even that was half-hearted. He blew a huge bluish puff of smoke up above him. "So?"

"Sir? You're my father."

Edward Montague did not even bat an eyelid. "So the fuck what? You want a job or not? Don't come in here with your fanciful ideas. I don't want to hear them!"

"But it's true!"

Edward picked up his phone. "Roger? Yes, I have a gentleman here who would like to be escorted from the premises immediately. He doesn't wish to ever come back so please make sure that his wishes are met."

Jordan was speechless. He stood up to leave as his father turned his back on him, only the smoke from the cigar could be seen floating away like Jordan's hopes.

Thirty minutes later and he was even more frustrated.

"Never do that again!" Miss Shannon shouted at her son. "You are forbidden to see that man again!"

Jordan stormed to his room. The next day he found out his mother had been given a large sum of money to keep quiet.

The day after, Jordan left Black Rock.

Chapter 54 – Joel

It seemed like a dire situation. Jordan had spent many years thinking up the plan, and so far, he'd thought it out well. Almost.

"What I don't understand is April," Joel said.

"What about her?"

"She's your half-sister, right?"

"Exactly, and look at her life? She's grown up thinking they're the bloody Kardashians! The expectation is rising for her. She hates it. She hates him!"

"What about her mother? Surely she doesn't want her to die?"

"Yeah, that was an annoying thing, I must admit. I had to make up a story to get her mum away for the night. It cost me a bloody weekend at a spa!"

"How nice of you. So now what? The place explodes, but what about us? Don't you think it would look a bit sus if we are found here handcuffed?"

Jim Ody

"It would if that's what was going to happen."

"What is going to happen then? Come on you're the director of this movie. You're the one in charge." Joel was allowing his frustration to come through. Jordan could sense it and was beginning to enjoy every single minute of it.

"Have you ever considered why I chose you, Joel Baxter, investigative journalist extraordinaire?"

"My dashing good looks?"

"Not quite. I didn't."

"I don't follow."

This amused Jordan. "This might surprise you, but I'd never heard of you. Then I was approached by a mutual friend. It would appear he had. Not only that, he was willing to pay me a large sum of money to get you off the streets, as it were."

"Who is your friend?" Joel couldn't think of anybody that could want him dead. Perhaps a few might want to punch him in the face, but killing someone for uncovering the truth was a bit drastic.

"Don't be ridiculous, I'm hardly likely to give you a name, although, in truth I don't know it, but he drives a rather nice big black Bentley Continental."

Something rang a bell with Joel but it wasn't concrete. He could picture the car. Unconsciously, he'd seen it a handful of times. Large and expensive - it wasn't something that you often see.

His heart sped up. He felt himself sweat.

The day of the crash. He'd seen it at a junction. Then again at the services they'd stopped at.

"Oh dear, what's up, Joel? You look a little off colour suddenly!" Jordan was now loving the situation. "Have you been poking your nose in other places you shouldn't have?"

That's when Jordan stepped forward and for no other reason than for entertainment zapped him again.

"Aagh!" Joel shouted.

"Sorry, I slipped. Anyway, I have a few things to get ready. A murder scene for instance. Tell me, Joel? How do you think you'd kill those two out there?"

"Don't you touch them!" Joel shouted, but Jordan just grinned once more. He turned and walked out of the room.

That was when Joel was left with his thoughts. The ones that worm their way around your mind: toxic and of no use to anyone.

What if the crash hadn't been an accident? Had someone really wanted to kill him? Had he known what this mysterious person had planned, then he would've jacked it all in. He'd have sat in a boring office doing a mundane nine-to-five job. Anything just to be with his wife and child again. But he'd never been given the option. Instead, somebody had decided to play God with him, and now they were looking to finish him off.

What he couldn't understand was why he'd not been targeted in the last year? Surely that was a time when being vulnerable, he would've been easy to take out. He did nothing but eat shit, and mope around.

Maybe that was it.

Perhaps they thought he was through with it all. He'd stop it all together, either become an author or get a real job.

And then he started looking at little things. He slowly began to investigate again.

That got them worried. Really worried. Enough to be part of this elaborate plan. And let's face it, it was elaborate.

Chapter 55 – Kip

Kip was worried. Something deep inside didn't sit right. He'd barely had time to tell Rob where he was going. Rob was desperate to come, too, but had to finish his shift. The police were short-staffed as it was.

He remembered the same drive a few years back when his sister had rung him in tears. He thought he felt bad then, but at least he was going to pick her up. A hug and shared tears would cure that. Now, he had no idea whether or not she was okay. Joel had lost her, and he knew his friend well enough to hear the worry in his voice.

The town of Black Rock brought nothing but bad luck to Melody. He knew for a time she was completely in love, and it all ended so badly.

Kip and Melody had always been close. There was only a couple of years between them, and they both felt equal measures of discrimination and had steered each other through it. Kip had secretly been a little hurt that he'd not been there to see his sister get married. Should he and Rob ever tie the knot, then she would be his best man. He never said anything as he knew it would upset Melody. She was besotted with Colson. He couldn't blame her, the guy was handsome, and appeared to be a great catch.

Melody was such a free spirit. Kip wished he was a little more like that and felt dull in comparison. She had been the one to colour her hair when she was barely a teen. She'd pierced her ears herself, and then later on began to collect tattoos. In comparison, he blended into the background. He often wondered whether he did that because his sister appeared so wild, or whether it was to hide his sexuality. He wasn't ashamed by it, but he also understood that whilst he never lied about it, if no one asked then he would never outwardly offer the information.

He saw the signs for Black Rock but continued to the next road, the road that led to the gated community of Beach View that liked to pretend they were a town all by themselves. This time he passed it and continued on and then turned into a small lane that led to the only house.

He slowed down to a crawl and eventually stopped to glance again at the picture Joel had sent him. It was getting dark, but he was able to make out this was the correct place.

It looked the same, and the old tin mine was there a few hundred yards to the left.

He could have parked somewhere and walked down, but there was little cover so a lone figure could be seen for miles. No matter what route you took, the chance of a covert approach was unlikely.

The Crazy Season

He was hardly Jack Reacher.

He'd only ever had one fight. And by one fight that would be being punched in the nose and grabbing it in pain. The guy had maybe expected a punch back, and when it didn't come, and Melody came bounding in, the guy soon legged it out of there.

The house was large but perfect in its design.

He looked over at the mine. Would that not be the perfect place to take someone?

He walked over tentatively. If he'd had an ounce of courage, then it had been lost like grain through a hole in his pocket.

He knew that to go underground was a stupid idea. The escape route was only here. The potential for something to go wrong was massive.

He looked around and saw nothing but an idyllic landscape, and an incline with a hill of sand dunes at the bottom, and a beach behind that. That was where he should be heading. If only it was high noon and not a dark evening, he'd be stripping off and swimming in the sea before coming out and diving into his current book, *Echoes of Home*, a wonderfully spooky read.

Instead, the mouth of the mine swallowed him up.

He carefully placed his feet on the steps and walked down the metal staircase.

He turned down a corridor, glanced back over his shoulder, then continued on. He passed a junction box that held the electricity fuse box.

There were lights on, and they gave off a dirty orange glow. The ground was compact dirt scuffed with footprints.

Jim Ody

At the end it opened up into a huge cave-like area. A wheelbarrow held dirt, and there were a number of shovels and tools. From there, it went off into a couple of smaller rooms (both empty), and then down a couple more corridors, which looked more like tunnels.

Kip didn't have a good feeling about it. He felt like he was being led into a trap. And he also felt alone.

The first tunnel wound around and the lights abruptly ended. He pulled out his phone and shone it but all he saw was a pile of large stones. There was nothing further there.

The next tunnel was straighter and did have a smaller room coming off of it but it still looked under construction.

He made the journey all the way back. He was getting tired now.

When he was back at the staircase and the lift, he looked downwards. It continued further down, but he felt a reluctance to go further.

He looked up, then stood still.

Silence.

It didn't make sense.

With a deep sigh, he took the staircase and went lower. It went down another twenty feet before he felt like he was at the bottom.

Ahead was a large area, but when he looked around there was nothing obvious coming off it.

He could see piles of rocks that looked like they might hold tunnels behind them, but for safety these were often blocked up.

The Crazy Season

There was nobody here, he concluded and made his way back up to the top.

It was pitch black when he came out. The evening had crept up on him.

The house. They had to be there.

Again, there was no point sneaking around. If someone was home then they would've heard his car approach.

He rang the bell and patiently waited.

Nothing.

He tried it again.

Nothing.

Next, he pulled out his mobile and tried both Melody's and Joel's phones.

Both went to voicemail.

Finally, he tried the door.

It was unlocked.

Kip watched it swing open. He turned around and looked left and right before entering. Was it breaking and entering if the door was unlocked? He wasn't sure, he'd have to ask Rob. If nothing else it was trespassing.

The house was clean. Sparkling clean. Everything had a place. It looked more like a holiday let, rather than somebody's humble abode.

"Hello?" Kip said. He didn't want to suddenly be caught out. He was already running answers through his mind about what he'd say. Each one was weak, and slightly more unbelievable than the one before.

The lounge was large with a huge fireplace as a centre-piece, a flat-screen mounted on the wall, and a sofa that looked like it had never been used. He could see all the way through to some double doors at the

Jim Ody

back. A staircase split the room, and as he walked around, he saw it was open plan with a large kitchen area. It looked like it was straight out of *Country Life* magazine. Marble worktops, a range oven and a large island with a couple of stools. It was spacious. On the wall were some floating shelves, but the whole place looked brand new.

Walking through, he came to a formal dining room, and then next to it was a cloakroom, and then an office. The latter was haphazard with paperwork, and open books. It looked like the only room in the house that was used.

The downstairs was clear.

He looked out of the window. Would someone be upstairs? What exactly was he expecting? Melody and Joel, gagged and tied up in a wardrobe?

He jogged up the stairs. A single light on the landing was on. "Hello?" he called, but again wondered how he'd explain why he was going up a stranger's staircase.

There were two smaller bedrooms, albeit good size. Then next was a messy room that looked like it might be owned by a teenager. Then there was a master bedroom with a huge bed and *ensuit*. Then looking around the landing, there was a family bathroom and a final bedroom that was completely white. It had a huge bed with brilliant white linen, and a single chair and mirror.

He checked wardrobes as he went, but there was nothing unexpected there. He didn't like the feeling of looking through other people's stuff, and it occurred to him then that he had nothing. No reason at all to be there. Just a picture from Joel.

The Crazy Season

He suddenly panicked inside, jogged down the stairs and out of the house.

He felt slightly better as he sat in his car and tried Melody and Joel on their mobiles again.

He got voicemail on both.

He glanced around one last time, started the engine, switched on his lights and drove away.

He wondered whether to go to the house he'd picked Melody up from a couple of years ago, but instead decided to continue to the B&B as was the original plan.

Chapter 56

The party – what actually happened

Timothy stood outside the door to his teacher's house. That very act felt strange. A single ring of the bell and the door was swung open. Mr Townsend stood smiling at him and with a bottle in his hand. It was like this was the most normal thing in the world.

"Timothy! Great you could join us!" he stood back and Timothy walked slowly inside. His teacher wore a T-shirt that showed a muscular physique Timothy had no idea the teacher possessed. It made him uncomfortable but he didn't know why.

The sound of a slow song played in the background. It was a mournful ballad, and the volume was loud. A deep bassline reverberated around the place. The gravelly female vocals swam over the top and sang about murder like she had no other choice.

Ethan nodded to him from the sofa, but it was mechanical. The guy still looked like he wanted to punch him in the face. It still all felt like a big trap he was being coaxed into.

From the kitchen came Stevie. He had a bottle of beer, too. He looked awkward holding it.

"Hey, Timothy!" he said looking glad that someone else was there. They both mirrored awkward feelings.

"Hey, Stevie."

From behind, his teacher called out. "Go get yourself a beer, too, Timothy. Or something stronger if you want. My house is your house!" he stood back with open arms. The affable host.

"Thank you," he replied. He walked into the kitchen and looked at all the alcohol. There was a lot.

The doorbell went again and there was laughter and giggling following it.

April, Becky, and Colson tumbled in and their enthusiasm kicked the gathering into a party.

"Now the fun can really begin!" Mr Townsend said, winking at them.

Both Timothy and Stevie shared a glance. Both were wondering which girl would be theirs by the end of the night.

"Hey, guys!" April sang as she wiggled through. She wore a tight top, and even tighter trousers. Becky followed, already a bundle of giggles, her skin smoothed out with make-up, and her hair fiercely straightened. The lads' eyes were instantly drawn to her plunging top that barely held her boobs.

Jim Ody

"Who's ready for some fun!" she grinned. She and April had already had a couple of shots of vodka before they left.

"Hey," both lads replied, their worries sneaking away. Ethan too suddenly seemed to liven up a bit.

The last to arrive was Natasha. She crept in with the same trepidation as the boys had.

"Hey, girl!" Becky said, walking over and throwing her arms around her. Natasha held her and felt a little more at ease. "Let's get you a drink."

Natasha glanced over to Ethan who let a sly smile slip out. She felt herself glow inside.

For the next half an hour, they all sat, drank, and listened to music. Deep in the shadows the elephant stood. No one wanted to bring it up. They all wanted to pretend they were there to drink and be merry, but they all knew that wasn't the case.

Snacks were passed around them all. Then after a few more songs they all did shots. Not many, but enough.

Timothy and Stevie had grins on their faces. The girls had snuggled up to them, and even Natasha had loosened up, Ethan's hand had found a home on her knee.

When the sweets were passed around, nobody said anything. They were all ready for anything.

Nobody noticed that neither Mr Townsend, Colson nor Ethan had one.

The sweets were good. Becky grabbed a couple the next time, and Stevie was quick to follow suit.

The world was becoming fuzzy. They felt completely drunk, but happy. Really happy.

The Crazy Season

"Let's move this downstairs," Jordan said, clapping his hands. He'd told them not to call him Mr Townsend for the rest of the evening.

"Ooh, downstairs!" Stevie grinned. He didn't even know there was a downstairs. Natasha grinned, too. She thought perhaps she misheard him.

Jordan took them into the kitchen, and to the door under the stairs. He opened it and turned on a light. There they could see a staircase.

"A cellar! Cool!" Somebody shouted.

Jordan laughed. "It's a bit more elaborate than that!" And they all followed him down and into the unknown.

The room below was large, probably the size of the whole house above it. There was a curtain all along the back wall and a closed door to the side. Around them were a couple of pews.

"Welcome," Jordan said and bent down towards a trunk. He opened it up and pulled out a cloak.

"These are for you!" he said proudly. Timothy giggled nervously. The mix of alcohol and tablets were taking away all of his inhibitions. It felt like dress-up.

Someone said, "Cool." And someone else cheered.

Jordan looked proud as one by one he handed them out.

"Okay, let's have another toast!" Jordan said, and Colson brought out a large brown bottle without a label, and handed it to him.

Jordan uncorked it, appeared to take a swig and said, "I am here for the order of Jordan!" He looked at them. "You all do that and then say your names

Jim Ody

and take another swig. *'I Jordon Townsend do solemnly swear to fuck Beach View to all eternity, and follow the teachings of Jordism instead!'* Then pass the bottle on!"

He handed it to Colson, who went through the words, and took swigs from the bottle. Then Ethan followed on, who then passed the bottle to April. She coughed after the initial drink, but managed to speak again before another cough. It was stronger than she was expecting. She passed the bottle to Timothy, then to Becky, Stevie, and finally Natasha. All of them coughing after their sips. It was nothing like any of them had ever tasted before.

Not one of them questioned why the first three hadn't coughed at all.

"Excellent!" Jordan said when they were all done. "Now, slowly and carefully all come up here."

Stevie jumped up with enthusiasm but the room began to move. He felt like he was dreaming. Nothing felt real. He looked around and the others were suddenly looking more serious and moving in a strange and exaggerated way.

They all stood, slightly swaying and looking to Jordan for direction.

"Colson," he said, and Colson pressed a button and they watched as the lights dimmed and the curtains drew back.

And there, laid out on a large table, wearing only knickers, was Annabelle.

They all stared at her, and nobody said a word.

Colson had brought her to the house earlier. He had talked her into coming down, and then he'd drugged her. Something slipped into her favourite wine.

Natasha stood looking over the woman and didn't know how she was meant to feel. Stevie was amazed at the perfection of her body, he wanted to reach out and touch her. *Was this an offering?* he wondered.

Jordan swung an arm towards her. "This woman represents the wealth that is slowly strangling you all. We've talked about this and I know you all want to break away from this place, right? Well, I am giving you that power! Right here, right now!"

Timothy looked at the others to gauge their reaction. They were all stone-faced. Apart from Stevie who was mumbling the *Fatboy Slim* song. He felt himself stepping out of his body, and when Jordan called his name his body went to him. His arm was no longer his. He gripped the handle of the knife offered, and without any thought of consequences, he plunged it hard into the woman's stomach.

Everyone remained silent as Timothy stood with a knife dripping with blood. Next up, April stood, her face contorted into hatred as she sunk the knife into a breast and pulled it out again.

One by one they all did it. Not one of them refusing to do it, nor thinking about what it meant and how their actions would change their lives.

When it was done, they all looked at each other as Jordan grinned, and Ethan and Colson both looked amused. The curtain drew closed, and suddenly there was music piped down from above. Now it was happy party music. Ethan handed out another pill to them all and they took it without question, wine and

Jim Ody

beer was distributed, and suddenly everyone was delirious

The cloaks were removed and placed back into the trunk.

Colours flashed from some light effects, and everyone laughed with hysteria. Clothes were shed and lips touched as friends kissed. Nothing more than roaming hands, but suddenly it didn't matter. They were teenagers again letting loose with teenage desires.

An hour later and they were all overcome with tiredness. They had come down from it all. The mental and physical fatigue gripped tightly to them.

And then it was the early hours.

Except it wasn't just morning. Each woke up with a thumping headache. And memories permanently tattooed into their brains. It was like a dream, and they now questioned the clarity of their memories, and whether or not it had happened.

Natasha was the first to cry. Huge sobs.

"It doesn't matter," Jordan said. "We're all in this together." He pointed towards the camera placed high above them in the corner of the room. "You all passed your initiation. Congratulations! Next we put the plan into action!"

"The plan?" Becky said having already covered up her naked chest with her T-shirt and grabbed her bra in her hands. She noticed the horror in the faces of the two boys. Both of whom looked about twelve this morning.

"Oh yes!" Jordan said. "I'm sure I mentioned it last night."

The Crazy Season

Although she knew part of it, April still frowned, and said, "I'm not sure you did."

"I didn't? Oh, I'm sorry! Okay, well the plan is - and you'll all like this - to blow up the country club!" He grinned like it was the most wondrous thing.

Eyes shot open wide with fear.

"No," Timothy said. "We can't do that."

"Why not, sport? They're controlling you! Your houses have cameras in them. They watch you whilst you're playing with yourself and looking at nudies on your laptop."

"No," Timothy said again.

"Yes," Jordan reinforced. "It's a dog-eat-dog world out there. You either control, or you're controlled. This is the only way to get your freedom back! Your identity!"

"What if we don't want to?" Stevie said in a small voice. He sounded like he might cry.

"Then don't. Except you're on camera killing an innocent girl. That's what. Life in prison for you all. Due to your age, probably fifteen years minimum."

"You bastard!" Becky shouted.

Jordan's face turned crazy and evil. "You all wanted to be part of this! The truth is, the video is insurance, but if I get the impression you are talking about this or backing out, then trust me, you will disappear. No one will find you."

"No. No. No." Timothy said, physically shaking. Tears were rolling uncontrollably down his cheeks. He was taking it worse than anyone.

"I will catch up with you all individually, but one last thing…" He looked around at them. His eyes drilled into theirs. "You can all fuck off out of here now!"

The sun hadn't even risen in the sky.

One by one they grabbed their clothes, and were half dressed as they walked out of the room and up the stairs.

Colson was nowhere to be seen, and Ethan was asleep on the sofa.

The fresh air hit them as they left the house and headed back over the field.

"What are we going to do?" Becky said, but April soon shushed her.

"Nothing," she said. "We get on with our lives. We stay away from each other. Then we do what we're told and go our separate ways."

"That simple, huh? We killed..." She didn't finish her sentence as April slapped her hard across the face.

"You don't speak. You don't say a single word of this to anyone. ANYONE!"

Too scared to speak any further, they trundled on with their heads down and slowly split up to sneak back into their houses.

Everything had changed.

Chapter 57 - Colson

The years slowly added up in his life. He got older, and arguably, he got wiser, but one feeling never left his body. That push and pull from those around him.

He hated it. There was always someone who had this overriding expectation of him. So much so he'd forgotten exactly who he was. His own identity had been discarded along the line whilst he was made to be a chameleon.

The pressure he'd felt growing up had given him anxiety, but he refused to use it as an excuse. Nobody knew that about it. Well, nobody except one.

He had been a fool. Even that was too weak. He'd been a total arsehole. He'd done things for all the wrong reasons, and then he'd not admitted to his failures.

The one person who he let in to his world, he had shat on. Well and truly. That was her phrase, too. He loved that about her. She truly couldn't give a shit.

Jim Ody

Melody was never a woman he thought he'd be attracted to. She wasn't going to be all dressed up in a flowing dress. A human accessory to him and hanging off his arm. She wouldn't just smile sweetly, nod and curtsey in all the right circles, and be well-versed in proper etiquette. She wouldn't wait to be asked a question and then bring the conversation automatically to her boyfriend.

At the last meal they went to at the country club, she'd turned up braless in a tight T-shirt. A Mexican wave of whispers flushed around the room as she walked in, and his parents shook their head in shame.

His uncle Edward walked over, blanked her and said, "There's a time and a place for hookers, Colson."

"It's Freebie-Friday," she grinned, demanding that he look at her.

"Still overpriced," he scoffed and stormed off.

"You can't say that to him," Colson had said, and all too quickly realised how it sounded like he was whining and not seeing it from her point of view.

"He can't speak to me like that, either! The funny thing is, he still couldn't keep his eyes of my tits!"

Colson hadn't responded. He should've done, he knew that. Instead, like a petulant child he walked over to the bar leaving her standing there, fending off the daggers from the upper-class females.

It was too late now, he knew it. But that didn't mean he still couldn't try and do the right thing.

To a point he understood. His half-cousin, Jordan, had felt the same way he had, the difference being he'd been rejected. Jordan wanted to be part of the

The Crazy Season

family empire, but his father didn't like the mixed blood.

Jordan was troubled. Even with a son, he hadn't calmed down. In fact, since they had come back, they were both angry and bitter. It was a scary anger.

What started as a joke turned ugly quickly. He realised that, like the others he'd been told what he wanted to hear. They'd fed him the lines that made him agree to it. Slowly the plan changed. It got darker and more serious until they were all in too deep.

It was that damn party. Why had he been caught up in it, too?

Annabelle was the reason. He was needed to bring her in, and her role would be enough to hold everyone else there.

He was able to get her out on the date. He was the one who could slip something into her drink. She trusted him, and he took advantage of her. Not Jordan, not Ethan or the others. The whole thing was set up so well that when it was over, Timothy, Stevie, Natasha, and Becky would do whatever they wanted of them. And if they didn't, or showed signs of weakness, then they would be eliminated, and made to disappear.

The sad thing was, if Colson hadn't been part of it then he would be sat in the Country Club now, unbeknownst to him that the place was about to be blown to smithereens.

Like all good powerful men, Jordan knew Colson was caught. He talked him into contacting the guy Joel pretending to be Timothy.

Jim Ody

The concoction of the hallucinogenic homebrew, the pills, and the vodka shots was easily enough to make the teens do whatever Jordan wanted. They were sheep beforehand. He only had to suggest where they were to go, and they'd do it without question.

Of course, what the teens didn't know was that it was a set-up. Annabelle was drugged and had no idea she'd been stripped and laid out on a table. But she'd not been harmed. Well, not fatally.

The knife had a blade that went up into the handle and the motion squeezed out blood. Some of the teens had been forceful so had left bruising. Annabelle had been pissed off. She'd woken naked in one of the spare rooms with Colson. She was dubious of his tale of their own party the night before, and scolded him for being so rough with her. By that time the teens had gone. She'd left being annoyed with him. Once again, another woman storming out without him following.

Jordan was obsessed with the suicides from twenty years before. He knew that some of the teens would be weak, it was the reason he'd chosen the three shy students. It was the benefit of being a teacher. He watched the kids and saw how they interacted.

Colson hated himself for allowing Jordan to continue to choose the weak and manipulate them to join in. He knew he could use his step-sister and her friend to attract the boys. A vague notion that they might get some flesh was all you needed. They had too. Then Natasha was added. Ethan had started a correspondence with her. A simple text at first had hooked her, spinning a fantasy she wanted to hear. Another weak one, except she'd turned out to be stronger than they were expecting. It had been Becky who had buckled underneath it all. April grew worried about the whole plan and turned her back on her friend. Becky couldn't cope on her own, and she'd disappeared.

Colson thought back to the day he heard about Stevie. The guilt was consuming. He couldn't believe he'd been part of it. He had blood on his hands.

And then the news of Timothy. His broken body was found at the bottom of the cliff.

Jordan was amused by it all. To him everything was falling into place. The teens had been set up. The bomb was already planted, and Melody and Baxter were there at his house held hostage. Even Natasha. Ethan had snuck her into the hotel, and then on a promise had slipped in and drugged her. They'd slipped her out at night with the help of the Black Rock owner, his gran, Angela. When Natasha had come around, she'd threatened Jordan, and that was when he made the decision to keep her. To show her what happens to girls who try to threaten a man.

Colson still struggled to understand what Jordan wanted. He knew there was a part of Jordan who saw himself as a leader of a cult. It was something he'd talked about. But he also wanted to show his old man he couldn't be bought. He wanted the whole of Beach View to be disrupted, their leader dead, and their country club blown up.

That was certainly disruption.

But what wasn't clear was the big picture, and the night before he'd spent tossing and turning over the ramifications of it all. It was escalating. He'd been blind to it before, but now he could see that hopes of starting a cult and manipulating teens had only been the beginning. It had led to kidnapping, and whilst he hadn't actually murdered anyone, he had certainly assisted in it. Now he was talking about murder. He had said he was going to get rid of the three hostages, and then on the busiest night of the month, he was going to set off a bomb that could kill, or at least injure, over a hundred people…

Colson was tired. He wished he'd told Joel the truth earlier. He wished he'd contacted Melody and told her not to come. He wished he'd never spoken to Annabelle and brought her over to Jordan's house.

And above all, he wished he'd not got talking to Jordan. Sucked in by his charismatic charm, he'd been taken on this crazy journey.

Colson was a fuck-up. In his parents' eyes, the whole of Beach View's eyes, in Melody's eyes, even in Anabelle's eyes. But worse was how he saw himself. A big fat failure. He'd been born with it all and somehow, had systematically lost it. Now, he was shunned by the community that raised him. He no longer shone. That's why he'd grown the beard longer. He'd had it before but now it was untrimmed and on the edge of wild. Even his personal hygiene had taken a backseat. He'd given up.

Until now.

The truth was he wanted to finish this himself. It was why he'd tried not to implicate Joel and Melody. He had some notion they'd come, ask a few questions, receive even fewer answers and leave. Turn their backs, drive off in the red Jeep and forget

The Crazy Season

all about the rancid underbelly of Black Rock. Hopefully a bigger story was just around the corner.

But that hadn't happened.

As he walked across the field towards Jordan's house, he saw the tin mine in the background. Even in the darkness, once your eyes adjusted it was prominent. Jordan had plans to build underground. He wanted to build a commune of people there. Eventually, they'd spill into building on land, and by then the residents of Beach View would be unable to do anything about it. But that was before he got sidetracked.

A car he didn't recognise pulled away. Colson wondered whether this was another plan being put into action. He couldn't trust Jordan, and it only reinforced what he was about to do.

Now, as if in a trance, he pulled out his mobile. He pressed the three digits.

"Police," he said. He gave the address and told them what they'd find. "There's also a bomb," he added and felt the weight lift even though he knew he was going to be in trouble. The operator calmly took the details, but he knew she thought it might be a crank call. He was about to put the phone down when instead he said his name. *Fuck it,* he thought. *It ends now.*

He walked up to the front door and didn't even bother to ring the bell, but walked straight in like he owned the place.

He knew where he was going.

He walked through the lounge, and turned towards the kitchen and to the door under the stairs. He saw nothing around him. His tunnel vision kept him focused.

He walked down the stairs and into the large room with the pews. He continued to the door and opened it.

The corridor behind was dirty and the floor made from dirt.

This was the new part.

The orange glow from the lights made the place even more unwelcoming.

He heard a shout and the sound of electricity zapping. It would be so easy to turn back. Instead, he gritted his teeth, squeezed his fists tightly and pursued his quest.

He walked past one door, and then another. He knew both held the women.

He stood next to the open door.

Slowly he peaked around it, and saw Jordan standing over Joel.

Then he carefully turned and crept in. He had the knife in his hand. A proper knife this time. No prop with disappearing blade and squirting pig's blood.

Without warning Jordan whipped around.

"You think you can creep up on me!" Jordan shouted. He held out the electric baton. Colson realised this was not the way he'd planned it at all.

But as Jordan went to move forward, Joel kicked out his leg which tripped Jordan and sent him sprawling on the floor. Colson was on him in a flash.

He heard the electricity go off as he plunged the knife into Jordan's back, his muscles contracting onto the button of the baton.

"You fucking idiot!" he managed as Colson was able to pull the baton from him. He stood up and unleashed the electricity into him.

"See how you like it!" Colson shouted, his anger flowing out of him.

Jordan screamed in pain as Joel looked on unsure what was going to happen next.

Jim Ody

Chapter 58 – Joel

It wasn't what he had expected. Of all the scenarios he'd thought of throughout the day, being saved by Melody's husband was not one of them.

Jordan had come back. His sadistic nature had found he enjoyed inflicting pain. It was as if he was taking out everything bad that had happened to him on other people. Somehow, he justified this as being okay.

Joel had just been blasted again with the baton when he saw the figure of Colson standing behind Jordan. He also saw that Jordan had heard him. He wanted to warn him and to shout but he couldn't because everything buzzed about his body. Slowly though, he felt in control of his own body again.

As Jordan turned and shouted at him, Joel did all he could to send every ounce of strength to his leg. In truth, it was less about strength and more about timing. It completely messed with Jordan's balance as the moment the weight came off his lead leg, Joel kicked it. And down he went.

Colson was on him and stabbing him in the back. A cowardly move, but Joel was in no position to make the point. He heard the baton go off, but Colson was in the way, and Joel couldn't see whether or not it was touching anyone.

Then Colson jerked and, leaving the knife buried in Jordan's back, he grabbed the baton and sent electricity into his captive's body. Jordan's arms and legs flapped uncontrollably in a way Joel knew only too well.

A form of justice.

"I'm sorry," Colson said, as he searched through Jordan's pockets for the keys. "I should've told you earlier."

Joel managed to sit up. "A lot of people should've told us a lot of things, it seems."

"We're raised to keep secrets. It's in our DNA. Money turns people into liars. Big fat greedy liars."

Colson jangled some keys triumphantly, and then bent down to find the right key for the cuffs.

Joel heard the click and felt the clasp snap open. He pulled his wrists apart, then slowly stood up. His legs were weak, and he had to use the wall to almost pull himself upright.

"Come on," Colson said. "Let's free the others."

Joel tried to keep up but he was feeling the effects of the being blasted three times with electricity. He heard the lock of the first door being opened and heard Melody gasp. He wasn't sure whether that was in shock at seeing her husband for the first time in a long time, or the fact he was covered in blood and looking bedraggled.

Joel watched them hug and wished to God he could have his wife hug him back again. Just one more time.

Awkwardly, Colson pulled away and glanced at Joel, before walking past and to the room with Natasha in it.

"Well, this is a fine mess we've got ourselves into, isn't it?" Melody said walking over to him.

"I met your husband earlier today."

Melody pulled a face. "Yeah, about that. I probably should've told you."

"*You think?*"

She flung her arms around him and squeezed him tightly. "I'm sorry, Joel. Really sorry. I'm so glad to see you though!" She pulled back and they held a moment together. Two partners on a case, deep underground in a man-made prison.

Just a normal and regular thing.

"Come on," Joel said. "I don't know about you, but I want to breath fresh air again."

They met Colson and a scared looking Natasha outside the room.

"Come on," Colson said. "I'll show you the way out."

Slowly they walked through the door, out into the large room with the pews, and then up the staircase and into the house.

"Shit, I thought we were in the mine," Joel commented as they found themselves in the clean and spacious kitchen.

"Me, too."

The Crazy Season

They walked around the spacious layout of the house, through the lounge, and out of the front door. Joel pulled out his phone.

"I've already rung the police," Colson said with a sigh. "I have to face up to it all."

Joel glanced at his phone. "Oh no. This is my backup phone. I switched it to voice record just before he opened the door."

Melody grinned. "You recorded his confession?"

Joel nodded. "At least I hope I did. The thing was stuck down my pants."

"You can keep it away from me then!" she laughed.

Colson pulled out his phone again and frantically tapped some numbers.

"April? It's me. Look, whatever you do, don't go to the club… what? No… it's over… Yes, it's over. Just go back home. Please."

"Your cousin," Joel said. "What was she doing?"

"She was setting the bomb."

"I thought it was already there?"

"It was but it needs a receiver to be in the building. One that will pick up the signal when Jordan was going to trigger it."

"So essentially, it's not activated?"

"Not quite. It's activated, it's just not set up with the trigger."

"Still dangerous then?" Colson nodded.

A small voice from behind them spoke up. "I had to take pictures. Mr Townsend told me to.

Joel nodded and tried to look reassuringly at Natasha. "He got you on camera, too. The wayward teen implicated."

Jim Ody

Colson answered anyway. "It almost worked."

A few minutes later they heard the sound of sirens cutting through the evening.

In the distance they saw lights turning into the Beach View, whilst a couple more vehicles were heading their way.

Everything happened hard and fast. Vehicles screeched in, and policemen swarmed them, barking orders for them to get on the ground and show their hands. Colson did his best to explain the situation, but the police wanted to make sure they weren't armed first.

A few minutes later, and Jordan was found. He wasn't dead, but he wasn't in a good way either. Colson had been separated from Joel, Melody and Natasha.

Word got out that the country club had been cleared and they were waiting for the bomb squad to turn up.

It was a few hours before the body of Becky was found. She had been dead a few days. Under the bed in one of Jordan's spare rooms. A suicide note was next to her, again, it explained exactly what had happened.

Chapter 59 – Joel

It was after half-ten by the time the red Jeep left the coastal town of Black Rock.

"I apologise for not saying about Colson earlier," Melody said stifling a yawn.

"It doesn't matter, although had I known then I wouldn't have let you go to see April alone."

"He was waiting for both of us, you know?"

Joel nodded. "I can't believe how complicated the whole thing was. Jordan missing out on the wealth and the father he thought he deserved. Many kids go through that…"

"But they rebel by getting into fights, pushing boundaries, not kidnap and murder."

"Strange place. I can see why you fitted in for a while," Joel jested trying to lighten the mood.

She smiled. "I loved the way you handled Miss Shannon!" When the police let them go, they had gone straight back to the B&B to get their things.

Jim Ody

"The bitch was in on it! Setting me up with those plans!"

Melody put on the exact voice of Miss Shannon, "What do you mean, you're not paying?"

"I know."

She laughed. "Then you told her to go fuck herself! She crossed herself and looked at you like you were Satan!"

"And that's the last time you pick the hotel on a case!"

Then both looked at the road ahead. The cars were few, but the ones that were there were driving well over the speed limit. Everyone was in a hurry.

"You keep looking at the clock," Melody commented. "You got a hot date lined up?"

"Sort of. I know it's stupid but I wanted to look in on Cherry."

Melody sat back, her head resting on the back of the seat. "It's such a wonderful thing. Colson wouldn't have ever been like that."

"It's what you do when you're in love."

Eventually, they pulled up outside her house.

"You want to meet up tomorrow for a debrief?" she said hopefully.

"It makes sense, doesn't it?"

She liked that he could tell. She waved as he turned around, and he was deliberately slow in pulling away until he saw she was safely inside.

Then he was gone like greased lightning.

He looked at the clock as he pulled into the hospital car park. It was still the same day. For some reason that meant something to him.

Despite all the spare spaces, he still chose his usual spot. He couldn't *not* park there, could he?

He got out and jogged to the reception area.

"Hey, Pete!" He said to the old guy with Brylcreamed hair, and glasses designed in the 60s.

"Hey, Joel! Bit late for you, isn't it?"

"It's never too late." He took the stairs and found himself at his second home.

"Well, well, well," Claudia, one of the nurses said. "I heard you were on an important case!"

"I was. And now I'm here."

"You solve it?" She enquired.

Joel was always modest. "The bad guys are in custody," was all he said, and pointed to Cherry's room. "Can I?"

"Of course! By all means. And well done!"

He pushed open the door to her room. He walked up, leant in to her, and despite all the tubes and wires hugged his wife. It felt like days since he'd seen her.

"I miss you, Cherry," he said. The last forty-eight hours of adrenaline mixed with his absence left him a mess. He sobbed over and over again.

He took her hand and gently rubbed it.

"I've come to realise that our love is everything I've ever wanted. I wish others could have what we have found... Cherry? If you need to go and be with Robyn, then go. I love you, and I miss you but you can't hang around for me. It's not fair to anyone."

Joel sat back down in the chair. It was the first time he'd stopped and relaxed since the last time he was there. Tears spilled from his eyes as he looked over at Cherry. She was everything to him, but he wondered how much of her was still there. Was he just visiting a 3D picture of her each day?

He heard movement from behind him and looked back. He made no effort to wipe the tears away.

"Shall I come back?" Carol said to him, but he shook his head.

"No, come in. Please."

"How did you get on?" she asked sitting down in the chair. "You look tired, Joel. In fact, you look dead on your feet, if you weren't sitting down!"

He smiled and nodded. "I'm shattered, but…" he struggled for the right words.

Carol looked over at Cherry and back at him. "Alive?"

His smile grew larger. "Yes, I think that's it… I did it. I solved the case, with the help from Melody too…" he began to relax as he went through all the details, and all the while looking over at Cherry, too, like he was sharing the story with both of them.

"Wow!" Carol said when he finished. "I'm pleased for the case, but I'm also pleased for you. I know you're tired, but you have something in your eyes. A fire, and a need to help others. Are you going to continue with big cases again?"

Joel paused for a few seconds. He hadn't considered past the visit to the hospital. He shrugged, but it was a gesture that held so much more behind it.

"Maybe, but I don't want to go too far from here. I'd hate to not be here if Cherry woke up… or if she…"

Carol understood. "I know. This is a dilemma. You cannot show Cherry any more love than you already do." Carol got up. "But there is a whole

The Crazy Season

world of people out there that could probably use your help. Do you stay here and mourn, or do you go and save them? You need to ask yourself which you think your wife would want." She made it sound so easy.

"Whilst she's here, I will always be with her."

Carol accepted that. She was a good woman with kind eyes. "Good bye, Joel." She said and she was gone.

Joel stayed for a bit longer and then he kissed Cherry on the cheek. "I love you Cherry, and I always will."

He left the room, said his goodbyes and ten minutes later was on the way home.

He pulled up to his house and then it hit him that he'd not played *their* song for her. It was the first time he'd ever forgotten.

He was tired, but he didn't want to go to bed just yet. He made a coffee and went out to the lighthouse and walked all the way to the top, albeit a lot slower than he normally did. That night it was a hard slog.

He opened his laptop and began to write notes.

He glanced out of the window. He turned off his lamp so he felt closer to the world outside.

His eyes adjusted as the moonlight sparkled silver on the sea. He looked over at the hospital. At her window.

He wanted to be there. He wanted to get into the hospital bed and hold her. Even with all the pipes and wires.

Then her window lit up. Maybe it was stress or exhaustion. Maybe his mind was playing tricks on him. But the bright light moved out from the window and arched up over the sea and into the night's sky.

It took his breath away.

He felt a tickle on his neck. The hairs stood up on his arms, and then he felt happy. He couldn't understand it. Well and truly ecstatic.

The radio on the side fell onto the floor which made him jump. He looked at it. The sound of the dial changing for a station and then through the sea of static came the beautiful voice of Sophie B Hawkins singing *As I Lay Me Down*.

He picked up his phone as the song ended. It rang before he could do anything.

"I'm sorry, Joel," the nurse said. "It's Cherry. She's passed."

"Okay," was all he could think to say. The nurse went on speaking about brain activity and a fit. She talked about them trying to bring her back but all the words were lost. His angel was finally where she belonged. He wondered if she'd been listening to him.

Chapter 60 – Joel

Joel slept up in the top of the lighthouse. It felt right. He slept deeply. He slept soundly.

The next morning, he was up early. He felt slightly numb, but also free. He felt happy for Cherry. But suddenly his whole life had changed.

He made coffee, and he sent a text message to Kip, who rang him straightaway.

"I'm so sorry, mate," Kip said.

"It's fine. Honestly. I'm pleased for her. How long should she have to stay there? It was over a year of being in that same room. Day after day."

"Listening to that same song you played her!"

"Yeah," Joel said, and then realised that Kip was worried he'd hurt his feelings. "Maybe I should've played something a bit more upbeat."

Silence fell between them, then Kip said, "D'you want me to come over?"

"No, that's fine. I'm going to pop to the hospital, and then Melody and I are going to go over the case."

Jim Ody

"I'm sure the case can wait."

Joel liked the fact Kip was thinking about it. "Yeah, I know. The old keeping-busy thing, you know?" He had a funeral to organise for his wife. It was such a heavy thought. A job no husband ever wants to have to do.

An hour later, Joel was parked for the last time in his parking space. He grabbed the flowers and the large box of chocolates and walked slowly towards the hospital. He was usually so enthusiastic to be there, but knowing it was his last time slowed him down. It wasn't that he loved the place, but the finality of never seeing Cherry again was there on his mind.

He walked into the building and for a change took the lift.

He walked down the corridor and saw the nurses' station. They were laughing but stopped instantly when he got there.

"Oh, Joel," Jules said standing up and waddling around. She barely came up to his shoulders but swung her arms around him and squeezed him tightly. "We're so sorry."

The other nurses nodded and looked sombre.

"That's fine," he said. "Thank you for everything. Really."

He handed over the chocolates. "These are for you all."

"Joel, you shouldn't have. Thank you."

"Thanks Joel," the younger nurse said.

Joel looked around. "I don't suppose Carol is around, is she?"

Jules looked at him funny. "Carol?"

"Yes, Carol... you know what? I don't even know her surname!"

Jules and the other nurse shared a strange look. "There's no nurse called Carol, Joel. Not in this department."

Joel frowned then looked past them to an old picture of them all smiling. It had been some sort of celebration. He saw her there. "Here," he said, and pointed to the woman with the kind face who had become such a dear friend to him.

"Oh, Joel... Yes, that's Carol..." They both looked like they were going to be sick.

"So..."

"Joel, she died a year ago. Just before Cherry came here, in fact."

What were they saying? Joel thought. "Eh? No, that can't be right."

He thought back to their conversations, specifically when he'd asked about her husband:

"How is your husband?" Joel had asked on many occasions.

"Not so good, if I'm honest. He gets so lonely now he's not working."

"And you're here working long hours."

She always smiled back. *"I cannot leave this place, Joel."* She couldn't leave because she was dead. Her husband was lonely living without her and she refused to leave. Was she staying to look after Cherry?

"But I've..."

Jules looked concerned. "Do you want to take a seat?"

He shook his head. "She sat with me every time I was here," Joel said slowly.

"She was a good woman," the other nurse said.

"So sad," Jules added. "She jumped from the cliff out there, and nobody knows why."

"She committed suicide?" Joel looked up with shock again. "No."

They both nodded. Again, he thought back to another conversation he'd had:

"What is so bad that it makes somebody take their own life?" Carol had looked over almost speechless.

"Everybody has a reason." She'd said. *"Try not to judge them on that."*

"I know but it's so… final?" He felt so bad now having not picked up on it before.

But she felt so real.

So very real.

He said his goodbyes and walked off. He had a lot to do, but also he knew there were hundreds of stories waiting to be written.

When he met up with Melody again, she flung her arms around him.

"Joel, I am so, so sorry," she said. "Anything you need, I'm here for you."

"You know what I need?"

"What?"

"You to be honest with me from now on."

"Of course."

"And one more thing."

She looked up at him, a naughty twinkle in her eyes. "It's a bit soon, isn't it?"

The Crazy Season

He rolled his eyes. "No. I want you to be my right-hand girl. I've realised that this is a two-person job. You fancy it?"

"Damn right I do!" she beamed and tried an awkward high-five. "But we definitely need a name. Something cool…"

He chuckled. This was going to be hard work. "We'll see," he said. "We'll see.

From deep in the sand dunes, a man dressed all in black watched them through binoculars. He took in the scene, noting it all down, ready to report back to his boss.

It looked like Joel hadn't got the message. He was like some bloody rubber ball; no matter how hard you hit him, he always bounced back.

His boss would need to take him out once and for all.

But that would be for another day.

Jim Ody

The Crazy Season

Epilogue

Barry had been idly scrolling through pages after pages of photos of women on his laptop. All going from clothed to a state of undress within less than a handful of photographs. He liked like. Normal looking women exposing what's beneath everyday clothes. So much better than over glamourised women who had so much plastic surgery done that they no longer represented being a woman, and they all looked decidedly the same.

But after half an hour he was bored. He closed the laptop lid down and put it to the side. He wanted something more from his life than a smelly flat.

He stretched over and picked up the warm 2ltr bottle of cola. It was misshapen from where he'd replaced the lid whilst the bottle was still squeezed out of shape from his grip. He belched, and his hand idly scratched his balls.

If he was honest with himself, he'd admit he was scared. Just a little bit.

The Crazy Season

At first it had been exciting, but now he wasn't so sure.

He reached over again to where he'd just placed down the bottle. Next to it was a cupboard. He didn't know why he hid them away but he did. Even his pornographic magazines were easier to locate than these.

He didn't like taking pills. They distorted reality and people stopped believing what you said to them.

He undid the lid with a pop, and shook a couple out into the palm of his hand. He threw them into his mouth and swallowed.

He turned off his light and thought nice thoughts. Normal women walking into his flat.

Eventually, he fell asleep.

*

The next morning Barry's bed was empty. His bedroom was untidy, but it was always like that.

But Barry's bedroom window was open. Wide open. The hinges broken allowing for a human to pass through it.

A gentle breeze floated inside and freshened up the room from the stale smell of a single man.

This time Barry never came back.

His sister looked out of the window expecting to see Barry's body laid out on the ground below. Broken and twisted.

But he wasn't there.

But Barry was gone.

His door was still locked and the chain was hooked from the inside.

Jim Ody

> Nobody knew where he was.
> Barry was never seen again.

The end

Acknowledgements

A big thank you to my family and friends. Your support is massive and continues to motivate me.

A huge thanks to the members of *Jim Ody's Spooky Circus* - my street team, and specifically my group of advisors Simon Leonard, Angela Hill, AJ Griffiths-Jones, Cheryl Elaine, Dee Groocock, Terry Hetherington and Ellie Shepherd who listen to all my crazy ideas and advise me whether or not they are worth pursuing!

I had some wonderful BETA readers for this, so thank you to Sarah MacKenzie, Deb Day, Caroline Maston, Sue Scott, Donna Morfett and Ang Lamb.

A nod of appreciation to the hard work of my admin team: Donna Morfett, Zoe-Lee O'Farrell and Kate Eveleigh.

A special thanks to the wonderful Mel Comley who has given me such great sage-like advice.

Thank you to Caroline, David and Jason for your continued support. Also, to Andy Barrett, Maggie James, Sarah Hardy, Valerie Dickenson, and Kerry Watts who also try to steer me in the right direction. Or try.

Thank you to Matt Rayner for your friendship, design and support with Question Mark Press. Everybody else at Question Mark Press: we are a great family! Especially, to Donna, Zoe and Kate – Top administrators!

A special mention to Emmy Ellis @ studioenp for her wonderful design direction. You truly bring my book covers to life! Not to mention being a great author, and a wonderful friend.

Thank to Shelagh Corker for adding the final polish to my books.

And finally thank you to you, the readers. For reading, for enjoying, and for getting behind me. Without you there would really be no point!

ABOUT THE AUTHOR

Jim writes dark psychological/thrillers, Horror and YA books that have endings you won't see coming, and favours stories packed with wit. He has written over a dozen novels and many more short-stories spanning many genres.

Jim has a very strange sense of humour and is often considered a little odd. When not writing he will be found playing the drums, watching football and eating chocolate. He lives with his long-suffering wife, three beautiful children and two indignant cats in Swindon, Wiltshire UK.

He is also the owner of Question Mark Press and enjoys helping new authors.

JIM ODY
Stories with a Twist

Connect with Jim Ody here:

Facebook: www.facebook.com/JimOdyAuthor
Jim Ody's Spooky Circus Street Team:
https://www.facebook.com/groups/1372500609494122/
Amazon Author Link: https://www.amazon.co.uk/Jim-Ody/e/B019A6AMSY/
Email: jim.ody@hotmail.co.uk
Twitter: @Jim_Ody_Author
Instagram: @jimodyauthor
Pintrest: https://www.pinterest.co.uk/jimodyauthor/
Bookbub: https://www.bookbub.com/profile/jim-ody
www.questionmarkpress.com

Want to read more books by this author?

Here are details of three more books for you to get your hands on!

A Lifetime Ago

(Hudson Bell Book 1)

This is a tale about how the events of one day have such catastrophic consequences on the future.

Hudson Bell is a consultant for the police. A former DI, he spends his days helping to find missing children.

May and her son go on a road trip to celebrate his birthday; Robert and Nadia buy their dream house by the sea.

But as each look to enjoy a new life, none of them can shake off what happened on that fateful day. One of them blames the others and will stop at nothing to seek revenge.

One accident and five lives changed forever.

?

Question Mark Press

The Place That Never Existed

For Paul and Debbie it was meant to be the happiest time of their lives.

A small village wedding in front of their family and friends, followed by a quiet honeymoon in Devon. Not everyone had been happy to see them together. A woman from their past refused to accept it. Her actions over the previous year had ended in tragedy, and had almost broken the happy couple apart.

Now, away from it all in a picturesque log cabin, Paul and Debbie look forward to time spent alone together... But she has found out where they are, and she will stop at nothing to make sure that the marriage is over... forever.

But Huntswood Cove isn't just a beautiful Devonshire fishing town, it has its own secret. Recently, people have begun to disappear, only to turn up dead in suspicious circumstances. The locals begin to question what is going on. Soon everything strange points to the abandoned house in the woods.

The house that nobody wants to talk about. To them, it is the place that never existed.

?

Question Mark Press

Mystery Island

The Island of dark secrets lies close to Maui. Few have ventured there, fewer have returned.

With a map in hand, extreme-sports enthusiasts, Kyle and Donna, descend to the depths of the Pacific Ocean in search of treasure. Will they find it? And will they survive?

Peering eyes are everywhere, lurking and in wait, ready to take back what's theirs.

Some things are better left buried.

?

Question Mark Press

How many have you read?

Other books from Question Mark Press

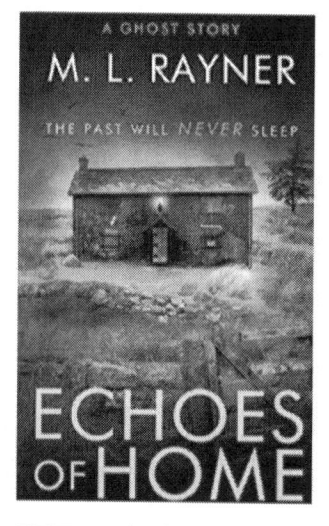

Coming soon:

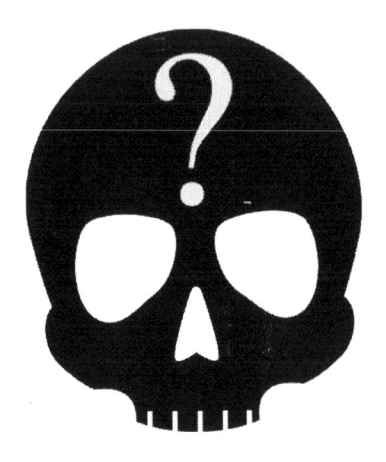

Question Mark Horror

A new series of YA Horror books. One series by a handful of authors.

Are you ready?